THE GENTLEMAN'S SCANDALOUS BRIDE

LAUREN ROYAL

DEVON ROYAL

June 2021 Edition

SWEET CHASE BRIDES

THE GENTLEMAN'S SCANDALOUS BRIDE by Lauren Royal & Devon Royal

Published by Novelty Books, a division of Novelty Publishers, LLC, 205 Avenida Del Mar #275, San Clemente, CA 92674

June 2021 Edition

Cover by Kimberly Killion

Learn more about the authors and their books at www.LaurenandDevonRoyal.com.

ISBN: 978-1-63469-181-9

MORE SWEET CHASE BRIDES BOOKS

∾

SWEET CHASE BRIDES

The Earl's Unsuitable Bride

The Marquess's Scottish Bride

The Laird's Fairytale Bride

The Duke's Reluctant Bride

The Viscount's Wallflower Bride

The Baron's Inconvenient Bride

The Gentleman's Scandalous Bride

The Cavalier's Christmas Bride

A Chase Brides Christmas

SWEET CHASE BRIDES: THE REGENCY

Alexandra

Juliana

Corinna

SWEET CHASE BRIDES: THE RENAISSANCE

Alice Betrothed (coming soon)

For Lynne & Bob,
in memory of Max

ONE

Trentingham Manor, the South of England
September 1677

STANDING IN HER family's small, crowded chapel, Rose Ashcroft shifted on her high Louis-heeled shoes, wishing she were in a cathedral so there would be somewhere to sit.

Wishing she were *anywhere* but here watching her sister get married.

"Randal John Charles, Baron of Newcliffe, wilt thou have this woman to thy wedded wife, to live together after God's ordinance in the holy estate of matrimony? Wilt thou love her, comfort her, honor, and keep her in sickness and in health; and, forsaking all others, keep thee only unto her, so long as ye both shall live?"

"I will." The confident words echoed through the magnificent oak-paneled chamber, binding Rand to Rose's sister Lily.

But Rose wasn't listening to the ceremony. Instead she heard *spinster, spinster, spinster* running through her head. Nineteen and a lonely spinster...while both her sisters had fine husbands.

Happy tears brightened their mother's brown eyes. She

leaned close, bumping against Rose's left side. "They're perfect together, aren't they?" she whispered.

Rose could only nod dumbly, gazing at her sister's petite figure laced into a stunning pale blue satin wedding dress embroidered with gleaming silver thread. The bride's hair, the same rich sable as Rose's, cascaded to her shoulders in glossy ringlets. Beside her, the groom beamed, looking tall and utterly divine in midnight blue velvet, his gray eyes steady and adoring.

The wretch.

Not that Rose still resented Rand. Though his rejection had crushed her, he was so clearly in love with Lily that it was obvious the two of them belonged together. Rose had made her peace with that fact. Truly, she wished her new brother-in-law every happiness.

But did he have to be *so* very handsome?

The priest cleared his throat and looked back down at his *Book of Common Prayer.* "Lady Lily Ashcroft, wilt thou have this man to thy wedded husband…"

Standing on Rose's right, her older sister Violet shifted one of her twin babies on her hip and smiled up at her husband of four years, Ford. Sun streamed through the stained-glass windows, glinting off her spectacles. "Oh, isn't this beautiful?" she said with a sigh.

Holding their other infant, Ford squeezed Violet around the shoulders. Seated cross-legged at their feet, their two-year-old son Nicky traced a finger over the patterns in the colorful glazed tile floor, obliviously happy.

Rose gritted her teeth.

Her friend Judith Carrington poked her from behind. "I cannot believe Lily's wedding is happening before mine," she whispered in a tone of dismay. "*I* was betrothed first!"

Rose couldn't believe Lily and Judith would *both* be married before she even received a proposal.

"…so long as ye both shall live?" the priest concluded expectantly.

In the hush that followed, even knowing it was unkind of

her, Rose half hoped some disturbance would occur to stop the wedding.

But nothing did, of course. "I will," Lily pledged, her voice as sweetly sincere as she was, ringing clear and true.

A few more words, a family heirloom ring slid onto her finger, and the deed was done. Lily was the new Lady Newcliffe.

And truly, Rose wished her sister every happiness.

But did she have to be her *younger* sister?

When Rand bent to kiss the bride, Rose turned away. Behind her, Judith was grinning up at her own betrothed—although only a little way up, since his stature was less impressive than Rand's. Lord Grenville was five-and-thirty to Judith's nineteen, and his pale brown hair was thinning on top, but Rose imagined that the way Judith looked at him made him feel like a king. And he gazed down at her in a way that surely made pretty, plump Judith feel like a queen.

Rose wanted someone who'd make her feel like a queen. Gemini, a duchess or countess would do. Or even a lowly baroness...

As the years crawled by without a husband on the horizon, she was getting less picky. Most any man would be acceptable to her now.

So long as he was handsome, titled, rich, and powerful.

The guests parted as Lily and Rand began making their way from the chapel. They'd taken but a few steps when a cat, a squirrel, and a chirping sparrow came to join them.

Rose moved to hug her sister. "It was lovely," she murmured. "I'm so happy for you."

And she was. Truly she was.

Lily leaned down to pick up the cat, straightening with a brilliant smile. "Your turn next."

A hurt retort came to Rose's mind, but she wouldn't snap at her sister on her wedding day. "I'm happy for you, too, Rand," she said instead, rising on her toes to give her sister's new husband a kiss on the cheek. But not too far up on her toes, because Rose was tall. Too tall, perhaps, or too slim, or too quick-tongued…or too *something*.

There had to be some reason she was still unmarried.

Too intelligent, most likely. It was precisely that failing, she suspected, that had driven Rand away. A handsome and high-born young linguistics professor ought to have been Rose's perfect match, given her unusual aptitude for foreign languages. But he'd never shown even a flicker of interest. He'd brushed right past her and gone straight for her little sister. Rose wasn't so arrogant as to expect *every* man to fall in love with her, but…

Well, she'd never had one ignore her completely.

Unfortunately, she hadn't taken his disinterest well. Desperation had driven her to proposition him in a most unseemly manner, and when that hadn't worked, in vexation and despair she'd attempted bribery and trickery of the worst kind.

She couldn't imagine what had come over her that day and had feared she'd never be able to look Rand in the face again. But to her utter relief he seemed at ease with her, as though he'd graciously forgotten that humiliating episode.

"I'm the luckiest man in the world," he said now, making Rose feel like the unluckiest woman.

Lily must have noticed her dejected expression, because her fingers stilled in the cat's striped fur. "You *will* be next," she said quietly, concern clouding her lovely blue eyes.

"Undoubtedly so, since I'm the only one left," Rose quipped. "Unless, that is, Rowan manages to find himself a bride before I find a groom."

Their ten-year-old brother stood nearby with Violet's young niece, Jewel, their dark heads close together in whispered consultation.

"He may have found himself a bride already," Rose added dryly.

Lily's giggle pealed through the chapel, bouncing around the molded dome ceiling. "Surely someone will claim you long before Rowan gets it in his head to wed. Why, you're the prettiest of us all!"

Rose shrugged. She'd always thought Lily the *most* pretty. Still, she wasn't about to turn down a compliment. Not today.

Besides, it took more than beauty, she'd learned, to land a good husband.

Well-wishers pressed closer. Rose began moving toward the drawing room and found Judith by her side. Forsaking her betrothed, Judith clutched Rose's arm. "Who is *that* charming fellow?" she whispered conspiratorially.

Rose cast a glance at the fellow in question. His gaze met hers, then skimmed her from head to toe in a way that might have made her heart skitter…if she were at all interested. "That's Mr. Christopher Martyn, a friend of Rand's—Rand calls him Kit. He's an architect," she added curtly.

Judith frowned. "The name sounds familiar…"

"King Charles recently awarded him a contract to renovate Whitehall Palace," Rose admitted. "Among other commissions." She happened to know that Windsor Castle and Hampton Court were also on Kit's account books. But she didn't want Judith to get the wrong idea. That he was someone important.

But Judith's blue eyes grew round with admiration. "He must be of great consequence to work for the king. And intelligent, too—no need to play the featherbrained country maiden for him."

"Don't be a goose," Rose retorted. "I've no interest in playing *anything* for him. And I've never acted featherbrained."

But perhaps now was the time to start. Her recent efforts to entice a certain gentleman—very well, to entice Rand—through intellectual conversation had failed. Hideously. So hideously that the object of her affection was at this very moment wed to her sister. What could be more hideous than that?

"You cannot tell me," Judith whispered, "that you don't think Mr. Martyn good-looking."

Dressed in forest-toned velvet, Kit Martyn was tall and lean, his hair dark as jet, his eyes a startling mix of brown and green. She shrugged. "I suppose he's handsome in a typical sort of way."

Judith sighed. "He looks ever so nice. Do you think he's nice?"

"He's nice enough." Except for those unusual eyes, which were decidedly *not* nice. They held a spark of something Rose couldn't quite name.

"And good heavens, he's building things for the king! I'm certain he has money—"

"Money," Rose interrupted pointedly, "does not make up for lack of a title."

Her sister Violet joined them, sans children for once. "Who needs a title?"

Judith crossed her arms. "Lady Rose apparently wishes to become Lady Something-Higher."

"Oh, well." Violet sent Rose an indulgent smile. "That's only because she has yet to fall in love."

Rose returned the smile, her lips feeling taut. "Given that it's as easy to fall in love with a titled man as one without, I've decided to concentrate on the former."

Violet and Judith exchanged a glance that set Rose's teeth on edge, then left her to return to their respective—*titled*—men.

Since Lily had given their mother barely two weeks to plan the event, the wedding party was small. Still, there were more than enough guests to fill the drawing room and spill out onto the Palladian portico and into the exquisite gardens. Trentingham Manor was known for its gardens, thanks to Rose's father and his passion for flowers and plants.

But it was a sunny day, and Rose feared for her creamy complexion, so she opted to stay indoors. She wandered the crowded drawing room, sipping from a goblet of the new and frightfully expensive champagne her parents favored for special celebrations. Although she enjoyed sharing a word or two with various relatives and neighbors, she was feeling rather at loose ends, not quite sure what to do with herself.

Noticing her father, she approached at once, glad of a comforting face—until she realized who he was talking to. "... one of those newfangled greenhouses," Father was saying. "On the east side of the house, I'm thinking, to catch the morning sun. Since autumn is nearly upon us, I'd be much obliged if you could start it immediately."

Rose made an indignant noise. This was the second time Father had pressed Mr. Martyn, architect to the king himself, to build a silly greenhouse!

She wished she could ball up the lacy handkerchief tucked in her sleeve and stuff it into her father's mouth. "Mr. Martyn works for *royalty*, Father! He builds palaces, for heaven's sake. He's far too—"

"Well, not quite palaces," the gentleman corrected her. "Renovations to palaces, additions to palaces, but I've yet to build an entire—"

"See?" Rose met her father's green eyes, speaking loudly and slowly to make sure he could hear her over the hubbub of the celebration. "Palaces. He hasn't the time to build you a greenhouse."

Mr. Martyn sipped from his own goblet of champagne, then grinned at Rose's father. "Oh, I think I might find the time," he argued, his words infused with a hint of laughter. "In exchange for a dance with your lovely daughter."

A pointed look at Rose made it clear which daughter he meant.

Lord Trentingham frowned. "My chubby doctor?"

Mr. Martyn looked confused, and Rose knew she should remind him that her father was hard of hearing at the best of times—and in a crowded room, he was all but deaf.

But she couldn't seem to speak. The impertinence—that he meant to barter for her company! Surely her father would never—

"I'll be most pleased to build your greenhouse," Mr. Martyn reiterated a bit louder, "if your lovely daughter will grant me a dance."

"Plant what in grass?"

Understanding dawned in the young man's eyes. "A dance!" he shouted. "May I have the honor of a dance with Lady Rose?"

"Oh, yes. Of course," Father said. "Now, about that greenhouse—"

"I'll do a preliminary design before I leave," Mr. Martyn all but bellowed.

"Excellent." Lord Trentingham turned a vague smile in Rose's direction. "Run along, my dear. Enjoy yourself."

Her mouth dropped open, then snapped shut when she found herself propelled from the drawing room by a warm hand at her back. Then she was stepping out onto the covered portico, which had been pressed into service as a dance floor.

Three musicians in one corner were playing a minuet, a graceful dance that facilitated conversation. The wedding guests chatted and flirted, their shoes brushing the brick paving in unison. Though the dance was already in progress, Mr. Martyn handed both their champagne goblets to a passing maid, took Rose's fingers, and swept her into the throng.

Touching his hand, skin to skin, reminded her of her first glimpse of him in Oxford. Her nerves were suddenly jangling, though she was not a nervous sort of girl, and she remembered she'd felt much the same when they'd first met.

But only until she'd discovered he was a plain mister. Since then, seeing him had had no effect on her at all.

So it was disconcerting to find that touching him now seemed to make the champagne bubbles dance in her stomach.

"Lovely Corinthian capitals on the columns and pilasters," Mr. Martyn noted, ever the architect. "Do you know who carved them?"

She pliéd and stepped forward with her right foot before finally finding her tongue. "Edward Marshall, who also carved the Ashcroft family arms in the pediment. And in future, please keep in mind that there's no cause to seek my father's permission for a dance," she added archly. "Ashcroft women make their own decisions."

"So Rand has told me," her partner said, breezing over the implication that she might have refused him.

They rose on their toes, and when he pulled her closer, she

caught a trace of his scent. A woodsy fragrance with a base of frankincense and myrrh. It smelled nice, she thought, wondering if she could duplicate it in her mother's perfumery.

"Your family is an odd one," he said conversationally. "I don't allow my sister to make her own decisions. Not the important ones, in any case."

She felt sorry for his sister. "Our family motto is *Interroga Conformationem*."

He hesitated.

"Question Convention," she translated, narrowing her eyes. Couldn't every educated gentleman speak Latin? Certainly any she'd consider husband material.

It was a good thing he wasn't in the running.

They dropped hands to turn in place, then he grasped her fingers again. "Is it true, as Rand says, that your father allows his daughters to choose their own husbands as well?"

She noticed Lily and Rand dancing together—much closer than the dance required. Surprisingly, envy didn't clutch at her heart this time. She smiled. "Yes."

"In future, I'll keep *that* in mind," Mr. Martyn responded with an irresistible grin.

Ignoring his impertinence, Rose glanced across the wide daisy-strewn lawn toward the Thames, noticing her brother Rowan racing onto the portico. He looked like a miniature version of their father in a burgundy suit, his long hair streaming behind him.

A quite ordinary-looking man followed more sedately, but as he wore red and white—the king's livery—he attracted more attention.

The musicians stopped playing, and the dancers ground to a halt.

"There he is," Rowan said, pointing toward Rose in the sudden silence. "Mr. Christopher Martyn, the man you seek."

TWO

"$\mathcal{I}$F I MAY speak with you in private, sir," the
messenger said. "I bring word from His Majesty."

Kit nodded and stepped off the portico, feeling the eyes of all
the wedding guests upon him. Ignoring their speculative
murmurs, he calmly led the way toward a summerhouse he'd
spotted earlier. The sudden appearance of the king's man didn't
alarm him as it did the others. He was, after all, completing
several royal projects. King Charles likely just wanted a change.

He hoped.

As Kit crossed Trentingham's celebrated gardens, he resisted
the urge to cast Rose a last look over his shoulder, just to gauge
her reaction. Not that it mattered what she thought of him—she
was an earl's daughter, after all. Unattainable. He was wasting
his time with her, and he was not normally the sort to waste
time.

But he'd watched Rose sipping champagne, and her mouth
had looked like a perfect red rosebud. Or the comparison *seemed*
to fit, anyhow. Kit didn't know much about flowers.

And she was fun to tease. She wore her hauteur like armor,
and he couldn't resist testing it, poking at its weak spots. Trying

to draw out what lay underneath. There was more to Rose, much more, than met the eye.

But perhaps he should leave well enough alone. It wasn't his role to draw her out. He knew his place in the world. Commoner, through and through.

A girl like Rose would never look twice at a fellow like him.

Which was another reason he didn't turn around. He didn't want to see that theory confirmed.

Though his best friend was a baron who'd grown up in a mansion, Kit had been raised in a single-room cottage. No Martyn had ever held a title, or even flirted with the possibility —much less with a beautiful, high-born lady.

The circular redbrick summerhouse was a small building with classic Palladian lines. Kit ushered the king's man inside. Owing to the commendable design—large arched windows over each of the four doors—it was bright beneath the cool, shaded dome.

Bright enough to make out the gravity in the messenger's eyes.

Apprehension soured the champagne in Kit's stomach. "Yes?" he prompted.

"It concerns one of your projects, sir. I've been sent to advise you that the ceiling at Windsor Castle is falling—"

"Falling?" The word hit Kit like a punch in the gut. "Falling how?"

The messenger shrugged apologetically. "I'm no builder. It looked to me as if only some plaster had fallen—not the ceiling itself. But there are many cracks."

Many cracks. That was bad, very bad. And inexplicable. "Was anyone hurt?"

"No, sir." The pressure in Kit's stomach let up just slightly. "But His Majesty wanted to make you aware—"

"I understand." Kit understood Charles's underlying message all too well. If he failed to complete this project on time and satisfactorily, his hope of being appointed Deputy Surveyor

—a step toward someday becoming Surveyor General of the King's Works, the official royal architect—would be as good as dead.

And the rest of his dreams would die along with it.

He yanked the door back open. "I shall depart for Windsor posthaste."

"Sir." The man bowed and preceded him outside.

Back at the house, Kit looked about for Rand, but his friend was nowhere to be found. He went instead to make his apologies to his hostess. "Forgive me, Lady Trentingham, but I must take my leave. There's a problem at Windsor Castle. I cannot seem to locate Rand—"

"He and Lily have a habit of disappearing," she told him with a rueful smile. But then her brown eyes turned sympathetic. "I'll explain," she added. "He'll understand."

In no time at all, Kit was settled in his carriage, rubbing the back of his neck as the vehicle lumbered its way toward Windsor.

Could he possibly have made an error in designing Windsor's new dining room? Had a flaw in the plans gone unnoticed? He unrolled the extra set he always carried, spreading the crisp linen over his lap. But he couldn't seem to concentrate.

Especially when his carriage jostled past the village of Hawkridge, where he'd grown up.

He gazed out the window at the familiar landscape, remembering nights whiled away in his family's snug cottage, he and Ellen playing on the floor while their mother read by the fire. Days spent with his father, learning carpentry and building. Afternoons fishing with the local nobleman's son, Lord Randal, both of them starved for companionship their age.

That felt like a lifetime ago. Now Rand was a married man, a man who looked as though he'd seen all his hopes and dreams realized—on the very day that Kit's seemed to be slipping away.

His hand went into his surcoat pocket, grasping at the small, worn bit of brick he always carried there. A chip off his very first project.

For twelve years—through school and university, through punishing hours and sleepless nights—he had dedicated himself to one goal. The Deputy Surveyor post was almost within his grasp.

He couldn't fail now.

THREE

"*Y*OU LOOK melancholy," Rose's mother said later that evening. Standing with Rose in her perfumery, Mum picked over the many flower arrangements on her large wooden worktable, plucking out the marigolds. "Why the long face, dear? Are you sad to see your creations destroyed?"

"Of course not." Rose added a purple aster to a pile of flowers and some ivy to a bunch of greens. She cleared her throat, then forced what she hoped sounded like a romantic sigh. "The wedding was beautiful, wasn't it?"

"Made more so by your lovely flowers." Rose had filled the house with towering creations made of posies cut from her father's gardens. "Which is why," her mother added, "I thought—"

"I don't care what becomes of my flower arrangements. Honestly, Mum, it makes no sense to let the blooms wither and die when we can turn them into essential oils for your perfumes. I don't mind in the least." With a bit more force than necessary, Rose tugged two lilies from the vases and tossed them onto the table. "Whatever happened to Christopher Martyn, do you know?" she asked in an attempt to change the subject.

"That messenger brought news of a problem with one of his projects. He had to leave."

"Which project?" Rose asked.

"He didn't say. Or perhaps I don't remember." Mum fixed her with a piercing gaze. A motherly gaze. "Does it signify?"

"Of course not. I was just curious, that's all." A touch of the headache began to pulse in Rose's temples. "Why should I care what happens to his projects?"

"You danced with him—"

"Father traded that dance for a greenhouse. I had no say in the matter."

Her mother nodded thoughtfully, beginning to pluck petals from a bunch of striped snapdragons. "You just look melancholy."

Rose pursed her lips, quashing her exasperation. She lifted the lid off the gleaming glass and metal distillery that Ford had made for her mother while he was courting Violet. "It's nothing, Mum."

"It doesn't bother you that your younger sister is wed?"

"Why should it?" She was chagrined to hear her voice crack. "I wish her happy, Mum. I do. I vow and swear it."

"It's no failing of yours, dear, that Lily met with love first."

"Stuck as we are in the countryside, it's a wonder she met anyone at all." It was an ancient complaint, but in her present mood Rose had no compunctions against dragging it out again. "We've hardly ever been to London, or anywhere else we might meet eligible—"

"You have a point," Mum interrupted.

"Pardon?" Rose blinked.

"You heard me. You haven't much opportunity here to meet gentlemen." Mum tossed the pink petals into the distillery's large glass bulb. "I'm thinking that we—you and I—should attend court."

"Court?" Rose decided she couldn't be hearing right. One of them had clearly drunk too much champagne. "As in King Charles's court?"

"I believe they're at Windsor now—they do move around, as you may know."

"What I *know* is that you and Father have always claimed court is no place for proper young ladies."

"Well, you're not so young anymore," Mum said, then came to wrap an arm around Rose when she winced. "I didn't mean it that way, dear. But you're nineteen now, a woman grown. And I *will* be there to chaperone. It's perfectly acceptable."

It was more than acceptable, Rose knew—girls as young as fifteen went to court, many of them *un*chaperoned. And she also knew the licentious men there treated them like full-grown women. Violet had been to court with Ford, and she'd come back with stories that had made Rose's hair curl.

A little part of her wondered if this was really such a grand idea.

But she wasn't going to argue when faced with such extraordinary good fortune. "Gemini, I'd best go talk to Harriet! She'll need to alter some of my gowns, and it will take hours to decide what to bring before she can even begin."

"There's no time for alterations, dear." In contrast to Rose, whose stomach was churning with excitement, Mum calmly plucked petals. "I mean to leave tomorrow."

"Tomorrow!" Rose dropped the stem in her hand. "Tomorrow?"

"There's no time like the present," her mother said with an enigmatic smile.

Normally, Rose might have been mortified by the implication that her spinsterhood was fast approaching. But this was no time to be touchy.

No, it was time to prepare.

She was going to court! Leaving her flowers on the table, she hastened to her chamber to pack.

FOUR

"**W**HAT A DAY." Chrystabel slipped beneath the counterpane to join her husband in bed, sinking into the mattress as she relaxed for the first time in what seemed like weeks. "Thank heaven they're married at last."

"I suspect you're really thanking heaven Lily's virtue is no longer at risk," Joseph teased, leaning up to kiss her lightly on the lips. He lowered himself onto an elbow, smiling into her eyes, his own a deep, sparkling green.

She pushed a lock of dark hair off his forehead. "Well, there is that," she admitted. Her eldest daughter's courtship had taught her the vulnerability of a girl's virtue—and her own motherly duty to protect it with every stratagem she possessed.

Chrystabel was a woman who could learn from her mistakes.

"But mostly," she added, "I'm just gladdened to see them happy at last. Everything worked out."

"It usually does," said her ever-practical husband.

She released a contented sigh. "Another wedding."

"Another wedding night," he responded with another kiss.

A tradition, their wedding nights. That was one of the reasons she so loved arranging other people's marriages.

Chrystabel kissed him back, her hands on his warm, stubbly cheeks. "I'll miss you," she murmured against his lips.

"Where are you going?" He pulled back slightly in alarm.

"I'm thinking to take Rose to court at Windsor. With your permission, of course," she rushed to add, knowing he would never deny her.

"Court? Do you expect that's wise? The men there—"

"I'll watch her like a hawk. And rest assured, there's not a man at court I want for Rose. She belongs with Kit Martyn. He's at Windsor as we speak, checking on a project—"

"Kit Martyn? You've mentioned him before. Chrysanthemum my love, I know you fancy yourself a matchmaker, but Rose has shown no interest—"

"Which is exactly why he's perfect for her."

Joseph lifted his head and searched her eyes in the dim, flickering light from the fire. "Come again?"

"You know how she is. As soon as she sets her sights on a gentleman, the act begins. The shameless flirting and flattery. Don't you see? She's doomed to chase away anyone worthy of her—unless he's someone she thinks she doesn't want. With Kit she'll be herself. Charming, intelligent, sharp-witted....why, he cannot fail to fall in love with her."

"I suspect he's taken with her already," Joseph said dryly. "But what good will that do if she doesn't fall for him? We've promised her she can choose her own husband."

"Making her fall," Chrystabel said, "will be Kit's problem, and I've no doubt he's up to the task. I need only provide the opportunity."

"You cannot push, Chrysanthemum."

Her laugh tinkled through the darkness. "I would never. I know full well our daughters pledged to avoid me arranging their marriages. Yet I managed to match both Violet and Lily without either being the wiser, didn't I? Have no fear, darling— Rose's romance will follow suit. And she'll have no idea I was behind it."

FIVE

K IT STOOD IN a corner of Windsor Castle's soon-to-be new dining room, watching two carpenters affix carvings of fruit to the paneled wall. The piece, exquisitely worked by Grinling Gibbons, was made of supple lime wood, a fine material.

He wished he could say the same for the rest of his project.

His gaze went to the sagging ceiling on the side of the room that had recently been part of a brick courtyard. Jagged cracks ran this way and that, and bits of broken plaster littered the floor underneath. On his orders, men were hastily erecting scaffolding to support the damaged ceiling until it could be repaired from above.

All day, Kit had measured and figured, tearing out parts of the ceiling to search for causes, to find where his planning had gone wrong. It hadn't, he'd finally discovered—the plans had been perfect. That was, if they'd been executed with the high quality materials he'd used in his calculations.

But Harold Washburn, his project's foreman, had apparently not seen fit to order those materials, no matter that he'd been supplied with the funds. Instead, the new portion of the room had been built with inferior goods that weren't strong enough to support the ceiling. Kit had found beams made of wormy wood that had obviously been hit by lightning, weakening it; and cheap, substandard plaster that might look fine on first inspection, but wouldn't hold up over the years, sagging ceiling or not.

And Washburn, no doubt, had pocketed the savings. Making Kit look the fool.

Calculations in hand, he stalked toward the foreman. "Washburn!"

The older man swung around, his beady gaze hooded. "Aye, young Martyn? Have you a plan to repair the faulty addition?"

"Faulty?" Seething, Kit loomed over the balding old cur. Washburn may have had the advantage in years, but Kit had the height. "The only thing faulty here is your honor—or appalling lack thereof. Do you know what the penalty is for bilking the Crown?"

Washburn had the gall to feign innocence. "Sir? What are these accusations? I would never—"

"Never again for me, at any rate," Kit interrupted. He gestured with his rolled-up sketches. "Be gone."

The man's breath huffed in and out through a large nose crisscrossed with tiny red veins. "You think you can just dismiss me?" he growled.

"Would you rather be swinging from the gallows? Or buried under several tons of wormy wood?" Kit spit on the ground at the man's feet. "You're lucky I'm only dismissing you."

Astonishingly, Washburn simply shouldered past him and marched out.

Was it Kit's imagination, or did the old cur actually look smug?

Kit consciously unclenched his jaw, reaching for the scrap of brick in his pocket. His fist clenched around it; he'd been itching for a fight.

In the end, though, the anger faded, replaced by relief. In truth, the crisis had resolved far more quickly and easily than he'd feared.

He took a deep breath, promoted a grateful mason to take

Washburn's place, then headed to the small chamber he'd been given to use as an office, revising the schedule in his head. The project would still finish on time.

That there were greedy men in the world wasn't news to Kit. He wouldn't let this particular one cost him the Deputy Surveyor post.

It would take worse than the likes of Harold Washburn to stand in Kit Martyn's way.

SIX

"*H*URRY," ROSE SAID. "Or by the time we get to court, the presentations will be finished."

"Stop worrying, dear." Seated together with Rose at the single dressing table in the rooms they'd been assigned at Windsor Castle, Mum held very still while her maid, Anne, used hot curling tongs to put the final touches on her hair. "We'll still be admitted, even if we're late."

With all the last minute preparations, they'd left home today much later than they'd planned. Mum had needed to leave instructions for the running of the entire household, and Harriet, Rose's maid, had taken forever to pack. It had been dark by the time they'd reached Windsor, and Rose, dying of curiosity, had hardly been able to see anything of the enormous castle as a warden showed them by torchlight to their small apartments.

"I don't *want* to be late," Rose complained. Beneath wine-colored satin sleeves fastened at intervals with jeweled clasps, her skin prickled with suppressed excitement. "I want to meet the king and queen."

"You will, dear." Mum met her gaze in the dressing table's mirror. "You look very pretty."

"Yes, you certainly do," Harriet added as she wove matching

burgundy ribbons through the bun on the back of Rose's head. "And just think of all the new men you're going to meet! I can hardly believe I'm here, so far from Trentingham."

Actually, it wasn't far at all—little more than a couple of hours downriver. Though Rose had never been inside the castle before, she and her sisters often came to Windsor to visit the shops. But Harriet had been born at Trentingham Manor and, at age nineteen, had never gone farther than the nearest village before today.

Rose reckoned that was half the reason for their late start. Harriet had been so flustered, she'd been unable to keep her mind on the preparations.

"You just might meet a nice young man, too," Mum told Harriet, a familiar light coming into her brown eyes. Chrystabel Trentingham was always happiest when matchmaking. She didn't care whether the couples were royalty or servants, so long as—thanks to her—two people were finding true love.

"Do you think so?" Harriet's fingers fumbled with the ribbons as a wistful expression unfocused her pale green eyes.

Rose had never thought of Harriet as pining for romance. Harriet was just Harriet, a sturdy girl with frizzy red hair and a wide face full of freckles.

But now that face had gone soft and dreamy. "How I would love to fall in love," the maid sighed.

"I shall keep that in mind," Mum promised her.

"There, Lady Trentingham, you're finished," her own maid Anne said. "And you look wonderful, too. As for Harriet," she added, aiming a wink at the girl, "my lady will find you someone special to love."

Anne's husband had been a coachman at the Liddington estate before Mum's ministrations brought the pair together. Now they both resided happily at Trentingham, and so far they had produced one boisterous stableboy-in-training and a darling little chambermaid-to-be.

Mum stood and smoothed her peach silk skirts, looking to Rose. "Come along, dear. Do you mean to make us late?"

Though a retort danced on the tip of Rose's tongue, she clamped her mouth shut and leapt to her feet. As she followed her mother across the Upper Ward, excitement churned in the pit of her stomach.

She was about to meet the king and queen of England.

When they reached the open courtyard called Horn Court, where two red-and-white liveried footmen stood guard at the door, she paused and pulled a curl forward to rest artfully on one shoulder. Her breath was coming short, and it had little to do with the rigid stomacher that stiffened the front of her bodice.

"Shall we?" Mum asked, gesturing toward the door.

One of the footmen pulled it open.

To Rose's disappointment, the monarchs weren't waiting right inside. Instead, she followed her mother into a tall, wide hall that held nothing but a staircase. But what a staircase. "Oooh," she breathed. "It's beautiful!"

"It's in the French style," Mum whispered back. "While exiled on the Continent, King Charles was much taken with Versailles."

French or English, Rose thought the staircase was magnificent. Twin flights of steps rose to their right and left, meeting at a central landing above. The rooms they had been given here were rather ancient, with plain plastered walls, but these walls were covered in colorful painted murals depicting Greeks and Trojans. Giants battled on the deeply coved ceiling that towered over her head.

As Rose climbed the steps, carefully holding her skirts, she felt very small and insignificant. She supposed that was the desired effect. Even here, outside his chambers, the king would want to project strength and power.

At the top of the stairs, she held her breath while another liveried footman opened another door.

But she was disappointed again. Beyond lay an enormous rectangular room with no furniture—and no king or queen, either. A handful of courtiers stood in little clusters, absorbed in low, murmured conversations.

Rose's and Mum's high-heeled shoes made clicking sounds on the planked floor as they crossed the chamber. Rose huffed out a sigh. "Where are the king and queen?"

"We're getting there, dear. This is the Guard Chamber."

She might have guessed. Military trophies covered every inch of the walls: helmets and drums, shields and armor, guns and lancets, swords and knives. "Are there any weapons left for the army?" she whispered.

Mum's laugh broke the hush of the chamber. "I certainly hope so!" She met Rose's gaze, her eyes glittering. "It's an impressive display, but all the same, I expect we're still well defended."

The painted ceiling featured Jupiter and Juno seated on thrones at either end. In the center, a glassed octagonal opening provided a view of the stars and, Rose imagined, a great splash of natural light in the daytime.

Reaching the door at the far end, Mum paused. "Lady Trentingham and Lady Rose Ashcroft," she announced, her voice laced with quiet dignity.

Finally. As one of the six guards bowed and opened the door, Rose lifted her satin skirts.

But the next room was deserted, save for an usher at the far end.

"What's this?" Rose demanded.

"The King's Presence Chamber." Mum curtsied in front of the sumptuous red velvet throne, taking Rose's hand to make certain she did, too.

Thinking it the most ridiculous thing she'd ever done, Rose pursed her lips as she straightened. "Despite the name of the chamber, the king," she said pointedly, nodding toward the empty throne, "does not seem to be present."

"Come along," her mother said with a half-concealed smile.

Rose looked to the heavens for patience, seeing instead an elegant painted ceiling where Mercury was presenting a portrait of the king to the four corners of the world.

A red-and-white-garbed usher grandly opened the next door.

By now, Rose wasn't expecting to see Their Majesties on the other side. She'd probably be a wrinkled old crone by the time she actually met them.

"The Audience Chamber," Mum intoned softly. "You'll curtsy to this vacant throne as well." She glided toward the canopied seat. "Charles does sit here to receive visitors in the daytime."

"Does he never sit in the other throne?"

"That throne is only symbolic, dear. Ceremonial."

Rose was still questioning the necessity of all the empty chairs when she glimpsed the next chamber. Her jaw dropped open—and it had nothing to do with the elaborate ornamentation, or even the spectacular clothing and jewels that adorned all the lords and ladies milling about.

Unable to avert her gaze, she drifted slowly through the room by her mother's side. There, in that dark corner, a woman sat sprawled on a man's lap, her head thrown back in laughter. Across the chamber, a fluttering curtain left the distinct impression that action of some sort was going on behind it.

Nearby, another couple was kissing with what one might call *great enthusiasm*. Rose's cheeks heated—and it took a lot to make her blush. She'd always pulled faces at her parents' shows of affection, but they'd never behaved anything like *this*...

Gemini!

The man's gaze had met Rose's for a moment. Or at least she thought it had—she couldn't be sure, given how quickly she'd shifted to focus on the ceiling overhead. But the artwork above did nothing to erase the shocking images in her head. There, the painted King Charles rode in a chariot, entirely surrounded by naked—

"They're angels, dear. You needn't gawk." Her mother's hand squeezed her arm. "We're about to be announced."

"Announced?" Rose had been so distracted, she hadn't even realized she'd finally made it to the chamber where Their Majesties waited.

Rose had always considered herself unshockable, but quite suddenly she felt like an innocent country mouse. Father had been right all along, she thought. Court was no place for a well-bred young lady.

Good thing she wasn't so young anymore.

The couple in front of her bowed and curtsied and moved out of the way, and she found herself approaching a red-canopied dais.

"Lady Trentingham!" the stuffy usher called. "Lady Rose Ashcroft!" Rose held out her skirts—so plain compared to the jewel-encrusted gowns of the other ladies—and dropped into a deep curtsy. When she came up, she managed to smile at King Charles, a bit startled to find that he seemed to be an actual human being.

She'd seen paintings, of course, but of a younger man, and somehow not such a real one. The king was forty-seven now, and a bit of gray-streaked hair peeked out from beneath his long, curled black periwig. His dark eyes were as sharp as ever, though—or at least as sharp as Rose had always heard. They swept her from head to toe, a gaze both approving and more than a bit flirtatious.

Well, he *was* known for that.

In contrast, Queen Catharine's eyes were a warm, liquid brown. She wasn't a beauty, but her appearance wasn't displeasing, either—she looked sad, and a little world-weary.

After fifteen years of marriage, she had yet to present her husband with a child.

Standing before Catharine, Rose imitated what her mother was doing with Charles and lifted the queen's hand to press a kiss to the back.

She was rewarded with a smile. "It's a pleasure to make your acquaintance," Catharine told her in flowing, Portuguese-accented English.

"The pleasure is mine," Rose returned sincerely. Really, she couldn't imagine why her sisters had gone all fluttery over the prospect of meeting the monarchs. They were just people!

She switched sides with her mother and bent her lips to the king's hand.

He surprised her by gripping her fingers. "You're as lovely as your mother."

Mum blushed. Rose grinned at Charles. "Your reputation is well deserved, Your Majesty."

Still holding her hand, he grinned back. "My reputation, my dear?"

"As a ladies' man."

Mum gasped. When Charles threw back his head and laughed, Rose shot her a triumphant smile.

Charles glanced around the room. "It seems you're the last to be presented," he said, looking not displeased by that fact. "Would you honor me with a dance?"

Now it was Rose's turn to gasp. She knew the protocol was for ladies to ask His Majesty to dance, not the opposite. Feeling light-headed, she curtsied again. "It would be my honor, Sire."

"The second dance, then," he said, rising from his throne. He held out a hand to Catharine, and she rose as well and allowed him to guide her to the dance floor, the gems on her exquisite lavender gown twinkling as she moved.

The incessant chatter in the room ceased as everyone turned to watch the king and queen dance the first dance. Rose drifted to join the small crowd that ringed the dance floor, hugging herself with excitement. After the king danced with her, surely other gentlemen would want to do the same. Maybe one of them would end up her husband.

In fact, before the first dance even ended, she felt a light tap on her shoulder. The hand's owner was tall, fair, and handsome, his attire dripping with lace, his manner oozing aristocracy.

He struck a pose, one hand resting lightly on the jeweled hilt of his court sword, the other on the head of his high, beribboned walking stick. "Lady Trentingham, may I have the honor of an introduction?"

Though the stranger seemed near in age to Rose, she wasn't surprised he was an acquaintance of her mother's. The woman made friends with everybody—young or old, rich or poor, male or female. Mum probably had more friends than Father had flowers.

She laid a hand on Rose's arm. "Lord Rosslyn, may I present my daughter, Lady Rose Ashcroft? Rose, this is the Earl of Rosslyn."

"It's a pleasure," the earl murmured, lifting Rose's hand to his lips. "I hope you and I shall—"

"And may we offer our congratulations, my lord?" Mum went on pleasantly, as if he hadn't spoken. Her smile showed all her teeth. "You must be *delighted* with your new bride."

Lord Rosslyn didn't bat an eye, or even drop Rose's hand. "Indeed, my lady." He inclined his head toward the left, where Rose saw a young woman entwined with a man wearing a bright pink suit. "We are perfectly compatible."

I'll say, Rose thought, half tempted to bash him over the head with his own walking stick. But she'd only just managed to extricate her hand when King Charles appeared by her side and bowed. "My lady?"

Rosslyn's eyes widened, making Rose feel rather smug as she joined the king on the dance floor.

It was a country dance, performed in two lines, one of women, one of men. When it was her turn to parade down the center with Charles, their joined hands held high, Rose felt the eyes of the entire chamber on her.

The king's eyes were on her as well. Dark and glinting, they captured hers quite effectively. The fabled Stuart charm. "It's a pleasure to have a new face at court, my lady. Especially one as lovely as yours." Charles danced superbly, quite graceful for so tall a man. His voice was just as smooth. "Why have you never graced us with your presence before?"

She blushed once again—becomingly, she hoped. "My father thought me too young."

"Young?" he echoed, sounding puzzled.

And then they had to return to their respective lines.

As she executed the simple steps, she furtively surveyed the throng. There were ladies of her mother's age, certainly, but there were also girls of fifteen and sixteen. Or perhaps she should term them women, since they hung on the arms of grown men, flirting madly and more.

Clearly, she wasn't too young.

The next time she met up with the king to parade down the center, she had a more plausible reason. "I've come to court to find a husband, Sire."

"Ah." His dark eyes glittered speculatively. "Interesting choice of word, my lady. Husbands we have, although many are already wed." He smiled at his own jest. "Take me, for example—"

"I won't be," she interrupted archly.

Though she immediately worried that he might take offense, he only laughed. "You *are* your mother's daughter," he conceded good-naturedly.

Among this social circle filled with promiscuous spouses, her parents were known as extraordinarily devoted.

When the dance came to an end, the king raised her hand, pressing warm lips to the back. "It was a pleasure, my lady. I wish you every success here at court."

For a moment, while he still held her hand, Rose found herself suffused with wonder. Here she was, in the King's Drawing Room at Windsor Castle, with none other than Charles himself. A night like this could go to a girl's head, she thought giddily.

Then he led her from the dance floor, and she watched him head straight to a girl of no more than seventeen and kiss her soundly on the lips. Rose couldn't help but notice his queen was studiously gazing elsewhere, resignation etched on her small, foreign-looking face.

Apparently all was not lightness and fun here at Windsor Castle.

But this was Rose's first evening at court, not a night to shoulder the worries of the world. She looked away, determined to enjoy the spectacle that was the royal court. Courtiers wore every color of the rainbow. Great lords swaggered about impressively while elegant ladies fluttered delicate painted fans.

"May I claim the pleasure of a dance?"

Startled, she turned to see a heartbreakingly handsome gentleman. "I'd be delighted, my lord...?"

"Bridgewater. The Duke of Bridgewater," he clarified with a warm smile and a smart bow.

Rose was pleased to see he wasn't carrying one of those foppish ribbon-topped walking sticks. And he was a duke! Not only a duke, but a youngish duke—of an age, Rose guessed, below thirty.

Most dukes, in her experience, were doddering old coots.

As he swept her into the dance, her heart skittered with excitement. Already she was dancing with exactly the sort of man she'd come here hoping to meet.

"My given name is Gabriel, and my family name is Fox," he informed her quite pleasantly. "You're Trentingham's daughter, aren't you?"

"Yes. Rose Ashcroft," she said, gazing up at him—for he was tall. Tall enough to make her feel nearly as petite as her sister Lily. Her gaze skimmed from the top of his very-English blond head, past blue eyes, and down a patrician nose to his smiling mouth, each detail making her even happier.

He was perfect!

She was certain she was falling in love already.

"My dear Rose—may I call you Rose?" he asked, and then continued without waiting for confirmation. "I hope your mother will approve of our dancing without a proper intro-duction."

He was not only perfect, but a perfect gentleman as well.

She gave a well-practiced flutter of her lashes. "To be sure, your grace." Imagine being called *your grace*—her stomach fluttered at the mere possibility. "My mother brought me here to meet gentlemen like you." *Exactly like you*, she revised silently, overjoyed to have caught the attention of such a man.

And she *did* have his attention. His hands gripped hers rather more tightly than was necessary, as though he were loath to let her escape. Not that she minded. To the contrary—his possessiveness made a little thrill run through her.

Court was *wonderful*. Even while dancing with Gabriel—for already, she thought of him as such—she couldn't help but be aware of her surroundings. The entire room glittered with the light of hundreds of candles in the chandeliers above and tall torches held by liveried yeoman, not to mention all the flashing precious metal and gemstones that adorned everyone in attendance.

That observation prompted her to scrutinize Gabriel's jewels. A heavy gold chain draped flat across the peacock blue velvet of his surcoat. Beneath that, a strand of fat pearls gleamed in the firelight, swaying a bit as he moved with the dance. His lacy white cravat was secured with a large diamond pin, and the buttons on his suit boasted sapphires and diamonds set in glittering gold. Froths of lace spilled from his sleeves onto hands adorned with various rings set with rubies, emeralds, and jet. His high-heeled shoes sported gold and sapphire buckles.

Not only was he a duke, he was a *rich* duke!

When the dance came to an end, Rose felt deflated. One never danced with the same partner two tunes in a row. But when Gabriel bowed over her hand and kissed it, she knew he would ask her again.

No sooner had he straightened than another courtier rushed over and begged the honor of a dance. She accepted happily, thinking she would be generous enough to give him a fair appraisal. Him, and any other fellow who sought her good graces.

But she knew—she just *knew*—that none of them would be as perfect for her as the delicious, delectable, utterly divine Duke of Bridgewater.

SEVEN

*K*IT WALKED BRISKLY through the dark castle grounds toward Sir Christopher Wren's apartments—the official apartments of the Surveyor General, apartments he hoped to occupy himself someday. Not that he'd actually live there. He had just put the finishing touches on a brand new house here in Windsor—a house of his very own, situated on an enviable plot of land on the banks of the River Thames.

In fact, his sister, Ellen, was waiting for him there now. At least, he hoped she was waiting for him. If she was off with that lousy Whittingham fellow again…

Reaching his destination, he put those brotherly concerns from his mind and gave the door two sharp knocks. When it opened, Kit was startled to see not Wren's secretary, but the man himself, dressed in shirtsleeves and no periwig. His dark hair was disheveled, as though he'd raked his hands through it repeatedly.

Wren didn't reside in these official apartments either, but instead used the rooms as his offices. Like Kit, Wren had recently built an impressive house for himself in town. But as the Dean of

Windsor's son, he'd been raised right here in the castle deanery, a playmate of the young Prince of Wales—now King Charles— and he and his monarch were still intimates. Kit was hoping their long-standing relationship would mean Wren could convince the king that Kit was the right candidate for the Deputy Surveyor post.

But the look on Wren's face wasn't reassuring.

"This new development does not bode well," Wren said without preamble. Waving Kit toward a chair, he settled himself against a large drafting table strewn with copious drawings, rubbing at the shadow of gray whiskers sprouting on his chin.

Though the Surveyor General was more than two decades his senior, Kit counted him a friend. Wren had been his favorite professor at university, while Kit had been Wren's prized pupil. After Oxford, Wren had done what he could to champion his young protégé—and thank heaven for that, or Kit would prob- ably still be designing pantries instead of palaces. Unlike his more privileged classmates, he hadn't started his career amidst a heap of impressive commissions. He'd actually had to *earn* his reputation.

"Until this unfortunate mishap," Wren continued, "you were the front-runner for the Deputy Surveyor appointment. But King Charles hasn't the patience for costly errors—the monarchy, I'm afraid, is as cash-strapped as ever."

Kit rubbed the back of his neck. "The error wasn't strictly mine—my foreman chose to use substandard materials. Not," he rushed to add, "that I don't take responsibility. Quite clearly I erred in hiring the man in the first place. I will make up the losses."

Wren nodded thoughtfully, his brown eyes sympathetic. "Last I saw, the dining room was coming along brilliantly— impeccable craftsmanship, exceptional eye to detail." His lips thinned. "Regardless, I'm now under pressure to award the appointment to Rosslyn."

Gaylord Craig, the young Earl of Rosslyn, had been a classmate of Kit's—and not a particularly stellar one. But he came from a prominent family of staunch Royalists, one of many such families King Charles owed for their support in the Civil War. And it was far cheaper to repay those families with political appointments than with gold.

Kit's fingers curled around the bit of brick in his pocket. "Can the king's mind be changed?"

"Anything is possible. Charles plans to inspect the project tomorrow, so if you can make certain the site is safe and any debris is cleared—"

"Of course."

"—perhaps we can divert his attention to the impressive design."

"I'll have everything under control," Kit assured him.

If necessary, he would comb the town for extra hands to work through the night. Sufficient scaffolding would be erected to assure no safety concerns, and the site would look pristine, whatever it took to make it that way. "What time have you scheduled the visit?"

"Noon."

"Then I shall be ready by ten."

"Make sure you are." Though Wren's words sounded serious, he tempered them with a small smile. "With any luck, we can pull this off."

"I've never put much stock in luck. Hard work and persistence have done well by me so far." Kit returned the smile with a wry one of his own. "But I suppose a little luck wouldn't come amiss just this once."

Wren rose and opened the door, giving Kit a companionable slap on the back as he ushered him through it. "I'll do what I can."

"I'm counting on it," Kit told him.

Hard work and persistence. He'd always believed that with both, anything could be his.

The castle grounds were quiet this time of night, the Round

Tower on its huge mound of earth looming tall and imposing between the Lower and Upper Wards. Kit's footfalls echoed off the cobblestones as he skirted the circular structure and cut through Horn Court on the way back to his site.

Nodding a familiar greeting, the usher there opened the door to admit him to the King's Staircase. Kit hurried up the steps and through the progression of chambers—rooms he didn't belong in, if one went strictly by rank. But as one of the king's architects, he had free access.

His mind on the hectic night ahead, he fairly sprinted through the Audience Chamber and into the King's Drawing Room, where court was in full swing this evening. There, he stopped short at the sight of Rose Ashcroft on the dance floor.

He very nearly tripped over his own feet.

Rose was stunning in burgundy satin. Her wide neckline exposed creamy skin, and her jewel-studded bodice tapered to a narrow, elegant waist. Most striking of all, her face was flushed with excitement, her rose-red mouth beaming. He'd never seen her looking so happy. As if she hadn't a care in all the world.

He wanted to be the one making her look that way.

But she was dancing with a gentleman—a tall, blond, and exceedingly aristocratic one. Kit hated him on sight.

As she spun in the stranger's arms, jealousy crawled over Kit's skin. Which was absurd, aggravating, and utterly unproductive. She would never be his—at least not until he had the one thing that could make a lowly commoner worthy of someone like Lady Rose Ashcroft.

A title.

There was reason to hope a knighthood might accompany the Deputy Surveyor appointment—Kit's good friend Sir Christopher Wren hadn't been *born* a knight, after all. If the king was sufficiently impressed with Kit's work, he might judge it prudent to raise his rank, granting him the status of a member of the court.

Which had, as it happened, always been Kit's long-term goal. Holding a title meant the Martyns would forever after be members of the enviable gentry class. Never again would he, his sister, or their descendants suffer the desperation and humiliation of poverty. The degradation of being pitied. Looked down upon. Inferior.

And suddenly it seemed vital that Kit achieve that goal *now*. Today. Yesterday! This very evening Rose might accept an offer from one of the many rich, eligible men who were presently ogling her. She could very soon be betrothed to the blond cur who was holding her—in Kit's opinion—quite a bit closer than was necessary.

Not that *Kit* was ready to propose. Perish the thought! He barely knew her, after all. All he knew so far was that she was beautiful, clever, and challenging. And that he wanted to know more. And that the thought of never having the chance to know more made his lungs mysteriously stop working.

If he wanted to keep breathing, he would have to win that appointment.

Determination made his jaw clench and his hands curl into fists. It would take more than cleaning up Washburn's mess to impress Charles. He must not only meet, but surpass expectations—and with Wren talking up Kit's merits to the king, likely those expectations had been raised high.

Windsor's new dining room would prove to be spectacular, that was a given. The renovations at Whitehall Palace and the new building at Hampton Court—apartments for Charles's longtime mistress and their five children—would have to be equally so.

Kit tore his gaze from Rose and strode through the glittering assembly, exiting the drawing room into the small, as-yet-unrenovated vestibule that led to his project.

"Martyn."

Kit turned to see Gaylord Craig, the Earl of Rosslyn, follow and close the heavy door behind him. After the hubbub of court, the vestibule seemed quiet, the music and voices muffled to a dull hum.

"Yes, Rosslyn?"

Slim, fair, and fine-featured, Rosslyn clapped Kit on the back. "I hear you've run into a spot of trouble, my friend."

Kit cast him a sharp glance. "And thought you'd come gloat over your rival's misfortune?"

"My rival?" Rosslyn snorted. "You think I care a fig for that piddling appointment? I'm overwhelmed with commissions as it is." His pale blue eyes raked Kit's plain clothes. "And I certainly have no need of a knighthood. Truth be told, it would suit me quite well if you took the Deputy Surveyor job off my hands."

"Then you'll be happy to know my project has suffered only a minor setback. I will finish by the deadline as planned."

"I'm glad of it."

Kit measured his old classmate, watching him toy with the ribbons that crowned his walking stick. "You could simply refuse the appointment, you know. If you don't want it."

"Refuse the king? Gads, Martyn, you *are* new to court." One square-toed high-heeled shoe tapped impatiently. "I shall have to serve if Charles commands it of me. But I'd much rather spend my time in more, ah, satisfying pursuits."

Kit didn't wonder what sort of *pursuits* Rosslyn had in mind. At Oxford, he and his cronies had shown far more enthusiasm for tumbling maids than attending lectures.

"Thus," the earl went on, "if I can assist you in any way, you need only ask. I believe our interests are in alignment." He offered a hand.

Kit shook it. "I say, Rosslyn, this is a relief. I didn't feel quite right competing against you for the post." Not that the two of them had ever been close. Though they'd attended Westminster School as well as university together, they'd never run in the same circles. Kit had been a King's Scholar with his tuition paid by the Crown, while Rosslyn stuck to his own high-born crowd. Still, Kit had always got on well with everyone, and he disliked the idea of making an enemy out of a friend.

But that wouldn't have stopped him from doing whatever it took to beat the competition. He'd been working toward this appointment all his life. Now he was so close.

"You always *were* too good for your own good." Rosslyn's handshake was limp. "Far better than I."

Kit grinned. "Well, then, may the best man win."

He knew he was the best man.

Now he just had to prove it.

EIGHT

𝒶 S THE EVENING wore on, Gabriel sought out Rose for a second dance and then a third. "People will talk," she told him as he guided her toward the dance floor for the fourth time.

"Would that trouble you?" he asked.

"Not at all, your grace." Rose's attention was drawn by a spectacle that was already becoming familiar: King Charles crossing the chamber followed by a bevy of yipping spaniels. Charmed, she smiled as she saw him stop before a petite woman and slide an arm around her possessively. "Who is that?" she asked.

The duke barely spared the couple a glance. "Have you never met Nell Gwyn?"

"Is that Nell Gwyn? Gemini!" Rose knew the name, of course; she doubted there was a soul in England who hadn't heard of the brothel-born actress who'd stolen His Majesty's heart. But she'd expected Nell to be exquisite.

Although the woman heartily kissing the king was pretty, Rose wouldn't call her beautiful. Her small figure was lushly curvy, her hair a riot of red-brown curls. Rose's eyes widened as King Charles backed his mistress toward a chair and pulled her onto his lap. Over the music, Nell's delighted laughter mixed with the ever-present yaps of the king's dogs.

"I had no idea she was allowed at court," Rose mused. "Has His Majesty granted her a title?"

"Of course not." Gabriel maneuvered her around to where she couldn't stare. "But the king made their young son the Earl of Burford, and Nell herself was appointed Lady of the Queen's Bedchamber these two years past."

Rose blinked. "And what does Queen Catharine think of that?"

"I don't expect our dear queen was given a say in the matter." The duke raised a brow as he looked down at her. "Wives usually aren't."

"Not all wives," she said archly. "I'll have you know my family's motto is *Interroga Conformationem*."

"Question Convention?" he translated, looking amused.

Rose smiled, pleased. On top of everything else wonderful about him, the duke knew his Latin.

After a few more dances with gentlemen who failed to measure up to Gabriel, Rose crept off toward the ladies' attiring room, needing a moment to catch her breath. Did court always last so long? She'd been here for hours, and the assembly showed no signs of slowing down.

As she approached the small chamber, Nell Gwyn's distinctive laughter drifted out. "Aye, my ladies, the tale is true."

"Tell us," someone squealed.

"Yes, do tell!" came a veritable chorus.

Wondering just how many ladies were crowded into the attiring room, Rose stopped outside the door and listened.

"I took His Majesty to a bawdy house," Nell confided, "and encouraged him to run up a bill treating everyone to drink. Incognito, of course—it wasn't the type of place his associates frequent, you understand." That was met with titters of laughter. "By and by, I took him up to a room and got him undressed—and then ran away with his clothes."

"You're a bold one, Nelly Gywn!" someone hooted.

"Hush," said another voice. "What happened next?"

"Well, the brothel owner didn't believe this man wrapped in a sheet was her sovereign—you cannot blame the poor fool, can you? He carried no money, so to pay his debt and for something to wear, he offered an emerald ring as security. It was all he had on him, you see."

"And fair enough," a lady pointed out.

"Well, the proprietor refused, claiming it was paste for certain. Our dear king nearly burst a vessel, he did, when fortunately someone recognized him and convinced the owner as to his identity. So all was well."

"He must have been furious," someone breathed.

"You don't know my dear Charles," Nell declared. "Once it was over, he thought it a fine jest indeed!"

Howls of laughter greeted Rose when she stepped into the room. "Good evening, ladies," she said to the nearest cluster of women.

Her smile slowly faded as the chamber fell silent and, in a rustle of expensive fabric, the occupants shouldered their way past her and out the door one by one.

Finally only Nell was left. She shrugged and made her way to Rose. "Don't pay them no mind, milady." Like a man, she held out a hand. "I'm Eleanor Gywn, Nell to my friends."

"I know," Rose replied guardedly. Nell's hand felt small and warm for the brief moment she clasped it. "I'm Rose Ashcroft."

"*Lady* Rose Ashcroft, I've been told." Nell's twinkling eyes nearly closed when she smiled. "They're only jealous of your beauty. And afraid you'll steal their men."

"Gemini!" Rose exclaimed. "Most of them are married!"

"Ah, a babe in the woods." Nell gave a theatrical sigh. "Here at court, that makes no difference. The women consider all male courtiers fair game, and the men hunt amongst the women just as freely. Fidelity went out with Cromwell," she concluded, then wiped her tongue and spit, having uttered the hated name.

Rose grimaced, torn between abhorring such vulgarity and appreciating the kind intention underneath. She slanted Nell an assessing glance. "*You* don't seem to worry that I'll help myself to a courtier or two."

Nell's giggle was infectious. "Bloody right, sweetheart, what do I need with the pompous fools? I bed with the king. It doesn't get any better than that!"

The shock must have been plain on Rose's face, because Nell's giggle rang out louder. Still, Rose couldn't help wondering at her meaning. The aging King Charles wasn't so handsome as he'd once been. Did he possess some sort of special aptitude in the bedchamber?

She was on the verge of asking when another lady barged in, her china-white complexion mottled with angry red. Giving Nell a glare that could curdle milk, she plopped onto a green baize bench with her back to them both, her dark ringlets shaking with barely controlled fury.

Nell made a rude noise, then sailed out the door with a reluctant Rose in tow.

"Who was that?" Rose kept her voice low and her shoulders hunched. Though relieved to escape the attiring room's tension, she didn't fancy the prospect of being seen on Nell's arm.

"Oh, just the high and mighty Louise de Kéroualle."

"The Duchess of Portsmouth?" Another of King Charles's mistresses. It seemed Rose couldn't turn a corner without running into one.

"She's hated by the people, you know," Nell said with relish.

"Because she's a shrew?" Rose scanned the room surreptitiously, worried Gabriel might spot them.

Nell guffawed. "Nay—though she *is*, of course. But it's her Catholicism they hate. Her grace could be the soul of compassion and they'd still hate her, whilst I get cheered through the streets because I'm the *Protestant* whore."

Rose was startled into laughter—though she'd not be repeating the jest to her mother.

"Poor Squintabella is in a snit," Nell explained, "because she arrived today after a long journey from Bath, but although

Charles took dinner with her, he didn't invite her to stay the night."

"Squintabella?" Rose echoed weakly, her head spinning with all this lurid court gossip.

"Did you not notice the slight cast in the duchess's eye? I was here at court before her, and I'll be here long after she's gone. She's managed to send Barbara running across the Channel, but she won't do away with me so easily."

"Barbara? The Duchess of Cleveland has left England?" Rose was having trouble keeping up. Barbara Palmer was Charles's longest-standing mistress, having accompanied him home for his Restoration.

"She's on the outs now, thanks to Louise. Living in Paris. But she'll return—she always does. And no matter what she's done, Charles always forgives her."

"You must find that maddening," Rose said.

"Nay, it's Barbara. She's had him wrapped around her finger for seventeen years. I know better than to expect that to change now." Nell grinned and pecked Rose on both cheeks, sang "Good luck in the woods!" and disappeared in the crowd.

No sooner had she left than Louise de Kéroualle took her place. "Enjoying court, Lady Rose?"

Rose turned in surprise. "Very much," she said distractedly. Baby-faced with almond-shaped eyes, full red lips, and enough jewelry hanging all over her to stock a small shop, the duchess would make any girl feel unsightly next to her beauty.

But her manner rather spoiled her looks. "You'd do best," she sneered in a lisping French accent, "not to fraternize with such as she."

"Do you speak of Nell Gwyn, your grace?" Rose couldn't help but notice the small squint Nell had mentioned.

"I cannot credit that he's taken up with such a coarse, common orange wench." Everyone knew that as a young girl, before she'd stepped on stage at the Theatre Royal, Nell had been employed there selling oranges. "She has no respect for her betters. Calling His Majesty Charles the Third—"

"The *third*, your grace?"

Her smile was full of venom. "The wench's former lovers include Charles Hart—a common actor—who then passed her to Charles Sackville, Lord Buckhurst. She called *him* her Charles the Second, and now the king has become her Charles the Third."

Rose's lips twitched.

"It's not amusing," the duchess said with a sniff. "Charles deserves his due—not least from a guttersnipe like her."

Rose bristled. Louise de Kéroualle, daughter of a distinguished house, quite obviously considered herself much above Nell Gwyn. But the duchess's virtue was just as stained as her rival's. In Rose's estimation, that made them equals—and at least the guttersnipe was *nice*.

Pretty is as pretty does, Mum had always told her three girls. Rose was watching the Frenchwoman's flawless face shrivel up to match her bitter insides when Gabriel appeared.

"Did you not promise me the next dance?" he asked Rose, although she hadn't. He nodded toward the duchess. "Your grace."

The pale beauty nodded back, a smile curving those blood-red lips. "Your grace," she echoed, her voice as sweet and smooth as honey.

The woman, Rose realized, was a natural-born predator. Though she knew tongues would wag when the duke led her off toward the dance floor yet again, she went more than willingly.

As she took her place across from him, her spirits soared with renewed excitement. She'd always said it was as easy to fall in love with a titled man as one without, and the Duke of Bridgewater certainly had a title worth falling for.

The dance was a branle, and all the running, gliding, and skipping left her breathless. Or maybe it was Gabriel...she couldn't be sure. She only knew that when he took her by the arm and drew her toward an exterior door, her heart gave a little lurch.

"Are you certain we should—" she started.

"Quite certain. Aren't you overwarm?" His smile looked innocent enough. "I'm roasting after that dance."

She glanced toward her mother, who was engaged in conversation across the drawing room. Rose didn't hesitate. Here was her chance to get the duke alone and…take a walk. Yes, just a walk. And a nice talk. Alone, together, getting to know each other. The first step toward trapping—*attracting*, that was, *not* trapping!—the perfect husband. Which was why she'd come to court in the first place.

So why was she suddenly uneasy?

Perhaps it was the dark. She'd never liked the dark, so she was dismayed to see naught but a few torches lighting the terrace. It was a mild evening, yet no one else seemed to be outdoors enjoying the weather.

"Should we be out here?" she asked nervously—though there was no reason to be nervous. What could be troubling about a pleasant walk with a nice, gentlemanly duke?

"It's open to the public. Charles expanded this terrace recently, and he's invited the townspeople to enjoy the views. Enormous as it is, it's crowded as Newgate in the daytime."

She'd bet it was—and for no plausible reason, she found herself wishing all those people were here now.

He took her hand and began walking. "How long have you been here at Windsor?"

"We only arrived today."

"Just as I thought—or I would surely have spotted you before now."

They fell quiet as Gabriel guided her toward the edge of the terrace and stopped by the railing. This castle, like most, was built on high land, and the terrace afforded magnificent views. Beneath the castle wall, parkland gave way to a few flickering lights and the moon reflecting off the Thames in the distance. Stars twinkled above.

"It's a lovely night," Rose said to fill the silence.

"Yes, it is." He smiled down at her, his face lit by the moon, his expression perfectly pleasant. "And made more so with such lovely company."

That was nice. Gabriel was nice.

There was no reason to feel uneasy, she reminded herself. No reason at all.

NINE

*K*IT HAD SIX men erecting scaffolding, two chipping off the ruined plaster, and another two hauling away the debris. At the same time, he had a team dispatched to London to fetch the building materials that should have been used in the first place. With any luck, they'd return on the morrow.

Construction work generally halted at dusk. There were no chandeliers in the room as yet, so the men worked by the light of torches and candelabrum. If Kit could persuade the rest of his crew to remain on the job twenty-four hours a day, he would. But of course they were snug in their beds while he fretted. Artists, especially, were temperamental creatures.

"Careful!" he warned, one eye on the late-night crew while he reworked the schedule again in his head, planning contingencies in case the new materials arrived late. "Your haste is appreciated, but I won't have injuries. Or a fire."

"Pardon me!" a musical voice exclaimed. He turned to see a swish of peach-colored skirts as Lady Trentingham swiveled away, narrowly missing being whacked in the head by three men carrying a beam. "I've apparently stumbled into the wrong room."

Emerging from the shadows, Kit strode toward her, his footfalls muffled by the protective tarpaulins on the new oak flooring. "It's perfectly all right, Lady Trentingham." Taking her arm, he drew her over to a safe corner.

"Mr. Martyn!" she said warmly. "I was searching for my daughter—"

"Lady Rose? I thought I glimpsed her earlier. What a surprise to find you both here."

She turned slowly, inspecting the chamber. "I've brought her to court to find a husband."

It was just as Kit had feared. He itched to know more—had Rose taken to anyone? That irksome blond fellow? Was he accident-prone, perchance? Or incurably ill?—but the countess cruelly kept her counsel. Instead of answering Kit's burning questions, she admired the room, her eyes widening with appreciation.

"This ceiling will be exquisite," she commented, gazing up at the half-painted details on the portion of the room that wasn't ruined. "A banquet of the gods, am I right? Fish and fowl…and look, a lobster! How very charming."

"I'm pleased you think so," he said warmly. The countess was back in his good graces. "I envisioned it both exquisite and somewhat amusing. The painter is Antonio Verrio. You may have heard of him?"

"Heavens, yes. The Duke of Montagu brought him from Paris, didn't he? I arranged his marriage. The duke's, not the artist's." She ran a hand down the intricate oak carving on the wall beside her, a melange of fruit and vegetables. "And who is responsible for this?"

"Grinling Gibbons, assisted by Henry Phillips."

She nodded approvingly, still looking around. "The cornice is his work as well, if I'm not mistaken. Are you interested in my daughter, Mr. Martyn?"

He blinked at the rapid change of subject. Not to mention the subject itself. "Lady Rose is indeed interesting," he replied cautiously. "And please, call me Kit."

"Kit." She dropped her gaze to meet his. "That isn't the sort of interest I was enquiring about, and"—a little smile curved her lips—"I suspect you know it. Do you fancy Rose?"

He wished there were furniture in the unfinished room, so he could sit down. "I, um…well…"

"I don't mean a passing fancy," she clarified, the corners of her eyes crinkling. She seemed to be enjoying his discomfort. "Would you fancy her for a wife?"

"A *wife*?" Furniture or no, if this line of questioning continued, he was going to have to sit. The floor was looking mighty tempting. His knees felt weaker than the plaster that was crumbling overhead.

And he hadn't the slightest idea what sort of answer Lady Trentingham sought. If he said yes, would she berate him for aspiring far above his station? If he said no, would she take offense on her daughter's behalf? He rubbed the back of his neck.

Would he fancy Rose for a wife?

Lady Trentingham's smile softened as if she already knew the answer. "You would make her a fine husband, Kit."

He blinked. Was this a jest? Or a hallucination? Had *he* been whacked by that beam? Or could she truly mean…

"But I'm low-born," he blurted. "Doesn't that bother you?"

She fluttered a hand dismissively, her rings winking in the torchlight. "I know a good man when I see one, and rank rarely has much to do with it. In my opinion, that is. As for my Rose's view…" The countess hesitated.

Hope vanished before it had even taken shape. "She cares about rank."

"She thinks she does." The woman looked as though she would have rolled her eyes if it weren't beneath her dignity. "But with persistence and a bit of ingenuity, you may succeed in changing her mind."

"How encouraging." Hands fisting in his pockets, Kit savagely ground a bit of plaster into dust beneath his shoe. "Forgive me, my lady, but why are you telling me all this? If I'm not what Rose wants..."

"What Rose wants is love. And I believe she'll find it with you."

He raised a brow. "I thought you believed in letting her find it herself. Rose told me she was raised to make her own choices, including the choice of who to marry."

"She *will* choose to marry you—just as soon as you've made her fall in love with you."

Kit snorted. "A minor detail."

"Naturally." Perfectly complacent, the countess smoothed her skirts. "After all, you two are meant for each other."

Feeling a strange bubble of hysteria, Kit crushed more plaster underfoot. He still wasn't entirely certain this conversation was real. "And what did your daughter say when you told her she was meant for me—a commoner?"

"Good heavens, I haven't told her. She has no idea I approve of this match. And she can never find out."

"I beg your pardon?"

"Have I mentioned that I'm rather known as a matchmaker?"

"No, but it does seem in character."

She cracked a smile. "Rose wants no part in my matchmaking efforts—she and her sisters vowed long ago never to become one of my 'statistics.' But I love my children too much to let their own stubbornness impede their happiness. I managed to arrange both Lily's and Violet's marriages without their knowledge, and I aim to make it three for three."

"So you were responsible for matching Rand with Lily?"

Her smile betrayed a hint of pride. "And didn't that turn out well?"

Laughing, Kit lifted his hands in a gesture of surrender. "I cannot deny they are exceptionally happy."

"You and Rose will be, too," she said earnestly, her dark eyes so like her daughter's, "if you take my advice."

"And if I conceal your involvement." Kit sighed, watching

his boots scuff the dusty floor. "You're asking me to lie to Rose. It doesn't feel right."

When he looked up again, Lady Trentingham was beaming. "I knew you were a good one. Yes, you'll do very nicely."

Feeling his face slowly heating, Kit cleared his throat. "Thank you, my lady, but—"

"How long have you been in the Crown's employ, Kit?" she interrupted.

"Almost two years." He eyed her suspiciously. "Why?"

She shrugged, searching for something in her pretty little drawstring purse. "I assume you've observed the goings-on here at court. The king and his merry ways? The courtiers and their...proclivities?"

"Let us say that I've observed far more than I ever wanted to."

Lady Trentingham glanced at the time on an enameled watch. "And what might you say," she went on, tucking it back in the purse, "if I told you Rose left the drawing room a quarter of an hour ago, accompanied by one of those courtiers?"

Kit scarcely hesitated.

Barking at a carpenter to take charge, he turned back to the countess and offered his arm. "Have you had a chance to enjoy the terrace, Lady Trentingham? The views are quite spectacular."

TEN

*a*S ROSE AND Gabriel walked, she found herself mentally bouncing back and forth between trying to be her most charming and marveling that the Duke of Bridgewater was choosing to spend so much time with her. As a result, she feared their conversation had been a bit stilted.

But that was only to be expected, wasn't it? After all, they hardly knew each other. Still, her family had always been rather vocal, discussing anything and everything with great enthusiasm, so the awkward silences made her uncomfortable.

"What do you think," she asked after a particularly long gap in their dialogue, "of the maritime agreement we've just signed with France?"

"Maritime agreement?" The duke's perfect brow creased in puzzlement.

Did people not discuss these matters at court? Didn't he read *The London Gazette*? She plucked a yellow bloom off a potted hollyhock plant. "English ships will now be permitted to carry Dutch cargoes without fear of French interference."

A little chuckle burst from his lips. "What would a woman know about that?"

She forced a simpering laugh in return. "Oh, just something I heard," she said and cursed herself silently.

Though she wasn't a student of history or prone to philosophical musings, she'd always been interested in what currently went on in the world. But she should have realized even unsophisticated political matters weren't appropriate topics for ladies to bring up. Would he now think her too intellectual?

She sniffed the flower daintily. "I was just wondering if you could tell me what the agreement might mean to us here in England." When he gave her a blank look, she worried that he might no longer like her. "The significance of such an action escapes me," she lied in a desperate effort to redeem herself.

"That's quite all right, my dear." He squeezed her hand. "Don't worry your pretty little head."

Did he still like her, then? she wondered.

But then he drew her between a turret and a potted tree, and she knew.

He still liked her.

In fact, he was going to kiss her.

She could tell when a gentleman was aiming to kiss her. After all, it had happened before. In truth, she'd lost count of how many young men had tried their luck with her lips—though most hadn't succeeded. Rose wasn't nearly as proper as her sisters, but nor was she apt to kiss every Tom, Dick, and Francis who looked her way.

So she'd been kissed a few times before, and she knew what to expect. But she had a dreadful secret.

She didn't like kissing.

"Gabriel," she whispered when he turned her to face him. "May I call you Gabriel?"

"But of course, dear Rose." His voice had deepened, and he raised a hand and skimmed her cheek. Then it curled around the back of her neck as he drew her closer, and before she could say anything further—before she could attempt to slow him down, to possibly suggest they get to know each other better before sharing this intimacy—he lowered his head.

His other arm went around her, and his hand pressed into the small of her back, drawing her against him. As the flower dropped from her fingers, his mouth came down on hers.

She stiffened, but he seemed to be enjoying himself too much to notice. When he deepened the kiss, she tried to relax and participate. She tried to learn to enjoy herself, too. But try as she might, kissing didn't feel as wondrous as everyone else said it did. In fact, it didn't feel like much at all beyond a damp, messy collision of mouths.

She was relieved when he pulled away—and even more relieved when her mother's distinctive silvery laughter floated to her on the night air.

She spun away and leapt back onto the terrace. "Mum! And...you," she added rather ungraciously as her gaze shifted to her mother's right.

There stood Kit Martyn, looking handsome and mysterious in the low torchlight. A commoner in a plain suit had no right to look so good. She felt those champagne bubbles again, and she hadn't even been drinking spirits.

"What are you doing here?" she asked him.

"Building a new dining room for the king. What have *you* been doing here?" he asked in a way that made it clear he thought he knew.

Rose felt herself turning red. For once, she appreciated the dark.

"She's with me," the duke said, sounding rather possessive. "Though what business is it of yours, I wonder?"

Picturing these two in a fistfight, Rose feared Kit might win. "Your grace," she said quickly, "may I present Mr. Christopher Martyn. Kit, the Duke of Bridgewater." She looked up at Gabriel. "He's just a family friend," she added, feeling it necessary to explain.

"And I asked Mr. Martyn to help me search for you," her mother put in. "I felt it unsafe, as a lady, to be out in the dark alone."

"Indeed, it wouldn't have been wise." Kit held Gabriel's gaze until the duke looked away. "I'm glad to have been of service, but I must be off. I've much to accomplish before tomorrow. Lady Trentingham, Lady Rose." He nodded toward them both, then addressed the duke with an elegant bow. "Your grace."

Slightly disconcerted, Rose watched him walk away.

"We should return as well," her mother told her. "I'm grateful to have found you in such safe hands."

If Mum's voice held a bit of warning, Rose chose to ignore it. She hadn't been doing anything her mother would disapprove of, anyhow. Mum always said one ought to kiss a man before marrying him, to make sure it wasn't disagreeable. Although Rose reckoned that in her own case, she'd just have to resign herself to her fate.

Seething with jealousy, she'd listened to Violet's sighs over her first kisses with Ford, and watched from afar Lily's tender kisses with Rand. But kisses had never been like that for Rose. In all honesty, she found them more than a little repulsive.

Of course, she'd never told her sisters as much, so she sometimes wondered if they, too, were concealing their disgust. But she thought not. Both her sisters were honest to a fault. How they could enjoy having their mouths mauled was beyond her, but apparently they did.

Still, on the way back to the drawing room, she couldn't help smiling up at the duke. She'd liked the way he'd made it clear to the others that she was with him. He truly was perfect.

It wasn't his fault she didn't enjoy kissing.

ELEVEN

"I'M PLEASED." King Charles nodded thoughtfully, his dark eyes skimming the dining room again with approval. "And I'm satisfied with your explanation, Mr. Martyn. Do be certain, however, to complete this project per schedule."

"I can assure Your Majesty that will not prove a problem." Kit walked with the king toward the double doors and threw them wide. "I thank you for taking the time to visit."

Kit smiled as he watched King Charles make his way through the vestibule, several of the man's ever-present spaniels yipping after him. After pulling the doors shut, he unfolded some tarpaulins and laid them near the side of the chamber that was supported by scaffolding. Then he strode through a door at the other end, along a corridor, and into Brick Court. "Come along, now! Beams, lumber—move!"

Dazed, he stepped aside to let the workmen through with the first of the new materials he'd ordered.

If it wouldn't be such a bad example, he'd slump against the wall.

He'd passed.

He wandered back along the corridor and into the dining room, keeping out of his crew's way. He'd been up all night—

supervising, reevaluating, working with his own hands—while his men secured the damaged area and hauled away all evidence of the mishap. He'd attached countless strips of decorative molding, polished all the oak paneling, stripped off the tarpaulins and polished the new floor, too. All in hopes of charming the king's eye.

He'd passed.

Dropping onto a fresh stack of wood and using it as a chair, he flipped blindly through a book of architectural renderings. He should go home; he was exhausted and needed to check in with his sister. Ellen had a habit of finding trouble when he wasn't around.

The drawings before him blurred.

He'd passed.

All was not lost.

When the double doors reopened, his heart seized as he wondered wildly whether the king had some complaint, after all. Two ladies entered instead, and he sagged with relief. Then sat straight when he recognized them.

Lady Trentingham and Rose, both dressed in bright, cheerful colors. Surely a sight for tired eyes.

"Oh!" the countess exclaimed, meeting his gaze. "I didn't expect to find you here."

He wouldn't wager on that.

"I just wanted to show Rose this beautiful chamber," she added.

Kit shut his book. "I was about to leave, anyway. It's time I went home."

"Home? Surely you're not finished here. It looks wonderful, but—"

"It's stunning, Mum! Even better than you described." Rose gazed up at the ceiling. "Beauty and whimsy all rolled into one. I'm beginning to think some of the decoration here at Windsor overdone, but this room doesn't take itself as seriously as the others."

"Thank you," Kit said. Relishing the admiration in her voice, he watched her wander the chamber, touching a carved panel, the white marble mantel, a bit of grooved wainscoting. Smiling, he turned to her mother. "The project is well in hand for the moment; I'm not abandoning it, I assure you. I live right here in Windsor. Not a ten minute walk."

"Is that so? I imagine your home must be lovely."

He knew a hint when he heard one. "Would you like to see it?"

"Mum, I don't think—"

"We'd love to," Lady Trentingham cut in. "Weren't you just saying, dear, how tedious it is here in the daytime?"

TWELVE

*K*IT LED THEM on the easy walk from the castle down the hill to the Thames. Rose decided it felt good to be out in the fresh air. And there truly was nothing to do at Windsor Castle in the daytime. With the exception of the palace staff, it seemed everyone was still abed, sleeping off the excesses of the night before.

When Rose had hit her pillow after midnight, court had still been in full swing. She would have to adjust her country hours and perhaps take a nap this evening before court got underway. They had just begun setting up gaming tables when she left. Although she'd never tried gambling, as the duke was a keen gambler she found herself suddenly eager to join in. Perhaps she could win enough money for a new gown.

The steep, curved street followed the castle wall. Across the road, townspeople were going about their business, entering and exiting rows of gabled shops with living accommodations above. Women carried baskets over their arms, gathering purchases as children and dogs played tag in the cobbled street.

No dirt road here, in this bustling town where the king kept a household.

"Look," she said as they reached the bottom of the hill. "A bookshop."

"John Young, Bookseller," Mum read off the old, cracked wooden sign.

Rose was always looking for new books to help practice her skills. "I wonder if they might have any books written in foreign languages."

"They do," Kit put in. "I found this there." He raised the book tucked under his arm. "It's Latin."

"You read Latin?"

"Certainly not," he said with a smile. "Latin was always my worst subject, and I've forgotten most all of it since leaving school."

Rose wasn't surprised, since he hadn't understood her family's Latin motto.

"I bought this book to examine the drawings," he explained, opening the volume and holding it up as they walked. "See? Classical architecture."

"But there are words," Mum pointed out. "Descriptions."

"True." He sighed as he closed the cover. "I believe, actually, that this book is meant to teach one how to accurately draw buildings. But I enjoy studying the pictures."

"Rose can read Latin," Mum said.

Rose avoided her mother's gaze, instead looking longingly inside the bookshop as they passed. "May we stop here on the way back, Mum?"

"Perhaps."

"We can stop now, if you wish," Kit offered, pleasantly surprising Rose. She thought fleetingly that were it the Duke of Bridgewater walking beside her, she wouldn't have dared show an enthusiasm for books.

It was freeing to be with a gentleman she had no interest in.

"Later," Mum said. "I'm anxious to see the house."

At last they came to the end of the street. On the bucolic River Thames, swans glided majestically. Rose gazed across the

Windsor Bridge toward the charming town of Eton. "Where do you live?" she asked Kit.

"Right here," he said, gesturing toward an impressive redbrick house that sat beside the river.

No, not a house. A *mansion*.

She consciously closed her gaping jaw. "It looks like Rand's house."

Her mother smiled. "Rand's house is white, not brick."

"But the style in which it's built..." Rose looked toward Kit, knowing he'd understand what she meant. "It looks nothing like Windsor's dining room."

"The dining room reflects the king's preferences, not my own."

"I like yours much better," she murmured as he led them under a small columned portico and into the house.

She paused on the threshold, admiring the clean, modern lines of the entry hall. The black marble floor was studded with small white marble diamonds. Smooth, pale stone walls were set off by classic dark oak molding. A high ceiling led to a corridor beyond, where Rose glimpsed a series of archways that vaguely reminded her of a vaulted cathedral.

As she'd said, it reminded her of the house Kit had built for Rand in Oxford. But better. Not to mention at least twice the size.

Kit Martyn was quite obviously a wealthy individual.

"Mr. Martyn." To Rose's surprise, a butler dressed in dark blue rushed to meet him. "Welcome home." His inquisitive pale blue gaze swept over the ladies. "Shall I have Mrs. Potts prepare dinner for three?"

"Thank you, Graves, but I don't believe the ladies are staying long."

"As you say, sir." The servant took himself off.

"You wanted to see the house?" Kit asked, directing the question to Mum.

"We'd love to," she assured him.

He led them through to a drawing room, all white paneled walls with a gray marble fireplace. The furniture was upholstered but not fussy, the windows large and tall, allowing sunshine to flood the room.

"I prefer natural light to candlelight," he told them. "Would you care to sit?"

"No," Rose said. "I'd like to see the rest."

He shared a smile with her mother.

Rose's favorite room on the ground floor was the dining room, a complete contrast to King Charles's in its simplicity. Other than wide crown molding, the ceiling was smooth and white—at night it would reflect the light of the single carved oak chandelier that hovered over the round table. The walls were covered with dark oak paneling, rich and simple except for a few ornately carved sections above the fireplace.

"Sixteenth century, all of it." Kit waved the book he still held, indicating the wood that graced the walls. "I rescued it from a house I renovated—the owner wanted something more extravagant."

Rose turned in a slow circle. "Something more like Windsor Castle's decorations?"

"Very much."

"That owner has no taste," she declared.

Kit grinned. "Would you like to see upstairs?"

A small, exquisite stained-glass window threw colored light onto the curving staircase. "Another item I rescued," Kit said, waving the book at it, too.

The bedchambers weren't simply sleeping rooms; they were suites—and there were many. His sister's was peacock blue with a lovely canopied bed, a sitting room with a settle, a desk, and a marble fireplace, and a mirrored dressing room that made both Rose and her mother jealous. This suite was also the only cluttered area in the house, with pretty little items decorating every flat surface. Rose wondered what his sister was like.

Kit's chamber boasted more classic oak paneling, a red-draped half-tester bed, and a beautiful sitting room surpassed only by the luxurious dressing room. It had the biggest bathtub

Rose had ever seen—not a tub that the servants had dragged upstairs, but a permanent one positioned before a fireplace.

Rose could imagine herself in a tub like that. She hoped the Duke of Bridgewater lived half so nicely. Many of the estates she'd visited were much too old and drafty, and she'd met quite a few men who seemed more than happy living with their grandmothers' choices in decor.

When the Ashcrofts had seen and admired everything, Kit led them downstairs. "Ellen isn't here," he muttered darkly as though to himself. "Anywhere."

"Ellen?" Rose asked.

"My sister," he explained, rubbing the back of his neck. "Graves!" he called. The butler reappeared. "Will you send someone to Whittingham's to seek out Ellen? Should she be there, I wish to see her directly."

"Of course, sir." The butler went off, presumably to fetch and instruct a footman.

"Well." Kit set the book on a small marble-topped table in the entry. "I hope you enjoyed the grand tour."

"I did." In truth, Rose was overwhelmed. She'd never imagined a commoner could own such a lovely home. And Kit not only owned it, he'd designed it. He was responsible for the pleasing proportions of each room, the tasteful wall and window treatments, the spare but perfect accessories.

All it needed, she thought absurdly, was flowers. Yes, beautiful arrangements of flowers would be the crowning touch. Her fingers itched to design them. She'd use silver vases in simple, classic shapes to match the house.

Mum lifted the book. "It's a shame you cannot read Latin."

"Not just Latin. All foreign languages elude me." Kit flashed a self-deprecating smile. "I'm astonished I managed to pick up English."

"Rose could read the book to you. Couldn't you, dear?"

Rose was still planning her flower arrangements. Red, she thought, would suit this entry perfectly. The black-and-white floor called for something bold.

"I desperately need to lie down," Mum said, "but why don't you stay here and translate this book for Kit? I'm certain he can find someone to escort me home."

"Stay here?" Rose echoed, wrested from her vision of the multicolored arrangement she'd create for the lovely dining room.

"It's early still, and you have nothing else to do until court this evening. It would be a kindness."

She collected her thoughts and considered. Rose was not known for being kind—a perception she'd been trying to remedy. Inside, she'd never felt like the spoiled, selfish harridan others apparently saw, though she did understand why her recent behavior might encourage that view. Particularly her behavior toward Lily and Rand.

All this was to say: Rose could stand to do someone a kindness.

And besides the fact that she *didn't* have anything else to do, she suspected translating a book about architecture might prove a fascinating challenge. She needn't hide her unfeminine intellectual curiosity from Kit. Last summer he'd watched her work with Rand to decode Rand's brother's diaries—he already knew she had brains. Besides, he was just her brother-in-law's friend and—now that he was building the greenhouse—her father's hireling. What did she care if he thought her unfeminine?

"Rose?" her mother queried.

"Very well."

Kit's eyes brightened, suddenly looking more green than brown. "Graves! It seems we'll be requiring dinner, after all."

THIRTEEN

$\mathcal{B}$EFORE ROSE COULD change her mind, her mother had departed, and she and Kit were in the beautiful paneled dining room, a lovely dinner of beef in claret and carrot pudding set before them.

To her surprise, she found Kit very good company.

"It's odd," she realized in the middle of their meal. "You're quite easy to talk to."

A forkful of carrot pudding halfway to his mouth, he laughed. "Do you always say exactly what's on your mind?"

"Usually." Unless she was with someone she thought of as husband material; then she had to watch her words. "Do you not find it odd at all? After all, we hardly know each other."

"Perhaps we should get to know each other, then." He sipped thoughtfully from a goblet of Madeira. "What's your favorite color?"

"Red. Why?"

He met her eyes. "Color can say a lot about a person."

"Oh, yes?" She took a swallow of the sweet wine. "What do you suppose red says about me?"

"I imagine that you're strong-willed…and perhaps a bit daring."

She liked that description. "What's *your* favorite color?"

"The clear blue of a summer sky."

"But your bedchamber is red," she remembered.

"So it is." He smiled and didn't elaborate. "Do you prefer sweet or savory?"

"Pardon?"

"To eat. Sweetmeats or real meats, which is it?"

"Oh, sweets, most definitely," she told him, relieved to be on a different subject. Enjoying this game, she eyed a cherry tart one of his serving maids had placed on the table. "But I'm not passionate about it."

He raised a brow. "Passionate?"

Feeling herself blush, Rose was certain he'd taken her statement the wrong way. "Violet's sister-in-law, Kendra—she'd have a wedge of that tart on her plate already. She always eats dessert first. In case she wouldn't have room for it later."

"Ah."

Rose swallowed more wine. "And you? Sweet or savory?"

"Give me a hunk of beef any day." He speared a bite of meat and popped it into his mouth. "Which do you enjoy more, Christmas or your birthday?"

"My birthday. It's mine alone."

He sipped, looking amused. "But Christmas is a time for sharing."

"Exactly." Two could play this game. "What's your favorite book?"

His eyes narrowed as he considered. "*The Odyssey*."

"Homer's *Odyssey*? In Greek?" she added teasingly.

He laughed, tipping his wine glass to her. "George Chapman's version."

"Homer's is more poetic." She scooped up her last bite of the buttery carrot pudding. "Why do you like it?"

"Odysseus faced terrible obstacles, but he persevered and triumphed in the end." Kit set down his fork. "I admire that sort of man, that sort of success."

He sounded very serious. "He did it for love," she reminded him.

"For his wife, Penelope, yes. She waited for him twenty years."

Though Rose dreamed of such enduring love, she couldn't imagine waiting twenty years for anything. "Penelope was more patient than I."

"What's *your* favorite book?"

"*Aristotle's Master-piece,*" she said without hesitation, even though it was a scandalous marriage manual. It seemed she could tell him anything. "I learned quite a bit from that book."

"Did you?" That brow went up again, making her wonder if he knew what the book was about or if he assumed it was Aristotelian philosophy. But his thoughtful expression didn't give him away. "Musically," he asked, "do you prefer instrumentals or songs?"

"Songs. I love to sing. I sang in the parlor after Lily's wedding, do you remember?"

"I left early," he reminded her. "I must have missed you."

"Oh." Absurdly, she felt disappointed. "Do you sing?"

"Not where anyone can hear me." His eyes looking very green, he sat back and twirled his goblet between his palms.

"My turn," she said, focusing on the pewter cup. "Red wine or white?"

"Red. Most definitely red. It's richer, deeper, more complicated." He fixed that vivid green gaze on her. "And you? Red or white?"

"Champagne," she said, feeling like she'd just sipped some.

"Rare and expensive. It fits."

Her face heated again. "The bubbles tickle."

He opened his mouth to respond, but then apparently changed his mind. "Are you early to bed or late to rise?" he asked instead.

"Both," she admitted with a chuckle. "But that's about to change. Last night I was so early to bed, I have no idea what time the court festivities ended. Do you know, or did you seek your bed beforetime, too?"

"I never sought my bed at all. I had work that kept me there through the night."

Her jaw dropped. "You haven't slept?" She began to rise. "I must leave you to get some sleep, then. Although my mother's heart was in the right place when she suggested I read to you, she was clearly unaware of the circumstances."

He rose and helped her to stand, his hand warm on her arm through the thin silk of her violet gown. Her skin seemed to prickle underneath.

"I would have you stay and read," he said. "If you're finished with your dinner, we'll adjourn to the drawing room."

"But you must be exhausted—"

"Think of it as a bedtime story, then." When she laughed, his eyes glimmered in response. "Honestly," he added, "tonight will be soon enough for me to rest. I'm accustomed to keeping long hours when a project demands it."

She thought about his words as she let him guide her into the light-flooded drawing room. The people in her life had no demands that would keep them up all the night—or at least none they hadn't put on themselves. She had nothing in common with Kit Martyn.

But despite that—despite *herself*—she liked him. His ease, his self-confidence, his quick sense of humor. In fact, she liked him a little too much. She felt uneasy when he was too close.

When he fetched the book and sat beside her on the pale moss green settle, she briefly considered moving to a chair. But considering they needed to work from the same book, that would be silly—not to mention insulting.

She took the volume from him. "'*Perspectiva Pictorum et Architectorum*,'" she read aloud, "which means, 'Perspective in Painting and Architecture' by Andrea Pozzo."

"Just as I thought," he said, reaching to open the cover and flip pages.

She caught a hint of his scent again—the same mix of frankincense and myrrh that she remembered him wearing at Lily's wedding. It was woodsy and masculine and made the champagne bubbles dance in her stomach, no matter that she'd been drinking Madeira instead.

She'd have to see if she could duplicate it in Mum's perfumery. Perhaps the Duke of Bridgewater would like some.

"See here," Kit said. "There's a sketch of how to properly mount paper on a board for drawing. I've done it, but I couldn't tell what to do after that." Rising, he strode across the room to a desk and lifted a piece of wood with sheets of parchment tacked to it. "What does that page say?"

"To the lovers of perspective," she translated. "The art of perspective does, with wonderful pleasure, deceive the eye, the most subtle of all our outward senses…"

While she read, Kit collected an inkwell and quill and wandered back to sit beside her.

She turned the page. "This section is called 'Explanation of the lines of the plan and horizon, and of the points of the eye and of the distance.'" She read on, turning the Latin into English as she went. "That you may better understand the principles of perspective, here is presented to your view a temple, on the inner wall of which…"

With quick, precise motions, he sketched the lines of the classic Greek temple pictured beside the Latin words. He nodded as he followed her translated instructions, adding a man —tiny, as fit the proportions—standing before the structure with its high, arched windows.

"Let me see," she said when she'd finished reading the page.

He set down the quill and turned the sketch board to face her. "What do you think?"

"It's lovely."

"Just lovely?"

"Well, you've drawn it skillfully, of course."

He smiled. "It's a perfectly proportioned structure. Can you see the way the arched windows echo the arches in the rest of the building? A true thing of beauty."

If she couldn't quite appreciate the structure itself, she couldn't help but notice his enthusiasm. "You find buildings beautiful."

"Not all buildings, but the well-designed ones." He cocked his head, piercing her with those all-seeing eyes. "What do you find beautiful?"

A little flutter skittered through her, but she ignored it. "Are we back to playing the getting-to-know-each-other game?"

"Tell me. Beauty is..."

"Oh, flowers, jewelry, rainbows—"

"No. Not what others find beautiful; what *you* find beautiful. For example, this curve of cheek to chin"—he reached a long finger to trace along her face—"is a thing of beauty."

She shivered.

"Tell me," he said softly.

Your eyes, she thought. *Your voice, when you talk like that. Your ideas...*

"Flowers," she repeated aloud. But then she added, "When they've just been kissed by the rain."

He nodded solemnly. "What else?"

"Children's laughter."

"And?"

"The sun reflecting off the Thames at dusk."

He seemed to be staring at her mouth. "Very good."

Her lips tingled. "And my sister, playing the harpsichord. Even more beautiful when Rand sings with her."

Kit nodded again. "He has an incredible voice."

"Yes, he does." And it didn't hurt anymore to think of him as Lily's husband.

"How about," Kit suggested, "the first blade of grass that pushes through the ground in the springtime?"

"Oh, yes." She'd never thought of it before, but a blade of grass could be a thing of beauty.

"Church bells ringing through the fog."

"Fog." She nodded. "Tendrils of fog creeping over the rooftops of London."

"The fog in London?" Laughing, he picked up his sketch board and ripped off the top sheet of paper. "Perhaps we're getting carried away. Read on, please."

She hesitated a moment, wishing the game could continue. "'*Figura Tertia*—The Third Figure.' The delineation of an oblong square in perspective..."

FOURTEEN

*K*IT SKETCHED while Rose read all that long, pleasant afternoon.

And the longer he spent with her, the more he wanted her.

Rose was much more than just a pretty face. He'd known that, somehow—known it in his gut before he'd even really known her. But now he knew for sure.

"You've never seen these buildings," she commented after translating nearly a dozen of the Latin explanations. "In person, I mean. Have you?"

"No." He placed the sketch board facedown on the table and stuck the quill into the inkwell. "I've always dreamed of traveling abroad to study the classical buildings, but"—he smiled sheepishly—"I don't know how I'd communicate."

"I've also never been outside of Britain." She flipped through more pages, her dark eyes lingering on the drawings of classical buildings. "I'd dearly love to go to Italy—to travel anywhere, really, where I could see the world and try speaking the languages I've learned to read and write."

"How many?" he asked.

"I've never counted." She lifted a shoulder in an elegant shrug. "Ten, eleven...maybe more. You get to a point where new languages become easier, where the words and grammar parallel ones you already know."

"*You* get to that point," he said, making her laugh.

She was charming in that easy dismissal of her abilities. And kind, too—willing to sit with him all day and patiently translate his book.

And she shared his dream, to travel. Although it was clear she wasn't talking about traveling with *him*, Kit couldn't help but think of her mother's matchmaking intentions. With such a talented wife at his side, Kit would gain access not only to knowledge like that of the *Perspectiva Pictorum*, but to the whole wide world beyond England's borders.

Not that he was really looking for a wife.

"You must have done well in school, though," she said, startling him from his musings, "in order to get where you are today."

He shook his head to clear it. "I was a good student. I had to be."

"What do you mean?"

"I lost both my parents in 'sixty-five—"

"The Great Plague?"

"Yes." That year of horror. "Did it not affect your family?"

"We went off to Tremayne, an estate my family owns near Wales. We were safe there. Isolated."

"We weren't," Kit said succinctly. "My father was a carpenter, my mother a secretary and housekeeper for a local noblewoman. They owned no land; we had no place to go."

"I'm sorry," she said. "Do you miss them terribly?"

"I did, but it's been twelve years. My sister, Ellen, was but four when they died. She doesn't miss them like she might if they'd passed when she was older."

"But you remember your parents well."

He nodded. "Oh, and she remembers them, too. I talk about them often—I've tried to keep them alive for her. My mother was the daughter of a cleric, and she taught us how to read. My father taught me how to build. They were good people."

Not that that had saved their lives. The few titled families in the area had escaped before falling ill, but common folk like the Martyns hadn't any choice but to stay behind. Kit and Ellen had survived, but their parents had not.

The Martyns, Kit had resolved—what remained of them—wouldn't be left behind ever again.

Leaning closer, Rose laid a hand over his. "What happened after they passed on?"

"I was thirteen and did my best to care for Ellen, but we had no income, after all. We were alone in our tiny cottage. We nearly starved."

Her fingers tightened on his, and she leaned closer still, swamping him with her floral scent. "Oh, Kit…"

He shrugged off the sympathy. It would do him no good. He'd long ago learned to face life's problems and work toward solutions. Wallowing in self-pity got one nowhere.

"When my mother's employer, a widow called Lady St. Vincent, returned to Hawkridge after the danger had passed, she felt great remorse for having left our family behind. To make amends, she took in Ellen and sent me to Westminster School. She saw to it that I was made a King's Scholar and promised to send me on to university if I did well. So I did," he concluded simply.

He'd been given a chance in life, and he hadn't been about to waste it.

"Did she follow through with her promise?"

"Indeed, she did. She sent me to Oxford, and not on charity, either. She paid my expenses and made sure I was treated as well as the best."

He waited a beat, hoping Rose would say he *was* the best, as good as all the titled lads at school. But she didn't, of course. She hadn't been raised in a world that believed that.

Glancing down to their connected hands, she looked startled and pulled hers back. "You enjoyed your time at Oxford," she said. "I can hear it in your voice."

"I was anxious to finish and get on with life, but Oxford was hardly a trial. Rand was there—we'd been friends since child-hood. And a few of my friends from Westminster School ended up there, too. Gaylord Craig—"

"The Earl of Rosslyn?" From the tone of her voice, he gath-ered she didn't like the fellow. "I met him last night. *He's* your friend?"

Kit grinned. "Rosslyn ruffles some people's feathers. We're not close friends, but I've always got on with everyone."

"I'm not surprised," she said, returning his smile. She had adorable dimples. He felt a sudden urge to kiss those two little indentations.

"Someone's here," she said.

He heard footsteps on the marble in the entry, and the low murmur of Graves's voice followed by one with a higher pitch.

"That will be my sister, Ellen," he told Rose, rising. "Will you excuse me?"

FIFTEEN

𝒶S ROSE WATCHED Kit leave the room, closing the door behind him, a clock somewhere in the house struck the hour, chiming six times.

Where had the afternoon gone? The bookshop would have closed by now, and she'd wanted some reading material to pass the long, empty days at the castle. Court would be commencing soon, and she'd wanted time to rest. And she needed time to choose a gown and ready herself.

Mum must have been very tired, because surely she'd have come to fetch her if she wasn't still napping.

Voices sifted through the drawing room's closed door. Rose couldn't tell what Kit was saying, but he didn't sound happy. She couldn't understand his sister's replies, either, but the girl was clearly giving as good as she got.

Rose hadn't even met Ellen, and she liked her already. Smiling to herself, she idly reached for Kit's sketch board and turned it face up.

Her heart skipped a beat. He hadn't been drawing Greek temples or Roman theaters. He'd been sketching *her*.

And he'd captured her perfectly.

Transfixed, she couldn't tear her gaze away. The young

woman gazing back at her wasn't the flirting Rose, the one with the big smile. Instead her lips curved as though she shared a secret. And her eyes glittered not with forced gaiety, but with simple pleasure in what she was doing.

Translating a book. Sharing a quiet afternoon.

It wasn't a painting, nor a work of careful artistry. The black ink on white gave no hint that her gown was a rich purple, her cheeks were pink with carefully applied cosmetics, her lips were dyed red and ripe. The drawing was plain and stark. True.

It was a Rose very few people ever saw.

How had he seen the real Rose? she wondered. And what had made him sketch her while she was describing how to draw classical buildings?

She blew out a shaky breath as Kit and his sister barged in.

"I'm entitled to live my own life," the girl said, continuing their argument as though Rose were invisible. "And you had no right having me fetched home as though I were your property."

"You *are* my property," Kit ground out. "Until you're wed—"

"Let me wed, then, and we'll both be happier."

"Not if you wed *him*."

"Him?" Rose asked.

They both turned to look at her, fire and surprise in their matching eyes.

"Thomas Whittingham." Kit's sister tossed her head of long jet hair. "The love of my life."

"He's a pawnbroker," Kit spat.

Rose set down Kit's sketch and stood. "I'm Rose Ashcroft," she said to the girl, who looked to be about a year or two her junior.

"My apologies for not introducing you." Kit's gaze nervously snapped between Rose's face and the drawing he'd done of her. He took a deep breath. "Lady Rose, this is my sister, Ellen. Ellen—"

"*Lady* Rose," Ellen drawled before her brother could complete the belated introduction. "Do you not think, Kit, that you're aiming a bit out of your range?"

"We're just friends," Rose rushed to clarify.

Surprisingly, she really *did* feel Kit was a friend. The pleasant afternoon had changed her view of him entirely.

And she found herself wishing to be Ellen's friend, too. With her sisters both married and moved away, and the women at court giving her the cold shoulder, she desperately needed a female friend. And she sensed Ellen could be one. She liked this forthright girl.

She sat again and patted the cushion beside her. "Tell me about this Thomas of yours."

Ellen slid onto the settle and folded her hands in her lap, a female version of Kit dressed in an innocent shade of yellow. "He's kind and generous and handsome, and I love him."

"She wants to marry him," Kit said derisively. He swept the sketch board off the table and crossed the room to place it face-down on the desk. "I will *not* see her wed to a pawnbroker. To go from this"—he waved a hand, indicating the house, the life he'd built for the two of them—"to living above a pawnshop, is—"

"—what I want," Ellen rushed to finish for him. Then she met Rose's eyes, her own pleading.

Apparently they were friends already.

"How old are you?" Rose asked.

"Sixteen."

"You're young yet," she said gently. "Can you not put off marriage for a little while? Perhaps you'll meet—"

"I *love* him. Kit has no right to dictate my life."

Ellen was wrong; legally, Kit had every right. When Rose looked to him, he spread his hands in an exasperated gesture. She turned back to Ellen, who looked so much like her brother. Just as hot-tempered too, from all indications. They probably butted heads precisely because they were so much alike.

Rose had fancied herself in love many times. But she knew now, having seen her sisters with their husbands, that she'd been mistaken. She knew now that she'd never been in love at all, not even once.

Ellen was young yet. And Rose had never before felt so old.

"Do you know, Ellen," she said carefully, "it's as easy to fall in love with a titled man as one without."

"Oh!" Ellen cried. "You don't understand!" Tears sprang to her eyes as she jumped up and ran from the room.

Rose and Kit listened to his sister's footsteps until they faded up the stairs. "She likes you," he finally said.

"And our navy will conquer the Dutch tomorrow." Rose sighed. "I think I'd best return home."

"OME" RIGHT NOW for Rose was Windsor Castle. That was what Kit wanted for Ellen: the rank that would give her the security of feeling at home in a royal castle. Or anywhere. The rank that would assure she'd never again be left behind.

And yet, when Rose had supported his position, he'd found himself not grateful, but vexed.

Her voice still echoed in his ears, so measured and reasonable: *It's as easy to fall in love with a titled man as one without.*

Never mind that it was exactly what Ellen needed to hear, Rose's stance didn't bode well for his own suit.

The sun was setting as he walked Rose back to the apartments she shared with her mother, the two of them chatting amiably. All the way past the Round Tower, into an Upper Ward building, and up a staircase, he listened to her amusing banter and watched her fluttering lips.

Those lips…

When she reached for the door latch, he stopped her with a hand over hers. She turned and looked up at him, her dark eyes questioning.

"Thank you for a pleasant day," he said quietly, watching the light dance over her face from the single torch that illuminated the deserted corridor. "And also for the translation. It was much appreciated."

"You're very welcome," she said, looking relieved. "I enjoyed myself."

When he felt her trying to draw her hand away, he held it tight in his. There was something between them, whether she knew it—or wanted it—or not.

"I'm happy to hear that," he told her.

She offered him a tentative smile. "No, I mean I *truly* enjoyed myself. I can see why Rand is happy to count you as a friend."

He flushed with pleasure—and a touch of guilt. He still didn't feel quite right about his furtive encounter with Lady Trentingham. But if he confessed, would his hopes be dashed?

As it turned out, he needn't have fretted, because his hopes were dashed anyway by the next words out of Rose's mouth. "You're the best, Kit," she said, giving him a friendly pat on the arm. "Like a brother, but better."

A brother? He didn't want to be her brother.

Had the countess misread her daughter's feelings? She'd seemed so certain they were right for each other. Then again, she had also endeavored to check his expectations, warning him that Rose would be resistant. Her mother could scheme and maneuver all she wanted, but in the end, the decision belonged to Rose alone.

Like a brother.

He had to respect that, didn't he? Respect *her*. His heart heavy, he released her hand, then leaned to give her an innocent, brotherly peck on the cheek.

When his mouth brushed her silky skin, he smelled flowers. And he felt something—a jolt of energy between them, an involuntary shift of her body toward his—that made all his resolve simply melt away.

Then somehow his lips were on hers, and something else inside him melted, too.

And Rose's world turned over.

She didn't like kissing. She'd always found it messy and awkward and unpleasant. But this kiss was...none of those things. These lips were soft and warm and seemed to fit hers. They moved *with* her lips, using just enough pressure to guide her, as if he were leading her through a dance. A dance that was slow and intimate, that made her knees feel weak, that sent dreamy swirls of sensation through her body.

A thing of beauty, she thought dizzily.

When it ended, she didn't feel relieved. She felt let down. And stunned. And like she wanted Kit to keep kissing her.

Kit? Gemini, had those lips really been Kit's?

His eyes glittered green in the torchlight, his gaze piercing into her as though he could read her thoughts. Which seemed unlikely, since she could scarcely begin to decipher them herself.

His mouth curved into a faint smile that might have been the slightest bit smug.

"Good night," he said and walked away.

SEVENTEEN

ROSE CLOSED THE lodging's door and leaned back against it, releasing a long, long sigh. Then she was grinning from ear to ear.

She didn't hate kissing! There was nothing wrong with her after all.

Apparently, she'd just never kissed anyone who was any good at it—until today.

She was still astonished that it was Kit Martyn who had finally made her feel all those wondrous things her sisters talked of. Who would have thought? But she supposed kissing ability had little to do with one's birth. And though Kit had had no business kissing her, she couldn't find it in herself to be sorry he'd done so. She'd watched him walk away, knowing she should call after him, berate him for taking such liberties, inform him in no uncertain terms that he was never to do so again.

But she'd been too busy being so, so very happy. Everything had changed. Kissing wasn't dreadful. She wasn't doomed to a lifetime of forced participation in a romantic ritual she found revolting.

She'd actually enjoyed it!

She could hardly credit that she'd ever imagined herself

defective. How silly she'd been to jump to such a conclusion. Obviously one's enjoyment of a kiss depended upon the skill of one's partner. How lucky her sisters had been to receive their first kisses from gentlemen of such great talent. And how unlucky that she had never met a gifted man until now.

"Are you out there, dear?"

"Yes, Mum." Rose took a deep, calming breath and crossed the small sitting room toward the even smaller bedchamber she and her mother were sharing.

Mum was seated at the heavy carved wood dressing table. While her maid Anne twisted the back section of her hair up into a bun, she tore a small sheet of red Spanish paper from a tiny booklet and rubbed it lightly on her cheeks. "Did you have a nice time, dear?"

Feeling heat flare in her face, Rose was glad her mother was busy looking in the mirror. "It was a fine day," she said carefully, not wanting to sound too enthusiastic.

She certainly didn't want her mother finding out she'd allowed Kit—a commoner!—to kiss her.

Mum set down the Spanish paper and lifted a kohl pencil. "What did you do?" she asked, carefully rimming an eye.

"Oh, we had dinner and then I translated part of the book." The sound of an ungraceful snore drew Rose's gaze to Harriet, dead to the world on a pallet laid out on the floor. Shaking her head, she crossed to her trunk and rummaged through it herself. "I met Kit's sister, Ellen."

"Was she nice?"

Rose held up a frosty pink gown and then rejected it; she was feeling much bolder than that. "I liked her. But she's sixteen and fancies herself in love. With a *pawnbroker*."

"Perhaps she *is* in love. And in a bustling town like this, a pawnshop is likely to be a thriving business."

"Surely she can do much better than to live life above a pawnshop. Look at the house she's living in now!"

Mum turned to her, raising one kohl-darkened brow. "You liked it, then."

"Kit's house?" Rose shook out a bright red gown. Perfect. She laid it on the old canopied bed. "It was very impressive. It must be lovely to live right on the river like that and yet in a bustling town, too. And the house is beautifully designed."

Another thing of beauty, she thought, standing over her sleeping maid. "Harriet," she called softly.

The girl bolted upright. "Yes, milady." She scrambled to her feet. "Forgive me, milady. I was tired."

Rose waved a dismissive hand, thinking she was a mite tired herself.

"You like the house's designer, too," her mother said.

"Kit? He's pleasant." Memories flashed: his smile, his laughter, his eyes...his lips. Rose shivered, then made a show of rubbing her arms, moving closer to the fire on the grate. Curling tongs sat heating in the embers. "It's cold in this stone building, don't you think?"

"Not particularly."

Her mother's gaze was making her uncomfortable, so she turned to let Harriet unlace her gown. "I've been thinking, Mum..."

Shifting back to the mirror, her mother opened a little jar of pomade. "Yes?"

"You've always cautioned us to kiss a man before we agree to marry him. I think that is *excellent* advice. I believe that if I see Ellen again, I shall tell her. Perhaps she'll find she doesn't love the pawnbroker, after all."

Mum slicked the pomade on her lips, then stood and waved Rose toward the stool in her stead. "Love has to do with more than kisses, dear."

"Well, of course it does!" Rose settled herself, watching in the mirror as Harriet slid the pins from her hair. "But since a wife is expected to kiss her husband, she should at least make sure she likes his technique."

Leaning forward, Rose darkened her lashes with the end of a burnt cork while Harriet used the hot tongs to fashion perfect ringlets. What a pity the Duke of Bridgewater was such an abysmal kisser. He'd seemed so perfect.

Well, there were other suitable, handsome gentlemen at court. With any luck, she wouldn't have to kiss them all before she found one as talented as Kit.

"Ah, kisses," Harriet murmured with a sigh.

Mum stepped into high Louis-heeled shoes fashioned of golden brocade to match her gown. "Have you met any young men here at Windsor yet, Harriet?"

The girl's freckles went three shades darker. "Not yet."

"Harriet's shy," Anne put in.

"Well." Mum straightened and gave her skirts a shake. "We shall have to see about an introduction."

Rose rolled her eyes. Whoever heard of "introductions" for servants? Only her hopelessly romantic mother would even think of such a thing.

"Mum," she started.

"Yes, dear?"

On the other hand...at least Mum didn't seem to be foisting any introductions upon *her*. Perhaps it was a blessing that the matchmaker had found someone else to torment with her schemes. Better Harriet than Rose.

"Never mind," Rose said lightly.

The last thing she needed was her mother interfering in her love life.

EIGHTEEN

*T*HREE DAYS LATER, Kit looked down the hill toward Ellen dragging along behind. "Come along, will you?" Walking backward, he squinted at her in the darkness. "What is that you're carrying?"

"A book."

"A book?" He stopped to wait for her to catch up. "Since when do you spend your time reading?"

"Since you went stark raving mad and decided I should spend half the night watching you work. Since then."

He chose not to respond.

It was too dark to see her expression, but he could hear the pout in her voice. After returning home to find her absent one time too many, yesterday he'd finally decided to bring her with him to work so he could keep an eye on her. She'd acted positively feral, shouting and disrupting the worksite, so tonight's pouting was a vast improvement. Perhaps she was learning resignation.

"Why won't you let me stay home?" she suddenly shrieked.

Then again, perhaps not.

"I'd let you stay home if you *would* stay home. But I know

you, and you won't. I'd return to find you're at the pawnshop again."

"I love him," she said for the hundredth time. Or maybe the millionth.

"I want better for you," he said for the millionth time, too.

As they passed through the gate at Windsor, the drowsy old scarlet-uniformed guard snapped to attention. "Evening, Mr. Martyn."

"Evening, Richards."

The man narrowed his rheumy eyes. "Who goes with you?"

"My sister."

"Pretty thing." He smiled, displaying half a mouth of teeth. "Go on through."

"My thanks." In the torchlight of the gateway, Kit glanced again at the book clutched to Ellen's chest. "Where'd you get that? It's not even English."

She clutched the book tighter, as though she were afraid he might snatch it from her hands. "You don't want to know."

"Whittingham?"

"Maybe."

"Can pawnbrokers even read? Why would he give you a foreign book?"

He thought perhaps she blushed, but they were still walking and had left the circle of torchlight, so he couldn't be sure.

"I'm hoping your friend Rose can translate it for me," she said, neatly evading his question.

"Rose isn't my friend." He didn't want to be Rose's friend. He didn't want to be her brother, either. He hoped he'd made that clear three nights ago when he'd kissed her on her doorstep.

"You drew a picture of her."

"You weren't supposed to see that."

"It was good," Ellen said grudgingly. "You should draw pictures more often. Of things besides buildings, I mean."

"I'm too busy trying to make you a good life."

Her reply to that was sullen silence.

He sighed as they skirted the Round Tower. "You cannot see

Rose tonight. You'll be at my construction site. She'll be at court." He wouldn't walk Ellen through the king's chambers— they'd take the long way around. "Ellen Martyn doesn't belong at court. Until, that is, she marries a title."

"I'm marrying a pawnbroker," she said.

NINETEEN

*R*OSE HAD KISSED three gentlemen since Kit—one last night behind the huge bay window's velvet curtains, one in the little unfinished vestibule the evening before, and one out on the terrace the evening before that…and all three nights had ended in failure.

It seemed good kissers were *exceedingly* rare at court.

But at least her quest was getting easier. The first two gentlemen had been pleasantly shocked when she'd asked them for a kiss, but the third had come to *her*.

And here came another, swaggering her way. Trying to appear casual, she leaned a hand on the solid silver table by the wall where she stood. It felt cold—and very expensive—beneath her fingers.

"Lovely table, isn't it?" the fellow asked, coming to a stop before her. She looked him up and down. Although he wasn't any taller than she, he wasn't shorter either, and he had a pleasing face.

"The engraved top is nice," she said, unable to summon yet another charming and flirtatious reply. Court chatter was exhaustingly repetitive.

He tried again. "Louis the Fourteenth has silver furniture like this all over Versailles."

"Does he? Gemini, that palace must be even more overblown than this one."

The gentleman appeared nonplussed. "I don't believe I've had the pleasure of an introduction."

She lazily waved her fan while she considered him. He was young enough. His hair was covered by a long, curled periwig, but she guessed from his fair complexion that it was blond. His periwinkle suit wasn't too ostentatious, adorned with just enough jewels to make known his wealth.

He would do.

"Lady Rose Ashcroft," she replied with a calculated smile.

He took her free hand and raised it to his lips, pressing a kiss to the back. A bit wet, but not totally disgusting. "Lord Craven-hurst, at your service."

His voice wasn't too grating, and, unlike the last fellow, she guessed he'd bathed within the week. His perfume was light and not too cloying. Perhaps he'd ask her to dance before claiming a kiss. That would be nice.

But she was not to be so lucky. He leaned close, sneaking a peek at himself in the silver-framed mirror above the table. "I hear you enjoy kissing," he uttered in a confidential tone.

Rose fluttered her lashes. "Why, yes, actually, I do." With the right partner.

Maybe he would be the one.

Although she would prefer a dance—or sitting somewhere alone where she could put her feet up—she allowed him to guide her behind the curtain again. She wasn't exactly keen on the idea of kissing a virtual stranger, but after three wasted evenings, her patience was dwindling. Wasn't it silly to spend hours getting to know a gentleman if her lips could rule him out in ten seconds flat?

Nervous, she turned toward the window and pretended to admire the view over Eton. It *was* a nice view, but apparently Lord Cravenhurst didn't feel like looking. One arm clamped around her tight, and his mouth descended on hers.

Her fan dropped to the floor. He tasted funny, and his mouth felt slimy. When he tried to snake a hand down her bodice, she gasped and shoved him away. "How dare you!"

He didn't look at all fazed. "I was told you were a wild one."

"By whom?" Taking out a handkerchief, she wiped her mouth vigorously, not caring if she offended him.

He shrugged. "It's all the buzz."

"Well, the buzz is wrong. A kiss is not an invitation to be manhandled." She tossed open the curtain. "Now go out there and tell everyone they were mistaken."

"And reveal that you refused my advances? I think not," he huffed and stalked away.

She barely had time to catch her breath before another gentleman hurried over. The Earl of Rosslyn, Kit's friend.

Since they'd already been introduced, he wasted no time on preliminaries. "My lady," he said with a bow, "I have it on good faith that you particularly enjoy kissing."

The scoundrel. "You're married!"

He grinned. "Then you know I have much experience."

"What I *know* is that you're an adulterer."

"Why should that matter?"

Indeed. Looking around the chamber, one could observe all manner of embracing couples—and Rose had grave doubts that most of them were married. To each other, at least.

And where on earth was her mother? She might as well have come here by herself for all the chaperoning she was receiving.

She scooped her folded fan off the floor, half tempted to bash Rosslyn on the nose with it. "Go away," she told him instead.

To her vast relief, he did. She aimed a shaky smile at two passing women, but they both pointedly avoided her gaze, whispering behind their fans. And yet another gentleman was headed in her direction.

Her tension eased as she realized it was the Duke of Bridgewater. At least Gabriel was a *real* gentleman. He was wearing russet tonight and looked aristocratic as ever. As he drew nearer, she opened her fan and composed herself.

"Your grace," she greeted him with a smile. "Where have you been these past few evenings?"

"I've been about. It's you who seem constantly occupied," he pointed out good-naturedly, "and I've dearly missed your company. Was Rosslyn bothering you?"

In truth, she could take care of herself—hadn't she just proven it? But she sidled up to him, waving the fan coquettishly. "I'm glad you arrived to protect me."

"You're in good hands, my dear." Looking pleased, he linked an arm through hers and began guiding her toward the terrace.

Good heavens, the blasted terrace again.

"Wouldn't you rather dance?" she asked, then whirled at hearing the meaty sound of a fist connecting with someone's skull.

Nell Gwyn's voice carried across the chamber. "Don't make me sorry I talked Charles into releasing you from the Tower!" she spat as she stalked off.

The Duke of Buckingham stood watching her go, his mouth hanging open, one hand held to the spot above his ear where petite Nell's punch must have landed.

What a woman.

Gabriel reclaimed her arm. "Come along."

"What happened?" she asked, resisting his propulsion.

"The idiot tried to kiss her." The duke managed to harrumph in a genteel manner. "Everyone knows that unlike Louise and Barbara, Nell is completely devoted to King Charles."

"Is she?" Rose wondered, pleased to learn that a single other courtier besides herself valued fidelity—even if Nell *was* a fallen woman. At least she was falling *honestly*.

"Oh, yes. She hasn't touched another man since the king made her his mistress. Nearly nine years, if you can believe it."

Gabriel's apparent amazement gave Rose pause, but she consoled herself that at least he seemed to admire the achievement. She glanced back at the Duke of Buckingham, who still stood rooted in place. Even with his long black periwig all mussed, he looked entirely too dignified to have recently been a prisoner. "Why on earth was he in the Tower of London?"

"He's not the first man King Charles has clapped in there, and he certainly won't be the last. It's political, my dear. You wouldn't understand."

Certain she *would* understand, Rose was about to ask for an explanation when he added, "Are you and your dear mother coming along to Hampton Court?"

Rose blinked, effectively diverted. "Hampton Court?"

"Haven't you heard? The court is moving tomorrow—getting ever closer to London, as it were. The household will spend a few weeks at Hampton Court and then move to Whitehall for the winter, in time for the royal wedding on the fourth of November and the queen's birthday celebration on the fourteenth." He guided her toward the door. "Will you be coming along?"

"I'm not sure. I suppose I'll have to ask Mum."

"Well, I certainly hope she'll agree. I'd feel bereft without your company."

He sounded sincere, and she couldn't help but respond to his flattery. He really was the most handsome of all the courtiers. And the tallest—only King Charles was taller—not to mention the highest ranked.

There was the kissing problem, of course, but having experienced an excellent kiss herself, maybe she could teach him how to perform one.

It was worth a try, she decided as he drew her out to the blasted terrace.

She was getting nowhere in her search.

TWENTY

"*B*URNING THE midnight oil, eh, Martyn?"

Working in the blaze of torches and candelabrum, Kit looked up from his plans to see Gaylord Craig, the Earl of Rosslyn. He offered his old friend a wry smile. "Oil lamps are a bit dim for my purpose, but you've got the gist of it, yes."

Rosslyn paced the chamber with an elegant swagger, his tall walking stick clicking as he went. He paused, watching men and supplies go in and out of the two sizable holes cut in the ceiling that gave access to the area above, where Kit's crew was busy reinforcing the structure. "The repairs seem to be coming along nicely."

"Thank you." Kit rubbed his eyes, realizing he must force himself to rest more in the daytimes. Even he couldn't keep up this relentless pace forever. "And your own projects, Rosslyn?"

"Oh, fine, fine." Rosslyn pulled a tortoiseshell snuffbox from his pocket. "You've done an excellent job recovering here, Martyn. But then, you always were up to the task."

Kit could remember a few occasions, back in their school days, when Rosslyn *hadn't* been up to the task. But then, he'd had no compelling reason to excel, as Kit had. The secure life of a peer had been awaiting him.

"What made you become an architect?" Kit asked. Surely an earl didn't need a profession.

Having partaken of a pinch of snuff, Rosslyn sneezed. "Monuments."

"Monuments?"

"I wish to leave something behind. Something so men will say there went Gaylord, the Earl of Rosslyn."

The fellow wasn't as shallow as Kit had thought. "Your theater in London is a masterpiece," he conceded.

"I rather prefer my last church. But I thank you." He tucked the snuffbox back into his pocket. "Well, the ladies are waiting. I shall leave you to it." He turned on a high heel and swaggered toward the door, letting loose another sneeze followed by an "Oof!"

"Pardon me!" Lady Trentingham exclaimed.

"My apologies, my lady." Holding his walking stick in a wide stance, Rosslyn swept her a deep bow. "I was just leaving."

She turned and watched the earl mince away.

"Lady Trentingham," Kit called over the bangs and scrapes of construction.

The countess looked over and smiled. "Good evening," she greeted him, her own voice carrying well. He supposed that came of dealing with her half-deaf husband. She walked farther into the dining room, lifting the hem of her gown to step over a few boards and skirt her way around a sawhorse. "My, your men are busy as bees."

"That's why I'm here," he told her, shooting a glance to his crew. "I long ago learned that my presence makes all the difference." He rolled up the plans. "Can I help you with something?"

She met his gaze, her own forthright. "I'm wondering why you've spent the past three days avoiding my daughter."

Kit slanted a look at Ellen. She'd stopped sulking and had her nose buried in her book. He would have to take a look and see what she was finding so fascinating.

In the meantime, though, he'd rather not have her privy to this conversation. "Would you mind stepping out onto the terrace?" he asked Rose's mother. "I've a hankering for some fresh air."

The pounding of hammers and scraping of saws receded as they exited the room, leaving a pleasant calm in their wake. The deserted terrace was silent but for their footsteps, the thud of his heavy boots and the click of her feminine heels.

"Well?" Lady Trentingham prompted. "Tell me what's happened. I gather you kissed her."

Kit froze. "H-how do you know that?" He felt as if the bottom had dropped out of his stomach. Would he ever have an exchange with this woman that didn't take years off his life? Or was this to be their last exchange anyhow? She must be furious that he'd taken such liberties with her innocent, high-born daughter.

"My lady, I offer my deepest apologies. My conduct was shameful, and I don't—"

Her chuckle was startling. "I'm not angry, Kit. I've always told my daughters they ought to kiss a man before agreeing to marry him—no more than kiss, you understand," she added sternly. But she was still smiling. "And I'd say yours was an effective tactical move, given that Rose has been babbling about it ever since."

Though Kit's face was on fire, his ears perked up. "About kissing me?"

"About kissing her future husband. Presently, she seems to be seeking another gentleman with your skill. Interviewing them, you might say."

His ears were suddenly filled with an odd rushing sound. "She's kissing other men?"

"With very little success, from what I can tell. Though she unfortunately seems to be acquiring quite a reputation. As a mother, I'm rather concerned about that. I'm considering taking Rose home for a spell, rather than following the king directly to Hampton Court. Might you come see us at Trentingham?"

Kit's head was spinning. Though he knew full well he had no

right to be vexed at Rose for kissing other men, he couldn't control his gut reaction.

His gut didn't like it.

But nor did it like the thought of Rose leaving court.

He drifted to the edge of the terrace and gazed over the half wall at the darkened Thames Valley. "Even if I could think of a suitable pretext for visiting—"

"Such as my husband's greenhouse?" she chimed in sweetly, coming up beside him.

His fingers clenched the stone railing. Just once, he'd like to be one step ahead of *her* for a change. "*Such as,* yes. Still, the fact remains that I'm needed here to oversee my work for the Crown. That's why I haven't had time to call on Rose in recent days. Raising my status at court is the best chance I have of winning her—and impressing the king is the first step toward that goal."

The countess sighed. "I hate to separate you two just as you've caught her attention."

Kit didn't like the idea any more than she did. Though he'd spent no more than a few hours in Rose's company, somehow—absurdly—he missed her. It seemed all he looked forward to was seeing her again. He'd never felt less enthusiasm for his work, or had so much trouble maintaining his focus. Stray thoughts kept intruding, thoughts of rosebud lips and adorable dimples and the scent of flowers…

And that kiss. That kiss had been…

He shook himself, wrenching his mind back to the present. Gripping the top of the wall so tightly that stone dug into flesh, he reminded himself that if he wanted the chance to *keep* kissing Rose, he had to put her from his mind for the present. He had to concentrate on getting back into the king's good graces.

But if he neglected her too long, would he lose his chance anyhow?

"I've barely got this project back on schedule," he muttered, then realized his fingers had begun to ache. He released the railing and stuffed his hands in his pockets. "Give me a few days to ensure that it stays that way. Then I shall visit and pay court to Rose."

"Very well." Though dissatisfied, Lady Trentingham sounded resigned. "We will take our leave tomorrow afternoon." Then she suddenly brightened. "But we still have tonight."

TWENTY-ONE

*E*VEN THE KING had tried to steal a kiss!

As His Majesty and Rose had ended a minuet, he'd murmured his intentions in a low, velvet-edged voice and leaned close, apparently unconcerned that anyone might be watching. Right then, Gabriel had appeared to claim she'd promised him the next dance, which had been lucky for Rose, because she had no idea how to gracefully refuse a king.

And she'd had more than enough kissing for one night.

A good loser, Charles had gone away happily enough, smiling when he spotted Nell Gwyn sashaying into the chamber.

Now, as Rose and Gabriel performed the complicated steps of the galliard, she was aware of all the gazes on the two of them. Jealous gazes. The ladies were jealous because she'd captivated the most coveted bachelor at court. The gentlemen were jealous because he'd made his intentions crystal clear—and one didn't elbow aside a duke.

All the attention was positively heady, and part of Rose was thrilled beyond belief. A duke, and such a handsome one at that!

If only the man could kiss.

She'd allowed four more attempts, trying vainly to coax him to change his style. When that hadn't worked, she'd tried—really tried—to learn to enjoy his technique. Because, truth be told, she couldn't imagine why she didn't. It seemed to her that his kiss wasn't actually all that different from Kit's.

Some of the others had been positively boorish in their approach, but Gabriel didn't fit in that category. He wasn't too slobbery, his breath was pleasant, and he had the manner of a gentleman, if an impassioned one. So she couldn't put her finger on what Kit had done specifically that made his kiss magic while Gabriel's had no effect on her at all.

Or at least not the *desired* effect.

There was only one solution: She'd have to allow Kit to kiss her again. Once she'd discerned his method, it ought to be a simple matter to explain to Gabriel what she wanted. Practice, after all, should make perfect.

If only the practice weren't so disagreeable.

"Thank you, your grace," she said kindly when the dance came to an end. She loved calling him *your grace*, not to mention imagining being called *your grace* herself. She noticed the musicians set down their instruments. "Is the dancing over so early?" she asked with a frown.

"Only temporarily." Gabriel gestured to another corner of the room. "I believe Nell is about to grace us with an entertainment."

Chairs had been arranged to leave the corner open as a stage of sorts. Rose and the duke drifted closer as the performance began, a clever comedy mocking court life and filled with bits of song and dance. It seemed Nell had brought friends, for other actors and actresses took the makeshift stage along with her. When the brief play ended, the chamber burst into applause, the king's the loudest of all.

"Extraordinary!" he exclaimed, the remnants of laughter still on his face. "Extraordinary!"

Laughing herself, Nell swept him an exaggerated bow. "Then, sir, to show you don't speak like a courtier, I hope you'll make the performers a handsome present."

Charles made a great show of patting his velvet clothing. "I have no money about me." He turned to his brother, the Duke of York. "Have you any coin, my dear James?"

His eyes dancing, the duke shrugged. "I believe, sir, not above a guinea or two."

Laughing harder, Nell turned in a circle, her arms outstretched. "Od's fish," she cried, borrowing the king's favorite oath, "what company have I got into?"

Rose laughed along with everyone else. Nell's charm was difficult to resist.

Gabriel tucked a hand beneath her elbow. "Shall we adjourn to the North Terrace?" he asked politely.

Not again. Her high spirits quickly faded. "I think not. I feel, um, a bit peaked. I should like to find my mother and see if she's ready to leave."

"Already? The gaming hasn't even started."

And she'd wanted to try that. But not as much as she wanted to escape now. Somewhere—anywhere—where she could find a few moments of peace.

"I believe I saw my mother head in that direction," she said, indicating the portion of the castle that was under construction— an area she suspected the fastidious duke would have no wish to enter. "I thank you for the dances."

Without looking back, she hurried away, hoping he wouldn't follow and heaving a sigh of relief when she made it into the unfinished vestibule without hearing any footsteps behind her. Thinking to hide herself even better, she slipped into the half-built dining room and sagged against an exquisitely carved wall.

This late at night, she'd expected the room to be deserted, but it wasn't. Across the chamber, Kit and Ellen were having words.

"Let me see it," he said, reaching toward his sister. "Why should it be a secret?"

"It's mine," Ellen shot back, clutching a book to her chest. "Why do you have to stick your nose into everything that's mine?"

Dazed, Rose just watched. It struck her that in his fine but plain suit, with his gleaming black hair free instead of tucked beneath a wig, Kit looked anything but aristocratic. His skin was browned from working outdoors, and he carried his lean, rangy form with a steady ease, not the controlled posture necessary to carry off the weight of layers of heavy fabric and ornamentation.

In an odd way, she found the lack of fussiness appealing. But she wanted an aristocratic husband.

It was a good thing he was just a friend.

"Rose!" Ellen exclaimed, spotting her and abandoning Kit to hurry over. "I was hoping to see you tonight."

"Were you?" Rose asked.

"I brought a book I'd like you to translate."

"Did you?" Her gaze still fastened on Kit, Rose seemed to be reduced to two-word responses.

"Will you try?" Grabbing Rose by the arm, Ellen pulled her down the length of the chamber. "I'm dying to find some fresh air—this place is filled with sawdust."

Before Rose could protest, Ellen had propelled her out a door at the end of the chamber. As it shut behind them, Rose sneaked another glance at Kit. The last she saw of him was those glittering green-brown eyes.

It should be a crime for a commoner to be so attractive.

$\mathscr{E}$LLEN LED ROSE down a long back corridor, around a corner, and out into a small brick courtyard. Unlike Horn Court with its uniformed guards and staircase to the king's chambers, this area was lit by a single torch and held nothing but stacks of building supplies and a weathered wooden table with two chairs. Rose gratefully dropped onto one of them, amused to hear assorted bangs, scrapes, and curses coming from the building to her right.

"We're nearly back where we started, aren't we?"

Ellen took the second chair. "The dining room is on the other side of that new wall, yes."

Despite the sounds of construction, the courtyard seemed private enough. "So…why wouldn't you show Kit the book?"

"He wouldn't like it. He'd probably lock me in my chambers so I could never see Thomas again."

"Oh?" Though Rose felt drained, her curiosity was stronger. "May I see it?"

"In a minute." Ellen laid the book on the table and ran a finger over the gold lettering that gleamed in the torchlight. "Kit drew a picture of you."

"I know. I saw it. It was very well done. I had no idea he was an artist."

"He's not. Or not anymore. He used to draw all the time, and paint, too." Ellen's voice was so melancholy, Rose's throat tightened just hearing it. "Da used to bring extra wood home from his work—he'd spend hours sanding it smooth and cutting it to size so Kit could paint on it. And Mama would bring home old paints. The lady she worked for painted landscapes as a pastime."

"They sound like they were very devoted parents."

Ellen nodded, still absently tracing the gilt title. "They were. But Kit hasn't painted since they died. Not anything. He says he's too busy, but I'm not sure I believe him."

"He *does* seem very busy," Rose said gently.

Ellen's eyes, so like Kit's, went from sad to furious in a heartbeat. Brown to green. "All he wants to do," she said between gritted teeth, "is make money and add it to my dowry. He thinks he can buy me a titled husband. I don't *want* a titled husband. I want Thomas."

Rose had never been afraid to ask questions when she wanted answers. "How much is your dowry?"

"He adds to it constantly. Half of every penny that comes his way. Last I heard, it was up to eleven thousand."

"*Pounds?*"

"Pounds."

"Gemini," Rose breathed, stunned. "Mine is only three thousand." Hardly a pittance—three thousand pounds was ten years' income for a gentleman. "I have another ten from my grandfather, but that money is mine to control."

Ellen pushed back her unruly dark hair. "Kit doesn't let me control anything."

"He only wants what's best for you." Rose was sure of it. She was also sure Kit was going about it in a typical male, pigheaded way, but she wouldn't say that, at least not now.

"What's best for me is Thomas. I've told Kit that over and over, but he won't listen. He thinks he knows better than me."

"Well, you *are* still fairly young—"

"But I'm not a baby. Why can't he see that I've grown up? I *hate* being at odds with him. I hate the harsh words. I love him—but I love Thomas, too." Ellen fought back tears. "Will you help me persuade him?"

"Me?" Rose blinked. "Why should Kit listen to me?"

"He *drew* you," Ellen reminded her. "He hasn't drawn anything but buildings in twelve whole years."

And he'd kissed her, too, but Rose wouldn't be telling Ellen that. "I suppose I can try," she promised her. "But I'm not at all sure I can make any difference."

Pigheaded. That was Kit. But Rose also thought he was right—at least where Thomas was concerned.

A pawnbroker, for heaven's sake!

"Do you know, Ellen," she ventured carefully, "it might be a good idea for you to kiss Thomas before you decide you want to marry him."

"Kiss him?" Dashing away the tears, Ellen burst out laughing. "Mercy me, that's precious."

For a moment Rose was confused, but then she just felt like a fool. Of course Ellen had kissed her love. The girl was sixteen, and Rose had received her first kiss at sixteen.

Which, incidentally, had been the last time she'd ever sought one.

"Show me the book," she said.

Sobering, Ellen pushed it slowly across the table. "I'd like to read the words that go with the pictures," she said, for the first time sounding a bit shy. "But it's a different language."

"As long as it's not another architecture book," Rose jested, trying to lighten the mood, "because I've seen enough buildings." Her eyes scanned the title. "'*I Sonetti Lussuriosi* di Pietro Aretino,'" she read aloud. "It's Italian."

"Ah. I was wondering." Ellen scooted closer. "What does it mean?"

"It's authored by a man named Pietro Aretino, and it's called *The Licentious Sonnets*," Rose translated with some relish. This sounded good, maybe as good as *Aristotle's Master-piece*, the marriage manual her older sister had brought home years ago. She flipped open the cover—and gasped.

When her hands flew to her mouth the book fell on the floor, but it landed open at the same page. There, above the first sonnet, was an engraving of two people.

Nude people. On a bed.

Hearing muffled sounds, she looked up to see Ellen shaking with suppressed laughter. Suddenly, instead of feeling like the older, wiser woman of nineteen to Ellen's sixteen, Rose felt about five years old.

"I'm—sorry—" Ellen choked out, a few giggles spilling out along with her words. "Just—your face—" With a visible effort, she calmed herself, wiping more tears from her eyes. "You were so shocked."

"And why aren't you?" Rose snapped, her temper flaring from mortification more than outrage. "What on earth is a respectable young woman doing with a book like this?" Feeling the first twinges of headache coming on, she closed her eyes and rubbed her temples. And mentally repeated what she'd just said aloud, wondering when she had inexplicably turned into her mother.

"Please don't be mad. This is the only way I can learn."

"I beg your pardon?" Rose opened her eyes. "Learn what?"

Ellen chewed her lip. "About...men and woman. What happens when you get married. Kit won't tell me anything, you see, and I just want to know..."

Rose felt for the girl. She'd grown up sheltered, too, but at least she'd had Mum to explain things. Not that she'd ever actually asked her mother about *things*—instead she'd got all her knowledge from the manual—but still, she'd always *had* Mum. Who did Ellen have?

Wait...the manual!

"I've got a better book for you," Rose declared, crouching to retrieve *I Sonetti*. With an air of finality, she closed the book's cover. "Believe me, you'll find it much more informative than sonnets."

Ellen's eyes lit with interest. "Ooo, what's it called? Do you have it here?"

"Well, no. But—"

"When can you get it?"

"I don't know. I'll have to borrow it from my sister's house, and I'm not sure when I'll next be there. Or when I'll be able to bring it back to Windsor..."

"Oh."

Ellen sounded so deflated that Rose wanted to hug her—and she was not normally one for hugging. "Perhaps...perhaps I could give the sonnets a try. The words might not be as shocking as the pictures."

Ellen perked right up. "Oh, would you? I'd be ever so grateful!"

Rose cracked the book again, quickly covering the picture with her hand. She took a deep breath and read the first line. "'Fottiamci anima mia, fottiamci presto; Poi che tutti per fotter nati siamo.' Let us make love, my beloved, quickly, for we were made to make love." She looked up. "That's not *too* shocking."

"Not at all." Looking disappointed, Ellen reached to turn the page. "Maybe try this one."

When Rose saw the engraving, she slammed the book shut again. "You've looked at all the pictures?"

"Of course."

After taking a moment to collect herself, Rose drew a shaky breath. "Where did you get this?" she asked Ellen.

"I found it in Thomas's shop."

"Someone *pawned* this book?"

"People pawn everything. Jewels and pottery and pistols and swords...it's like a treasure trove, I'm telling you. My favorite place in the world. You should pay a visit, Rose. The shop is right on the High Street."

Rose had never thought she'd like a pawnshop—they were

seedy places, from what she'd heard. Disreputable, along with their owners. "Does Thomas have other foreign books?"

"Not like this one," Ellen said with a wicked smile. "But yes, I've noticed other books that aren't in English. This book was part of a whole library someone pawned; I don't think Thomas ever looked through the titles to see what he had." Her eyes filled with hope. "Please, would you translate the rest of the first poem?"

Rose felt her cheeks heat; in fact, she couldn't remember blushing so much in her whole life as she'd done since coming to court.

She was caught out. This book made her mighty uncomfortable, though the words seemed perhaps less objectionable than the pictures. Part of her felt she ought to go straight to Kit so he could take the book away from Ellen—but another part recoiled at the very idea. Given how protective he was of his sister, there was no telling how he'd react.

Rose needed to consider this carefully.

"I shall take the book back to my apartments," she told Ellen, "and write down the translation. That will give me a chance to puzzle out some of the less common words." And decide what should be done about all this, she added silently.

And in the meantime, young Ellen would be prevented from further study of those unseemly engravings.

"When will you bring me the translation?" Ellen asked eagerly. "Tomorrow morning, at the pawnshop?"

"It's past midnight already." Rose stood with a yawn. "And will Kit even allow you to go to the pawnshop?"

"He has to sleep sometime," Ellen said with a mischievous smile. "And when he does succumb, he sleeps like the dead. I manage to sneak out easily enough. After he wakes, though, he'll surely drag me back here while he works all the day."

"And half the night," Rose agreed.

Kit was the hardest working person she'd ever met.

"Probably." Ellen sighed. "Will you visit the pawnshop tomorrow, then? In the morning?"

"I'll try," Rose hedged, thinking she was rather curious to meet this Thomas Whittingham. Collecting the book, she led her younger friend back to the dining room.

Kit was up on a ladder inspecting something or other. He'd removed his surcoat and wore only shirtsleeves rolled up nearly to his elbows. Rose couldn't help noticing he had muscular forearms sprinkled with crisp black hair.

"Did you two have a nice visit?" he asked. As he climbed down the ladder, Rose saw muscles moving under his thin white cambric shirt, too. She hadn't sipped any champagne tonight, but her stomach seemed to think she had, anyway.

"Very," Ellen said, but Rose couldn't remember what the girl was responding to. She was thinking Kit must carry big beams all the day to have developed such muscles. And she was thinking about how she'd decided to let him kiss her again. Just to find out what he did differently from Gabriel.

And then she was remembering how soft his lips had felt, and how he'd drawn a picture of the real Rose.

She didn't like where these thoughts were leading.

"How did the translation go, then?" he wondered, his gaze on the book in Rose's hands.

She knew he was hoping to get *his* hands on it. "It was more difficult than Ellen had anticipated, so I'm going to take it home to work on it. Please excuse me. I must go find my mother."

She felt very relieved to escape. At least until she walked back into the drawing room and saw two gentlemen descending on her. Gabriel approached from one side, and from the other came someone she had yet to meet.

Though the stranger wasn't as handsome as the duke—or Kit —he might be a good kisser. But for some reason she had no interest in finding out. Not to mention she was holding a scandalous book clutched to her chest.

She had to get rid of it.

When Gabriel got to her first, the other suitor turned away dejectedly. "Pardon me, your grace," she said quickly. "I was just heading to the ladies' attiring room."

"Are you quite all right?" Gabriel asked, his blue eyes radiating concern.

He really was terribly nice. "Oh, yes. I'm just feeling a bit, um, peaked."

"Still?"

"It's all the excitement, I'm certain," she told him with a romantic sigh.

When he smiled, she knew she'd succeeded in convincing him he was responsible for her excitement. Leaning close, he lowered his voice to an intimate murmur. "I do hope you'll be feeling better soon."

She didn't care for his perfume. It was too sweet. "Oh, I'm certain I will," she said blithely and sailed out of the chamber.

Blessedly, the attiring room was empty. She stuffed the book under her cloak and dropped onto one of the green baize benches.

She really *was* feeling a little bit peaked.

TWENTY-THREE

"*K*IT," **HIS SISTER** said a few minutes later. "I need to talk to you."

"One moment, Ellen." He turned back to inspecting the latest materials that had arrived.

"I need to talk to you *now*," she yelled across the courtyard.

"It will do nicely," he told his new foreman, then took a deep breath and strode over to his sister, thinking, not for the first time, that he was mad to keep bringing her here every night. "What in your little selfish world is so important you had to interrupt me?"

Instead of bristling, she looked smug. "Lady Trentingham wishes to see you."

He slanted her a suspicious look. "Lady Trentingham doesn't even know who you are."

"Could that be because you weren't polite enough to introduce me?" She straightened her slim shoulders. "Well, she noticed me, anyway. Came right up and introduced herself, then asked where she might find you. I gather she looked in the dining room, but of course you were out here."

"Where did she find *you*?"

"On the terrace. She's waiting for you there."

He headed in that direction, wondering just what Ellen had been doing out on the terrace now that she no longer had her book to occupy her.

He admitted to himself that this arrangement must be even more frustrating for her than it was for him. It couldn't be pleasant having to entertain oneself all evening long. But he didn't feel as though he had a choice. If he left her at home, she'd surely run off to enjoy the company of that wretched pawn dealer. Doing goodness knew what.

He certainly didn't want to know.

Life had been so much simpler when he was off at school and Lady St. Vincent was still alive and caring for Ellen. He and his sister had spent glorious times together during the weeks he'd been able to visit. They'd never argued.

Well, rarely. Only when she'd begged him to take her back to school with him.

He stopped in the dining room long enough to shrug back into his surcoat before stepping out to the terrace.

Lady Trentingham turned in a swish of golden brocade skirts. "Kit. Ellen found you."

"I apologize for not introducing you earlier."

She waved that off. "I knew at first glance you were related. She looks just like you. A little prettier," she added with a smile.

He grinned back. "I should hope so."

"I wanted to let you know that my daughter is in the ladies' attiring room. If you can play truant for a bit, I'd like you to be there when she comes out."

Kit hesitated, suspecting from Lady Trentingham's tone that this was more of an order than a request. He was dying to spend time with Rose, but still determined to avoid distractions. "Rose was here a while ago, my lady," he said instead of answering. "She mentioned that she was looking for you."

"Is that so?" The countess reached to straighten his cravat. "Well, she's going to find *you* instead."

TWENTY-FOUR

*R*OSE HAD NEARLY steeled herself to venture forth from the attiring room when two young women walked in.

"Oh," the blond one said when she spotted her. "*You're* here."

Rose didn't care for her tone. She wanted to slap her across her pinched face. But she also wanted to be liked here at court, so she plastered on a smile. "I'm Rose Ashcroft. And you are...?"

"Lady Wyncherly."

"And I'm Lady Wembley." The other girl joined her friend at the large gilt-framed mirror. Her hair was so black Rose imagined she dyed it *and* used a lead comb.

"I'm pleased to make your acquaintance, Lady..." *Willoughby? Wemperley?* "Ladies. You're both married, then?"

"Yes," they said in unison, and then the dark-haired one added, "and you're not."

For once, Rose could think of worse things than being unmarried. Like being one of these harpies.

The blond Lady W touched a pimple on the other's face. "Right there," she said.

Her friend glared at herself in the mirror. "Stuff and bother, another one."

The blonde pulled a tiny silver box out of her drawstring purse. "Here, choose a patch."

While the pimpled Lady W rummaged through the box with a fingertip, the blond one turned to Rose. "Why aren't you busy kissing someone?"

Rose was rapidly concluding it was just as well none of the women here seemed to like her, because she certainly didn't like them. But she decided to ignore the slur. "I'm resting until the gaming."

"There won't be any gaming tonight," pimpled Lady W said, choosing a crescent-shaped patch.

"No gaming?" Rose echoed, dismayed.

Blond Lady W pulled some adhesive from her purse and dotted it on the back. "Haven't you heard?" She stuck the black velvet on her friend's face. "This will be an early evening, because we're all leaving for Hampton Court tomorrow. Will you be coming along?"

She sounded as though she hoped not.

"I'm not sure," Rose told her. She'd found no opportunity to discuss it yet with Mum. Half of her wanted to go to Hampton Court just to spite these two, while the other half thought the peace of Trentingham Manor sounded like heaven.

Unfortunately, there were no potential husbands at home.

The blonde chose a patch for herself—a cupid—even though she was already wearing nine and had no pimple to cover. Patches were quite in fashion, and Rose wore one herself—a small heart at the outside edge of her right eyebrow—but she thought the woman's face looked diseased with so many black shapes all over it.

Maybe blond Lady W *was* diseased. Maybe most of the patches were hiding hideous smallpox scars. Although Rose knew it wasn't nice of her, the thought made her smile.

"What?" the Lady Ws barked together.

Rose shrugged and sauntered out of the little chamber. She was certain they started talking about her the moment she cleared the door—and she doubted they had anything positive to say. It was a good thing she didn't care.

Stepping into the drawing room, she stopped short at the sight of Kit. He shifted from foot to foot, gazing into space and looking uncomfortable. Well, he didn't belong here at court, so that wasn't such a surprise. Perhaps the king wanted the drawing room renovated too, and he was studying it.

She noticed Kit was taller than she, but not terribly much taller. Maybe half a head, while she only came up to Gabriel's chin. Kit didn't make her feel petite like the duke did.

He finally observed her. "Rose," he greeted with a smile.

No *Lady*. Did that mean he considered her a friend now?

"Kit. Finished working already? It's not even dawn." Suddenly remembering her plans, she dropped her teasing tone. "Will you kiss me?"

"Here? Now?" His eyes widened, becoming more green than brown.

"I didn't mean it like that," she rushed out, cursing herself silently for her habit of speaking before she thought. "I just… well, I just want to see how you do it."

He looked amused. "Like anyone else does it, I imagine."

He was wrong, *so wrong*, about that. As he moved closer, the little bubbles began dancing in her stomach.

He was very, very wrong.

His gaze locked on hers, now purest green with only flecks of brown. Flecks she was close enough to see. Though his scent was light, it still overwhelmed her—that woodsy perfume mixed with the dust of the construction site and a sweet tinge of ink.

"Are you certain you want a kiss now?" he teased back. "Right here, in front of the entire court?"

"Haven't you heard?" a gentleman cut in. "Our Lady Rose quite enjoys kissing."

Startled, Rose turned to find Lord Davenport standing behind her. She'd kissed him last night and been disappointed, but at least he'd had good manners.

"Greetings, my dear Lady Rose," he said and bent to kiss her again, right there—as Kit had said—in front of the entire court.

But before his lips could touch hers, she felt herself pulled out of the way. She would have fallen if not for Kit's steadying hands... but then, it was he who had yanked her off balance in the first place.

"Why on earth did you do that?" she snapped, though she'd been about to dodge the unwanted kiss herself. Wriggling out of Kit's arms, she turned to glare at him. "You've insulted Lord Davenport!"

Kit's mouth fell open. "But he...you weren't..." Pausing to gather himself, he rubbed the back of his neck. "Rose, I—"

"Ah, there you are."

She whirled to find that Lord Davenport had fled...only to be replaced by the Duke of Bridgewater.

Gabriel wore a charming smile. "You promised me this dance, if I'm remembering right?"

She hadn't, but before she could say so he was leading her away.

"I don't like seeing other men touch you," Gabriel said.

"Then don't look," she suggested, laughing when he began to protest. "I didn't encourage him," she soothed.

"Shall I call him out, then?"

"Gemini, no!" She laughed again, furtively searching for Kit. He was nowhere to be found. "You're ten times the man he is, your grace. He's not worth your time."

The duke's pretty blue eyes sparkled, telling her he liked hearing that.

They danced an almain and once again received jealous glances from gentlemen and ladies alike. Gabriel was a perfect gentleman. But after the dance, when he contrived to draw her behind the curtains, she sighed.

If only she enjoyed his kisses instead of dreading them, life would be so much better.

They weren't the only couple in the big bay window. In one corner, two figures were locked in a passionate embrace.

"Don't look," Gabriel whispered, turning her to face the other corner.

There, another couple was entwined, and the lady's skirts appeared to be hiked up to her knees! Rose was uncomfortably reminded of the engravings in Ellen's book.

She needed air.

"I wish to go outdoors," she told Gabriel.

"Excellent idea. There's a distinct lack of privacy in this area."

She hadn't meant with him; she'd endured four of his kisses tonight, and she didn't intend to suffer a fifth.

As they emerged from behind the curtains, Rose looked around for rescue, relieved to meet the gaze of Viscount Hathersham. She'd kissed him two nights ago, and he hadn't been *that* bad. At least not bad enough that she couldn't risk encouraging him a little if it might save her from another private outing with the duke.

"Lord Hathersham!" she called, waving him closer. "I completely forgot that I'd promised you the next dance."

She hadn't, of course, but thankfully he wasn't dim enough to say so. He bowed and took her by the hand, raising it to his lips. His kiss was a bit damper than she'd remembered, but at least it was to her hand, not her mouth. "The next dance will be my pleasure, Lady Rose. And well worth the wait."

As they moved toward the dance floor, Rose sent Gabriel what she hoped he would take as an apologetic look.

"I never asked you to dance," the viscount said in a low tone that she imagined he thought seductive.

"Well, you should have," she told him with a smile.

"You feel we two are suited, then?"

"For a dance."

Though a vigorous country dance would have been more to her liking, the musicians had chosen a minuet. As the dancers went to their toes, the viscount pulled Rose near. "I'm hoping I can persuade you we're suited for more than a dance." One of his hands slipped around her and rested on the small of her back. "You move nicely," he said.

"Thank you, my lord."

"I have nice moves as well." When she tried to gain some distance, he pressed her even closer. "Especially," he added, "in bed."

Panicking, she forced a girlish giggle. "Oh, my lord! There's no bed here at court."

"We can find one," he murmured as his hand began to drift lower.

"My lord!" She twisted subtly out of his embrace, not wanting to make a scene. "That is *hardly* appropriate," she told him in a voice colder than the ice sculpture that decorated the refreshment table.

"But, my lady—"

"Hush up and dance!"

She held herself in check, though she wanted to rant and rave —and perhaps bash him over the head with something good and heavy. The Chinese vase on that silver table would do nicely.

The nerve of him!

When the dance ended, she muttered a stiff "Thank you, my lord," and bolted for the solitude of the terrace.

TWENTY-FIVE

"SHE'S DISTRESSED," Lady Trentingham said, standing with Kit in a dark corner of the drawing room. "And she'll be alone out there on the terrace. Go to her."

"I'd wager she won't be alone for long," Kit predicted. A safe bet, given the Duke of Bridgewater was wandering toward the door already.

"I'm sure she'd appreciate you whisking her away for a spell."

"She didn't seem to appreciate me earlier," he said sourly, remembering her hostility outside the ladies' attiring room.

A short laugh escaped the countess's lips. "My prickly Rose. But surely a resilient fellow like you can't be frightened off by a few thorns?" She didn't wait for an answer. "You can find solitude, yes? You know this castle better than anyone."

Kit eyed the woman curiously. "Aren't you a mite concerned about letting your daughter go off alone with a young man? I thought chaperones were supposed to abhor that sort of thing."

Lady Trentingham's lips quirked. "Are you saying you'll divest Rose of her innocence at the first opportunity?"

"Of course not!" He was fairly certain he'd just blushed all the way down to his toes. "I would never—"

"Indeed, I trust that you wouldn't. Though of course everyone gets carried away at times." Her expression subtly shifted, her eyes glittering with something that wasn't quite menace, but wasn't friendliness, either. "I believe in giving my children the freedom to learn from their own mistakes. Rose is nineteen, and thus entitled to a measure of privacy. But please know, Kit, that I am not remiss in my chaperoning duties. I may not always be by my daughter's side, but I *always* know what she's getting up to."

Kit swallowed hard. "I see."

She gave him a little push. "Now, go. I'll keep an eye on Ellen."

He went, quickly, feeling foolish as he elbowed his way past the more sedate duke and handily beat him outdoors. This whole endeavor had become an exercise in humiliation. Here he was, a grown man shirking his responsibilities, jeopardizing his livelihood, and literally shoving people out of the way, all in pursuit of a girl. A girl who, though she appeared perfectly willing to flirt with him in private, never hesitated to point out his inferior status in company. On top of which, there was her mother—*her mother*—orchestrating their relationship and critiquing Kit's every move.

His masculine pride was more than bruised. It was beaten to a pulp.

But that all floated to the back of his mind when he saw her standing at the edge of the terrace. Silhouetted in the moonlight, she gazed over the darkened Thames Valley.

"Rose," he called softly as he approached.

She started, then turned, looking amused. "Kit? You always turn up."

Mercifully, she seemed to have forgotten she'd been angry with him. He glanced back, noting the duke had made it out to the terrace. "Would you fancy a stroll?" he asked her quickly, already taking her arm.

She fell into step beside him. "Where will we stroll to?"

"Just around the courtyards, or—"

"Lady Rose!"

"It's Gabriel," she whispered, walking faster. "Ignore him."

"Don't you like him?"

"Of course I like him! He's a duke!" She sped up, walking amazingly quickly considering her high heels. "I just need to leave court for a while, that's all."

Her mother really was quite perceptive. "And why is that?" he asked, steering her around a corner.

"I'm making a fool of myself here," she said with a sigh, never one to mince words. "I wish to break the cycle."

He laughed, casting another glance back. Thankfully, they seemed to have lost the duke. "A fool?" he echoed, enjoying the coincidence of their similar mental states. Perhaps love made a fool out of everyone.

Not that he was in love. He hadn't meant *love*. Not *love* love. Just—romance. Courtship. That sort of thing.

He tugged at his cravat, feeling suddenly hot though it was a cool evening. "I think you're mistaken. It's quite obvious all the men like you."

Men like that popinjay who had tried to kiss her.

"And all the ladies hate me." He could hear the pout in her voice.

"They're only jealous," he soothed.

"I know that."

As he led her through a small courtyard, he laughed again, enjoying her candor.

"They're vulgar bores, anyway," she declared. "But a girl needs friends. I miss my sisters. I enjoyed talking with Ellen."

"She enjoyed you, too. She's in a much better mood now. Thank you for that."

She waved a hand. "I cannot think what I did, besides possibly offer friendship."

"She needs friends, too. Of late, she spends all her time with *him*." He steered her around the Round Tower. "What was the title of the book she brought along?"

"I won't know until I translate it," Rose said glibly.

So glibly he suspected it was a fib. That book was making him more and more curious.

She stopped before the castle gate and turned to face him. Torchlight danced over her fine features, highlighting her puzzled smile and the charming little indents it made in her cheeks.

"Where are we going?" she asked.

He hadn't known, but now he did. "To the river, if it pleases you."

TWENTY-SIX

*R*OSE KNEW SHE shouldn't have left the castle, especially with a man. But she'd wanted so much to escape. And Kit was a friend.

She'd never had a male friend before.

"It's quiet out here," she said.

"Unlike your friends at court, most of the townfolk rise with the dawn and seek their beds when the sun sets."

"I guess that's why none of the windows are lit." The hill was steep, the uneven cobblestones treacherous. "It's so dark." A little wobble in her voice matched a sudden lurch in her gait.

He reached to steady her. "You're not afraid of the dark, are you?"

"No," she snapped, then added, "Well, maybe. A little," when she caught him looking at her sideways.

What was it about him that made her spill her most embarrassing secrets?

She waited for him to laugh, but he didn't. "I'd know the way with my eyes closed," he said. "Here, take my hand."

She did, though she knew she shouldn't be doing that either. But Kit's fingers felt nice linked with hers, comforting instead of intimidating, though his palm was rougher than those of the court gentlemen. Work worn, she supposed. And while she was holding his hand, the night didn't seem quite as dark.

At the bottom of the hill, rowdy laughter drifted from a tavern called Bel and the Dragon. The sound of common men thick with drink. Kit was common, too, but for now she didn't care. It was peaceful here, away from court. And no one was threatening to kiss her.

Not even the one person she wished would.

When they reached Kit's house and he turned and started up the steps, Rose pulled her hand from his. "You said we were going to the river."

"We're stopping here only a minute." He fished a key from his pocket and unlocked the door; it was late enough that Graves wasn't there to open it. "Wait here," Kit whispered, ushering her into the entry. A single oil lamp burned on the small marble-topped table. "I'll be right back."

Hugging herself, she watched him walk deeper into the house. Through an open window, more laughter floated from the river, faint and joyous. People celebrating on a barge, she imagined.

She didn't have to wait long. A minute later Kit was back, a cloth sack in one hand and a cloak in the other. "Ellen's," he explained. "I thought you might be cold."

He moved close and settled it over her shoulders, wrapping her in its warmth. Fine gray wool with black and silver braid, it was much heavier than her own velvet one and smelled faintly of Ellen, a light, carefree fragrance compared to her own bolder perfume. But Kit being so near, his own scent seemed stronger—robust, woodsy, and deliciously overwhelming.

She was on the verge of asking for a kiss again when he stepped away.

"Thank you," she said quietly as he guided her back outdoors. "It was very kind of you to take me for a walk. Away from…all that."

"I needed a break from my work," he said too quickly, as though he'd readied the excuse in advance.

She slanted him a sidelong glance. Had he sought her out for a different reason? Or was it something else he was keeping from her? "Then you mean to return to work afterwards?" she asked in a neutral tone.

He shrugged. "Likely not for long. Lack of sleep is finally catching up with me."

Ellen was counting on that, Rose thought, wondering why she felt disloyal. Whose side was she on regarding this brother–sister tug of war? She wasn't sure. She only knew that right here, right now, she was in the right place.

The streets were deserted this time of night, the river slow and dark, the moon illuminating its ripples. Kit guided her past the bridge that led to Eton, its shops dark and shuttered. They came to a wooden gate with white lettering that gleamed in the moonlight. "Romney Walk," Rose read aloud.

The gate creaked when Kit opened it. "There's a place near Trentingham named Romney as well, isn't there?"

"There are many such places, I believe." Beyond the gate, the path angled closer to the river. Although the moon provided enough light that she could trod the packed dirt without tripping, she allowed Kit to keep a steadying hand on her elbow. "The word derives from a Saxon word, *rumnea*, meaning water."

He looked at her with admiration. "You know ancient languages, too?"

She smiled, liking that look. She couldn't remember a gentleman ever admiring her for more than her appearance.

It was the difference between a suitor and a friend.

"No, Rand told me about that. I'm not so much interested in old tongues—I'd rather learn languages I can use someday when I travel. What's in the sack?"

"Bread. For the swans." Several had been following them as they walked, gliding soundlessly on the water. One of them honked now, as though he'd heard Kit and knew food was in the offing. "I thought you might like to feed them."

"It would never occur to me to bring bread. Lily would think like that."

"She loves animals, doesn't she?"

"Almost as much as she loves Rand." Rose released a long sigh. "She's nice to everyone and everything, human and animal alike. I could never live up to her perfection."

"No one is perfect. Not Lily or anyone else." He reached into the sack and handed her a few cubes of stale bread. "Shall we sit?"

The bank rose here, forming a little grassy hill that over-looked the river. Rose lowered herself to the springy ground, tucking Ellen's cloak beneath her. She tossed a bread cube out on the water and watched the swans rush to gobble it. "What is it about you that makes me such a chatterer?" she wondered.

He sat beside her. "You don't seem tongue-tied with anyone else."

Pursing her lips, she tossed another cube. "I don't generally admit to people that I'm imperfect."

"I hesitate to disillusion you," he said wryly, "but I imagine they could figure that out without you informing them."

Laughing, she shoved at his shoulder. Swans honked, demanding more bread. Across the river, a tiny bridge was barely visible over small rapids gleaming white in the moon-light. The sounds of running water were soothing.

After a moment of silence, Kit reached over and took her hand. When she didn't pull away, he raised it to his mouth and pressed his warm lips to the back.

She knew she shouldn't allow it. But his kiss on her hand felt different from Lord Hathersham's, so different it made her shiver.

"Are you cold?" he asked.

"No. Will you kiss me?"

"Shy as usual," Kit teased, looking rather pleased with himself.

Though his tone made her blush, it was anticipation making her heart pound. "I didn't mean..." Agitated, she scrambled to her feet. "Gemini, I just want to see how you do it."

He rose, too, moving closer. "Like anyone else, as I told you."

With a hand beneath her chin, he tilted her face up. His breath teased her lips. "A kiss is a kiss."

"Oh, no," she whispered, "it isn't."

Then she couldn't say more, because his mouth was covering hers.

She did her best to concentrate on analyzing his technique. But as his hands came up to cradle her cheeks, as his lips coaxed hers with slow and deliberate care, as her fingers gripped his solid shoulders, then gripped harder when she feared her knees might buckle...

What was it she was supposed to be concentrating on, again?

Kiss, her muddled mind reminded her. *How...*

Mmm. Was he more gentle? Not really—and not at all once he'd gathered her into his arms, pulling her closer to deepen the kiss. Was he more skilled? She had to think so, but she couldn't seem to discern how. Did he taste different? Well, certainly. He tasted like Kit.

She felt his heart beating, and then she couldn't think any longer. She could only feel. She shifted so that her own heartbeat was next to his. They were beating in tandem. A perfect moment.

A thing of beauty.

When he broke the kiss, she tugged him back for another. He obliged her briefly before drawing away with a laugh. "So I'm different, am I?"

"Somehow." She sighed. "But I cannot figure out the difference. It makes no sense. I don't even *like* kissing!"

"Oh, I think you do."

"Only with you—so far." He kissed her neck now, and she liked that, too. Little damp kisses she should have loathed, but she didn't. Instead, she shivered with delight. "What's your secret?"

"Maybe," he murmured, his lips warm against her throat, "the secret is that we belong together."

"No." It couldn't be. She couldn't *belong* with a commoner. Kit was her friend, and she liked kissing him, and that was all. "I think not."

"No?" He raised his head to meet her gaze. But then the intensity in his eyes suddenly dissipated. He adopted a lazy smile. "Shall I kiss you again to prove it?"

"Oh, Kit," she scolded, half grumble, half sigh. She wondered what he'd almost said before he'd changed his mind.

He pressed a warm, clinging kiss to her mouth. "Hmm?"

"I think we should go back." She didn't want to go back, but she had to. This wasn't where she belonged. "Please, take me back. I don't think this is right. I mean...*we* aren't right."

It was a long, heart-stopping moment before he drew away. Then he took her hand and started down the path. She didn't pull her hand from his. She knew she should. But she didn't.

"I think we *are* right," he said after a while. "And I think that in time you'll agree."

It was a good thing he was just a friend, because she feared she might agree already.

TWENTY-SEVEN

"*L*ADY TRENTINGHAM?"

Chrystabel turned to the Duke of Bridgewater and took note of his troubled expression. "Yes, your grace?"

"I thought I should let you know your daughter is missing."

"Oh?" Poor young man, he really seemed to care. "Whatever makes you think that?"

"She went off more than an hour ago. I was hoping she'd return within a reasonable time, so I'd have no need to alarm you—"

"Did she go off with Kit Martyn?" Feeling sorry for him, she laid a hand on his arm. "Mr. Martyn is a friend of the family. I asked him to escort her."

"Back to your apartments?" When she didn't answer, he apparently took that for an affirmative. "She did say she felt peaked. Will she be returning later this evening?"

"I'm not certain," Chrystabel said slowly, feeling a twinge of guilt for misleading him.

But she hadn't really lied, had she? She'd merely allowed him to jump to a conclusion. He truly did seem concerned. A pity he was all wrong for Rose—too dull and unchallenging.

Although her daughter would make her own decision,

Chrystabel had no doubt that, with her subtle help, in the end Rose would choose the right husband.

Bridgewater suddenly frowned. "It seems that, besides Lady Rose, a number of other ladies have gone missing."

Chrystabel looked around, surprised to find he was right. There were noticeably fewer women than earlier. The abandoned gentlemen shifted restlessly, standing in little groups and talking about God knew what.

"Do you expect they're all feeling peaked?" Bridgewater asked. "Perhaps the prawns were bad."

"You men ate prawns, too, did you not?" Dull, just as she'd thought. But his heart was in the right place. Looking over to her right, she brightened. "Oh, here comes Rose now."

Her daughter's step was lighter, her cheeks pinkened from the fresh night air—and perhaps a tender moment with Kit.

Chrystabel could only hope.

Bridgewater swept Rose a bow. "We missed you, my lady."

"Did you?" she murmured distractedly.

Chrystabel took that as a good sign. If Rose was failing to flirt with a *duke*, she must have someone else on her mind.

"Are you feeling better?" he asked politely.

"I...um...not really, I'm afraid. I...I just returned for my cloak."

"You're wearing a cloak," he pointed out.

"Oh." She blinked. "I borrowed this one." She unfastened the gray wool garment and shrugged it off, handing it to Chrystabel. "Will you both excuse me?"

TWENTY-EIGHT

*T*HE ATTIRING ROOM was so crowded, Rose had to edge her way inside.

"Marry come up!" a lady was saying. "Will you look at this? And this"—there was a pause during which Rose heard pages flipping—"how would this even *work*?"

"Very well, I can assure you," another lady said smugly.

Amid laughter, Rose worked herself toward the center. And then froze. Eleven—no, twelve—courtiers were huddled over Ellen's book.

She was beginning to back away when one of them glanced up. "Lady Rose! Could this book be yours?"

"Mine?"

The pimply, black-haired Lady W held up Rose's purple cloak. "We found it under this. It's yours, isn't it?"

"The cloak, yes. But the book..." Oh, dash it—she couldn't leave it here, so there was no sense in lying. "It belongs to a friend," she said, holding her head high. After all, given the behavior these women exhibited here at court, they were hardly apt to condemn her for possessing such a book.

"A friend? Wherever did he find it?"

"She," Rose corrected. "And why? Have you heard of this book?"

"Heard of it?" a plump brunette said. "Why, *I Sonetti Lussuriosi* is known far and wide." She pronounced the Italian words with a dreadful English accent. "It was suppressed by the Vatican in the last century; didn't you know? There are few copies surviving, and many men searching for them."

"And women," someone added, prompting giggles.

"Lord Chauncey has a set of the engravings on his bedchamber walls," one lady slyly informed them. "I've seen them."

"A crude set," a second lady put in. "Copies. Nothing like the fine artistry of these originals."

"You've seen them, too?" a third lady asked.

"You haven't?" a fourth replied with an arched brow.

From the laughter that ensued, Rose concluded that Lady Number Three—and she—were the only women at court who hadn't found their way into Lord Chauncey's bedchamber.

Perversely, she was beginning to think she might have more in common with a woman like Nell than with these high-born ladies of her own class.

A wistful sigh came from one of the women. "I do so wish I could read Italian. These sonnets must be fascinating."

"And far more tasteful than the pictures," Rose said dryly.

As one, the assembled group stopped focusing on the book and swung to her instead. A few of them sidled closer, looking at Rose with more interest than resentment for a change.

"Can *you* read Italian?" one of them asked. Or rather, slurred. She was wearing the newly fashionable plumpers—cork balls inside her cheeks to round out her face.

Rose nodded. "Yes, I can read it." Perhaps it wasn't considered ladylike to study languages, but she was far past trying to impress these women.

And oddly enough, they didn't seem disapproving. Quite the contrary. "Will you read this book to us?" one asked.

Rose's face flamed at the thought. "I...I don't read Italian that well," she fibbed. "Not well enough to translate aloud."

They all sighed together rather theatrically, their good-natured expressions hardening.

"But I'm translating the first sonnet tonight," Rose found herself telling them. "For my friend. I could bring a copy to court, too, if you'd like."

The brunette's overly made-up eyes widened at this offer. "Would you?"

The pimply Lady W smiled. "We'd be most grateful."

"Mosht grateful," slurred the woman with the plumpers.

The blond Lady W stepped forward. "I must say, Lady Rose, that's a very kind offer, indeed. I'm so pleased to have made your acquaintance here at court."

TWENTY-NINE

"DIDN'T YOU SLEEP well, dear?" Mum frowned as Rose yawned for the dozenth time. "Perhaps you should go back to bed."

"I slept fine, Mum." And she had—for the three hours she'd actually slept. "I overslept, in fact. It's past ten already, and I mean to visit Ellen at the pawnshop this morning."

"The pawnshop?"

She crossed to the window to check the weather. "I never made it back to the bookshop yesterday, and Ellen said the pawnshop has books. Foreign books. And I need to return her cloak." It looked sunny, so she decided against wearing her own.

"It's amazing how quickly you've become friends." Mum sounded pleased.

Rose made no reply. Friends didn't lie to each other, yet she was about to do just that.

"Sometimes friendships are meant to be," Mum went on. "Just like some men and women belong together."

"Like the ones you introduce to be married?" With a forced laugh, Rose turned from the window. She collected her little purse and slid the cord over her wrist, then draped Ellen's cloak over one arm. "The court leaves today for Hampton, as I hear it?"

"That's right."

"Will we go with them?"

"We could. Or we could catch our breaths at Trentingham first. What do you wish to do?"

"Oh, I don't know," Rose hedged. She watched her mother reach for her own drawstring purse. "Where are you going?"

"You didn't think I'd let you go to the pawnshop alone, did you? A young lady doesn't parade around town on her own."

Plenty of young ladies did, but Rose didn't feel like arguing. She only hoped she could contrive a way to speak with Ellen in private. She'd die if her mother found out about *I Sonetti*—which was why she was somewhat keen on the idea of leaving court for a while. With all the ladies atwitter over the scandalous book, it might prove difficult to keep Mum in the dark.

Outdoors, the courtyards were teeming with servants hauling luggage, but there was no sign of any courtiers. "Have they left already?" Rose wondered, half hoping it was true. Maybe she'd arisen too late to go to Hampton Court, and the question would be decided, at least for today.

But as they skirted the Round Tower, Mum laughed. "I imagine they're all still fast asleep."

"I thought everyone was planning to leave early."

"That, Lady Rose," came a male voice, "depends on your definition of *early*."

Rose turned to see the Duke of Bridgewater fall into step beside them. He looked very dapper this morning, with a broad-brimmed, ostrich-plumed hat shielding his golden head from the sun.

"And what is your definition of early, your grace?"

"Oh, before noon, I suppose. I'm certainly proud of myself for being up and about before the sun reaches its zenith." Gabriel grinned, his blue eyes twinkling. "Most of us wake as the sun sets. I fear the court will find it tedious to have to rise and travel in broad daylight today."

She laughed, enjoying the company of so pleasant and impressive a gentleman. Even for traveling, he was dressed to the height of fashion. His bright burgundy suit sported rows of gold buttons along the front edges of both the long waistcoat and the embroidered surcoat that went over it. The breeches beneath were secured at the knee with gold buttons, too. His lace cravat was tied at his neck in a wide bow, and, unlike Kit, he wore shoes instead of boots—heeled, with a double sole and small gold spurs.

She smoothed her scarlet silk day gown, wishing it were adorned with pearls or something else extravagant. She'd always thought herself fashionable, but the ladies here made her feel like a country frump.

"I'm so glad to see you're feeling better this morning." The duke took her arm. "Please tell me you're coming along to Hampton Court."

She exchanged a glance with her mother, who shrugged, apparently leaving the decision up to her. "We're just on our way to the pawnshop," she said, evading an answer.

"The pawnshop?"

If Rose could judge by the duke's tone, he and Kit held similar opinions regarding pawnshops. "We're not pawning anything," she assured him with a laugh. "Just visiting a friend there."

"A friend?" Sounding slightly disturbed, he gripped her arm tighter. "I shall accompany you, then, at least as far as the door."

"That's not necessary," Rose protested.

"I was planning to take a walk in the Great Park, anyway. A brisk morning stroll does wonders for a fellow's constitution. I usually leave from the castle, but I can enter off Park Street, no harm done."

There was no arguing with him, it seemed. They walked through the Lower Ward, Rose wishing some of the ladies were around to see her on the arm of the tall, handsome duke. Was she a fool to consider leaving court when it appeared she may be on the verge of snagging him?

Beyond the gateway, it was a short stroll down Castle Hill and a left onto the High Street. The pawnshop was right there, as Ellen had said. Three golden balls—the pawn trade's age-old symbol—dangled from a bracket that projected from the building. As they approached, Rose couldn't help but notice the business looked prosperous. A wooden sign overhead said WHITTINGHAM'S PAWN SHOP in fresh gold paint.

Then she lowered her gaze from the sign to find a gorgeous pair of earrings in the window. Set in delicate gold filigree dangles, rubies sparkled and pearls gleamed. "Oooh," she breathed, fingering her few coins through the thin fabric of her drawstring purse.

Dozens of items crammed the window, but the earrings stood alone as dainty works of art. She fairly itched to own them.

"Aren't these earrings beautiful?" She gazed at them on their bed of black velvet. "If there's gaming at Hampton Court tonight, maybe I'll be lucky enough to win them."

"They match your gown superbly," Gabriel observed. "I think this *is* your lucky day."

"Pardon?"

He grinned. "I've never patronized a pawnshop before, but wait here, ladies, if you will." He bowed and then entered the shop, a bell jingling as he pushed the door open.

Rose pressed back against the building to avoid a careening carriage. "Mum, do you expect he's going to buy those earrings for me?"

Her mother shrugged and smiled. "It seems so."

An unfamiliar hand went into the window, square with pale hair sprinkled on the back. Rose watched the earrings and the hand disappear. "I hope he won't think I belong to him afterwards."

"Does that mean you don't want to?" Mum raised a brow but didn't wait for an answer. "In any case, they're only earrings. A trifling item for a man like the duke."

Rose breathed a sigh of relief, for the truth was, she wanted the earrings. She could hardly wait to see them on her ears. She hoped someone had pawned a mirror.

A moment later, the duke stepped back outside and presented the jewelry to her with a flourish. "Enjoy, my lady."

The rubies sparkled even more in the sunshine; the pearls shone like they held secrets; the gold was intricate, fashioned by a talented hand. Mum slipped into the shop as Rose fumbled with the first earring.

"Here, let me help." Gabriel took it from her and stepped close to fasten it on her lobe.

He still smelled of too much perfume, but Rose didn't care. "Thank you, your grace."

"It's nothing." He reached for the other earring. "Beautiful ladies deserve beautiful things."

She turned her head to allow him greater access. "I love them."

"I'm glad. I want to see you happy, Lady Rose."

She smiled. He truly was very nice, and generous and handsome and a duke, too. When he was finished, she tucked her long ringlet curls behind her ears, the better to display her new treasures.

"Stunning," he pronounced. Then he leaned close and pressed his lips to hers.

She tried to act enthusiastic, because truly, a kiss was a small price to pay for such beautiful earrings. But she was glad that Ellen's cloak over her arm gave her an excuse not to embrace him.

Thankfully, the kiss was chaste. Gabriel was too polite to attempt more in broad daylight on Windsor's High Street. But short as it was, all Rose could think was that his kiss was nothing like Kit's.

When Gabriel pulled away, he reached into one of the deep pockets in his breeches and pulled out a handful of coins. A small, secret smile curved his lips as he counted them, dropping each into a little leather pouch. "It's just as I thought."

Rose touched her new earrings, assuring herself they were still there. "What's that?"

"The fool gave me too much change. A crown more than I was due."

"It was good of you to notice. I'm sure he'll appreciate its return."

He blinked his nice blue eyes. "Return? Why on earth should I return it?"

"It's dishonest not to. Besides, I imagine he needs it much more than you do."

"A pawnbroker? I think not." He tucked the pouch into his pocket. "The knaves prey on the most unfortunate, paying pence on the pound for their goods, then charging exorbitant fees for their return. Ten percent a month—and when the poor clodpolls cannot pay, the brokers sell their goods at an enormous profit."

Rose reached up to toy with the ruby earrings. She didn't like to think of them as belonging to a poor clodpoll. Surely they hadn't. "So you'll just keep the money?"

"His loss, my gain. A wise man is more careful when doing business." The duke patted the leather pouch where it was hidden inside his pocket. "Now I must be off for my walk. I'll need to get back to the castle in time to see all my luggage is safely transported." He executed a small, formal bow. "Your servant, my lady. I hope to see you at Hampton Court late this afternoon."

"Thank you for the earrings," Rose called as he walked away. Then she went into the shop.

The bell on the door was still jingling as she headed toward a pockmarked blond youth who was polishing a glass counter. Though he was younger than she had pictured Ellen's Thomas, he looked very industrious indeed. And certainly not like a knave who preyed on the unfortunate.

"Lady Rose!" Ellen came running over. "Thomas and I were just having the most lovely conversation with your mother. And the duke bought you earrings, did he?" Her eyes danced. "Mercy me, imagine that."

"Kit loaned me this last night," Rose said, handing over Ellen's cloak.

Ellen looked at her sharply. "When?"

"Later, when it grew cold." Rose dug in her drawstring purse and pulled out a silver crown. "Mr. Whittingham gave Bridgewater too much change. He asked me to return it."

Ellen set the cloak aside, effectively distracted from wondering how she'd come by it. "That wasn't Thomas's doing, but the new apprentice he's training." Her disapproving gaze went to the young man behind the counter. "Thomas will have a word with him for certain."

Rose felt sorry for the boy. "I'm sure it was an honest mistake."

"Fear not, Thomas doesn't beat the lad. But he must learn to be more careful." Ellen took the coin gratefully. "Please thank his grace for returning this, next time you should see him. Thomas needs every penny, because he dreams of moving the shop to London—to the Strand, no less!" She laughed as she walked over to add the crown to the till.

Noticing a fine gilt-framed mirror perched on the wall, Rose went over to admire her new earrings. She turned her head this way and that, watching the rubies catch the light. "Where is your Thomas?"

"In the back, talking with your mother. Come, I cannot wait for you to meet him."

"Just a minute." She sidled closer to Ellen and lowered her voice. "I'm afraid I wasn't able to finish the first sonnet. It took longer than expected and the hour grew too late."

"Oh." Ellen's eyes clouded with disappointment, then cleared. "May I read what you've finished so far?"

"I didn't bring it with me," Rose said quickly, though she had the full translation hidden in her sleeve. In truth, the work had taken no more than a quarter of an hour. The rest of the night she'd spent agonizing over whether to show it to Ellen...or to her brother.

In the end she hadn't been able to decide, so her decision

had been to put the decision off. The copy in her sleeve was for the court ladies—nothing in its text could shock *them* overmuch.

"How long will it take to finish?" Ellen wondered.

"It depends," Rose said evasively. "I'll keep working at it."

"Very well," Ellen said after a moment, looking confused. She turned to make her way toward the back, and Rose followed, feeling like a worm.

The shop was deceiving, because although it looked large enough on the inside, even more space was hidden behind. Here, apparently, was where Thomas kept the goods that he was holding for customers to return and claim—and he had more in that category than goods for sale. Items were piled up on shelves and stacked in trays and spilling out of trunks—a treasure trove, as Ellen had said.

"Mr. Whittingham has been telling me all about the history of pawning," Mum said after the introductions.

Rose traced the silver embroidery on a deep green velvet surcoat. "There's a history?"

"Most certainly." Thomas had brown hair, blue eyes, and a strong chin that lent him a mature air, though he looked no older than twenty. "Pawnbroking can be traced back over three thousand years to ancient China, and there are also records of it in early Greek and Roman history."

Thomas seemed intelligent, too. More learned than she'd supposed a pawnbroker would be—and certainly more learned than Kit seemed to give him credit for. "And the three gold balls?" she asked. "From where did that symbol come?"

"In times past, the Medici family in Italy were well-known moneylenders. Legend says one of the Medicis battled a giant and slew him with three sacks of rocks. The three balls became part of their family crest, and eventually, the sign of pawnbroking."

"It's an honorable business," Ellen put in. "Where else can the common people find money should they need it? It's not as though they can approach noblemen for loans. Pawning has

saved many families' homes and farms—they consider themselves lucky to have a broker to turn to."

Rose remembered Gabriel's opinions about preying on poor
clodpolls. "Even when they cannot afford to redeem their
pawned goods?"

"Sometimes they just choose not to." Ellen lifted her chin.
"It's a business, after all. Thomas is entitled to make a living."

"Of course he is," Mum said.

Rose turned to Ellen's love. "Forgive my saying so, but you
seem young to have your own shop."

"It was my father's, and his father's before him."

She hadn't thought of a pawnshop as something a man could
inherit. In fact, she'd never thought about pawnbroking at all. It
was unlikely she would ever require such a service. But she had
to admit, standing here amongst neatly tagged jewels and guns,
tools, household goods, swords, and clothing...the business
wasn't nearly as seedy as she'd assumed.

She wondered if Kit had ever really looked at Thomas's shop
with an open mind. Not to mention listened to the fellow's ambi-
tions. She smiled at him. "Ellen was telling me you dream of
moving to London."

"I do, as did my father before me. He saved for twenty years
towards that goal. Trade in London would be much brisker—
there are so many more people."

"So many more *destitute* people," Rose put in.

"We can help them," Ellen said. "This trade isn't about taking
advantage, no matter its reputation."

Rose hadn't missed the *we*. "Why the Strand?" she asked.

Thomas waved an arm at the trays and trays of jewelry—
clearly the most often pawned item. "The Strand is home to
many of London's goldsmiths. Whittingham's could compete
favorably, drawing customers—paying customers, not pawning
ones—from the patrons who frequent the area. The real estate
there, however, can be prohibitively expensive. My father never
did manage to save enough to make the move. And prices are

still rising—the Great Fire made London's remaining developed land even more precious."

"But after we're wed…" Ellen murmured, then left it at that.

Rose knew she was thinking about her dowry. Eleven thousand pounds—surely more than enough to open the fanciest shop on the Strand. But she also knew that Kit wasn't going to be happy turning that money over to Thomas Whittingham.

The bell tinkled in the outer room, signaling another customer. "Pray excuse me," Thomas said.

As he left, Mum turned to examine a sword with a jewel-encrusted hilt. "Isn't this beautiful?"

"It is, Mum."

She hefted its shining weight, watching sapphires and emeralds twinkle in the light from the small, barred windows. "If this isn't claimed, I'll be tempted to buy it for your father."

Rose couldn't imagine he'd be too impressed—the sword wasn't a flower or plant, after all—but she knew her mother liked for him to look nice when they went out in public. "I'm certain he'd love it, Mum."

Her mother looked up from the sword. "You've a fine young man, Ellen."

"Thank you. I think so. I just wish I could convince Kit." She sighed, then took Rose's arm. "Come out front. Thomas has so many wonderful things for you to see."

"I want to see the books. Especially foreign ones."

But as they stepped back into the main room, they spotted Kit through the window, striding purposefully toward the door. Ellen gripped Rose's arm tighter. "Mercy me, I'm in trouble. I was hoping to return home before he woke."

Even the bell sounded angry when Kit slammed into the shop. "Come, Ellen. I've had word there's a problem at Whitehall. A fire."

Ellen's green-brown eyes widened. "Whitehall has burned?"

"Not the entire palace. Just the east end of the Chapel Royal where I'm building the new altar." He swore under his breath. "Come along. We must leave immediately."

Ellen set her jaw. "I don't want to go to London. I'll stay here."

"No, you won't." Despite his normal tanned complexion, Kit looked paler even than Bridgewater. And he hadn't noticed Rose. He shot a glance to Thomas instead, then glared back at his sister. "Do you think me a simpleton? I'll not leave you alone with *him*. You're coming to London."

"We're going to London as well," Mum announced, surprising Rose.

Kit looked surprised, too. "Lady Trentingham. And Lady Rose." His startled gaze met Rose's, disturbing her as much as ever. Something seemed to be fluttering in her stomach.

Her mother moved closer and put a hand on Rose's shoulder. "My daughter's favorite seamstress, Madame Beaumont, resides in London. Rose needs to order some new gowns if we're to spend more time at court."

That was news to Rose, but she wasn't displeased. A few days' distance would give the court gossips time to move from *I Sonetti* to the next scandal. Meanwhile, Rose would have some time to think about Gabriel...and Kit, blast him. He might be frantic with worry and wearing a simple blue wool suit instead of embroidered silk and gold, but she couldn't keep pretending she felt nothing for him. She needed to figure out what these feelings meant—and whether she might ever feel them with Gabriel.

Mum squeezed her shoulder. "Perhaps," she added, "we can have Kit and Ellen to supper, since they'll be in London, too."

"That would be nice," Kit said with polite impatience, "assuming I can leave the project. Assuming there's still a project to leave. Now, we must be off. Excuse us, please."

As she watched him herd his sister out the door, Rose realized he hadn't even taken Ellen to task for escaping to the pawnshop this morning.

He had to be very worried indeed.

THIRTY

*T*HREE DAYS LATER, Ellen strode into Whitehall's Chapel Royal. "I'm ready, Kit."

Kit swept the newly framed altar with one more glance before turning to his sister. "You're all packed?"

"Yes. My maid is seeing everything brought to the carriage. How about you? You've spent two solid days in this chapel. Have you eaten? Slept? Are *your* things all packed?"

"I have enough at the house in Windsor," he said, neatly evading her other questions. If he needed to forgo food and rest to accomplish his goals, so be it. What he *didn't* need was Ellen nagging him.

She bent to scoop up some wood scraps and toss them onto a pile. "I'm so glad we're returning to Windsor."

Reaching into his pocket, Kit touched the heavy vellum invitation that had arrived yesterday, a gracious request from Lady Trentingham to join her and her daughter for supper. If his plans worked out, Ellen wouldn't be returning to Windsor, but he wouldn't argue with her now. "I thought you loved staying here at Whitehall, where you can pretend you're a fine courtier."

"I loved it before I loved Thomas. Now I know that was only a childish game."

Evening was falling, and he'd dismissed his crew for the day, so he picked up the last of the tools himself. "It's not a game, Ellen," he said as he put them into a crate. "You could be that woman."

"I don't want to be that woman. I want to be Thomas's woman."

He bit back a retort, preferring to savor a good day's work. The situation here at Whitehall hadn't been as bad as he'd feared. Although the fire had destroyed the half-built altar, the building had remained intact. Yesterday he'd hired extra men—triple his original crew—and procured new materials. The progress today had been gratifying, surpassing his revamped schedule. Save for elusive bits of ash and the lingering scent of burnt wood, all evidence of the fire was gone, and the new altar was framed already.

Disaster had been averted again. But he didn't like the way things were going. The continued mishaps were reflecting poorly on him, and now he'd been forced to leave the Windsor project in a fragile state. He was anxious to return and ensure that the work remained on course. Even a small setback now could prove to be the feather that would break the horse's back.

But first, he had other matters to attend to: tonight, a visit with Rose, and tomorrow, a visit of a far less pleasant kind.

Kit had found no clear cause of the fire, as he had of the dining room's sagging ceiling. But he suspected something foul was afoot, and there was only one man he'd made an enemy of in recent memory: Harold Washburn, the foreman he'd fired at Windsor. Kit intended to seek out the old cur. And he preferred not to have his sister along to distract him. Not there at the scene and not at his house in Windsor, either—for he knew better than to believe she'd stay meekly at home. Not with the wretched pawnbroker so close.

Kit wasn't the sort of man to lock his sister in a guarded bedchamber, even for her own good. Sometimes he cursed himself for that weakness.

He folded the drawing of the new altar and slipped it into his pocket, then rolled the rest of the plans and tucked them under one arm. "Let's go. Lady Trentingham will be waiting."

Since the king and his followers were lodged at Hampton Court, Whitehall Palace was quiet. They exited into a large, grassy courtyard, their footfalls crunching on the gravel path as they followed it toward the gate. "I don't like traveling late at night. There could be highwaymen." Ellen pouted. "Can't we just go straight to Windsor?"

Kit heard: *Can't we just go straight to Thomas?* "It would be rude to refuse Lady Trentingham's invitation. Besides, don't you want to see Rose?"

"*You* want to see Rose."

"So what if I do?"

"She'll never be yours. Can't you see, Kit? Your winning her is as unrealistic as your wanting me to marry a title."

"Who said I want to win her?"

She snorted. "You look at her the same way Thomas looks at me."

He didn't like to think of any fellow looking that way at his sister. "If I'm appointed Deputy Surveyor, perhaps I'll soon be *Sir* Christopher Martyn."

"Is that what you're counting on? It won't change you."

"Exactly my point. I'm good enough for anyone now, and so are you. But you cannot argue that perception makes all the difference, and a change in rank will affect how outsiders look at us both."

"I don't care what outsiders think. I care only about Thomas."

Every discussion with Ellen was circular—back around to Thomas. Kit counted to ten, and then, as they crunched past the Banqueting House, changed the subject. "I wish I'd built that."

"It's pretty," she conceded. "But considering the rest of the palace is so old, it stands out like a sore thumb."

"Inigo Jones designed it with a basilica in mind." He nodded a greeting to the guard at the gate. "I heard the construction costs ran to more than fifteen thousand pounds. I believe it was the first modern building in all of London."

"When Thomas builds his shop on the Strand, it will be modern, too."

Thomas, Thomas, Thomas. Taking Ellen's arm, Kit helped her into the waiting carriage with a little more force than necessary. He pulled the door shut and dropped down across from her. "Just where do you suppose your Thomas will find the funds to build such an impressive shop?"

It was too dim inside the coach to read her expression, but he could see the tilt of her head. And hear the flippancy in her voice. "If the Banqueting House cost fifteen thousand, I expect eleven will more than do for a pawnshop."

"Eleven?" For a moment he could say no more. But then the words came out in a rush. "If you think Thomas Whittingham will ever see the money I've saved for your dowry, you'd best think again."

If the scoundrel was courting her for her money, *he'd* best think again, too.

"You wouldn't keep it from me," Ellen said smugly.

"You cannot know that," he shot back, although he feared she knew him all too well.

A tense quiet stretched between them, a silent battle of wills. When Ellen finally replied, her voice was so soft he had to strain to hear it over the rattles and squeaks of the carriage.

"If you do," she said, "I will never speak to you again."

THIRTY-ONE

*B*UILT JUST A few years earlier, the Ashcrofts' gray stone town house in St. James's Square was the height of modernity. Kit insisted on a tour before they all sat down to supper. He admired the ornamental scrolled ironwork on the staircase, the intricate pediments over the doorways, and all the chimneypieces carved with festoons of fruit and flowers.

For Rose's part, she'd decided it was all a bit overdone compared to the clean simplicity of his house.

"We cannot stay too long," Ellen said when they were finally seated. "We need to be on the road to Windsor before it gets too late."

"I understand." Mum smiled as she lifted her goblet, looking pleased the Martyn siblings had come at all.

As Rose served herself a tansy—a sweet omelet flavored with tansy juice—she wondered why Mum had taken such an interest in these commoners. But then she supposed it wasn't out of character for her mother. After all, the woman did "introductions" for servants. She might be an Ashcroft by marriage rather than blood, but their family motto, Question Convention, described her to a T.

Mum sipped. "Have you solved the issues at Whitehall?" she asked Kit.

"I hope so." He speared a bite of chicken fricassee, managing to graze Rose's arm for the third time in the process. "The issue of getting it finished on schedule, in any case. The issue of how and why the fire started is another matter entirely —one I'm hoping to solve in Windsor. There's a man there who's less than happy with me—the foreman I fired after the ceiling collapsed."

Rose wasn't sure if he was touching her on purpose or not, but either way, she was having trouble eating with the little bubbles dancing in her stomach. "You think he set the fire?"

Kit met her gaze, his eyes looking more green than brown. "A dishonest man like Washburn is the type to take revenge, and sabotaging another of my projects is effective revenge, indeed."

She sipped from her goblet, half expecting to taste champagne instead of the sweet Rhenish wine.

"This artichoke pudding is delicious," Ellen said with a hum of delight. "Almost worth delaying my return to Windsor."

"I'm so glad you're enjoying it." Mum poured more wine. "I'd be happy to teach you how to make it."

The girl paused with a forkful of tansy halfway to her lips. "Oh, would you? I don't know how to cook at all."

"No? How is that?"

Ellen chewed and swallowed. "I was but four when my mother died. While Kit was in school and university and I lived with Lady St. Vincent, I wasn't even allowed in the kitchen. And since then I've lived with Kit…"

Without brushing Rose this time, Kit set down his fork. "My sister has no need of cooking. When she marries, she'll have an army of servants to prepare her meals."

"Not if you won't give me my dowry," Ellen said darkly.

Mum looked between them. "Preparing a few special dishes can be a joy," she told Kit carefully. "No matter whether one has staff in the kitchen. Most every lady has a number of signature recipes."

"I would love to learn how to cook this," Ellen said. "It was very kind of you to offer, Lady Trentingham."

Mum smiled. "We shall have to plan another visit soon."

"May we?" Ellen asked her brother.

"Perhaps sooner than you think." Kit cleared his throat, sweeping both Rose and her mother with a glance. "I hesitate to presume upon our acquaintance, but I'm wondering if Ellen might stay here with you for a day or two while I take care of my business in Windsor."

"No!" his sister burst out.

Seeing the determined set of Kit's jaw, Rose turned to Ellen with a smile. "It could be fun. We could visit the shops at the Royal Exchange, and you could come along to my fittings. Maybe Kit would allow you to order a new gown."

"Two," he offered quickly, obviously willing to placate his sister.

Ellen's eyes narrowed. "The only new gown I need is one for my wedding to Thomas."

Kit's eyes blazed.

"I could teach you how to cook," Mum put in before he could open his mouth. "We could start tonight."

"I'm lea—"

"You're staying here," Kit said.

If looks could kill, Rose thought, his sister would be dead as the chicken on the platter.

Ellen apparently knew when to give up. She swallowed hard and put down her fork. "You're very kind," she told Mum in a voice devoid of emotion. "Unlike my brother."

A strained silence stretched between the siblings. Before more hurtful words could be spoken, Rose turned to Kit and tried to distract him. "I've seen what you're doing at Windsor, but tell me about Whitehall."

"It's a small project, just a new altar for the Chapel Royal." He took a bracing swallow of wine. "It's not my design. Here is Wren's sketch." Setting down his goblet, he dug a folded piece of paper out of his pocket and handed it to her.

The drawing showed not only the architectural detail but also an elevation complete with an altar cloth, alms dish, candlesticks, candles, and books. The lovely columns, carving, and molding looked much more modern than she supposed the rest of Whitehall to be. "It's beautiful."

"Can you see the original Tudor window behind?" When he leaned close, touching a finger to the sketch, she smelled frankincense and Kit. "Wren designed this to be the same width, so the two would appear harmonious together."

Mum reached for the drawing and nodded. "Why didn't he build it himself?"

Kit waved a hand. "He has far more important projects. Besides, I've a suspicion King Charles wanted to see me spread thin. Projects at Windsor, Whitehall, and Hampton Court all at once...plus my own. It's a test, you understand? If I can complete all three of the Crown's projects successfully, and on time, he will know he's found the right Deputy Surveyor."

"And the fire threatened this deadline," Rose said.

"Seriously. But fortunately it's a small project, and the damage could have been worse. I hope to overcome my bad luck a second time."

He was still tense, his answers clipped, his gaze settling too often on his sister. Rose tried again. "Hampton Court is a larger project, isn't it?"

"The largest of the three. A whole new building. Apartments for the Duchess of Cleveland—"

"The king's longtime mistress," Ellen interrupted, apparently having recovered some spirit. Derision laced her voice. "*He* is allowed to be with whoever he wants."

"*He* married where he was advised to." Kit turned to his sister with a lethal raised brow. "If you wish to take Thomas as a lover *after* you wed a peer, I suppose I cannot prevent you."

Ellen made a noise of outrage. Her brother stabbed another bite of chicken. Rose shifted on her petit-point seat, exchanging a look with her mother.

Kit must be at the very limit of his forbearance to say such things to his sister, even in obvious jest. Rose and her own siblings squabbled, of course, but they rarely harbored true animosity. She wished these two would get along. "Is King Charles wanting large apartments for the duchess?" she asked delicately.

He chewed and swallowed. "Larger than my house. He wishes their five children to have rooms there as well. I'm certain he'll be scrutinizing this project most of all."

"Did Wren do those plans, too?"

"No, I did. Top to bottom, start to finish, the building is mine. Thankfully, nothing has gone wrong with it."

"Yet," Ellen said.

He set his jaw. "When I'm finished with Harold Washburn, he won't be making any more trouble."

Mum pushed back from the table, looking at Ellen. "Shall we begin your first lesson? Something sweet to complete supper?" When Ellen shrugged and began to rise, Mum looked to Rose. "Perhaps you can entertain Kit while we work. A turn in the square might be nice."

"Kit must leave," Ellen said. "He needs to get to Windsor."

Kit pulled out Rose's chair. "It's late already. I believe I'll return to Whitehall tonight and leave early in the morning."

For a moment Ellen stood there openmouthed.

"What?" Kit asked.

"You plotted all along to get me and my luggage here, didn't you? No wonder you didn't bring your own things. You had no intention of leaving for Windsor at all."

"We came tonight because we were invited. And I've urgent business in Windsor that I intend to take care of tomorrow. It doesn't matter whether I travel there tonight or tomorrow morn. But believe what you wish...you will, anyway." Sighing, he offered Rose an arm. "If I may, Lady Rose? I could use some fresh air."

THIRTY-TWO

*O*UTSIDE, TORCHES burned brightly before each of the houses around St. James's Square, bathing the neighborhood in a pale, hazy glow.

As they crossed to the fenced square, Rose felt Kit's hand warm on her back. He slipped his other hand into his pocket and pulled out a small rock. "It's quiet," he said, turning it over and over with his fingers.

"Until recently, we wouldn't dare come out here at night." She paused to unlock the gate. "There were no rails—the square was just a big open area between the houses, used as nothing more than a receptacle for offal and cinders, not to mention all the dead dogs and cats of Westminster." Rose silently congratulated herself on introducing what had to be the least romantic topic possible. "Squatters lived among the filth, and there were thieves galore," she added with relish.

Any gentleman would be put off by such an unappealing speech.

Unfortunately, she'd forgotten that Kit was no gentleman. He merely looked interested, glancing about at all the stately three-story redbrick and stone houses. "Are these not the homes of dukes and earls?"

"Mostly. It was a travesty." The gate banged closed behind them as they entered the square. "Once Parliament approved their application for permission to put up rails and plant trees, the dukes and earls wasted no time seeing it done."

The dirty pavement had been replaced by soft grass and wide, curving paths with benches scattered throughout. Young trees rustled in the light breeze. When Kit slung his free arm around her shoulders, she couldn't bring herself to pull away.

Her will seemed to vanish whenever he touched her.

He was still playing with the rock. "What is that?" she asked.

He looked down as though surprised to see it there. "A piece of my first building," he said with a small, sheepish smile. "Just a bit of brick." He passed it to her.

It held the warmth of his hand and felt smooth, though she knew it must once have been angular. "Was it a church? A mansion? A theater?"

A rueful laugh broke the quiet of the night. "It was a warehouse. But I assure you, it's the most beautiful warehouse to ever grace our good green earth."

"I'm sure it is," she said, imagining a redbrick warehouse with triangular pediments over the windows and white marble columns flanking the doors. Smiling, she handed back the brick.

He sobered as he slipped it into his pocket. "Will you watch over my sister?" he asked quietly.

"Why? Do you expect Ellen might run off and elope?"

She'd meant the question to be facetious, but he took it seriously. "From here? No. She won't have time to get a message to Whittingham and pull off such a trick before I return." His voice dropped. "I'm just worried for her. She's not herself."

"You care."

"Of course I care." He rubbed the back of his neck. "Did you doubt that? She's my sister. I love her."

A horse clip-clopped around the square with a carriage creaking behind. "You two quarrel all the time."

"Not all the time. Only since she met Whittingham."

"Have *you* met him?"

"Briefly. Long enough to know he doesn't have horns. But I want better for Ellen." Kit hesitated a moment while the carriage squeaked off down King Street. "I work hard so she can have better."

Rose had no doubt that the kind of money Kit had saved could win Ellen the husband he was envisioning. The Civil War had left many good families land-rich and cash-poor.

But Ellen was her friend, and she'd promised her support. "Thomas is actually quite nice. And, from what I can tell, he's a very astute businessman."

"He's a pawnbroker."

"He's educated. If you'd talk to him, you'd discover that."

"He's still a pawnbroker. There's no security in a life like that. My parents wed for love, then couldn't protect their family when times got hard. I can buy Ellen a husband with land and the king's ear—"

"There's no security in any life," Rose interrupted to point out. "Look to your own projects for the proof—going along fine one day, ruined the next. Titled men can be ruined, too. It happens all the time."

Kit was silent a moment before he stopped walking and turned her to face him, his hands on her shoulders. "You said it's as easy to fall in love with a titled man as one without. Have you changed your mind?"

His eyes searched hers, and frustration was evident in his voice. But he also sounded hopeful. Which was absurd. They would never be anything but friends.

"Of course not," she said quickly.

"Oh," he said. "I see."

"You see what?"

"*You* wouldn't settle for less, but Ellen and I, we're different. An educated pawnbroker is good enough for her, and as for me, I'm good enough for kissing, but nothing else."

He was confusing her—and worse, he was making her sound terrible. Although she couldn't imagine how Kit and Ellen had managed to become so close to her family so quickly, she *liked* them—and she didn't think herself any better than they.

Did she?

Kit's fingers tightened on her shoulders. "Rose?"

Her thoughts were in chaos. When she tried to twist away, he held her fast. His gaze commanded hers, looking gray in the darkness.

"Perhaps that was exhaustion speaking," he said. "I haven't slept in two days. Should I say I'm sorry?"

He didn't look sorry, and she didn't know. If he'd touched a nerve, maybe that said more about her than it did him.

"Why do you kiss me, Rose?" he asked softly.

Realizing she definitely had more to think about than just the Duke of Bridgewater, she took a ragged breath. "You're good at kissing."

The tension eased from his face, and his sudden grin flashed white in the night. "I like a girl who says what she thinks."

His hands slid from her shoulders down her arms, slowly. She held her breath until he locked his fingers with hers.

"You're rather good at kissing, too," he said conversationally. When he drew on both her hands, she didn't have to sway forward. But she did. His eyes watched her intently, so intense she'd swear she saw glints of green even in the darkness. "My forthright Rose," he whispered right before his mouth touched hers.

And it was magic. Those lips were pure, stomach-fluttering, senses-swirling magic. Nothing and no one else would ever make her feel this way. How could they? They weren't Kit.

It hadn't been her imagination: their mouths fit perfectly. "A thing of beauty," she breathed aloud against his lips.

"Oh, yes," he said, moving to press little kisses to her cheeks, the tip of her nose, across her temples. His warm breath on her ear made her shiver. "I don't remember you wearing earrings," he murmured.

"They were a gift from Gabriel." Absently she touched the ruby and pearl bob on the opposite lobe.

"Gabriel? The angel?"

"The duke. Bridgewater." She could melt, she thought as his lips moved to her neck. She could melt right here.

"The fellow has taste," he said dryly. "I'll give him that."

"*I* chose them."

"I should have known." His low chuckle vibrated against her throat. She'd never dreamed the skin there was so sensitive. Her hands skimmed over his back, hard planes with ridges of muscle. The body of a working man. She hadn't really touched Gabriel, but somehow she knew he'd be soft.

A sudden impulse made her bury her fingers in his hair and drag his lips back to hers.

Kit groaned and pulled away, closing his eyes momentarily. Before they opened, he thrust his hands in his pockets. "We must go back inside."

She blinked at him, disoriented and hurt. "Didn't you like that?"

"I liked it too much." He moved closer to kiss her softly, apologetically...and briefly. Too briefly. His hands stayed out of sight. "You have no idea what you do to me, Rose."

She did have an idea, because he did it to her, too.

THIRTY-THREE

*R*OSE AND KIT returned to the house to find Mum and Ellen laughing, a smudge of flour on Ellen's nose. Kit stayed just long enough to down two servings of the apple fritters they'd prepared. Just long enough to lock gazes several times with Rose. Just long enough to surreptitiously touch her a few times beneath the table.

The apple fritters were sweet and crispy, spiced with nutmeg, mace, and cinnamon. Yet Rose could hardly eat a bite. These were not typical interactions between friends.

But she didn't want anything more with Kit. Did she?

"That was delicious," he said at last, rising from the table. "Ellen, you can make apple fritters for me anytime. But I must leave. I'll need to start out for Windsor very early in the morning, and I must get some sleep."

"I know." Ellen's earlier gaiety disappeared as she and Rose walked him from the dining room to the door. "You'll be back soon?"

"Day after tomorrow." He stopped to kiss her on the forehead. "Be good, will you? In the meantime, I expect you to spend a lot of my money at the dressmaker's. I trust that will give you some measure of revenge."

Ellen just gave him a wan smile as he headed out the door, then sighed when his carriage rolled out of the square. "I hate it when he's nice. It almost makes me forget that I loathe him."

"You don't," Rose said gently.

"Not really. I'm just...very angry with him right now. He shouldn't have the right to dictate my life."

"But he does."

"But he *shouldn't*. And it makes me sad to be at odds with him, because I know he cares underneath."

"Underneath? He cares every way that matters, Ellen—any fool could see it." Just like he cared for her, Rose...any fool could see that, too. And Rose feared she was denying it much the same as Ellen.

"Whose side are you on?" Ellen asked. "I thought we were friends. You promised to intervene on my behalf."

"I did. Out in the square we talked of little but you and your situation." It wasn't quite a lie—they hadn't *talked* about much else. "He doesn't want to listen. But I'd lay odds he listens other times, your brother. He wants only what's best for you. What *he* thinks is best for you."

"I know." Ellen released another sigh, looking very pale.

Rose remembered Kit's concern for the girl's state of mind. "Shall we go find my mother?" she asked, thinking of how cheerful Ellen had appeared back in the kitchen. Mum was far more adept than Rose at raising people's spirits.

Ellen shrugged as if she didn't really care, and allowed her friend to lead her toward the stairs. "Have you made any progress on the translation?"

"Not really," Rose answered guiltily. "Mum and I lived in close quarters at Windsor, and since we've arrived here I've been getting fitted for new gowns and catching up on my sleep. Unlike your brother, I'm afraid I'm only human."

Actually, she'd finished translating several more of the verses —with a handkerchief covering the engravings, as she couldn't seem to concentrate with those lurid poses exposed. Though undoubtedly explicit, the poems had struck her as more romantic than shocking. But then, she had nineteen years, the *Master-piece*'s knowledge, and a married sister who'd never shied away from frank discussion—whereas Ellen was only sixteen and a complete innocent. While Rose wouldn't hesitate to furnish the worldly court ladies with racy reading material, it felt unsuitable to do the same for her young friend.

Though she'd had several more days to mull over the dilemma, she still hadn't found a solution. She couldn't fend off Ellen forever, but nor could she bring herself to turn the girl in. She wished to help mend Ellen's relationship with Kit, and such a revelation would surely drive the siblings further apart.

As they made their way upstairs, unlike her brother, Ellen showed little interest in the house itself. Instead, she skimmed a hand over a marquetry hall table. "Thomas had something like this," she said. And a Chinese vase. "And like this. He just sold it last week." And a silver lantern clock. "He has something like this now."

Mum called to them through an open door. "Good evening." She sniffed at a bottle and made a note on a little card. "Come in," she urged, choosing a vial and lowering a dropper into it.

"What's this?" Ellen asked as they stepped into the room.

"My mother makes perfume," Rose explained. "This is a laboratory of sorts." She waved at the racks of vials. "Those are her essential oils."

"Essential oils?"

"Distilled from flowers. In her perfumery at Trentingham, she has a fancy still that my brother-in-law built for her. That's where she makes the oils."

Squinting in the candlelight, Ellen peered at the rows of labels with their tiny, neat black lettering. "Are some of them made from herbs, too?"

"Oh, yes," Mum said. "Many herbs make lovely top notes. Rosemary, for example, has a lavenderlike fragrance, and tansy is both fruity and minty—"

"Tansy?" Ellen's head jerked up. "Like the tansy at supper?"

Mum nodded. "It's more commonly used in cooking, of

course." She added two drops to her blend and swirled the bottle. "Do you know much about perfumes?"

"Nothing." Ellen's gaze swept the assorted vials again. "Except that I like them."

"Shall I make a blend for you, then?" Mum set down the bottle and chose an empty one. Using a little silver funnel, she poured in alcohol and water from two pewter flagons, then turned back to Ellen. "Should we start with tansy?"

"No," Ellen said quickly. "I…" She swallowed hard. "I don't actually care for mint."

Mum nodded slowly. "You seem like a dreamer. A floral, then. Orange blossoms, and maybe some lilac. Vanilla, I think…" She went off into a dreamworld of her own as she concocted a mix that would fit Ellen perfectly.

Rose chose another empty bottle.

"I cannot believe how many oils she has," Ellen whispered to her, as though speaking aloud would break Mum's spell.

Rose took up the little funnel and a flagon. "She works all spring, summer, and autumn, converting the plants to oils," she said, filling the bottle with alcohol and water. "Some oils she has to buy—as talented as my father is in his gardens, he cannot make everything grow in England."

Ellen's gaze continued sweeping over the labels. "But so many. They're not alphabetical?"

Searching for frankincense, Rose shook her head. "My mother just knows where to lay her hands on whatever she wants. This is nothing, really. She has a whole little room at Trentingham where the walls are filled floor to ceiling with all her many supplies."

Ellen nodded distractedly.

"What do you think?" Mum asked, presenting her with the bottle.

Ellen sniffed. "It's lovely!"

"A good scent can go a long way toward cheering one up."

Rose added several drops of myrrh to her mix and swirled it gently while her mother jotted a few notes on a card.

"There," Mum said, looking up. Smiling at Ellen, she took the bottle from her, corked it, and handed it back. "Now I'll be able to duplicate the scent should you wish for more later. Or we can alter the ingredients if you think you'd like something else."

"Oh, no, this is perfect." Ellen smiled, but Rose couldn't help noticing it didn't quite reach her eyes. "Thank you very much."

"You're quite welcome, dear. I hope you'll enjoy it." Mum concealed a yawn with one elegant hand. "My, but this bustling city does tire one out. I believe I'll just finish this blend and turn in. Rose, you'll show Ellen to her chamber? I've had the room opposite yours prepared."

Rose corked her bottle, too. "Of course. Good night, Mum."

"Good night." Smiling absently, her mother returned to the perfume she'd been creating earlier.

Ellen was quiet as they made their way down the corridor. Rose slid her a sidelong glance. "Would you like to see my chamber?"

The girl shrugged.

Rose's bedchamber at Trentingham was hung with crimson silk, but here in town she had jewel tones—bright ruby, deep sapphire, and rich emerald. "This is beautiful," Ellen mumbled when they entered.

"Kit showed us your blue chamber when he gave us a tour of the house. It's beautiful, too."

"I like it." Though Ellen smiled, the expression quickly faded. "I suppose it's as well, since I'll likely live there all my days."

Taking Ellen's bottle, Rose set both on her bedside table. "Not all your days, surely."

"I suppose not. Just until Kit finds some hateful nobleman in need of money to marry me off to."

Rose sat on the bed, drawing Ellen down beside her. "He wouldn't wed you to anyone you hated."

"He's obsessed with raising our social status." Ellen shifted to face her. "He's convinced people judge him by that rather than his accomplishments."

"It's the way of the world. But he should be proud of those accomplishments—"

"Exactly what I tell him," Ellen interrupted. "He shouldn't care what people think. Do you know, I believe he doesn't look on the Deputy Surveyor post as an accomplishment so much as a chance to be knighted. Kit really believes that people will look at him differently if there's a *Sir* before his name."

Rose knew Ellen was waiting for her to disagree, but she couldn't. People *would* look at Kit differently. Even more so if he managed to dazzle King Charles into awarding him an even greater title.

She'd never thought about that possibility, but then she hadn't known the position of Deputy Surveyor carried with it a probability of knighthood. That and more was certainly within the king's power. If Kit were elevated to the aristocracy—

"Oh," Ellen moaned, "I'm so tired of this! It would all be over if I could only—" She swiped at damp eyes, hunching over, her head drooping. Then, after a moment, she straightened and seemed to gather herself. "Rose, tell me the truth. Are you *ever* going to finish the translation?"

Entirely caught out, Rose went rigid. "I..."

The younger girl burst into tears.

"Gemini! I'm so sorry." Rose seized Ellen's hands. "Of course I'll finish it," she fibbed, then cursed herself for the ill-considered lie, suspecting she would regret her words later. But right now she'd say anything to calm her friend. "You'll have it soon, you'll see. I would have worked faster if I knew it meant this much to you."

"It's not that. I just..." Ellen searched her eyes, her own overflowing. "I feel..." She appeared to swallow past a huge lump in her throat. "I just miss Thomas, is all," she whispered finally.

If this was love, Rose wasn't sure she wanted anything to do with it. Ellen looked more miserable than she'd thought possible. She'd never seen anyone so desperate—not even Lily when she feared Rand would have to marry someone else.

"You'll see Thomas soon," she soothed, squeezing Ellen's

hands. "You live in Windsor, after all. Kit cannot keep you away forever. I imagine he just wanted to conduct his business there quickly and then get back to Whitehall where he's needed."

"But he's *not* needed at Whitehall—not anymore. The crisis has passed, and the project will go smoothly without him."

"Well, that's good, then. He's coming back day after tomorrow. You heard him say that, didn't you? If he isn't needed here in London, then surely he'll take you back to Windsor."

"I think not." With a great effort, Ellen choked back the last of her tears. "He told me today that Thomas will never see a penny of my dowry."

Rose didn't think Kit would follow through with that threat, but it wasn't her place to say so. "Is that what this is about?"

"No. Well, maybe." She bit her lip, looking up at Rose through damp lashes. "What if Thomas doesn't want me without the money? We've spent so much time dreaming of the day when—"

"Don't be a goose." Rose reached to lift Ellen's chin. "I know the look of love in a man's eyes, and I can assure you Thomas is besotted. He doesn't want you for your money, Ellen—you need to put that right out of your head."

Ellen looked like she wanted to believe her. "Do you think?"

"I *know*." Rose felt her age and then some. Ellen was so young. So vulnerable. Rose thought of Kit's concerns and her promise to watch over his sister. "Would you like to sleep in here instead of the other room? We can talk all night like my sisters and I used to when one of us was upset."

Tears leaked again as Ellen nodded. "You're so kind, Rose."

Nobody had ever described Rose as kind. Her own eyes felt watery as she rang for her maid to prepare them both for bed.

THIRTY-FOUR

"**G**OOD MORNING, Ellen." Rose stretched beneath the quilt, then slowly rolled over. "Ellen?"

Ellen wasn't there.

Rose sat up and squinted at the clock on her mantel. Seeing it was only seven in the morning, she groaned. Breakfast wouldn't be served until nine.

Yawning, she absently lifted one of the bottles off her bedside table. The cork came free with a soft pop, and she inhaled deeply, closing her eyes.

Frankincense and myrrh. Kit. Almost. Something was missing. That woodsy something. She'd have to locate and add that elusive ingredient before she gave the bottle to the duke.

Thinking she'd better find Ellen, Rose yawned again and slid from the bed. She tied a red wrapper over her white night rail, slipped her feet into a pair of quilted satin mules, and padded out of her chamber, taking the bottle with her.

Ellen wasn't in the room opposite, either. Through the open door of her mother's sitting room, Rose glimpsed two maids busy about their day's work, one opening the shutters while the other cleaned the fire grate.

"Have either of you seen Ellen Martyn?" she asked.

"Nay, my lady," they chorused in unison. "Perhaps she's still abed?" one of them guessed.

"No, she's not."

For one panicked moment, Rose wondered if Ellen had escaped and gone to Thomas after all, but then she shook herself and headed for the staircase. Just because the upstairs maids hadn't seen her didn't mean that Ellen wasn't here. She could easily be in the dining room having an early breakfast. Or perhaps in the large basement kitchen. Their cook would be long awake, baking the day's bread, and she wasn't the type to let anyone in the house go hungry.

There was no need to fret. In fact, Rose thought, pausing in front of the perfumery and looking at the bottle in her hand, maybe she could take the time to perfect this scent. Half guilty knowing her mother would be a much more solicitous hostess, she pushed down on the door's latch and shoved it open.

The bottle crashed to the planked wood floor. "Ellen!"

Ellen held a dropper in one hand and a vial in the other. Looking away from Rose, she tilted her head back and deliberately emptied the last glistening drop into her mouth.

"Ellen!" Skidding on glass and perfume, Rose ran to her, not wanting to believe what she'd just seen. "Whatever are you doing?" She grabbed the vial from her hand. "Tansy?" Her heart pounded. "Are you trying to kill yourself? Essential oils are poison, tansy one of the worst!"

Ellen's skin looked as white as her night rail. Sweat beaded on her forehead. As her red-rimmed eyes met Rose's, the glass dropper fell from her slack fingers and shattered on the floor.

She doubled over. "I think I'm going to be sick."

"It's just as well, else I'd stick my finger down your throat and *make* you sick!" Rose ran for the chamber pot that sat beneath a sideboard and rushed back to plunk it on the worktable.

She held Ellen's head—and her own tongue—while spasms wracked the girl's body, purging her of the poison. Over and over, but it wasn't enough for Rose. When Ellen swallowed convulsively, holding back another spasm while she slumped over the table, Rose hauled her back up.

"All of it," she demanded. Ellen's knees buckled, and Rose kept her upright by sheer force of will. "More! I want to see that there's nothing left in your stomach. Nothing, Ellen, you hear me? Else my finger will go down your throat. More!"

At long last, a series of dry heaves left Rose satisfied. She slung an arm around Ellen's shoulders and led her to a chair.

Still shuddering and frightfully pale, Ellen sank down. "I'm sorry," she murmured, a shaky hand to her mouth. Tears spilled and ran down her cheeks. "I'm so sorry."

Rose took the chair beside her, a hand to her still-racing heart. She thought she'd caught Ellen in time. She'd call her mother and a doctor to make sure, but first she had to catch her breath.

She'd never been so scared in her life.

"Confound it, Ellen, I know you're unhappy, but surely things aren't bad enough to end it all."

Ellen's eyes widened. "I wasn't trying to," she whispered. "I swear it. I didn't know tansy was dangerous."

Cautious relief sang through Rose's veins, but something still didn't fit. "Why, then?" Suddenly chilled, she hugged herself, running her hands up and down her arms. "Tansy is powerful stuff. What could have possessed you to drink a whole vile?"

Ellen clenched her hands together in her lap and stared at them. "What do you know about it?"

"I know what my perfumer mother drilled into her children's heads so we wouldn't accidentally do ourselves in. Tansy oil is incredibly potent and *never* safe to eat. In herb form, small doses can be used to flavor food and brew remedies." Rose's brows snapped together. "Are you ill?"

Ellen shook her head. "A midwife told me tansy tea helps a woman conceive." The tears flowed faster, and words spilled out between her sobs. "But I didn't have any leaves, and then I saw your mother's oils…"

"Conceive?" Rose felt utterly lost. "But I thought…you and Thomas haven't…"

"No," Ellen whimpered, "not yet. I don't know how to do it yet, since you haven't finished—" She stopped abruptly, dropping her head in her hands.

Rose's breath faltered as she stared at her friend's miserable, huddled form—and understanding dawned.

"Oh, *Ellen!*" Aghast, Rose slid from her chair to kneel at Ellen's feet and pull her hands away from her face. "Why?" The girl's tears fell on their clasped fingers as Rose searched her eyes. Her friend hadn't been attempting suicide, thank heavens, but... "Why on earth would you behave so recklessly?"

A sudden spark of anger made her friend's eyes flash green. "It's the only way, don't you see? If I'm carrying Thomas's child, Kit will *have* to let me marry him."

She wrenched her hands from Rose's and dashed at her tears.

"Which is worse, Rose? Sacrificing my virtue in exchange for a happy marriage, or saving it for a rotten one? Because I vow and swear, if Kit marries me to some rich poltroon, I will not be a dutiful wife. I will *never* lie with my husband. How could I, knowing I was meant to be with another? I will run back to Thomas, and then my virtue will be sullied anyhow."

Rose swallowed, trying to understand, trying to be a good friend. "So you felt the only way to persuade Kit was to get yourself with child?"

"Can *you* think of another way?" Ellen's tears flowed even faster. "I've tried for months to talk him around—*I've tried!* He'll never listen to me. And I'll never give up Thomas. It's hopeless."

Not knowing what she could say to help, Rose patted the girl's shoulder. She appreciated the depth of Ellen's frustration— her situation *was* hopeless. "Does Thomas know of your plan?" she asked gently.

"Of course not." Ellen sniffled and wiped her nose on her sleeve, evidently too wretched to care. "He would never have agreed. That's why I needed the book. I was going to persuade him, you know, the way women persuade men. Only I don't know how."

"And you won't need to," Rose said through gritted teeth.

Ellen was her friend, and she'd promised Kit she'd watch over her. He wouldn't want to see his sister like this—especially knowing he'd had a hand in causing her distress. "I'm afraid you're not getting that book back, Ellen."

The girl's face hardened, though she didn't refuse the hand-kerchief Rose offered. She blew her nose loudly. "Perhaps I had the right idea with the tansy."

Though Rose didn't think Ellen was serious, she was glad no more tansy oil remained in the house. Thankfully, her friend seemed to be out of danger. A little color had sneaked back into her cheeks. Though her face was wet with tears, her forehead was no longer slicked with sweat. Her body had stopped shuddering.

All Ellen needed was rest. And hope.

Rose got to her feet, bringing Ellen up with her, and wrapped her into a fierce hug. "You will not sacrifice your virtue," she decreed into Ellen's wavy dark hair. Drawing away, she offered a shaky smile. "And you will marry Thomas."

"Kit won't—"

"Kit *will*. I shall talk to him."

Ellen stepped back, startled. "And tell him what?"

"Everything," Rose said firmly. "But first, we send for the doctor."

THIRTY-FIVE

"GOOD AFTERNOON, Mr. Martyn," the guard at Windsor Castle's gate greeted.

"Afternoon," Kit muttered back.

After all, there was nothing *good* about it.

He'd arrived at Harold Washburn's meager rooms on Peascod Street only to find them empty. The only neighbor he could locate informed him that Washburn had carted his belongings out days before.

Of course. As he walked from the Lower Ward to the Upper, Kit cursed himself for a fool. It was obvious enough that if the man had set fire to Whitehall, he'd left Windsor in the time since Kit had dismissed him. Kit had assumed Washburn would return home, but without employment, there was no longer anything to hold him here.

He could still be in London—or anywhere.

Though Kit itched to confront the old cur, he hadn't time to mount a full-scale search, not while seeing his projects to successful completion. He would have to hope that the arson at Whitehall had satisfied the man's thirst for revenge—that he wouldn't try anything more.

When he finally reached Windsor's dining room, he breathed

a sigh of relief. Here, at least, everything seemed to be going right. The ceiling was nearing completion. The scaffolding was coming down, and new plaster was going up. In one corner, men labored to put a fine finish on the last pieces of oak paneling. Pleasant aromas of fresh-cut wood and sawdust filled the air.

The scent of building. It never failed to revive him.

"Well done," he told his new foreman. They spread out the plans and went over them together, then discussed the final schedule.

"Seen Washburn lately?" Kit asked when they were finished.

Though he hadn't expected an affirmative answer, the foreman nodded. "Just yesterday, in fact. Been parading about town with some mighty fancy doxies."

Celebrating his successful revenge, Kit thought, seeing red. And spending the money he'd pocketed by purchasing inferior materials.

Through the anger, though, the new knowledge lifted his spirits. Apparently Washburn was here in Windsor, after all.

"Saw him not an hour ago," another man volunteered through nails held between his teeth. "At the Old King's Head on Church Street."

Better news yet. Kit thanked the men for a job well done, then hied himself off to Church Street, feeling more optimistic than he had in days.

His projects were well in hand, his sister was safely ensconced in London, and best of all, last night's outing with Rose in the square could not have gone better. Sweet heaven, that girl could make him lose his head. Though he'd always adored her bold nature, somehow he'd been unprepared for *physical* boldness—perhaps due to her seeming innocence? In any case, that moment when she'd grabbed him by the hair and wrenched him to her...

Well, to be blunt, it had been the most thrilling moment of his life.

And he could only but take it as proof of her feelings growing bolder as well. The only pitfall he could see was this deuced uncomfortable secret between them. That night they'd walked together by the Thames, in a heated moment he'd nearly taken leave of his wits and betrayed her mother's confidence.

Thank goodness he'd caught himself at the last moment. Though it rankled him to lie to Rose, he couldn't risk spoiling things with her now that he was finally, *finally* making progress.

"Good afternoon, Richards," he said to the guard this time.

"Afternoon," the man returned with a gap-toothed smile.

Within sight of the castle gates, The Old King's Head was a typical inn—a few chambers above a darkly paneled taproom. It was known as the meeting place where the Roundheads had sanctioned King Charles I's execution. Given its association with his father's beheading, one might presume the current King Charles would avoid the area. But the opposite was true. Nell Gwyn owned the house next door, where she stayed—and the king paid nocturnal visits—whenever the court was lodged at Windsor.

But His Majesty had moved on to Hampton Court, so the infamous Nell wasn't here now. Kit could only hope Washburn still was.

He pushed open the door and scanned the dim taproom. Few patrons sat at the long wooden tables this quiet afternoon, and the man Kit sought was nowhere to be seen.

"Can I get you something, milord?" A plump blond serving maid sidled up to him.

Milord, he thought with an inward smile, though the honorific was surely no more than calculated flattery. Someday he would have a right to that form of address. "I'm looking for Harold Washburn."

"Ah, His High and Mighty." The girl rolled her lively blue eyes. "He's staying above." She gestured up a staircase. "The Bard's chamber, no less."

It was said that Shakespeare had resided in this inn while writing *The Merry Wives of Windsor*. Kit wasn't sure he believed that, but he *was* sure the establishment charged a pretty penny for the room supposedly rented by the playwright.

Washburn had apparently come up in the world. The cur must have pilfered even more money than Kit had realized. Seeing red again, he took the stairs two at a time.

"Wait, milord!" the serving maid called, lifting her skirts to run after him. "You cannot just go up there!"

Try and stop me, he thought as he reached the top and began pounding on the first door. "Washburn! Are you in there?" When nobody answered, he tested the latch and found the room open and empty.

He strode to the next, rapping so hard he bruised his knuckles. It was a welcome pain, one that fueled his anger. "Washburn!"

The serving maid caught up and tugged on his arm. "Milord, the proprietor—"

"A pox on the proprietor!" Shaking himself free, he opened the door. Finding this room vacant as well, he moved on, banging his fist against the next. "Washburn!"

A loud, startled squeal came from inside. A female squeal. And then Washburn's voice, a low hiss. "Shut your trap, you hateful wench."

For the costliest room in the house, Shakespeare's chamber sure had a thin door.

Kit tried the latch and found the door locked. "Washburn, open up!"

Again, the serving maid tugged on his sleeve. "Milord, you cannot—"

"Oh, but I can. Watch me." His patience at an end, Kit raised a booted foot and rammed it into the door.

It gave incredibly easily, slamming back against the wall and making the cheap porcelain knickknacks dance on Shakespeare's marble mantel. Another squeal followed, snapping Kit's gaze to the gaudy purple velvet–draped bed, where a blowzy woman sat straight up, the counterpane held to her bosom.

And beside her lay a half-bare Washburn sporting a day-old beard and a sheen of sweat on his bald head. Huddled beneath the covers, he looked, if possible, even more petrified than the woman. The tiny red veins on his oversized nose seemed to pulse with terror.

Under other circumstances, Kit might have doubled over with laughter.

But these weren't other circumstances.

"You mangy old cur," he gritted out. "I swear on the graves of every thief ever hanged by the High Sheriff of Berkshire, if you interfere with *one* more of my projects—"

"More?" Washburn squeaked, sounding utterly pathetic. "Why would I—"

"Set fire to the Chapel Royal at Whitehall?" Kit spat, moving closer. "I know not. Why don't you tell me? Or are you so sotted on women and drink that you've lost your half-witted memory?"

The man rose, taking the counterpane with him and baring his companion in the process. Kit averted his eyes as she squealed again and slid off the mattress, cowering on the far side of the bed.

The purple velvet clenched in one fist, Washburn brandished the other threateningly. "To the devil with you, Martyn. I've no knowledge of a fire at Whitehall, and I sure as rot didn't set it."

Something in his foe's eyes gave Kit pause. "Where were you four days ago?"

"Here," Washburn growled.

"And what fine, upstanding citizen can you find to vouch for that?"

The ex-foreman swung to glare at his woman. "Me," she squeaked, peeking over the edge of the bed.

Kit snorted. "You think me maggot-brained enough to believe such as her?"

"How about me?" the serving maid said from behind him. "Will you believe me?"

Kit turned to her. "About what?" In his red-hot rage, he'd forgotten she was there.

"About him." She pointed at Washburn with a work-chapped finger. "He's been here since last week. Hasn't left except to buy some gewgaws for his ladies. An hour here or there."

Kit stepped closer and bore into her spirited blue eyes with his own. "Do you swear?" When she nodded fiercely, he turned back to Washburn. "You hired someone to do it for you, then."

"I'm no arsonist, Martyn."

Kit snorted. "Just a liar and a cheat, then." His breath was still coming hard, but blast if he wasn't beginning to believe the old man. The serving maid seemed too honest, and Washburn seemed too shocked.

Kit dug into his belt purse. "For the damage," he said, shoving a few coins at the maid. "With my apologies." He gave her a curt tip of his hat.

Gripping the piece of brick in his pocket, he made for the stairs without another word.

THIRTY-SIX

*T*HE NEXT DAY, Rose answered the door herself, all but dragging Kit into the town house without so much as a good morning. "I need to talk to you."

He grinned as she pulled him toward the drawing room. "Missed me, did you?"

"No," she said, although in truth she'd missed him entirely too much. She shut the door behind them and waved him toward a blue brocade chair. "Sit, please."

"Sit? Then you didn't drag me in here for a kiss?" Lowering himself, he linked his fingers and rested his elbows on the chair's arms, looking nauseatingly good in his simple dark blue suit. "It isn't like you not to be looking for a kiss."

She gazed at him, wondering how to break this to him gently while half wishing he were an ugly harebrained hayseed with no talent at all for kissing.

Of course she wanted a kiss.

"No, I'm not looking for a kiss." His sister was more important than kissing. "This is serious, Kit. You must let Ellen wed Thomas. She loves him, and—"

"I've told Ellen time and again that I won't see her wed to a pawnbroker." The good humor leaving his face, he unlinked his fingers and crossed his arms instead. "I haven't changed my mind."

Something else had changed instead. And she hadn't realized how significant that change was until it had almost cost Ellen her life.

"Thomas isn't only a pawnbroker," she said carefully. "He's also a man—the man your sister loves. You're judging him the way you complain people judge you."

He raised a brow. "The way *you* judge me?"

"We're talking about Ellen." She wouldn't let him turn this around. "Ellen really and truly loves Thomas. Why should it matter what the fellow does for a living? He's decent, he's respectable. Don't you want your sister to be happy?"

He remained quiet for a moment, just gazing at her. As the silence stretched, she thought maybe she'd struck a chord.

Until he finally spoke. "What happened," he asked slowly, "to your conviction that it's as easy to fall in love with a titled man as one without?" He rose and slid off his surcoat, tossing it over the arm of the chair. "If those words no longer apply to Ellen, can I assume they no longer apply to you, too?"

She backed up. "No. Of course they still apply. But in Ellen's case—"

"Why should Ellen be different?" Kit advanced, taking perverse pleasure in watching Rose retreat. He'd caught her—twice—insisting Ellen should marry for love, and this time he wasn't going to let her get away with claiming it shouldn't work the same way for her.

"Ellen isn't different." She backed into a marquetry desk and braced her hands on the surface. "But Ellen has already fallen in love." She lifted her chin. "She never had a chance to fall in love with a titled man first."

He brought his face to within an inch of hers. "Who will *you* fall in love with first, Rose?"

Though he was too close to see it, he heard her nervous swallow. "We're talking about Ellen."

"Not anymore," he said, and bent his head to meet her lips.

Her eyes closed, and a tiny sound rose up from her throat. Her hands came to rest on his chest, seeming to burn through the thin cambric of his shirt.

Then she pushed him away, her eyes popping open. "Kit! Listen to me. You must let Ellen wed Thomas—she almost killed herself."

He stumbled back, not from the force of her shove, but from the impact of her words.

He couldn't have heard right. His baby sister had tried to...?

He fell back onto the chair.

"Gemini," Rose said, putting her hands to her cheeks and looking entirely unRoselike. "I'm sorry. I didn't mean to say it like that. She didn't do it on purpose. But she did nearly die."

He rubbed his face. "You're making me more confused. Just...please, tell me what happened."

Rose took a deep breath and started from the beginning. By the time she finished, he was less confused. But even more shocked.

"You say she's all right, though?"

"The doctor thinks so. Though I feel she's quite melancholy."

"Show me the book."

Rose produced a tome from somewhere in her skirts, and he reflected, not for the first time, that ladies' clothing was an utter mystery. But once he'd opened the book's cover, he could no longer think about clothing.

Because nobody in the engravings wore any. Clothing, that was.

He flipped back to the title page. "*I Sonetti*? Weren't virtually all the copies burned by the Vatican? Where on earth did she find one?"

This was obviously the book Ellen had brought that evening to Windsor, the one she'd asked Rose to translate. He should have known it was something licentious. Ellen had never been bookish, and yet she'd been engrossed.

He flipped through a few more pages before slamming the book shut. "*This* is what my baby sister's been reading?"

"Technically, she hasn't read any of it," Rose soothed. "Only looked at the pictures."

"Well, isn't that a relief!" he said sarcastically.

She sat in the chair next to his and angled to face him. "Kit, what's in the book isn't as important as what's in Ellen's heart. She will do anything—*anything*—to wed Thomas. She's willing to push moral boundaries, risk her reputation, risk her own life..."

His heart hammering, Kit came halfway off the chair. "I thought she didn't know the tansy was dangerous."

"She didn't." Rose darted forward to push him back down again. "A midwife told her that tansy tea aids in conception, so she took one of my mother's essential oils. They're stronger than the herbs by a hundred times or more. It would likely have taken her life had it not been purged at once."

"Thanks to you."

Rose waved that away. "My point is this: Your sister will marry the man she loves, or she will die trying."

Kit blinked at her. "But it was an accident. She wasn't thinking."

"Because she's too desperate to think. She's gone this far, Kit. She won't stop now. Her latest plan failed, so she'll move on to the next harebrained scheme." Resettling herself in her seat, Rose put a hand on Kit's. "I know she's young, and I know it seems like she's throwing her future away, but I fear the sort of future you envisioned is no longer possible. If you could give her happiness or a title—but not both—which would you choose?"

"What a ridiculous question," he snapped. "Of course I'd choose happiness." Gripping the chair's arms, he willed himself to calm. It wasn't Rose he wanted to shout at, after all. "But I shouldn't have to choose. I could give her both."

"No, Kit. You can't." After a gentle pause, she leaned back in her chair and continued in a lighter tone. "And don't you go blaming yourself for this fix. I vow and swear, if your sister had fallen for a viscount, you'd condemn yourself for not snagging her an earl."

When Rose paused again, he managed a weak chuckle.

Evidently she could tell it was forced. Her expression sobered. "At least you can be certain she'll have love in her life."

"She already does. *I* love her."

Her dark eyes held his captive. "So does Thomas."

Kit wasn't so sure. But Rose's judgement of Ellen rang true. Kit should have seen that she'd never let this go. But he hadn't wanted to see, and his stubbornness had nearly cost him his sister. His only family. The one person he was supposed to protect at all costs.

Guilt was a vise squeezing the air from his lungs.

If it hadn't been for Rose...

She'd saved his sister's life. Because she was good, because she was caring, because there was a heroic person hiding inside this exasperating young woman who insisted she wanted a duke.

His throat tightened, and something else settled in his chest —an odd rush of tenderness laced with a flicker of panic. He reached for Rose, wrapped his arms around her, and buried his nose in her flowery hair.

"Thank you," he whispered, afraid he'd just fallen in love.

Wanting was one thing, love quite another. It scared him to death. He'd wanted her before, yes. Wanted her for her beauty, her intelligence, her refreshingly bold nature, her family's position in society. And, of course, because she'd made him burn like the sun in August from the first time he'd laid eyes on her.

But suddenly he wanted her in an entirely different way. The want had turned into need.

He'd been tasked with making her fall in love with him, but he hadn't expected to fall himself. What would he do now if she couldn't be convinced?

Feeling his throat tighten more, he pressed his lips to the top of her head.

"You must let them marry," she said quietly. "If you have even a glimmer of an idea what they feel for each other, you cannot deny them."

He had a glimmer, all right. A sudden new glimmer that was singularly terrifying. If Rose was right—if Ellen really did experience the emotions Kit was feeling at this very moment—he wouldn't dare stand between his sister and her love.

That was, as long as Thomas Whittingham loved her back.

He motioned to the marquetry desk. "Is there paper and quill in there?"

"Yes." Rose slanted him a look. "Why?"

"I wish to write a letter."

Her expression made clear she wasn't satisfied with that answer.

"Trust me," he added. "And fetch Ellen, please?"

Sighing, Rose stood. "Try not to be too hard on her."

THIRTY-SEVEN

HEN ROSE BROUGHT Ellen in, Kit's sister looked pale, wan, and subdued. And small, wrapped in a velvet dressing gown that must have belonged to Rose, for it pooled at Ellen's feet.

He'd meant to be stern, but all resolve fled the moment he saw her looking so fragile. He leapt from his seat and wrapped her in his arms, then all but carried her to one of the blue brocade chairs. "You shouldn't be up and about. I wasn't thinking. I ought to have—"

"I'm perfectly recovered." Avoiding eye contact, her listless gaze scanned the room and lit on *I Sonetti*. Her only reaction was a sullen glance at Rose.

"You don't look it. You're not dressed…"

"I just didn't feel like getting dressed today, that's all." But she was lying. Something about her was different. Flat and dull, as if she couldn't summon enough energy even to feel irritated with him. As if she couldn't be bothered.

Had he done this to her?

Feeling worse than ever, he shuffled back to the writing desk to retrieve the hastily scribbled missive. When he handed it to Ellen, she scanned the single page with disinterest.

Then a soft gasp escaped her lips.

"What is it?" Rose asked.

"A letter to Thomas." Ellen looked up at Kit, her uncomprehending eyes a murky brown. "You're...you're allowing the marriage?"

"Insisting on it," Kit corrected. "On one condition."

She swallowed hard, clutching the paper to her chest. "What?"

Kit gazed down at her, his heart pounding a mile a minute. He'd thought reading the note would make her happy. Shouldn't she be acting happy? Instead she still seemed different and wrong. Was she through being his sister? Or...heaven forbid, could it be the poison? Could it have hurt her mind somehow? Changed her permanently?

"How?" he asked abruptly. "How could you have been so stupid?"

"I don't know." Her eyes filled. "I thought I had no other choice."

The tears wrenched at him, but at least they were a sign of emotion. Any emotion was an improvement over that awful nothingness. He decided to go on yelling. "No other choice but to abandon your honor and risk your life? And all for a blasted pawnbroker?"

"Kit," Rose said in warning.

But her interference wasn't necessary, since Ellen had already launched herself from her chair. "How dare you?" she bellowed, eyes blazing a hot, liquid green.

Kit wanted to cheer.

Except then Ellen would have killed him.

So he cheered on the inside, where he also breathed a sigh of relief. He would recognize that righteous fury anywhere. That was one hundred percent Ellen, his Ellen. He hadn't lost her after all.

But he could have.

The sobering thought made him clench the chip of brick in

his pocket until it could have turned to dust. "Don't you know how much I love you?"

Her gaze dropped to the floor. It was so quiet he could hear the ticking of the mantel clock. Finally she nodded—then looked up. "Don't you know how much I love him?"

Kit rubbed the back of his neck until Rose prodded him with a foot. He sighed. "Are you sure, Ellen? You're only sixteen, and you can't change your mind later. Are you sure?"

"I'm sure."

He nodded. "Very well."

"Very well...?"

"You have my blessing," Kit said grudgingly, then nearly toppled over when his sister plowed into his chest.

She gushed gratitude and apologies, and for a while he just let her, holding her and savoring the fact that she was all right. And occasionally meeting Rose's eyes, which looked bright with either tears or amusement. Or both.

After Ellen had calmed down, pulled away, and blown her nose, she brought out the letter to Whittingham again and perused it happily.

Kit turned to Rose. "Can you send a rider to Windsor to deliver the note? And an extra horse so Whittingham can ride back with him. I left my carriage at Whitehall, and it's too slow in any case."

She looked between him and his sister. "Of course."

"Good," he said to her, and to Ellen, "I will see you wed today."

Both girls stared at him incredulously. Rose spoke for the two. "They cannot marry today!"

"Tonight, then. However long it takes the groom to show up, we'll wait."

"What's the rush?" Ellen's eyes turned suspicious. "Does it have to do with your condition—"

"It will take weeks," Rose was saying, "for the banns to be called. Unless Thomas can manage to obtain a special license from the Archbishop of Canterbury."

Kit scoffed. "Have you never heard of a privileged church? There are one or two directly outside the City walls. Places where a couple can marry without posting banns, without a license. Without waiting."

"Kit," Ellen began.

"That doesn't sound legal," Rose said, frowning at Kit.

He shrugged. "They claim to be outside the jurisdiction of the Bishop of London and therefore free to make their own rules."

"Kit," Ellen repeated.

Deferring her with a hand, he continued, "The marriages stand, and that's good enough for me. Now, the church I'm thinking of was called...Saint something, I believe. Anyway, it was in the Minories. I'll find it." Kit turned to his sister. "I was hoping to see you wed in a cathedral, but a privileged church will have to do."

"*Kit,*" she cried.

He blinked. "What?"

"The condition," she gritted out. "You mentioned a condition?"

"Oh." He grimaced, unwilling to start another fight with Ellen just now. "You'll find out soon enough," he told her, and refused to say more.

THIRTY-EIGHT

KIT EVENTUALLY remembered that the privileged church was called St. Trinity. Following a bit of deliberation, it was decided he'd go ahead and arrange matters while Rose and his sister waited for Whittingham. They would all meet Kit at the church.

It took an hour for him to reach St. Trinity—an hour during which he cursed himself ten times for not watching more closely over his sister. For not protecting her better. For allowing her to maneuver him to the point where he had no choice.

But there was nothing left to do except make the best of it. If Whittingham could prove he truly loved Ellen, he could have her. And Kit would make sure the two of them had a wonderful, carefree life together.

Or rather, his eleven thousand pounds would.

But he wouldn't tell them that now. Either of them. His sister had said over and over that she wanted to marry for love—and marry for love she would.

Kit arrived to find St. Trinity in surprisingly good repair for such an old building. The walls and columns were freshly painted, costly leaded glass filled the windows, and votive candles flickered around the sanctuary.

A privileged church was quite obviously a lucrative business.

He stood in the back, watching a wedding in progress. Several more couples seemed to be waiting their turns. One bride was well gone with child, another quietly weeping. A third wedding party included a man who didn't look much happier. If Kit didn't miss his guess, the bride's father was surreptitiously holding a pistol on the poor fellow.

The moment the current wedding concluded, Kit barged down the aisle.

The priest looked up and frowned. "You're not next."

"I'm not marrying at all. But my sister will be here later today, and I wish to make certain you'll stay to perform the ceremony no matter how late she arrives."

The man shook his balding head. "I've too many weddings this day already. She'll have to come tomorrow. Or try St. James instead."

Ellen and her groom weren't going to St. James—they were coming here. "What is your customary charge?" Kit asked flatly.

The plump clergyman sized him up. "Six crowns."

Gasps from behind told Kit the quote was high, perhaps by double or more. "I'll pay you ten," he told the man. "And half of that now." He fished his pouch from his surcoat and began counting out coins. "I'll expect her to be wed the moment she appears."

"By all means, good sir," the priest said, licking his fleshy lips. When he took the gold and hefted its weight in a hand, a wide smile emerged, revealing large, uneven teeth. "Bring two witnesses, and—since you seem to value speed—a pistol," he added with a wink.

Despite himself, Kit laughed. "We've no need of a pistol—I'm the only party reluctant to this match."

Hours later, Kit was waiting on the church's steps when the Ashcrofts' carriage pulled up. His sister stepped to the cobblestones, followed by Rose, who was carrying a bunch of flowers. He wasn't surprised when Lady Trentingham emerged next, although he hadn't expressly invited her.

Finally, Whittingham stepped down, dressed in a green wool suit that was ten or more years out of fashion. His brown hair was tied back in a neat queue. Somehow he managed to look both pleased and scared spitless.

Kit was happy to see that. Perhaps the fellow really did care.

Ellen marched up the steps and dragged Kit inside the church. Her gaze swept the sanctuary before swinging to fasten on him. "What on earth have you planned here?" she whispered fiercely.

"What a blushing bride you make," he said, arching one brow. She'd changed into what had to be another borrowed garment, a confection of pale green satin with silver embroidery. It wouldn't suit Rose's high coloring at all, but looked perfect on his sister. The hue brought out the green in her eyes—or maybe they looked green because she was angry.

Well, she was about to get angrier.

"I'm going to ask Whittingham if he'll take you without your dowry," he informed her in an even tone. "And if he hesitates as much as a moment—*one* moment, Ellen—the wedding is off."

"That's so unfair!" she burst out.

Heads turned. "Hush!" he cautioned.

She moderated her voice, but not her demeanor. "You gave us your blessing."

"With a condition. Should Whittingham love you, I wish you the best. But if not…well, I'd rather suffer your wrath than see you bound to a man only interested in your money."

She crossed her arms, narrowed her eyes, and shut her mouth decisively. Remembering her words when he'd talked of withholding her dowry—*I will never speak to you again*—he figured she was following through on her threat.

That wouldn't last. A married woman was no longer a child, and couldn't afford to act like one.

"I've paid good money to see you wed quickly." He put a hand on her arm, then frowned when she shoved it off. "Let's adjourn outside and see this thing through."

THIRTY-NINE

*R*OSE WATCHED brother and sister emerge from St. Trinity, Kit looking determined, Ellen furious. She wondered what had been said during their short time inside.

Thomas stepped forward. "Ellen has informed me you're putting a condition on our marriage," he said, looking directly at Kit.

He was a direct sort of person. Rose had come to know him a little better on the ride from the town house to the church, and she believed he would make a good husband for her friend.

If only Kit would allow it.

"That's true," Kit said. "You must be willing to take my sister without her dowry."

Rose suspected Kit's aim was to test the groom's devotion, but Ellen released an angry huff. Yet Thomas, bless him, didn't so much as blink. "I would take your sister if she came with a mound of debt. Ellen's dowry would be welcome—I won't lie—but I don't want your sister for money, sir. I want her because I love her."

It was such a pretty speech, Rose wanted to applaud.

But Kit just nodded, somehow contriving to appear pleased,

relieved, disappointed, and resigned all at once. "Come along, then. Let's get this done."

Ellen let out a little squeal, then ran to Thomas and threw her arms around him.

"*After* the wedding," Kit said, but not without a hint of good humor.

Regardless, Ellen chose to glare at him.

"Good luck, Ellen." Rose handed her the bouquet of flowers she'd arranged while they were waiting for Thomas. It wouldn't feel like a real wedding without flowers.

Though the bride smiled, she looked apprehensive until Thomas had drawn her down the aisle to stand before the priest. Then she took his hand and released a heartfelt sigh.

Some other people began to protest, but Kit pressed a small pile of gold into the priest's plump hand—and that was that. The man wasted no time beginning the ceremony. He was the no-nonsense sort, with a booming voice, a big belly under his robe, and flushed, well-fed cheeks.

Standing in the little old chapel, Rose shifted on her high-heeled shoes, wondering if she'd ever be a bride.

"Thomas Whittingham, wilt thou have this woman to thy wedded wife, to live together after God's ordinance in the holy estate of matrimony? Wilt thou love her, comfort her, honor, and keep her in sickness and in health; and, forsaking all others, keep thee only unto her, so long as ye both shall live?"

"I will." The confident words boomed off the plain, white-washed walls, binding Thomas to Kit's sister.

But Rose wasn't listening to the ceremony. Instead, she focused on the bride and groom—their linked hands, their bodies ranged close, their eyes shining with a potent mixture of disbelief and euphoria.

Smiling as though she'd arranged this wedding herself, Mum leaned close and nudged Rose's shoulder. "They're perfect together, aren't they?" she whispered.

Rose could only nod dumbly. Ellen and her pawnbroker were

clearly in love…for Ellen, at least, it hadn't been as easy to fall in love with a titled man as a commoner.

The priest cleared his throat and looked back down at his *Book of Common Prayer*. "Ellen Martyn, wilt thou have this man to thy wedded husband…"

Standing on Rose's right, Kit sighed. "Have I done the right thing?"

"Oh, yes," she breathed, wondering if *she* would do the right thing. For she feared that, like Ellen, she wasn't finding it easy to fall in love with a title. The Duke of Bridgewater was handsome and rich and kind, and she'd tried to make herself fall in love with him, to no avail. And yet, with Kit…

Her feelings didn't bear thinking about.

"…so long as ye both shall live?" the priest concluded expectantly.

"I will," Ellen pledged, sounding happier than Rose remembered ever feeling.

A few more words, a ring slid onto her finger—something chosen from the pawnshop, no doubt—and Ellen was clearly and truly wed now, the new Mrs. Thomas Whittingham.

And Rose was more confused than ever.

When Thomas's lips met Ellen's, Kit looked to Rose. Her breath caught in her throat. His eyes seemed full of promises… but they were promises she couldn't return.

She didn't breathe easily again until they'd all headed back down the steps to her family's carriage. The newlyweds received congratulations and hugs from the ladies while Kit stood stiffly off to one side.

"I'm so happy for you." Rose embraced the bride with a happy sigh. Then she lowered her voice. "Are you nervous about your wedding night?"

"Hmm?" Ellen had been gazing dreamily at her new husband. "Oh, not a bit. Who needs those old sonnets when I've got Thomas?"

Rose chuckled, relieved that her friend wasn't vexed with her for handing over *I Sonetti*. "Where will you go tonight?"

"Home. To the pawnshop in Windsor." She smiled up at Thomas, then glanced at Kit and lifted her chin before turning back to Rose. "It will doubtless be late by the time we arrive, but I've no wish to stay in London."

"We're going home to Trentingham tomorrow," Mum announced.

"Are we?" Rose asked, surprised. But right now the idea of home sounded wonderful.

"I miss your father. And Rowan. And I'm going to have your sisters and their husbands over for supper as soon as possible. In fact, I'll send notes to them before we leave. Perhaps they can join us tomorrow night." Without missing a beat, Mum turned to Kit. "Will you join us as well? My husband is likely impatient to see his greenhouse take shape. You *did* promise to work up a design before you left Lily's wedding."

"I did, didn't I?" he said wryly. "But—"

"Rose mentioned you've got Whitehall under control. And you won't be far from Windsor. Or Hampton Court, for that matter."

Mum could be persuasive when she put her mind to it. Kit nodded. "I suppose since no red-and-white-liveried king's man has shown up with bad news, I can take a day to sketch a design."

"And one night to relax before jumping back into the fray."

"And one night," he agreed, his gaze straying to Rose.

She ordered herself not to blush.

It took a few more minutes for plans to be nailed down. Rose and her mother would take Ellen and Thomas back to the town house to fetch Ellen's things. Kit would return to Whitehall, spend the balance of the day making certain everything there would proceed smoothly, then go on to Trentingham Manor in the morning.

Rose was settled in the carriage and halfway to St. James's Square before she realized that in all the time since before the wedding began, Ellen hadn't said one word to her brother.

FORTY

*R*OSE'S FAMILY was almost more than Kit could take. They were loud. They were boisterous. And there were so blasted *many* of them.

Rose's older sister, Violet, had brought along her husband Ford, the Viscount Lakefield, and their three children—two of whom were infant twins and prone to wailing—plus Ford's niece, ten-year-old Jewel.

Kit's friend Rand was there with his new wife, Rose's younger sister, Lily. Lily, as usual, was surrounded by animals— a cat she'd brought, along with a sparrow and a squirrel that had followed her. Her mother had ordered the latter two outside during supper, but they were watching through a window.

And then, of course, there were Lord and Lady Trentingham. And their ten-year-old son, Rowan.

With Rose and Kit—and not counting the creatures—that made eleven people around the table in Trentingham Manor's white-paneled dining room, plus two in cradles nearby. Kit was unwillingly reminded of his school days, eating in an enormous hammerbeam-ceilinged hall with shouts and conversation coming from all angles. He half expected a food fight to break out.

It seemed quite a racket to one who was used to dining with only his sister.

Ellen. She'd be settled in at the pawnshop by now, and he wondered how she was doing. Was she happy with her pawnbroker husband? They'd be happier, of course, when he gave them the money he'd saved for her dowry, but he thought he'd wait a little while for that. A week or two, at least. Let them get used to each other first—such a windfall was likely to be unsettling, indeed.

In the meantime, he hadn't wanted to be alone at his house in Windsor, imagining his baby sister and her new husband getting "settled" down the street. So Lady Trentingham's invitation had been welcome, even though heaven knew he had better things to do.

But his projects were under control, and the day had gone well enough. Lord Trentingham had been happy with Kit's ideas for the greenhouse, and Kit had gone only half hoarse shouting all his explanations. He'd order the materials and hire a foreman when he returned to Windsor. The earl was anxious to get his plants inside before winter, so Kit had promised him an accelerated schedule. The groundbreaking was planned for ten days hence.

"This all must be very disturbing," Rand said.

"Hmm?" Kit had been so deep in his thoughts he hadn't even noticed that sweets had been put on the table. "Are you talking to me?"

"Wake up, you dolt." Rand elbowed him in the ribs and laughed. "We've been talking about the problems you had at both Windsor and Whitehall."

"They're resolved now," Kit said. His plate had been removed by a footman, and he hadn't noticed that, either. Someone set a smaller, clean plate in front of him.

"Are you sure?" Jewel's deep green eyes were wide in her delicate, heart-shaped face.

She seemed as concerned as an adult might, so he answered

her seriously. "I'm convinced Washburn didn't set the fire, so I don't expect him to try anything else."

"But how can you be sure?"

Seated to Kit's left, Rose passed him a platter of small currant cakes, her soft floral fragrance wafting to his nose along with the fruity scent of the baked goods. "The fire was probably not intended," she told Jewel.

"Exactly." He took three cakes and passed the plate to Rand. "My men aren't supposed to smoke on the job, but I wasn't there to watch."

Lord Trentingham frowned. "Is it a bath house?"

Kit blinked. "Pardon?"

"Your building project, is it a bath house? You said the men aren't supposed to soak?"

"*Smoke*, darling, not soak." His wife leaned to brush a few cake crumbs off her husband's cravat.

"It could have been someone else." Taking six cakes for himself, young Rowan sounded a bit gleeful at the prospect of uncovering intrigue. "Not this Washburn, but someone else."

"Let's hope not." Kit used one of the cakes to scoop sweet whipped cream from a dish. "It was most probably accidental. These things happen."

"Bee stings do happen," the earl put in. "They're a right nuisance out in the garden."

No one corrected him this time.

Jewel waved a currant cake. "Accidents at two of your buildings? Aren't you wondering if your other building might have a problem, too?"

Out of the mouths of babes. Kit sighed. "Perhaps I should go to Hampton Court and make certain everything there is progressing smoothly."

"Rose and I are going to Hampton Court," Lady Trentingham volunteered cheerfully.

Kit wasn't surprised.

Her husband had actually heard that. "Not too soon, I hope, Chrysanthemum."

"Well, we won't want to wait too long. The court is there, after all, and Rose will want to see the duke."

Rose's sisters turned to her in unison.

"The duke?" Violet asked, leaning down to swipe her son's spoon off the floor for at least the tenth time.

Lily fed a bit of cake to her cat under the table. "What duke?"

"The Duke of Bridgewater." Rose hid her face by raising her goblet to her lips—although Kit knew it was empty. "We'll talk about this later."

FORTY-ONE

*N*OT TOO MUCH later, Rose found herself upstairs flanked by her sisters, the three of them lying crosswise on her oak four-poster bed, staring straight up.

"Tell us about the duke," Violet said to the underside of Rose's crimson velvet canopy.

"He's very generous and handsome and kind," Rose returned morosely. "He gave me these ruby and pearl earrings."

Her sisters both turned to look. Violet touched a finger to one of the delicate drops. "They're lovely."

"Goodness!" Lily exclaimed. "He sounds perfect. Exactly what you were looking for. Do you think he likes you?"

"Very much." Rose sighed. "I won't be surprised if at Hampton Court I receive my first proposal."

Violet came up on an elbow. "Then why do you sound so gloomy?"

When Rose turned her head to see Violet, her sister's warm brown eyes looked too concerned behind the lenses of her spectacles. She focused back up on the canopy. "I don't care for the way he kisses."

"Oh..." her sisters said together in a way that made it clear they considered this as important a problem as she did.

Rose wasn't sure whether she was glad or frustrated at that fact. Part of her wished they'd tell her to marry the duke and be done with it.

"Is his kissing...sloppy?" Lily asked.

"No."

"Rough?" Violet wondered.

"No."

"Then what?" they both chimed.

"I'm not sure. There's nothing wrong with his kissing that I can point out specifically—I just don't enjoy it." Rose crossed her feet where they hung off the end of the bed. She uncrossed them. Her voice dropped miserably. "For the longest time, I didn't like *anyone's* kissing. I thought something was wrong with me. Until..."

Now Lily came up on an elbow. "Until what?"

Rose felt hemmed in. She looked at her older sister, then her younger, then back to the canopy. "I've met one man who's different. Whose kissing makes me..."

"Swoon?" Violet suggested.

Rose pulled a face. "I suppose. But he's totally unsuitable."

"In what way?" Lily's voice was sweetly sympathetic.

"In every way. He's a commoner. And he *works* for a living."

"Rand works," Lily said defensively. "Don't you think being a professor is a lot of hard work?"

"But Rand doesn't *have* to work. He works because he wants to. Gemini, he's a baron, and someday he'll be a marquess."

"That wasn't always the case, and he never minded working. And it didn't bother me to think of marrying him when he did have to work. In fact, it didn't bother you, either, if I recall correctly. You were perfectly willing to chase Rand when he was only a professor."

"He was never only a professor." Rose didn't care for Lily's affronted tone, nor for the reminder of how foolishly she'd pursued her sister's husband. "Even before he became an earl, he was Lord Randal Nesbitt."

"There's nothing wrong with work," Lily insisted.

"Of course there isn't!" Frustrated, Rose pushed herself up to sit on the edge of the bed. She rubbed her face as her sisters came up beside her. "It's only that I had a plan for my life, and this man isn't part of it."

"Is he poor?" Violet asked.

"No," she said, thankful she could say that at least, else she'd get the same kind of tirade from Violet that she'd just heard from Lily. Violet's husband, after all, had been poor as a churchmouse when they met.

"It's Kit, isn't it?" Lily suddenly guessed.

"No," Rose denied quickly, then sighed at Lily's perceptive gaze and added, "How did you know?"

"I've both eyes and ears in my head. You're surprisingly familiar with his projects, and you cannot deny you thought him handsome the day you met. And he was drawn to you, too. I was there, if you'll remember. And he is *not* totally unsuitable."

"I want to love the duke," Rose wailed.

"Sometimes," Violet said softly, "we cannot choose these things."

All three of them sighed in unison.

Lily reached to cover Rose's hands where she'd clenched them together in her lap. "At least Mum isn't trying to match you with Kit," she offered with forced cheerfulness.

"That's right," Violet said. The one thing they'd all agreed on, from the time they were small girls, was that they didn't want any part of their mother's matchmaking schemes. "She's taking you to Hampton Court to spend more time with the duke."

"But she invited Kit here," Rose realized suddenly. "And to supper in London."

"True," Violet conceded. "But she probably just wanted to make sure he got started on Father's greenhouse."

"Oh, you're probably right. Plus she's taken a liking to Kit's sister. Perhaps she felt sorry for Ellen and invited her to the town house to cheer her up. Kit would naturally have had to come along."

"That makes sense," Lily agreed.

Rose breathed a sigh of relief. If it turned out Mum was trying to marry her off to Kit, she'd have to stop seeing him. Once her mother got something like that into her head, the pressure would be unbearable.

Not that Rose had decided she *did* want to keep seeing Kit.

She just wasn't ready to decide that she didn't.

FORTY-TWO

*A*T FORD'S SUGGESTION, the young men took their brandy in Lady Trentingham's perfumery. Ever the scientist, Ford tinkered with the distillery he'd made for his mother-in-law, searching for a reported leak. Rand reclined in a green velvet chair, sipping his drink.

Kit paced.

The contraption Ford was working on, and the large utilitarian table on which it sat, looked out of place in the otherwise elegant room. Kit ran a hand down the silk and linen brocatelle wall-coverings. "How is married life?" he asked Rand.

"Splendid," Rand said, looking nauseatingly relaxed.

Feeling decidedly *un*relaxed, Kit gazed up at the black and gold cornice around the plastered ceiling. A fine display of workmanship. Something like it would look magnificent in the apartments he was building for the Duchess of Cleveland at Hampton Court, not to mention in his own house in Windsor.

"You should try it," Rand added.

"Marriage?" Kit looked down to his old friend. "If I have my way, I believe I will."

"What?" Rand half bolted out of the chair.

"Sit," Kit said.

Frowning, Ford removed a lid and disconnected a copper tube. "Whom are you hoping to wed?"

Kit took a deep breath. "Your sister-in-law. Rose."

Ford looked up, astonished. "Rose?"

"Rose?" Rand echoed. He gulped a swallow of brandy. "I knew you thought her pretty, but—"

"She's *very* pretty." Kit's tone brooked no argument. "But more than that, she's extraordinary. She saved my sister's life. And she wants to travel, as I do—and can even speak the language when we get there."

Ford looked at him through a large glass bulb that was part of the device. "When you get where?"

Shrugging, Kit stooped to examine the marble fireplace. "Rome, Florence, France...wherever."

"If all you want is a translator, you can hire a linguist." Rand set his goblet on a small inlaid table. "I've students who would jump at a chance to spend a summer—"

"I'd rather spend it with Rose. I think...I think I might love her." Kit straightened, still facing the fireplace. "She's fun and beautiful and bright, and something about her just..." He trailed off, realizing how he must sound to these well-bred, aristocratic men.

Like a delusional, babbling idiot.

He turned to catch the two brothers-in-law exchanging a look. Ford raised a single brow. "He said the *L* word."

Rand nodded. "So I heard."

Kit reddened. "Look, I know what you're thinking. I'm a nobody, and she's—"

"Whoa," Rand said indignantly. "That's not what *I* was thinking."

"Me neither." Ford held up his hands in a gesture of innocence.

"Well, it's what Rose thinks," Kit said flatly. "But that could all change. If I'm awarded the Deputy Surveyor post and a knighthood—"

"You're sure she cares about all that?" Ford crossed his arms.

"I mean, I know she's Rose, but she's still an Ashcroft. They're a rather open-minded lot."

"Unconventional," Rand corrected.

Ford smiled. "That too."

"I'm sure she cares about that." Kit ran his fingers across a rack of little glass vials, all neatly labeled. LAVENDER, LILAC, MUSK. He plucked out the one that said ROSE. "Lady Trentingham told me herself."

"*Oh*," Ford said, the single syllable full of meaning. "You're working with the mother, then?"

Kit whipped around, his fingers clenching the vial. "What do you mean?" he asked nervously. Would Ford reveal Kit's deception to Rose? She was his sister-in-law, after all, while Ford had met Kit only a couple of times.

"I mean that Lady Trentingham is helping you win her daughter's affections." Ford grinned. "Don't look so guilty. The countess helped me, too, you know."

Rand made a choking sound that suggested he'd nearly spat out his drink. When he was finished coughing, he looked up at Ford through the ends of his longish hair. "She *helped* you?"

"Of course. She gave me advice when I was having trouble persuading Violet to marry me." Ford cocked his head. "Did she not do the same for you?"

"No!" As Rand wiped his mouth with a handkerchief, his brow furrowed. "Except…well, she did leave Lily and me alone together an awful lot. And she kept Rose away—"

He suddenly stopped, exchanging another look with Ford.

Sensing an odd tension in the room, Kit glanced between the two of them. "What?" When neither answered, he narrowed his eyes. "What were you saying about Rose?"

Since his friend remained guiltily silent, it was Ford who finally explained. "Rose sort of…used to fancy Rand."

Kit swallowed hard. "Really?"

"Only a little," Rand rushed to add. "Nothing happened between us."

"Nothing?" There seemed to be an odd rushing sound filling Kit's ears. "Then how do you know she had feelings for you?"

"Oh." Rand looked flustered. "She may have, um—just once —cornered me in the summerhouse and asked for a kiss."

The rushing grew louder. Rose had a habit of asking Kit for kisses, too. He'd believed there was something special between them, but what if she'd had the same feelings for Rand—Kit's best friend?

"When?" he heard himself asking.

"Over the summer." When Rand chanced a look at Kit's face, what he saw there seemed to alarm him. "But honestly it seems a lifetime ago. I'm married to Lily now, and Rose and I are just like brother and sister."

"He's telling the truth, man," Ford put in, bent over the distillery again. "There was nothing between them—or nothing of consequence, anyway." He replaced a copper tube with a little *snap*. "Rand had already been pining for Lily for years—"

"I wouldn't say *pining*," Rand grumbled.

Ford rolled his eyes. "I would. And for Rose's part, she was simply in a husband-hunting mood when Rand happened to be the first eligible gentleman to come along."

Kit grunted, remembering all the eligible gentlemen she'd been kissing at court. "That does sound like Rose," he had to admit.

"But listen, Martyn." Ford glanced up from his task. "Her mother obviously thinks you two are right for each other, or else she wouldn't be helping you. And with her assistance, I'd say the odds are in your favor. After all"—he gestured to himself and Rand—"she's two for two so far."

"Apparently so," Rand said ruefully, swirling his brandy.

"I hope you're right, Lakefield." Though Kit's tone was grim, the encouragement had given him a little surge of confidence. Retrieving his own brandy from a marble-topped table, he took a healthy gulp. "The girl's got half the bachelors at court panting after her, including a blasted duke. My only ray of hope is that his grace is reportedly a lousy kisser."

As the others laughed, feminine laughter drifted from upstairs.

Rand smiled. "Our ladies seem to be enjoying themselves."

"Where is everyone else?" Kit wondered suddenly.

"Jewel and Rowan are probably off somewhere planning a fiendish prank." Rand downed the rest of his drink.

"No doubt." Ford straightened, dusting off his hands. "The younger children were put to bed."

"And Lord and Lady Trentingham?"

"In bed as well."

Excellent. Perhaps Kit could manage to sneak off and get Rose on her own. And hopefully make a little more progress toward convincing her they were meant to be.

"Don't even think about it."

Kit looked around to see Rand grinning at him. "Trust me, Kit, you'll never tear her away from her sisters."

"Thick as thieves, those three." Lifting his empty cup, Ford moved toward the brandy jug. "Especially during their sleeping parties."

"Very well." Kit shrugged, masking his disappointment. "Another drink, gentlemen?"

FORTY-THREE

*C*HRYSTABEL SLID beneath the counterpane in her bedchamber, happily resting her head on her husband's shoulder.

Joseph kissed her forehead. "Two weeks."

"Pardon?"

"You were gone nearly two weeks. It's the longest you've ever been gone from me."

Chrystabel laughed softly. "You leave me for several weeks every year when you go to Tremayne."

She felt him shrug. "That seems different somehow."

"Because you're the one leaving and busy." She knew he had to go, that Tremayne, a castle near the Welsh border, was as much his responsibility as Trentingham or his duty to Parliament. But that didn't mean she liked it. "Now that the girls are grown, perhaps I'll come along. And bring Rowan," she said, warming to the idea. "After all, he's now Lord Tremayne. He should learn the ins and outs of running the estate."

"An excellent notion, Chrysanthemum."

Her husband's breathing was slowing, his head beginning to loll. She had always envied the way he could go straight to sleep the moment he climbed into bed. Meanwhile, she'd lay awake for long minutes—sometimes hours—her mind churning with thoughts of the day past and plans for the day to come. She'd never figured out what made them so different.

"I'll have to leave again, though," she said mournfully. "Soon."

His eyes opened halfway. "Hmm?"

"Rose is so close to making the right decision. Another few days at court ought to convince her there's no one there meant to share her life."

"Mmm." His arms snaked around her, pinning her securely against his warmth.

"I'm quite disappointed, though, that she hasn't found a moment here to go off with Kit. Lily and Violet are monopolizing her—perhaps I was shortsighted to invite them." She gave an expressive sigh, wiggling herself into a more comfortable position within the circle Joseph's arms. "I believe I shall have to wait until they all turn in for the night and then devise a way to get Rose and Kit out of their beds for a short while. I imagine he'll be leaving in the morning for Hampton Court. Perhaps we'll wait a few days before following...give Rose some time to miss him. What do you think, darling?"

Her husband's answer was a soft snore. He was fast asleep.

Oh, well. She was quite used to plotting these things without him. Men were dear creatures, but the vast majority of them didn't seem to have much of an imagination.

After conceiving her strategy, she dozed until the voices and giggles died down, signaling all were abed. Joseph had rolled over, leaving her free to slip out of bed without disturbing him. Tying a wrapper over her night rail, she padded across the chamber in her bare feet, her toes curling at the chill in the stone floor.

The house was amazingly quiet. Rose's room was right beyond hers, so Chrystabel tiptoed to the door and tapped her fingernails against it—*rat-a-tat-tat*. Then she moved to the door of the room she'd assigned to Kit and did the same thing.

Nothing. Rose was a heavy sleeper, and Kit must be, too. She tapped on both their doors again, then a third time. Finally, the sound of a latch sent her scurrying back to her room. Suppressing a giddy giggle, she pulled the door shut behind her —but not quite all the way.

Her ear pressed to the slit of an opening, she heard someone pad into the corridor and knock loudly on another door.

"Rowan!" came a harsh whisper. Then louder, "Rowan, open up!"

It was Jewel's voice, not Rose's. Chrystabel sighed as she listened.

Another door opened. "What?" Rowan demanded rather ungraciously.

"I heard a noise."

"What kind of noise?" he asked through a yawn.

"I'm not sure. Maybe a ghost."

That idea was greeted by a snort. "There are no ghosts at Trentingham."

"I heard something, Rowan! Listen, will you?"

A long spell passed where there was no sound. Of course, Chrystabel wasn't tapping on doors.

"It was nothing," Rowan said at last. "Go back to bed."

"I'm afraid of ghosts. I cannot sleep. Will you stay with me?"

"I cannot visit your chamber in the middle of the night. That wouldn't be proper." Even at the tender age of ten, Rowan knew that.

Good boy, his mother thought.

"What if I hear it again?"

The boy's sigh would have done a grown man justice. "Are you hungry?"

Jewel seemed to consider that question a moment. "I suppose I am."

"Maybe it was your stomach rumbling. Let's go downstairs and find something to eat."

Chrystabel waited until their footfalls had proceeded down the staircase before easing open her door. It seemed neither Rose nor Kit had awakened even with Rowan and Jewel talking outside their rooms. Something louder than those benign little taps would be necessary.

She scratched her fingernails down the front of Rose's door, a nice, satisfying scrape as she raked down the carved linenfold design. After repeating the motion, she moved to Kit's door and did it twice more.

Hearing a latch again, she darted back into her room.

"Just take a look, Rand! There must be something there. I cannot sleep with these noises!" It was Lily this time, Chrystabel realized with more than a little frustration. "Do you see anything?"

"Nothing. Would you like to come and look for yourself?"

"No," Lily said. "But those sounds cannot come from nowhere."

"Houses settle. You told me there have been no ghosts at Trentingham in the past, and there's no reason to believe one would suddenly arrive now. Hang it, now that you've wakened me, I'm hungry. Shall we go downstairs and find something to eat?"

For a brand-new son-in-law, Rand certainly felt at home here, Chrystabel thought wryly. While she waited for them to start downstairs, she looked around her chamber for something that would make more noise.

Her silver comb ought to do it. She snatched it up and peeked out her door. All was clear.

Drawn sideways across the wooden linenfold grooves, the comb made quite a racket. It wasn't long at all before the click of another latch sent her to safety behind her own door.

"There's no such thing as ghosts," she heard Ford say.

She barely stifled a groan.

A long minute or two passed while she listened to footsteps pacing up and down the corridor. Ford, the scientific one, was a much more thorough ghost-hunter than either of his brothers-in-law. "All's clear," she finally heard him tell Violet. "I swear it. You hungry? Let's go downstairs and find something to eat."

Slumped against the door, Chrystabel pictured her oldest

daughter slipping from her childhood bed and into a wrapper. Joseph snored peacefully behind her, and Rose apparently still slept in her room. Vexing girl must take after her father.

By the time Violet and Ford clattered down the steps—being none too quiet about it—Chrystabel had decided drastic measures were in order. Leaving the comb behind, she ventured once more into the corridor.

She paused by Rose's door, then pushed down on the latch and opened it a smidgen. "Whooooooooo," she called inside, a breathy, piercing whistle.

The fourth child of five, Chrystabel had long ago mastered the art of impersonating an eerie apparition. How better to get back at her older sisters than by scaring them silly? It was a far more lasting retribution than pinching or hair-pulling.

"Whooooooooo," she called twice more for good measure, then hurried to Kit's room.

"Whooooooooo. Whooooooooo." She'd drawn breath for another exhalation when footsteps sounded in Rose's room down the corridor.

She barely made it back into her own chamber before her daughter's door slammed open. "What was that? Who's there?"

Unlike her sisters, Rose didn't sound scared. Her voice wasn't tentative and frightened. Aggravated would better describe it.

Rose's footfalls paced the corridor up and halfway back before Chrystabel heard another door opening. Kit's, thank goodness. It had to be—his was the only occupied room left.

"What on earth is going on out here?" he said. "I thought I heard a ghost."

"There's no such thing as ghosts," Rose said peevishly.

"Obviously," Kit drawled, "you have never torn down an old building."

"Obviously," Rose returned, "you have a lively imagination."

Kit only laughed. Lightning strike her down, Chrystabel thought, if these two weren't perfect for each other.

No lightning bolts came down the chimney.

"Are you hungry?" Rose asked.

"I could eat."

There wasn't a male alive who couldn't find space for food, no matter how recently his belly was last filled. Chrystabel credited her daughter for knowing the way to a man's heart.

But as they made their way downstairs, her own heart sank. A jovial family midnight snack was not what she'd had in mind for Rose and Kit. And she might have few, if any, chances left to arrange another meeting before her daughter wised up and figured out what was going on.

A lot of terms could be used to describe Rose, but slow-witted wasn't one of them. And Chrystabel knew well what would happen should her daughter discover that she and Kit were in league. The marriage would never occur.

She shut her door and made her way back to bed, her mind churning with plans once more.

FORTY-FOUR

$\mathcal{A}$S KIT AND ROSE approached the kitchen, they heard laughter. Boisterous, rollicking laughter.

Kit peeked in the door to find nearly the entire Ashcroft family around a big, scarred wooden table. Pies, bread, and left-over dishes from supper littered the surface. Ale and chatter flowed.

Deciding he wasn't hungry, he shut the door quietly, muffling the laughter to a dull roar. "I've changed my mind. Let's go for a walk instead."

Rose's dark eyes looked huge in the light of the single candle she was carrying. "Outside? In my night rail in the dead of the night?"

"It's been unseasonably warm. I'll wait while you get your cloak."

"We've no shoes!" she protested, making Kit look down in surprise. Suddenly he could hardly fathom that he was here in Rose Ashcroft's home in bare feet.

Though her night rail and dressing gown revealed less skin than the current fashions—court fashions most especially—there was something undeniably intimate about the ensemble. Something that made him belt his own robe more tightly.

"We can go back upstairs for our shoes," he suggested.

"I think not."

For a moment, he thought she would open the kitchen door and join the impromptu party. It had been her idea to come down here, after all. Looking forward to some quiet time with her in this noisy house, he'd agreed—but perhaps her interest in food surpassed her interest in him.

Happily, in the end she didn't disappoint him. "I have another idea," she whispered, taking his arm to lead him away. "We can walk in my father's orangery."

"Your father grows oranges?"

"Not very successfully. That's why he's so keen to get that greenhouse."

The orangery was a long, narrow chamber that occupied the entire ground floor of the west wing. "It used to be called the Stone Gallery," Rose told him as they entered. There were candlesticks mounted on the walls at intervals, and she lit them as she walked. "I suppose that after you build the greenhouse we'll call it the Stone Gallery again."

Tall windows, dark now, lined the gallery along the west side and half of the east as well. The ceiling was intricately carved oak. Kit recognized it and the chamber as dating from Tudor times—a room the occupants would have used to take exercise in inclement weather. But now it was filled with a variety of trees and plants, all interspersed with statuary that looked like it had been brought from Italy.

"Would you like an orange?" Rose asked laughingly, pulling a small, rather shriveled example from a scraggly branch. "Don't worry—they don't taste as bad as they look."

He peeled it as they walked, the black and white marble floor cold beneath his bare feet. "It's quiet here," he said.

"Yes." She sounded amused at the observation. "It's not easy to find a quiet place at Trentingham, is it?"

"You've a large family. But I like it," he added, realizing suddenly that he did. "Even the noise. There's a lot of life here. Vitality."

He'd felt that lack of vitality since his parents' deaths. He'd been busy, yes—but there was a difference.

"It's real," he added, tossing the peel into an empty clay pot.

"Real?"

He divided the little orange and handed her half. "Charles's court, for example, is lively. But it's forced gaiety, don't you think? The liveliness here is real."

"Ah. Yes. I see," she said thoughtfully.

Popping the juicy, sweet fruit into his mouth, he hoped she also saw that court was a life she'd just as soon live without—because she'd have to if she married him. Even supposing he got his knighthood, he hadn't the time to flit from one place to another at the whim of his monarch. He had his lifework to pursue.

And no matter that it was fashionable, he had no intention of living a separate life from his wife.

He heard her swallow. "Are you not happy, Kit?"

She sounded like she cared. He hoped it was as more than a friend. More than *like a brother, but better.* "I'm happy right now," he said, licking his fingers.

"And Ellen is happy now."

"I don't want to think about Ellen."

"But you must." They'd reached the end of the gallery. She lit the last candle and set the one she'd carried on top of a headless statue. "I know you're angry with her, with what she did. But you cannot remain estranged, you cannot remain silent—"

"I'm not angry. Disappointed, yes, but not angry." He took her arm, turning her to stroll back the direction they'd come. "And *I'm* not the one who isn't talking."

"You cannot really mean to keep all that money—"

"Will you be quiet, Rose?" he asked and then turned her toward him to quiet her with a kiss.

She wound her arms around his neck and cooperated fully. She tasted of Rose and orange, a flavor uniquely hers. A flavor he couldn't get enough of.

He backed her against one of the walls between two

windows. Above their heads, a haughty Roman emperor gazed down from a terra-cotta medallion—a souvenir of earlier times. Kit wanted to make new times with Rose. A new life, a happy life—one full of the vitality he'd been missing.

He kissed the sweet stickiness from her lips, then he kissed her chin, then her long, slender throat. He felt her pulse beating in the silky hollow where her shoulder met her neck. When her eyes drifted closed and she breathed his name, his own pulse leapt in response.

He pulled her closer, relishing how soft she felt in his arms. Suddenly he realized there were naught but two thin layers of fabric between his hands and her skin. No stiff stomacher, no intricate lacing, no thick, quilted stays. The thought made him warm all over.

Then *she* was the one pressing closer, leaning into him, her intrepid hands roaming over his shoulders and back and leaving a trail of heat. When he felt a fiery shock, he realized one of those hands had slipped beneath the collar of his robe to graze bare skin.

"Rose," he groaned against her lips. "You feel too good. Too good…"

"Mmm," was her only response, but it was a sound of such perfect contentment that it made his heart swell with emotion.

"I love you," he heard himself saying, and it sounded true. Sounded right. The phrase was only three simple words, but somehow it encapsulated everything he was feeling. Everything that had changed inside him as Rose gradually became a part of his life. The most important thing in his life.

The love of his life.

Love was a true thing of beauty.

"You *what*?"

Kit slammed back to reality to find Rose recoiling from him, her eyes filled with pain and confusion, her contentment turning to panic. "No. I…no. Gemini, what am I doing?" Shuddering, she wrapped her dressing gown tighter and crossed her arms over her torso like a shield. Or like she was going to be sick. Either way, she looked utterly miserable. "I'm sorry. I must go."

She pushed past him and ran from the chamber, her bare footfalls slapping all down its long length. At the other end, he heard the door slam shut.

And then he was alone with the flickering candles and his tight throat and his disturbed thoughts.

And his crushed heart.

Blast Rand and Ford for encouraging him! He'd *known* Rose wouldn't have him—at least not in his current circumstances. But he'd let himself fall prey to their false optimism. He'd let his actions be guided by emotion rather than judgment, and now he may have scared her away for good.

What would Lady Trentingham say?

And more importantly, what would he *do?*

The candlelight that had seemed so intimate earlier now seemed harsh. He slowly moved to douse the many small flames. Should he tell Rose of his pending knighthood, even with his project deadlines approaching and all the problems threatening his appointment? Not to mention the fact that a knighthood might not be enough for her, anyway. The Deputy Surveyor post was only a first step—it could be years before he raised himself further.

By then it would be too late for him and Rose.

Too, too late.

FORTY-FIVE

$\mathcal{R}$OSE SPENT A restless, tormented night. When she
awakened, the note she found slipped beneath her
door did nothing to ease her distress. ROSE, it said in the neat,
all-caps printing she'd seen on Kit's architectural renderings:

MUST CHECK PROGRESS AT HAMPTON COURT. PLEASE GIVE YOUR
FAMILY MY THANKS AND ASSURE YOUR FATHER THAT THE GREENHOUSE
WILL PROCEED ON SCHEDULE AS PLANNED.
-K

There was nothing more. No "Dearest Rose." No "I love you,
Kit," or even just "Love, Kit."

Did he hate her now?

She couldn't begin to decipher what the note meant about his
feelings. She couldn't even begin to decipher *her own* feelings.

She washed and slowly dressed without help, so lost in her
thoughts she couldn't bear conversation with Harriet. *I love you.*
She supposed she had no right to expect Kit to repeat the declaration in a letter when his first attempt had been met with
silence. No, worse than silence—with horror.

The look on his face had nearly killed her. His words had

taken her completely by surprise. She supposed, on reflection, that they shouldn't have...

But she'd been expecting her first declaration of love to come from a duke.

Confusion was a weight in her chest. Did she love Kit? In the bliss of the moment, it had been on the tip of her tongue to echo those three words. But she hadn't, because she wasn't sure, and in any case it wouldn't matter.

He wasn't the right man for her.

He'd had no right to expect a different answer. She might have reached the advanced age of nineteen, but she wasn't yet desperate enough to marry a commoner. She'd be a fool to do that when Bridgewater, a lofty peer of the realm, was likely to offer for her hand. She squared her shoulders as she headed down to the dining room for breakfast.

Happy as bees in a bed of flowers, her sisters and their families were already eating, having risen early to prepare for their journeys home. The elder Ashcrofts had either slept late or already breakfasted. Rowan and Jewel chatted cheerfully, so focused on each other the rest of the room might as well have been empty.

Everyone in this house—everyone but Rose—was in love.

The conversation died as she scraped back a chair and plopped onto it. A footman offered a cup of chocolate, and she clenched it so hard her knuckles turned white.

"Where is Kit?" Lily asked.

Rose felt her jaw tightening. "What makes you think I should know?" she gritted out, suddenly visualizing herself biting her sister's head off. She gulped the hot liquid, scalding her tongue. "He left a note. It seems he's gone on to Hampton Court."

"Oh," Lily said.

"Did you hear a ghost last night?" Rowan asked.

Rose imagined biting his head off, too. "There's no such thing as ghosts."

"Rose is right," Ford put in.

He could live.

"I heard tapping," Rowan insisted.

"Me, too," Jewel said, gazing at him worshipfully.

That pixie-faced girl had fallen in love at six. Six! Off with her pixie head.

"We heard tapping *and* scratching," Rand said. "Lily and I both."

"And I heard a terrible scraping noise." Violet turned to Rose. "Did you not hear anything at all?"

A whoosh. But she'd never admit it. She didn't believe in ghosts.

Or marrying beneath her expectations, either.

FORTY-SIX

*T*HE SUN WAS SETTING upon Hampton Court's red brick when Rose and her mother arrived three days later. As they stood in one of Base Court's covered galleries waiting for a palace warden to open their lodging, a woman came out of the apartments next door.

"Oh!" she exclaimed, one hand to the pillowy bosom revealed in the low neckline of her orange brocade gown. Rose couldn't recall her name, but she remembered seeing her in the ladies' attiring room at Windsor. "Lady Rose! I'm so glad you've followed us. I hope we'll be seeing you at court this evening."

"Yes, you will," Rose said, pleased. Court was going to be so much more pleasant now that the women here liked her.

"And will you be bringing the translations?"

"Gemini!" With all the turmoil surrounding Ellen, she'd nearly forgot *how* she'd convinced the women to like her. "I'll send what I've finished to the ladies' attiring room," she promised, with a nervous glance at her mother.

"Excellent," the lady said before sauntering off, the train on her fur-trimmed cloak dragging behind her.

"What translations?" Mum asked.

"Some poetry. Italian. Nothing important."

"Oh, I see," her mother said as though she didn't see at all. "Come along, then, let's ready ourselves."

Their lodging was again just a sitting room and one bedchamber, no fancier than the one they'd been assigned at Windsor Castle. But at least the rooms were larger. In no time at all, Mum was settled at a creaky wooden dressing table with Anne working on her hair, while Harriet helped Rose into a new emerald gown she'd had made in London.

When a knock came at the door, Harriet went to answer and came back with a vase full of colorful fall flowers. "For you, Lady Rose."

Rose rushed to take them. "Lovely!" She rearranged the greenery more evenly and moved a yellow bloom from the right side to the left before reaching for the card. "They must be from the duke."

But they weren't.

For dear Lady Rose, the card said in a heavy, dark hand. *I wished for red roses to match your lips, but alas, they are not in season. Please accept this small token of my affection with my hopes of spending some time in your company this evening. Yours, Lord Somerville.*

"How did he know I was here?" she wondered.

"News travels swiftly at court," her mother said.

Harriet's pale green eyes looked wistful in her freckled face. "Oh," she said with a heartfelt sigh. "How I would love for a man to send me flowers."

She'd barely finished lacing the back of Rose's gown when another knock came at the door. This time she returned with a small wooden box. Inside was a dainty pearl bracelet.

"It goes well with my earrings," Rose said, wondering if she should wear the rubies tonight even though they didn't match her green dress. "How very thoughtful of Gabriel."

But the bracelet wasn't from him, either. The creamy sheet of vellum that had arrived with the box was lettered neatly in fine black ink. *For Lady Rose, though pearls cannot match the luster in your eyes. Passionately, Baron Fortescue.*

"Passionately?" Wasn't Lord Fortescue the one she'd ruled out on the first night of her quest for a courtier who could kiss? Frowning, she held out her wrist so Harriet could fasten the bracelet's clasp. "If I recall correctly, we were bored to death by one another."

"Oh," Harriet said, "how I would love for a man to give me jewelry."

A third knock on the door brought a platter of delicate sweetmeats and another note: *No sugar can match the sweetness of your demeanor.*

No one had ever called Rose sweet. "I vow and swear," she declared, popping a marzipan swan into her mouth, "I've never heard such ridiculous comparisons in my life."

Her mother moved to give her a turn at the dressing table. "They're just trying to impress you, dear."

"If any of them could kiss half decently, I would find that a lot more impressive."

"Oh," Harriet said, "how I would love for a man to kiss me."

By the time Rose was ready for court, she had two new bracelets, a sapphire stomacher brooch, and four bouquets of flowers in addition to the half-eaten platter of sweets.

None of it was from Gabriel.

Hampton Court had no keeps, no crenelated curtain wall, nothing like the huge central mound of earth at Windsor with its tall Round Tower. Instead, the palace was a virtual rabbit warren of buildings surrounding courtyards large and small.

Rose walked from Base Court through Clock Court with her mother, the pearls on her lavish new gown gleaming in the light from torches set on the walls at intervals. They climbed the Great Stairs. As they were crossing the cavernous blue-ceilinged great hall on their way to the Presence Chamber, a lord walking the other direction stopped and doffed his plumed hat.

"I hear you have a copy of *I Sonetti*, my lady."

Rose couldn't remember having met him, and the gentleman had a distinct gleam in his eye; one that made her uneasy. "I did," she told him cautiously.

The gleam faltered. "The book is no longer in your possession?"

"I returned it to the friend it was borrowed from." This wasn't exactly a lie, seeing as she'd given it to the friend's brother.

The gentleman brightened. "Then you could borrow it again."

"I think not," she snapped and swished past him.

"*I Sonetti?*" Mum asked when they reached the other end of the chamber.

"It means *The Sonnets.* Italian poetry."

"Why did the fellow's interest upset you?"

"I don't even know him!" Rose burst out, and then added in as calm a voice as possible, "I'm here to see the duke. If he means to make me his wife, he'll not like seeing me doing favors for other men."

The Presence Chamber was stunning, with great tapestries on the walls and a gilded ceiling. The king and queen sat under a canopy fashioned of cloth-of-gold. After the ceremony of presentation—which Rose found more tedious than thrilling this time —Mum wandered off, leaving her daughter at liberty to look for Gabriel. But she'd barely scanned the chamber when Baron Fortescue appeared and made a bow. "My dear Lady Rose, I'm most honored to see you wearing my bracelet."

He was dressed in mulberry satin with bunched loops of aqua ribbons. Rose had always admired men of fashion, but it seemed to her that lately the fashions had turned rather frivolous. And she remembered Lord Fortescue better now, most specifically that he was, as Lily had put it, a sloppy kisser.

She didn't wish to hurt the fellow, but she certainly didn't want to encourage him. "The bracelet matched my gown," she told him. "Thank you."

"My pleasure. I hear, dear lady, that you've learned the secrets of *I Sonetti.*" He grinned, displaying buck teeth. "I'm hoping you'll be willing to share them."

Was that why he'd given her the bracelet? She was tempted

to tear it off, but there was no reason, after all, to ruin such a pretty trinket. "If I knew any secrets," she told him archly, "I'd scarcely share them with a man who wasn't my husband."

To her consternation, his grin widened. "I entertain fond hopes of being that man."

"You *what*?"

"Will you marry me, dear Lady Rose?"

Good heavens, she'd just received her first proposal. This was it—the achievement she'd despaired of ever reaching. The moment she'd looked forward to ever since little Robin Beding-field had pushed her in a puddle and made her cry, and Mum explained why all the boys were mean to her.

A proposal!

And she felt about as happy as she had sitting in that dirty, freezing puddle.

Better she live all her days as a spinster than bind herself to Lord Fortescue and his sloppy kisses. "Please accept my apolo-gies," she said, "but my heart belongs to another."

Though he sighed, he didn't look surprised. "Best wishes, then, my lady."

No sooner had Lord Fortescue taken his leave than Lord Somerville made his way over. He raised her hand and kissed it reverently. "I hope you received my flowers."

"They're beautiful, my lord. I thank you." If she remembered correctly, he was an affable fellow whose kiss had been humdrum but not especially off-putting. And his suit was adorned with gold braid rather than ribbons. Perhaps he would ask her to dance. She had always dearly loved to dance.

"I hear you've a copy of *I Sonetti*," he said instead.

"Not anymore." If she had his flowers here, she would have dumped them on his head. "And before you ask, I've no secrets to share with the likes of you."

"Ah, I've heard tell of your desire for the state of matrimony. In that case, dear Lady Rose, I must ask you to do me the honor of becoming my wife."

Rose's first instinct was to scream at the top of her lungs, but causing a scene would only serve to increase her mortification. "It would be an honor," she said tightly, "but I'm afraid my heart belongs to another."

"I see." He swept her a courtly bow. "The duke is a lucky man."

Dazed, she made her way to a velvet-covered settle. A month ago she'd despaired of ever receiving a proposal, and now she'd collected two in the space of five minutes!

In the next hour, Gabriel failed to appear and four more courtiers proposed to Rose. Two of them were superb catches, men of positions as attractive as their persons. Men Rose would have thrown herself at a month ago. But suddenly she couldn't stomach the thought of marrying any of them.

And the ones who *didn't* propose were even worse, apparently taking her for some sort of lust-crazed doxy. Rose had warned off three of that type already when two more approached as a team. "We hear you have a copy of *I Sonetti*," one of them started, a lascivious gleam in his eye.

They both crowded close—so close Rose could tell one of them truly needed a bath. "We were wondering—" the second man began.

"Leave her alone," Nell Gwyn interrupted, shoving herself between them.

The first one turned on her. "Criminy, Nelly, we were only—"

"Hoping to share her, you beasts." Raising her dainty hands, she pushed on both their chests. "Go on. Be gone."

"I don't even have it anymore!" Rose hollered after them as they scurried away.

"But you did?" Nell asked the moment they were out of earshot.

"What?"

"Have a copy of *I Sonetti*. It's all they've talked of for days."

"Yes, I did." Rose sighed, fearing her mother was bound to hear the gossip. Judging by the dearth of ladies, at least half the women at court were presently crammed into the attiring room, squealing over her translated sonnets. "But I cannot imagine why everyone finds it so blasted fascinating."

"The ladies, they're just curious. They want to know what's behind all the whispers and scandal. But the gentlemen...well, if you're not looking for a tumble or two, you'd best stay in company and be watchful."

From what Rose had seen, there was nothing *gentlemanly* about these animals. "Surely not all men are such base creatures."

"Some may approach you with flowery words, but they are men. Inflamed most easily."

"Then perhaps I should carry a bucket of water."

Nell laughed, making Rose appreciate the woman's easy temper, not to mention her helpful advice. Once again, Rose wondered how one so thoroughly indecent could be the only decent person at court.

"Do you know," Rose said, "you are one of few here who haven't asked to see *I Sonetti*. Don't *you* want to view the scandalous engravings and read the poems?"

"I've no need of such things," Nell assured her blithely.

"Most ladies seem to think they'd learn something pleasing to their men."

"Not I." Nell leaned closer. "Charles"—she dropped her voice to a confidential murmur—"is a very catholic lover."

Rose frowned. "I thought you were both Protestant."

Nell's lips curved into a fond half smile. "I mean that he's not very imaginative. His tastes run to the simple. However, he more than makes up for that with his prodigious appetite and enthusiasm."

Rose felt her eyes widening. "Oh," was all she could think of to say, before quickly changing the subject. "Will there be gaming tonight?"

"Of course. And tomorrow night, there will be a masked ball."

"Gemini! Whatever shall I wear?"

"Not everyone wears a costume. Just a mask will do, although I suspect you'll find some of the garb amusing."

Rose's mind turned to the gowns she and Mum had brought and what she could possibly create from them. Maybe if she concealed her identity well enough, she'd have an evening free from being questioned about *I Sonetti*. She watched absently as a beautiful woman walked in and made her curtsy before the king.

Or rather, her bow.

Rose blinked. "Whoever is that?" she asked, staring. Though the tall woman was dressed in silks and satins, the sumptuous turquoise apparel wasn't a lady's. "It's a Cavalier's suit she wears! She must think the masked ball is today instead of tomorrow."

"I think not." Nell chuckled. "I gather you have yet to meet Hortense Mancini, the Duchess Mazarin?"

"That's the duchess?" Rose had never seen a woman dressed like a man, but the effect was stunning. A jeweled sword dangled from her belt, and a dark little Moorish boy dressed to match trotted beside her, completing the bizarre picture.

"Are you not jealous of her?" Rose asked candidly, knowing the Duchess Mazarin was yet another of the king's mistresses.

Nell gave a good-natured shrug. "She has Charles's attention for the moment, but when all is said and done, he will always come searching for my bed. For I love him, and I don't believe the lovely Hortense has it in her to love anyone. She has a brilliant mind, but beneath it she's colder than the Thames in January."

Rose slanted a glance to Louise de Kéroualle, who was watching Hortense and glowering. "It seems the Duchess of Portsmouth doesn't share your lack of concern."

"*She* has something to fret about," Nell said with a saucy grin. Taking Rose by the arm, she started toward the Duchess Mazarin. "Louise is a passing fancy for Charles as well, and the coming of Hortense may well mean the end of her reign. Even a king can spread himself only so thin," she added with a laugh.

"Why does King Charles like either of them?" Rose wondered aloud.

"He's a man," Nell told her with another shrug. "His head is turned by a pretty face. Louise is a beauty, and as for Hortense, you must agree she's extraordinary."

Drawing closer to the duchess's rare loveliness, Rose could only nod. Waist-length raven hair framed Hortense's perfect face. Her flawless Mediterranean skin set off large violet eyes that seemed to change color as she moved.

Nell lowered her voice. "Charles fancied himself in love with her years ago, while she was but fifteen and he still in exile on the Continent. He proposed to her twice. But she thought his prospects poor, and more importantly, so did her guardian, the Cardinal Mazarin. If either had foreseen that Charles would someday regain his crown, today she'd be a queen. Instead, she's forced to live off her keepers."

They drew up before the duchess just as she sent her little Moorish boy off to fetch refreshment. As the child trotted away obediently, Nell swept Hortense a theatrical curtsy. "Your grace, may I present Lady Rose Ashcroft, the Earl of Trentingham's daughter. Lady Rose, this is Hortense, the Duchess Mazarin."

"Lady Rose. I'm pleased to make your acquaintance." The duchess's accent was melodious, an intriguing mixture of her native Italian and the many years she'd spent in France. "I've been told," she added, raising one arched black brow, "that you're in possession of a rare copy of *I Sonetti*."

"I'm afraid your intelligence is out of date." Rose pursed her lips. Why should this stranger be the only soul at court—besides, fate willing, Chrystabel Trentingham—who hadn't heard? "I translated some of the book, but I no longer possess it."

"Then you speak Italian?"

"Among other languages." After saying that without thinking, Rose glanced quickly around and was relieved to see that Gabriel still hadn't appeared.

"An intellectual!" Hortense exclaimed with such enthusiasm

Rose half expected her to clap her hands. "You must come to my salon, then."

"Your salon?"

"A weekly gathering of great minds in my apartments at St. James's Palace. We discuss all manner of subjects. Philosophy, religion, history, music, art, ancient and modern literature…"

It sounded like something Violet would love, but Rose didn't share her sister's passion for scholarly debate. Not to mention she suspected the Duke of Bridgewater would find it a bore. Still, it wouldn't do to snub a duchess. "Perhaps someday I'll join you," she said.

"I look forward to it," Hortense said as her little Moor returned with a cup of steaming coffee. "Why, thank you, Mustapha." She patted him on the head, prompting a smile. His teeth looked very large and white in his dark face as he reclaimed his post by her side.

As she sipped, Hortense's gaze strayed to Louise de Kéroualle. "Look at her," she said to Nell with a roll of her amazing eyes. "She's wearing black again."

Rose looked, too. Louise's gown was exquisite, but clearly meant to convey grief. "Why black?"

Nell snorted as only Nell could snort. "That hoity-toity French duchess sets up to be of superior quality. If you listen to her, everyone of rank in France is her cousin. The moment some grand lord or lady over there dies, she orders a new mourning gown."

"Who died?" Rose asked.

"Doubtless some minor prince." Nell set one of her small hands upon a curvy hip. "I wonder, I do, if Louise is of such high station, why is she such a trollop? I was born to a trollop, so I hold that I've done as one might expect. But she was reared to be a lady—don't you think she should blush in shame?"

Hortense laughed at that, and her laughter was no feminine tinkle. It did her outfit rather proud.

Rose glanced again at Louise. "Does her grace have a black eye?"

Nell nodded. "An *unfortunate accident,* she calls it. But I overheard two ladies saying she'd done it deliberately, to make her pale skin darker like the Duchess Mazarin."

To judge from her braying laughter, the Duchess Mazarin thought that a fine jest.

"Lady Rose."

Rose turned to see the Duke of Bridgewater. "Your grace! I was wondering if you'd attend tonight."

"You look as though you've been having a fine time without me."

His tone implied he was less than thrilled to find her socializing with two of the king's mistresses. And now that she thought on it, Rose was a bit scandalized herself. But the truth was she felt more comfortable with these women than she did with most of the others here at court.

Gabriel was the exception, though. Other than proving a tad more amorous than she'd prefer, he'd been the perfect gentleman. "I'm glad you came," she told him, meaning it.

He drew her a safe distance away. "Where are your earrings?"

She knew she should have worn them. "I adore them, your grace, but they didn't match my gown."

"Well, then, these should match whatever you choose to wear." He fished a tiny silk pouch from his pocket. "A token of my esteem, my lady."

Rose drew open the drawstring and poured a pair of diamond drops into her hand. The stones winked in the torchlight. "Your grace! They're exquisite!"

She should have known he would come up with something to outshine all those other men.

"I'm pleased that you like them," he said, moving close to fasten them on her ears. "Would you care to dance?"

FORTY-SEVEN

"ROSSLYN." KIT looked up from the sketch he was making of Rose and quickly flipped it over. "What brings you here tonight?"

Rosslyn wandered the drawing room of Kit's building-in-progress, touching a panel here, eyeing the level there. "Just seeing how you're coming along." He squinted up at the half-painted ceiling. "You've pulled it off, Martyn, haven't you? I knew you would."

Kit glanced overhead at the fat, smiling cherubs the Duchess of Cleveland had requested, thinking, not for the first time, that they didn't really fit her. The king's longtime mistress was known to be anything but cherubic. "Something wrong up there?"

"Not at all. It's stunning, in fact." Rosslyn lowered his pale blue gaze to meet Kit's. "Mind if I look around?"

"As you wish."

Kit lit a second candle and handed it to his friend, then followed closely behind. Not that he had anything to hide. But the last of his men had just left, and he always checked everything one final time before leaving himself.

During the past few days he'd been over every inch of the

apartments time and again. Nothing seemed out of place. The materials were up to standard, and there was no sign of sabotage, fire or otherwise. Apart from some understandable grumbling when Kit kept them long hours, no one on the job seemed unhappy. No one had sighted Harold Washburn, either.

Apparently the man hadn't set the fire at Whitehall—or, at the very least, he'd heeded Kit's warning and was keeping clear now.

"Very nice." In the master bedchamber, the young earl nodded at a carved mantelpiece. "Gibbons's work, I presume?"

"Yes."

His walking stick tapped as he continued his rambling inspection. "I suppose a Deputy Surveyor ought to insist on the best."

Kit grunted. "I haven't won the post yet." Trailing him into the dining room, Kit watched the long tails of Rosslyn's lavender surcoat flap behind him. "Anyhow, it's only an interim goal. I won't be satisfied until the Surveyor General post is mine."

His friend turned to face him. "I'll alert Mr. Wren that you're angling to take his place."

"*Sir* Christopher Wren," Kit reminded him. "But I doubt he'll find that a revelation."

Rosslyn waved an elegant hand. "I was jesting. Can you not take a jest?"

"Sorry. I suppose I'm a bit serious these days."

"Understandable, my friend." Rosslyn smiled. "Well, I expect I had better get back to court. Excellent job here, Martyn." Still tapping, he retraced his steps to the entrance. "Excellent job, indeed."

As the fellow walked out, Kit was only half surprised to see Rose's mother walk in. "Lady Trentingham. I didn't know you'd come to Hampton Court."

"Good evening, Kit." She watched Rosslyn's retreating back, then turned to Kit in a swish of yellow skirts. "A friend of yours, is he?"

"An old schoolfellow. Now my rival for the post I'm seeking."

"Lord Rosslyn doesn't seem to be working very hard to best you. From what I've seen, he spends all his time at court."

Kit shrugged. "An earl doesn't have to prove himself the way a common man does." He could be bitter about that, but he'd long ago decided not to waste his time raging over life's inequities. Better to spend one's energies overcoming them. "How did you get in here?" he asked. "The only way is through the privy gardens."

He hadn't thought to ask the same of Rosslyn.

Her brown eyes lit with intrigue. "I had the most lovely conversation with the guard at the gate. It seems he is lonely and desirous of a wife. Since by all appearances he's a perfectly nice young man, I promised to send Rose's maid Harriet over to meet him after I complete my business here. Lovely girl, Harriet."

"I'm sure she is." The privy garden was supposed to be private to the king. Kit wondered if he should alert King Charles that his guard was so easily bribed. "And what is your business?"

"Oh, I just wanted to see how you were faring. My husband, naturally, is anxious for you to get back to work on his greenhouse."

"Naturally."

"So how *are* you faring?"

"Without my presence here the project has fallen slightly behind schedule, but not so far that the time cannot be made up." The bonuses he'd promised would ensure it. "Everything seems to be in order."

"Seems?"

He rubbed the back of his neck. "This nagging voice in my head keeps insisting something is wrong." Something he was missing. No matter that his countless inspections proved other-wise, he couldn't shake the feeling that he should reject what was on the surface.

"Hmm. And with Rose?"

He would never get used to the countess's abrupt changes of subject. "Rose?"

"Are you making progress there?" Her tone made it clear she thought not.

He felt his face reddening as he recalled the excruciating scene in the orangery. He'd made progress, all right. "I'm working on it."

"Such a shame your work has kept you so occupied."

"Yes. Well..." Perhaps it was time to clarify this point. "Architecture is my life, Lady Trentingham. Though I hope to make Rose my life, too, she will always have to share my attention with my work."

"I wouldn't want to see her wed an idle fool...too much attention can be as detrimental as too little. But I hope you wouldn't ignore her, either."

"Never." Small chance of *that*. Rose Ashcroft was the type of woman no man could ignore.

"I'm glad of it." Her eyes scanning the room, the countess tapped her fan against her chin. "I've been thinking about my Rose. I do believe she's the most romantic of all my daughters."

"Romantic?"

"Indeed. Violet, you may not know, is quite pragmatic and logical. And Lily, bless her heart, is straightforward as they come. Love, for Lily, either is or isn't...though if a being is alive, she's likely to place it in the former category." She smiled, the soft smile of a doting mother. "But Rose..."

"You're saying a bit more"—Kit swallowed—"romancing is in order?" What might that entail? Flowers? Sonnets? He'd had never had much room in his life for romance.

"It would certainly not be amiss."

"I see. Well." He would have to think more on this tomorrow, after he'd satisfied himself that the Cleveland project was flawless. "My lady, I'm afraid I have much to do..."

"Oh, I've no doubt of that. Given that my daughter has already received several proposals this evening—"

"*What?*" Kit felt as though a bucket of ice water had been dumped over his head. "B-but—proposals?"

Lady Trentingham smiled. "I'm glad you grasp the urgency of the situation."

"Has she...?"

"Accepted? Heavens, no. But the Duke of Bridgewater has only just made an appearance."

A rushing sound filled Kit's ears as he tucked his sketch of Rose into the building's plans and hastily rolled them up together. "I believe I'm finished for the moment." He turned to Lady Trentingham without a trace of irony. "May I escort you back to court?"

The twinkle in her eye revealed amusement at his sudden change of plans. Clearly this was a woman who enjoyed watching her puppets dance at the ends of her strings.

"I'd be delighted," she said, taking his arm. "But might we first make a tiny detour to my apartments?"

Kit gritted his teeth. "By all means, my lady." Despite his feeling of urgency, courtesy forbade refusing such a reasonable request.

Her smile widened, telling him she saw through his polite facade. "It won't take a moment to fetch Harriet and see that she meets the charming guard at the gate."

At least she wielded her powers in the name of love rather than villainy.

FORTY-EIGHT

*A*S THE EVENING wore on, Rose received a brooch in
the shape of a bow set with precious gemstones, a locket
filled with a hopeful suitor's hair, another bouquet of flowers,
and two more proposals. Every bachelor at court, it seemed, had
proposed.

Except the duke.

There were a few new gentlemen in attendance here at the
palace, but they seemed ruder than those Rose had met at Windsor. One of them hadn't even asked her name before attempting
to maneuver her behind the tall, exquisitely painted screen that
set off one end of the Presence Chamber, serving the same
purpose as the curtains in Windsor's drawing room.

She hadn't allowed any kissing tonight, recoiling from the
prospect of intimacy with these boorish men. Perversely, just as *I
Sonetti* had mended her relations with the court ladies, it had
gone and spoiled them with the gentlemen. Rose wished heartily
that she'd never laid eyes on the troublesome book.

All her life she'd yearned to come to King Charles's dazzling
court, but now that the shine had worn off the place, it was
beginning to seem rather bleak. When she ought to be dancing
and flirting and falling in love, instead she found herself

dodging offensive proposals and seeking refuge in the company of the king's notorious mistresses.

"My lady." Another suitor bowed before her. "I don't believe I've had the pleasure of an introduction."

"Lady Rose Ashcroft," she said flatly, barely stifling a yawn. Her flirtatious nature seemed to have deserted her somewhere around the fourth or fifth proposal.

He swept her an even deeper bow. "The Earl of Featherstone-haugh. Would you honor me with a dance?"

He'd said the magic words. "I'd be delighted." A pity to saddle herself with such a preposterously long name—which she knew from an item in the *Gazette* was spelled Featherstonehaugh though it was pronounced Fanshaw—but she'd long since given up searching for perfection. At least he was polite enough to ask for a dance. And he hadn't mentioned the blasted book. Perhaps, being a newcomer, he hadn't heard about it.

She downed the rest of her wine, handed her cup to a serving maid, then let him lead her onto the dance floor. The musicians were playing a lively country tune, and the accompanying dance was performed in two lines, not affording much chance for conversation. Instead, she sized up the earl as they progressed.

He was a certified fop. His wide, powdered periwig draped in curls down his fuchsia brocade-clad chest. Long rows of fancy solid gold buttons adorned both his coat and waistcoat, and the coat flapped open with the movements of the dance, flashing a blinding yellow satin lining. In addition, there was enough white lace spilling from his cravat and cuffs to choke a horse.

His outfit, she decided, would look much better on the Duchess Mazarin.

But if he turned out to be a good kisser, perhaps she could teach him how to dress more to her liking. It would no doubt prove easier than teaching a good dresser how to kiss. Feeling a bit more cheerful, she gave him a wide smile as the dance ended.

Evidently he took her smile the wrong way, because the next thing she knew, she found herself propelled behind the screen. Heaving an internal sigh, she tilted her face up for his kiss. As long as he had her here, she might as well get the assessment over with. No sense mentally ordering new clothes if the fellow was lacking in other areas.

But he surprised her by lowering himself to a cushioned stool and pulling her onto his lap.

She let out a yelp of surprise. "What are you doing?"

One arm curled around her waist while his other hand reached for the hem of her skirts. He tilted her head back and fastened his mouth to hers.

"Let go!" she cried, wrenching her lips free. "What the deuce do you think you're doing?"

His fingers began inching their way up the front of her bodice. "Engraving Ten, my lady. Haven't you been dying to try it?"

With an outraged gasp, she twisted off his lap and whirled to slap him on the face.

As her hand connected with his cheek, the priceless screen crashed to the floor, the musicians stopped playing, and Gabriel arrived like an avenging angel. "Are you all right?"

"I'm fine," she spat out, rubbing her palm where it hurt. "He, however, is a rutting lout!"

The duke nodded, then turned to Lord Featherstonehaugh, murder in his eyes. "Choose your second," he grated through gritted teeth, his fingers working to untie the peace strings that prevented his sword from being drawn.

The entire court had gone quiet, frozen as though in a tableau. The Earl of Featherstonehaugh remained silent. All that could be heard was Gabriel's harsh breathing and the scraping sound of his rapier as he pulled it from its scabbard.

"Outside," he demanded. "Now."

And then everyone seemed to be moving.

Stunned, Rose just stood there a moment as it slowly sank in that the duke had challenged the earl to a duel.

Over her.

Ignoring all etiquette, Gabriel hadn't given him till morning. Instead he dragged the earl from the building and into

Clock Court. The courtiers followed en masse. Rose snapped from her trance and hurried after them, fearing for the duke's life.

She heard the clash of swords before she reached the court-yard, but the cheers and catcalls from the crowd of onlookers were even louder. The gentlemen's rapiers flashed in the torch-light. Her heart pounding, she wedged herself into the circle, wincing at each ringing bash.

It wasn't long, however, before her concern for Gabriel turned to terror on behalf of the poor earl.

The fellow obviously paid more attention to his wardrobe than his swordsmanship, because it rapidly became clear that the duke was but toying with him. A flick here, and a few of his precious buttons went missing from his coat. A swipe there, and half his lace cravat fluttered to the stones. Lord Featherstone-haugh waved his own sword so ineffectively that Rose reckoned even she could do better.

Raging anger was evident in Gabriel's eyes, in his clenched jaw, in his carefully controlled movements. Panic clutched at Rose's throat. The rutting lout had acted abominably, but she had no wish to witness his death, most especially if it happened in defense of *her*.

"Gabriel!" she shouted, taking a step forward and then another when he paid her no attention. "Don't kill him! Gabriel, don't—"

"Hush," came a voice from the crowd. Warm arms encircled her from behind, pulling her back into the circle as a familiar scent of frankincense and myrrh enveloped her.

"Don't distract him," Kit said quietly in her ear. "Even an expert can falter if his attention is elsewhere. You don't want to be responsible for the duke's death."

"I don't want to be responsible for the earl's murder, either!"

"Hush." One of his hands came up and tucked an errant curl behind her ear. "This cannot be more than a tiff. It won't come to that."

"But what if it does?" she wailed, trying to struggle free.

His arms tightened. "Just watch. The duke is all but finished."

And so he was. He'd run out of buttons to flick off the other man's coat, and although not a drop of blood had been spilled, the brocade itself was in shreds. In addition to being half naked, the earl was thoroughly humiliated.

Disgust marring his fine features, Gabriel knocked the sword from Lord Featherstonehaugh's hand with an easy twist of his wrist. Then, while the earl was busy gasping, he reached out and nicked him under his chin—a cut so tiny only a single bead of red leaked out.

"First blood," he claimed as he shoved his rapier back into its scabbard. "You lose. Touch her again and your head will come off next time."

It was over. Kit's arms dropped from around Rose as babbling broke out among the assembled courtiers. She couldn't tell whether the chatter signaled approval or disappointment. Maybe it was a bit of both.

Louise de Kéroualle turned to her, her eyes wide and sparkling. "Nothing this exciting has happened in weeks!"

Rose suspected the duchess was happy to see everyone's attention focused on something other than her embarrassing black eye, which had made her the butt of much nasty teasing. But better everyone look to Louise for their entertainment. Now that the spectacle had ended, more than one gaze shifted Rose's way. Ladies whispered behind their fans. She couldn't fathom what they were saying, but she wanted no part of this.

She turned to Kit. "Take me away from here."

"Lady Rose!" Courtiers dispersed as Gabriel strode toward her. "I'd like a word with you, if you will."

Kit shrugged, retrieved a roll of linen off the ground, and moved a few yards away.

Rose faced the duke. "Yes?"

"In private."

Still shaky, she let him take her arm and lead her from the courtyard, under Henry VIII's clock tower, and into Base Court.

Her high heels wobbled on the cobblestone paths that criss-crossed the grass, but Gabriel seemed happy enough to steady her. In the galleries, a few lights flickered from apartments where courtiers had sought their lodgings, but the night was still young, and most everyone was returning to the Presence Chamber.

"My dear Rose," Gabriel started.

"A duel!" she interrupted loudly, the words echoing in the deserted courtyard. "I cannot believe you challenged that fool to a duel."

He hurried her into one of the galleries. The corridor was breezy, but the torches along the walls gave off heat as well as light. "I will never let anyone impugn your honor," he said gallantly.

"I appreciate your sentiments, your grace, but a duel!" The red tiles here were smoother than the cobblestones beneath her feet. She felt steadier, more in control. True, part of her had been secretly thrilled to see a man—a duke, no less!—leap to defend her honor. But a larger part had been terrified. "Not only is dueling barbaric, it's illegal."

As they walked past a diamond-paned window, the glass reflected his elegant shrug. "I don't see anyone rushing to arrest me. Featherstonehaugh deserved it."

"That may be, but I was taking care of him myself."

"You shouldn't have to take care of yourself." They heard the low murmur of people talking in an apartment, and he waited until they'd strolled past it. "Rose, I want to take care of you. I wish to make you my wife."

She stopped walking, the corridor suddenly silent without the rhythmic clicks of her heels. "Are you asking me to marry you?"

He turned to face her and crowded her against the brick wall. It felt rough and cool behind her back. "Yes," he said. "I'm not very good at this, am I? I'm better with actions than words."

He was a duke, and surely that was good enough. *A duke,* asking for her hand. He tilted his head and moved nearer, brushing her lips with his. His technique really wasn't that bad. He didn't smell of frankincense and myrrh, but he didn't smell unpleasant, either. And he was a duke.

"Rose, will you marry me?"

Of course she would. She wasn't brainless. She opened her mouth. This was what she'd been waiting for. "No."

She blinked and felt as surprised as Gabriel looked. "I'm sorry," she added quickly. Out of habit she almost added that her heart belonged to another, but surely that wasn't true. "I must go," she said instead.

Avoiding his stunned gaze, she sidestepped free and ran down the gallery toward her lodging. The heavy old door creaked when she opened it. She slammed it shut and leaned back against the thick wood, a hand to her trembling mouth.

How could she have refused him? Had she not been waiting for this proposal? Had she not come here to Hampton Court hoping to receive it?

How could she have turned down a duke? And a perfectly nice one, at that! One who had fought and risked his life for her honor.

Not that his life had ever really been at risk, given the earl's complete incompetence—but still!

There was nothing for it. She would have to seek him out and change her answer to *yes*.

But not tonight. She couldn't face him tonight. Furious at herself, she straightened and wandered toward the bedchamber. "Mum? Harriet?"

It was empty. "Harriet, where are you?"

No one was here. Not her mother, not her maid, not her mother's maid, either. She threw herself facedown on the bed.

The boned bodice of her gown poked into her, so after a moment she rolled over. But there were whalebone splints in the back, too, not to mention the bulky lacing that ran down her spine.

Where on earth was Harriet? Rose cursed the maid along with whatever fool was responsible for dictating court fashion.

She'd claimed to be able to care for herself—well, she could slap an impudent courtier, all right, but she couldn't manage to undress herself when her blasted gown was laced down the back.

The apartment was too silent. She sat up and sighed. She didn't really want to undress—she was far too restless for sleep.

She decided to talk a walk—a calming walk, out in Hampton Court's immense public gardens—and steel herself to change her answer to Gabriel tomorrow.

She'd bet the Duchess of Bridgewater would never find herself without a maid.

FORTY-NINE

*N*OTEBOOK, RULER, and rope in hand, Kit left his assigned lodging in Master Carpenter's Court and made his winding way through the palace.

Base Court smelled of cut grass, and it was quiet after the excitement of the duel earlier. Or at least it should have been quiet. As Kit approached the covered passage known as the Great Chamber, an odd pounding reached his ears. "Open up!" a female voice shrieked. A voice that reminded him of Rose, except she was far less shrill.

But he was doing his utmost not to think of Rose...and how she'd nearly gone out of her mind at the sight of Bridgewater in danger. And how she'd let the duke whisk her away for a private word.

And how she'd probably already accepted his proposal.

She would be a duchess, and Kit would be shattered and alone.

Crossing in front of the Great Chamber in a bitter haze, he glanced up see who was making such a racket, then stopped and stared. The shrill voice *did* belong to Rose. There she stood, banging her fists on the huge oak doors that led to the bridge over Hampton Court's moat.

"Rose!" The shout was ripped from his throat as his legs carried him forward of their own accord. "Wherever do you think you're going?"

She turned, her hands clenched at her sides. "To the gardens, if a guard will ever be pleased to let me out. I wish to take a peaceful, solitary walk."

He stepped deeper into the musty passageway. Her eyes shone with a luster that matched the pearls on her fancy gown—and with a touch of hysteria that brought Kit up short. "It's not wise to go out there alone at night," he ventured. "The privy garden would be safer."

What was wrong with her? Shouldn't she be rapturous and triumphant over her betrothal? For that matter, shouldn't she be with her betrothed?

Those lustrous eyes flashed. "I cannot enter the privy garden. Don't you know the meaning of the word *privy*?"

"I can get you inside. I'm on my way there now."

"To do what?" she asked, with a pointed glance at the assortment of items he carried. She was obviously struggling to rein in her temper. Her cheeks glowed red, and her breaths came out in little puffs.

"My project is there. The new apartments for the king's old mistress, her grace the Duchess of Cleveland." He sighed as his other source of vexation—besides Rose, that was—came rushing back. "I wish to check…everything."

A trickle of water dripped from somewhere overhead. "Have you found something amiss?" she asked.

"Not yet. But I've a feeling in my bones that something's wrong. I intend to measure every square foot of the building." It was a fool's task, he feared, as well as a long, tedious one. But he wouldn't rest easy until he'd completed it. And he needed to do it when no one was watching, trying to distract him—or worse, covering something up. "Come along. Their Majesties are at court, so the garden will afford you the solitude you're seeking."

She seized a lantern off the ground. "I shall help you measure."

In the torchlight that danced on the old brick walls, he gazed at her. "Why?"

Her dark eyes grew hooded. "I have nothing else to do. I've no wish to return to court and I'm not ready to retire. And your task would go faster with help, would it not? I've been called selfish, but I like to think I would be there to help a friend."

He wondered about some of her brave speech, not least why she was avoiding court. But he focused on her last sentence. "Are we friends, Rose?"

"Yes," she said firmly, and then more uncertainly, "I hope so."

A part of him—the part that didn't know when to give up—still hoped for more than her friendship. But it would do for now. "Come on, then," he said. "Lead the way."

She raised the lantern and started across Base Court, teetering a little on the cobblestones in her fashionable high heels. Such a lady, his Rose.

"Does this feel like a cloister to you?" he found himself asking.

She glanced around as they walked. "Maybe. A little. Why?"

"I keep thinking Cardinal Wolsey built this place like an Italian cardinal's palace. Something about the feel of it, the layout. Henry the Eighth would have ruined it when he rebuilt, but underneath…"

They crossed Clock Court, Rose's measured steps matching the cadence of King Henry's great astronomical timepiece. "Are there records of the construction?"

"None of which I'm aware." He sighed. "Someday I hope to see an actual cardinal's palace. To journey to Italy and stand in the middle of one and see if I'm right, if it feels the same as this."

He waited for her to say she'd like to come with him, but she didn't. Her skirts swished against the cobblestones, and as they passed the fountain with its paltry gurgle of water, hoots of revelers filtered down from the Presence Chamber.

"The court seems in high spirits following the duel," he remarked.

"I'm sure they are," she replied dryly. "Louise de Kéroualle said it was the most exciting thing that's happened in weeks."

"Why aren't you with them?"

She clamped her lips and walked faster, entering Cloister Green Court.

And there she stopped. "Listen. Do you hear the king's dogs?" She cocked her pretty head. "The sound is coming from that wing next to the queen's. How odd—King Charles usually keeps his spaniels with him at court."

He suppressed a smile. "You're not hearing the king's dogs."

"I am. Can't you hear them yipping?"

"It's not dogs you hear, Rose. It's people."

"People? Doing what?" Her eyes narrowed and then widened. "You cannot mean..."

Though his face felt hot, he couldn't hold back a grin. "Yes."

"Oh." She froze, her mouth open in a little O shape. Until, in a complete reversal of mood, she burst into giggles.

Kit laughed along with her, from surprise as much as mirth. He'd expected shock and embarrassment or even offense. But perhaps after everything she'd seen and experienced at court, Rose was no longer so easily shaken.

"It's a couple in the marriage bed?" she gasped, wiping teary eyes. Trust Rose to say out loud what he'd made a point of politely skirting. "Gemini, do people really sound like that?"

Though he doubted the couple's bed was a *marriage* bed, he wouldn't burst Rose's innocent bubble. "Evidently some people do," he said, struggling to maintain his dignity.

As the yipping went on, he grabbed her hand and hurried her across the courtyard. Her giggles filled the open space, mad giggles, giggles that warmed his heart. "I-I'm n-never g-going to s-sound like that," she choked out.

He was laughing hard enough to make his stomach hurt. He'd never in his life laughed so much as he had since he met Rose. It felt good. Her hand in his felt good, too.

"With anyone else," she chortled as the yipping sounds faded out of range, "I'd have pretended I didn't hear that."

"You thought it was dogs," he reminded her. "You couldn't have pretended."

"Well, a courtier wouldn't have pointed out my mistake."

Kit's laughter died off into the night.

"I didn't intend that in a negative fashion," she said quickly in the sudden quiet. "I'm very glad we're friends."

Kit was glad, too, but he feared that was all they'd ever be.

After a spell of silence, she drew a deep, audible breath. "I feel small here," she whispered. "In the dark with the towering buildings all around looming over us."

He squeezed her hand. "I know what you mean."

"Look at all the different shaped chimneys silhouetted against the sky." She gazed up for a quiet moment, then darted a glance at him. "It must be wonderful to create something so monumental."

She knew. She knew how he felt. "I'm only creating one building," he reminded her.

"Still, it will be part of this whole." Her sigh sounded wistful, calmer than before their bout of laughter. "Show me what you're creating."

He led her out the back of the palace, nodding to the sleepy guard. Before them, lime trees stretched into the dark distance, and moonlight reflected off Charles's Long Water, a manmade canal inspired by one at Versailles. Kit drew Rose to the right, where at the corner of the palace another guarded gate marked the entrance to the privy gardens.

"Harriet!" Rose exclaimed. "Whatever are you doing here?"

In the torchlight from the gatehouse, her maid blushed. "Just passing the time, milady. Your mother introduced me to Walter." Harriet motioned to the guard. "You haven't need of me, have you?"

"I certainly do...not." Rose shook her head. "No, not right now."

When Kit pushed open the gate, Walter cleared his throat. "The garden is for the king's pleasure only, I'm afraid."

"I'm here to work," Kit said succinctly.

"At this hour?" The man looked between them. "With her? Pardon me, Mr. Martyn, but it doesn't seem as though—"

"She's volunteered to assist me." Kit raised his supplies.

"Ah, let them go," Harriet cajoled with much more familiarity than Kit expected from one so newly introduced. "Trust me, Walter, my mistress won't be dallying with the likes of him."

That perspective, unfortunately, Kit did expect. As he ushered Rose through the opened gate, the fragile closeness he'd felt in Cloister Green Court disappeared like sawdust in the wind.

"Trust my mother to find a suitor for my maid," Rose grumbled. "She thinks she can match every last soul with his or her perfect mate."

Kit shut the gate. "Do her introductions often result in marriages?"

"Usually, which is annoying as anything."

He hid a smile. "Not to the happy couple, I'll wager."

"Hmm, I don't think I shall take that bet." She hurried toward the new construction. "Show me what you're building."

He walked her through the new apartments, the main rooms and all the bedchambers for Barbara Palmer, the Duchess of Cleveland, and the five children she'd borne for King Charles. Most of them were all but grown already, but the king had granted them titles, and he played a large part in their lives.

"The chambers are bare yet," he told Rose, "but they will be rich. King Charles is sparing no expense."

"Isn't her grace living in Paris now?"

"Yes, but he knows she'll be back."

"I understand he doesn't stay at Hampton Court often. Word has it he prefers Windsor and Whitehall."

"All the more reason to give her a home here," he said, lifting a brow. It was common knowledge that the king was long finished with his old mistress, though he valued their offspring and would support her so long as she should live.

After the tour, Rose held the lantern for Kit while he measured and made notes.

"What are you looking for?" she asked.

"Something off. Not to plan. I won't be able to tell here, but I'll take the notes back to my quarters and review every inch." Her lovely rose scent was distracting. "What did you mean," he asked, "when you said earlier tonight that you didn't want to be responsible for the earl's death?"

Though he was busy measuring, he heard her tight swallow. "The duke wouldn't have been fighting the earl if not for me."

"You?" Jotting a note, he looked up. "The duel was over *you*?"

"Yes." Her face looked pale in the lamplight. "The earl took… liberties that were out of line."

"Liberties?" Kit looked away, stretching his rope to make another measurement.

"With my person. He was trying to…"

She didn't need to say more. Fearing the heat of his temper, Kit counted the knots spaced at one-foot intervals, added swiftly in his head, and recorded the sum before allowing himself to speak. "Bridgewater should have killed him," he said quietly.

"Not you, too," Rose grumbled, yanking the rope from him and moving to another beam. "Men will be men."

Following her, he took one end of the rope and pulled it taut. "Not around you, they won't," he said with an aggressive streak.

"Especially around me. The whole court thinks me a loose woman, merely because I had that wretched book and asked a *few* gentlemen to kiss me—"

"A few?"

"Only the unmarried ones," she said, managing to sound indignant.

The rushing sound returned to his ears. "*All* the unmarried ones?"

"There aren't that many. And heavens, Kit, they were just kisses."

Kit darted her a glance. Her too-defensive tone told him she was regretting those kisses. Shaking his head, he thought, much as it pained him to admit it… "I'm thankful the duke came to your rescue."

"He didn't rescue me—I rescued myself quite well, thank you. I believe the earl has my handprint on his face to prove it." He'd finished counting the knots, so she dropped her end of the rope. "The duel is the result of a misplaced sense of possession. The duke wishes to marry me."

In the midst of writing another measurement, Kit froze. Here was the truth he'd been dreading. "Bridgewater proposed, then?"

"Yes." Rose adjusted the lantern for a moment that felt like the longest of Kit's life. "I refused him."

His heart reawakened in his chest. "You seem to make that a habit," he managed to say coolly, though a chorus of angels had replaced the rushing in his ears.

"I do, don't I?" she said with a sigh.

He wished he knew what that sigh meant.

~

"MY, HARRIET, you've been out here a long time." The maid startled and pulled her lips from the guard's, smoothing down her skirt. "Please forgive me, Lady Trentingham."

Walter's face flamed red in the torchlight. "My lady—"

"I saw nothing." Chrystabel waved a hand. "I'm looking for Rose."

"Oh! Lady Rose is in the privy garden, working with Mr. Martyn." Harriet hurried to open the gate.

"Is she?" With a smile, Chrystabel reached out and shut it. "I'll just let her be, then. I imagine they're doing something important, and I wouldn't want to interrupt."

The news that Kit had managed to get Rose alone—tonight of all nights—lightened her heart. After witnessing the duel, she'd been approached by the duke himself with a complaint over Rose dismissing his suit. Even though he'd drawn his sword for her, he'd pointed out with an affronted sniff.

She'd silently sent up a cheer.

Things were looking up. "Thank you," she said, turning to leave.

"Lady Trentingham?"

She swiveled back. "Yes, Harriet?"

"I shall report to your lodging forthwith."

"Take your time, dear. I expect Rose will be busy for a spell. And you and Walter have much to discuss."

The maid exchanged a puzzled look with the guard. "Discuss?"

"Will he leave the king's employ and take a post at Trentingham, or will you find a position here? A major decision, don't you think?"

Chrystabel imagined both their mouths falling open as she made her way back into the palace. But she was certain their relationship would come to that, soon if not this night.

Her matchmaking instincts were all but infallible.

FIFTY

*B*Y THE TIME Kit made the last measurement, Rose had long since slipped off her high heels. Carrying them, she followed him out of the building to find the sun was peeking over the horizon, gilding the privy garden in golden morning light.

"*Parterre a l'anglais,*" she murmured, mentally comparing the area to her father's exquisitely planted gardens.

Kit shut the door behind them. "*Parterre a* what?"

"Literally it means 'English floor,' but you must imagine it said in a derisive French tone." She grinned at his quick smile, adding, "It refers to the English preference for smooth turf like this, rather than their own intricate figured *parterres*."

Hampton Court's privy garden was divided into simple, plain grass quarters, each with a single statue: Venus and Cleopatra in brass, and Adonis and Apollo in marble. In the center of it all sat Arethusa above a great black marble fountain with only a trickle of water.

"It is rather pathetic," Kit admitted. "I've heard the fountains in Italy gush water."

Rose shifted both her shoes to one hand. "I can see why King

Charles is putting his discarded mistress out here—I imagine he rarely visits this garden himself."

"I'd wager he does," he disagreed. "He needs places all his own, whether beautiful or not. The poor man cannot even dine or dress without people watching."

Rose had never thought of the king as *poor*, but she supposed Kit had a point. Court etiquette could be tedious, she thought through a yawn.

"It's morning," she suddenly realized. "We've been up all night."

"I'm used to it," Kit muttered.

"I'm not. Do you know, I've only stayed up all night once before, and I was with you then, too—the night we deciphered Rand's brother's diary. You're a bad influence," she accused with a weary smile.

"You can sleep today. Heaven knows nothing happens at Hampton Court while the sun shines. For the court, anyway. My crew will be arriving any minute, though; we'd best leave before we're discovered."

He put a hand to her back, guiding her toward the gate, and Rose realized it was the first time he'd touched her since they'd laughed in Cloister Green Court. They'd passed the long hours of the night working and talking. He hadn't tried to kiss her even once.

Perhaps he'd decided to abandon his pursuit of her. Which was a good thing, she told herself firmly. She was grateful to retain his friendship, and it was easier this way, because it would be hard to keep saying no.

But she was unaccountably forlorn at the thought of never kissing him again.

Walter was no longer at the gate; an older guard nodded as they passed though. No sooner had they rounded the corner of the building than they heard men's voices and the stomp of boots.

"The workmen." Kit grabbed her hand. "We cannot let them

see us." With that, he began running along the perimeter of the palace, pulling her along with him.

She dropped one of her shoes. "Wait!"

"We'll return for it!" he said without slowing.

By the time they rounded another corner and skidded to a stop, they were both huffing and puffing. When he released her hand, she felt a loss. "Safe," he declared with a breathless laugh. "I don't think they saw us."

Her chest was heaving, and she noticed him noticing. "Whyever does it matter?"

Chagrined, he returned his gaze to her face. "If one of them is sabotaging this project, I don't want him to know I'm investigating. They'll all be hard at work in a few minutes. Then we can sneak into the palace."

"Like spies," she said with a smile, wishing he was still touching her.

"Like spies." He grinned, glancing around the extensive public gardens. "In the meantime, I've been hankering to try the maze."

"Not the maze," she said with a groan. "I despise mazes. I always get lost."

"If you know the left-hand rule, it's impossible to get lost."

"How is that?"

"I'll show you. We won't get lost." Apparently noting her skeptical expression, he took her hand again and began walking. "Besides, I reckon I can make it fun to get lost."

Something had changed in the quality of his voice, something that made bubbles start pinging in Rose's stomach. The grass felt cool and springy beneath her stockinged feet. "I missed the gaming again," she realized.

"I'm sorry," he said, not sounding at all sincere.

"It's a favorite recreation of the duke's. I had hoped he would teach me so I could win enough for a new gown."

"Is that so?" Kit's eyes were an unreadable, murky green. "A gown is a mere pittance at the court gaming tables. Word has it the Duchess Mazarin lost ten thousand last week on a single bet."

"Ten thousand *pounds*?"

He nodded. "Pounds."

"That's my whole inheritance!" Perhaps it was just as well that she'd missed the gaming. "I've got better things to do with my money."

"You have big plans for it, then?"

"Unlike my dowry, it's mine. It won't belong to my husband."

He slanted her a glance. "I'm not in need of it. I cannot speak for the duke."

The thought startled her. The truth was, she had no idea whether the duke was in need of funds or not. He dressed richly and had given her diamond earrings, but that didn't necessarily mean anything. For all she knew, he could owe his tailor and jeweler a fortune.

"Well, he won't be getting it," she said.

"I admire your conviction. What do you plan to do with it?"

"Maybe I'll give it to Ellen," she said with a sly smile, "so she and Thomas can move their pawnshop to London."

"Be serious."

"Is this more of the getting-to-know-each-other game?"

They'd come to the entrance of the maze. "Tell me," he said softly.

Her sisters had both nurtured dreams since childhood: Violet wanted to publish a philosophy book, and Lily wished to build and staff a home for stray animals. But in truth, Rose had never made such high-minded plans. She'd only ever hoped to find love and be happy.

She'd just never dreamed that goal would prove so difficult.

"I want to travel," she said. "I wish to see the world."

"Travel can be fascinating, but it can also be tiring and tedious. Does the duke enjoy it?"

She had no idea. In fact, she realized now, she knew little of the duke at all. They'd never had a serious conversation, never shared a confidence, never discussed likes, dislikes, values—or much of anything at all.

But she'd spent hours talking to Kit, about anything and everything. They'd become friends before he ever kissed her. She knew he wanted to travel, to Italy and elsewhere.

"Let's go inside," she said. "I'd have you show me this left-hand rule."

The look he gave her made it clear he knew she was avoiding his question. But he took her remaining shoe and set it down with his own things, then led her inside the tall hedge maze.

"Put your left hand on the wall as we walk," he instructed. "And leave it there. Just follow that left wall without breaking contact, and I guarantee you'll find the center without getting lost. Go on," he urged when she hesitated. "I'll follow you."

Slanting him a wary glance, she did as he said, skimming her left hand along the leaves as she marched through the hornbeam hedges. When they reached a dead end, she turned on him. "It didn't work."

"Keep your hand on the wall," he repeated. "Follow it around."

"It's a dead end."

"I didn't say you'd never come to a dead end. I said you wouldn't get lost." He took her left hand, pressed a slow, warm kiss to the palm, then placed it back against the hedge. "Keep going."

She did, but not before releasing a long, shuddering breath. She could still feel his lips on her palm, even as she slid it along the leaves. Why had he done that?

Had he not given up on her?

The towering hedges made the path shady and intimate. At the second dead end, she turned to him again. "This cannot be the optimum route."

"Of course it isn't." He looked amused. "You'd have to know the pattern of the maze to take the optimum route. But this is a safe route. You won't wander the same way twice, and you'll find the center." He pressed a quick kiss to her lips, so fast and light she wondered if she might have imagined it. "Keep going."

At the third dead end she turned to him once more. "This is a waste of time."

"Of course it's a waste of time. It's a maze—there are few things more frivolous." Smiling, he trailed a finger down her cheek to her chin. A frisson of warmth followed. His thumb grazed her bottom lip. "But there's nothing quite so delightful as wasting time with someone you care for, is there?"

He cared for her. What did that mean, exactly? Too tired to think straight, she held her breath as he leaned close and slowly brushed her mouth with his.

She definitely wasn't imagining this.

Giddy with exhaustion, she wrapped her arms around his neck and pulled him closer. He was right: There was nothing else quite so delightful. Forgetting that she shouldn't encourage him, she sank into the kiss, into the intimate dance that made her head feel dreamy and her stomach flutter with excitement.

"Keep going," he whispered when at last he drew back.

Dizzily she trailed a hand along the cool leaves, the trodden dirt path hard under her stockinged feet. At the next dead end, she felt his hands on her shoulders, turning her into his arms. His fingers cradled her face, and as he lowered his mouth to meet hers, his woodsy scent filled her head.

The morning was chilly, but he was so very warm and solid. As he deepened the kiss, she surrendered all too willingly, leaning into the delicious heat of his body. When he bit down gently on her lower lip, her breath caught.

"Kit," she murmured.

"Hmm?" He kissed both sides of her mouth, where her dimples would be if she were smiling.

"I think..." She was so lightheaded, her thoughts refused to come together. Was it the exhaustion or the kissing? "Let's keep going."

She felt limp, so weak she could barely keep her hand to the hedges as she went along. Another dead end loomed ahead, and this time she turned to him before they even reached it.

He laughed, his smile affecting her nearly as much as his kisses. "I think you're enjoying this maze more than you anticipated." He reached to tap the lip he'd just bitten, traced her mouth, then trailed a finger down her chin to the delicate hollow of her throat. His gaze went a glittery green as he drew circles there.

She shivered and went on her toes to press her lips to his. It was a kiss that held nothing back, that carried all the force of her frustration, her resistance, and her inexplicable need. They were clasped to each other from top to toe, like they were molded together. Her every nerve was on fire at the feel of his muscles pressing up against her softer form.

By the time he broke away, she was gasping for breath, and she couldn't have held her hand to the wall had her life depended on it. He scooped her up in his arms, carried her a short distance to the center of the maze, and deposited her on a bench.

No one had ever carried her before—at least, not since she was a small child. It was beyond romantic. She'd felt safe and cherished enfolded in his arms, and she was sorry the experience hadn't lasted longer.

But she was also sorry there hadn't been more dead ends.

Feeling boneless, she placed her hands on either side of herself for support. The maze's center was an oval, grassy space, a tiny hidden garden with two old trees and the bench between them, nothing more. A secret place that exuded an air of tranquility and the scents of greenery.

Kit stood over her. "Told you we'd find the center."

She leaned back on her palms, blinking up at him. "That always works?"

"Well, not necessarily quite so enjoyably," he said with a grin. "But yes, it always works. From a mathematical standpoint, it must."

She shook her head, then stopped when it made her feel woozy. "I was never all that good at mathematics."

"And I cannot speak anything but English." Stepping back, he leaned casually against one of the trees, looking wide awake and irresistible. "We all have our strengths and our weaknesses. Don't underreckon yourself."

"You don't," she said, knowing it was true.

"I don't what?"

"Underreckon me."

"Of course I don't. I couldn't love a girl if I didn't admire her as well."

That single syllable, *love*, threw her. She was reeling under Kit's onslaught of affectionate actions and words. He quite obviously hadn't given up.

And he admired her.

Did she admire Gabriel? She didn't know. He'd proven himself kind and solicitous and generous, but he'd also kept a pawnbroker's change.

She hadn't slept in more than a day. She was so tired and confused and dizzy. Her knees still shaky, she stood and walked to the other tree, putting the bench between herself and Kit.

She turned away, running her fingers down the trunk, smiling dazedly at the carvings made by others who had found their way to the center. "Look at all the initials," she said quietly. "Hundreds of them. Do you suppose all these people made it here using the left-hand rule?"

His low laugh sounded by her ear, surprising her. "No," he said from right behind her, his voice reawakening that flutter in her middle. "I'm sure most of them were lost for hours, both on their way in and on their way back out."

She smiled, the only reaction she could manage at the moment. Not that it mattered, since she was facing away. "You're fooling."

"Maybe. You're tired."

"Definitely."

She felt his fingers on her face, warm and sure, his lips

brushing the back of her neck, trailing up her nape. She let her head fall back against him, breathing in frankincense and Kit.

"Romance," he muttered under his breath, pulling away.

Or at least she thought she'd heard him mutter. She straightened woozily and turned to face him. "What?"

"Nothing." He pulled his knife from his belt. "Who do you suppose made all these carvings?"

"I'm sure I don't know."

He moved around the tree, examining all the initials. "Do you think the king has left his mark?" He set his knife to the wood and began scratching. "Or his mistresses? Do you expect any two people have been here who fit together as perfect as we?"

She followed him around and stopped, swaying slightly as she stared. He'd engraved *RA* and *CM*, and now he was busy surrounding both with a heart.

Her own heart melted. "Kit," she whispered.

The knife dropped to the dirt as he turned her around to back her against the tree, his mouth on hers for a brief, fierce moment that drove the breath from her lungs.

Then he moved away and left her sagging against the tree, bracing herself on the rough bark to stay upright. "Come back," she said plaintively.

His crooked smile held satisfaction, amusement, and a tinge of exasperation. "No," he said, pushing his hands into his pockets. "Not until you admit you care for me."

"I…" Her senses were still spinning, making it hard to absorb his meaning. "I do care for you. As a friend."

"As more than that."

"But…"

"But nothing." One of his hands reappeared to rest on her cheek, and he pressed a sweet, lingering kiss to her forehead. Then he retreated, looking resolute. "Until you admit the truth, Rose, that's the last kiss you'll get from me."

She looked away and pushed an errant curl behind her ear, feeling like she should say something but not knowing what.

She'd made a complete fool of herself.

"A gift from the duke?" he asked, gesturing to her diamond earring.

She swallowed and nodded, not trusting herself to speak.

"I'm not giving up without a fight," he said, his voice husky and shaky. "We're too good together. I want to be with you."

Heaven help her, she wanted to be with him, too, and not just because his mere proximity made her forget her own name. Of all the young men she'd ever met, he was the only one who appreciated her for more than her beauty—who valued her intelligence, who was awed by her talent with languages. She wanted him more than she could remember ever wanting anything.

But in the end, she said nothing, because a duke had offered for her hand. And risked his life defending her honor.

How could she accept an architect over a duke?

She felt the headache coming on. "I think we'd best go back."

He scooped his knife off the ground and slid it back into its belt sheath.

She rubbed her temples. "How do we get out? The right-hand rule?"

Though his gaze still glinted with intensity, one corner of his mouth quirked. "How about the rule of knowing the way you came in?"

"How many times have you been in this maze?"

"Just the once. But it's a pattern. Geometry."

She nodded slowly. "You're good at geometry."

"You'll find I'm good at a lot of things." He wasn't smiling now. She searched his eyes, wondering what he meant, but he quickly turned away. "Follow me."

He led her out without one misstep.

Without running into one dead end.

Without any more kisses.

FIFTY-ONE

*L*ATER THAT DAY, Kit was in the midst of a calculation when a knock interrupted.

"One minute," he called, pausing to scribble down a number.

He rose and stretched for a brief moment, then padded across his small lodging to open the door. "Lady Trentingham." He blinked.

How had she found him? The courtiers weren't lodged near Master Carpenter's Court.

"May I come in?"

"Of course," he said, suddenly aware of his state of half-dress: no shoes, no stockings, no coat, no cravat. Just breeches and a shirt, the latter unlaced at the neck and the sleeves rolled up to his elbows. He began turning them down.

"No need to do that for me," she assured him as she stepped inside. "I've seen arms and feet before." Her warm brown eyes twinkled with humor.

He shrugged and waved her toward one of the two chairs that flanked the spartan room's small table, taking the other for himself. "If this is about me keeping Rose out all night, I assure you—"

"It isn't. I trust you, Kit." The countess sat, fluffing her skirts. "How went the romancing?"

He rolled his eyes, a habit he seemed to have picked up from Rose. "I carried her to the center of the maze. And I carved our initials into a tree trunk. The mere act had me choking back laughter, but she loved it."

"Excellent. You must do some more of that."

He wasn't sure he could come up with anything more. "I'm a very straightforward sort of fellow, my lady. I wasn't raised here at court. I'm no good at gallant gestures."

She glanced at the carefully drawn plans he'd spread on the table. "You seem creative enough to me. I'm sure if you put your mind to it, you'll do just fine."

Designing buildings wasn't creative—it was logical, mathematical. Certain requirements had to be met, certain loads had to be supported, certain shapes were inherently beautiful.

But he'd learned by now there was no arguing with Lady Trentingham. "I'll try," he told her.

"Excellent." She tapped a finger against her chin. "The fact that Rose refused the duke's proposal after he dueled on her behalf—I take that as a very good sign."

"The duel…" He rubbed the back of his neck. "I realize it's not my place to say this, my lady, but matters at court seem to be getting rather out of hand. I fear it might be best if you took Rose and left—as soon as possible."

"We're leaving tomorrow. Her friend Judith is marrying later this week, and she'd never forgive us if we missed her wedding."

"No, I mean you should leave today. Before…" Hoping Rose would forgive him, he plunged on. "Are you aware that your daughter was recently in possession of a book? A very—"

"*I Sonetti?*" she interrupted.

He gasped. "She shared the book with you?"

The countess's lips quirked. "Of course she didn't share it. But the court talks of little else. I'm not deaf, you know."

"And you aren't…angry?" He kept his expression carefully

blank, wondering if she'd learned how her daughter had come by the book.

Lady Trentingham sighed. "I'm hardly thrilled about the effect on her reputation."

He nodded his agreement. "Then you're aware of the danger. It seems that people—men—have decided Rose is...that she's..."

"Wild? A wanton?"

"And worse," he snapped. He didn't want to think of Rose like that. And he knew it wasn't remotely true.

"I'm well aware." The countess shook her head mournfully. "It's unfortunate, and certainly not in my plans. But she more than held her own against the unsavory Featherstonehaugh last night—besides which, I have no intention of allowing her to get into such a vulnerable position again."

"You feel you can ensure her safety?"

"I appreciate your concern, Kit. But never doubt that I'm watching over her. If you wish to help," she continued archly, "the best thing you can do is get on with those gallant gestures. Once you've secured her hand, she and I will leave court once and for all."

Kit's hand closed around the bit of brick in his pocket. "Take her home," he begged. "As soon as I've finished my inspection here, I'll come straight to Trentingham. Without these distractions, I'll be able to concentrate my efforts on the, um, romancing."

"Excellent. But we'll leave tomorrow. Rose would never forgive me if she missed the masked ball. Even now, she's wearing her fingers to nubs sewing blooms on a gown."

"Blooms?"

"Her costume. She's going as a flower arrangement."

Despite his anxiety, he smiled. It was so Rose. "I thought she would be sleeping."

"She did, for a while. But then she raided the palace's gardens and set both our maids to work. The three of them are stitching madly."

He sighed, seeing her mind was made up. "What are you going as?"

"A mother. I'll watch her, Kit."

"You do that," he said.

But he would watch her, too.

FIFTY-TWO

*E*VERYTHING LOOKED so beautiful!

The masked ball was held in the great hall rather than the Presence Chamber, and instead of candelabra and oil lamps, the huge room was lit by liveried yeomen holding tall, flaming torches. Overhead, the gold stars on the painted hammerbeam ceiling winked on their field of bright blue.

Dancers twirled in the blazing light. King Arthur was paired with a glittery-winged butterfly, and Robin Hood danced with Aphrodite. An angel and a devil were flirting rather madly, and Zeus had his arm around Anne Boleyn.

Decked out in a gown covered neckline to hemline with fresh flowers, Rose watched from a corner, drinking in the splendor and trying to puzzle out everyone's identities. All the faces were covered by full or half masks, but a few courtiers weren't difficult to spot.

Beneath Caesar's crown of laurel leaves, his half mask failed to cover King Charles's mustache, and as the tallest man in the room, the monarch's height would have given him away regardless.

The Duchess Mazarin had come as a shepherdess, and her boy Mustapha was her little black sheep. Apparently shepherdesses wore no stays of any sort, because Hortense's ample bosom moved against the thin fabric of her peasant blouse every time she laughed—which was often.

Rose was trying her best not to stare.

Other ladies were skimpily garbed as well. A tavern wench's décolletage peeked from her low, frilled bodice. A tipsy doxy flitted about in dishabille. A Greek goddess's robes couldn't seem to stay fastened—

"Enjoying yourself?" someone asked, and Rose turned to see Nell Gwyn. Since she was the smallest woman in the chamber, her identity wasn't in doubt. Her half mask of black matched her lovely black gown. But it was, after all, just an ordinary black gown, much like the one she'd made fun of Louise de Kéroualle wearing yesterday.

Rose cocked her head. "Who are you supposed to be?"

"I'm in mourning," Nell said gaily, "for poor Louise's lost hopes."

Rose laughed and looked for Louise. There she was, as a haughty Cleopatra. But Caesar, surrounded as usual by spaniels and drooling over the buxom shepherdess, seemed distinctly uninterested.

Lost hopes, indeed.

"What a clever costume," Nell said. "I don't believe anyone has ever before come as a flower arrangement." She leaned closer to Rose. "You smell delicious."

Pleased, Rose smiled beneath her mask. "You know who I am?"

"I know who everyone is," Nell boasted. "Except him." She gestured toward a gentleman standing before one of the massive gold- and silver-embroidered tapestries that covered the walls. "Handsome as sin, isn't he?"

Following Nell's gaze, Rose spotted a pirate. His breeches were tighter than the current fashion—skintight, as a matter of fact—hinting at long, muscular legs. His full white shirt was unlaced at the throat, revealing a little triangle of skin sprinkled with crisp black hair.

"Handsome, indeed." Rose wondered if he was a good kisser. "When do the masks come off?"

"Midnight," Nell said with a tinkling laugh, apparently divining Rose's thoughts. "But I've arranged a surprise first. It should be jolly fun. In the meantime"—she lifted her black skirts—"I'm going to meet that pirate."

As Rose watched her dance off, a medieval knight arrived bearing a goblet full of warm, spiced wine. He bowed elaborately, his chain mail clanking. "My lady."

He'd taken no pains to disguise his voice, so she knew it was Gabriel. "My thanks, Sir Knight," she said, taking the cup and sipping gratefully.

Or gulping might be a better description.

Instead of a mask, he wore a polished helmet complete with a visor that concealed his face. How very appropriate, she thought, for him to dress as a knight in shining armor after yesterday's duel.

And he wasted no time in reminding her. "I would slay dragons for you, my dear Lady Rose."

She sighed. "You recognize me?"

"But of course. I would know you anywhere." The visor creaked when he flipped it up, his blue eyes blazing with earnestness. "You're the damsel of my dreams…I hope you've reconsidered and decided to marry me."

He was so perfect. So gallant.

Was it terrible of her to be glad the helmet prevented any kissing?

She sipped more wine. "I'm thinking about it, your grace."

"I would have your answer soon. I would waste no time making you my wife."

Why couldn't she just say *yes*? She'd resolved to do so last night, hadn't she?

But she didn't know him. She only knew he was a duke. "Do you like to travel?" she asked.

"I visit my mother in Northumberland every year."

Oh, wouldn't *that* be exciting? "I meant overseas."

"I get seasick in the bath." He looked a little green at the mere thought. But then he mustered a bold face. "If you wish to travel, my dear Rose, I will manage."

She couldn't expect more. "What's your favorite book?" she asked, wracking her brain for some of Kit's questions.

"I don't read," he said, looking bewildered.

"You cannot read?"

"Of course I can read. I simply find other pursuits more interesting."

"Oh." That wasn't too bad, then, was it? She wasn't much of a reader herself, save for news sheets and foreign books. Everyone had different tastes. "Tastes," she murmured. "Do you prefer sweet or savory?"

His good humor seemed stretched to the breaking point. "What is it with these questions?"

"Nothing. Never mind. Thank you for the wine."

She wandered away, leaving him staring after her. So he wasn't much for conversation. Not every fellow liked to talk, she told herself sternly. It wasn't a crime to keep one's thoughts to oneself.

She just wondered whether he had any.

Musing, she bumped into someone, crushing more than a few of her flowers. "Pardon me," the gentleman said in an unnaturally deep voice. A disguised voice, she decided, looking up.

It was the pirate. Her heart skipped a beat. "It was my fault," she assured him with a flutter of her carefully darkened lashes. She hoped he could see them through the eyeholes of her mask. "I was daydreaming."

His own masked face was expressionless. "I hope they were sweet dreams."

Who was he? What courtier had come just today? She hadn't heard of any new arrivals, but she'd been busy catching up on her sleep and preparing her costume.

Her fingers itched to touch the triangle of skin that showed where his shirt was open at the top. She sipped again instead, feeling the wine go straight to her head. "Will you kiss me?" she asked boldly.

Again, that expressionless reply. "I don't kiss strangers, my lady. And I'd advise you to follow the same rule."

Well! She wanted to rip that mask off his handsome face.

Then again, she had no idea whether he was actually handsome under that mask. Maybe he wasn't. In fact, maybe he was hideous. And if he didn't want to kiss her, perhaps that was because he knew he had dismal technique.

Feeling better, she flounced away.

But as she flirted with Henry VIII, she felt the pirate watching her. And when a jester led her to the dance floor, she saw him glare. Wherever she went, his gaze seemed to follow.

The only person keeping a closer eye on her was her mother. Dressed in a sea-green gown with a demi-mask to match, Mum watched Rose the entire evening. Since her mother had seemed to all but ignore her so far at court, Rose found the sudden attentiveness disconcerting.

She danced with a monk and then with Thor, but she wasn't truly enjoying herself. When Merlin lifted his mask to try to kiss her and she discovered he was the Earl of Rosslyn—the married cur!—she almost decided to head back to her apartments.

But she wanted to see the unmasking. And Nell's surprise.

She was dancing with a Viking when, outside in Clock Court, the great astronomical timepiece struck midnight. Nell sharply clapped her hands. "Yeomen," she shouted. "Now!"

As one, the flaming torches were extinguished, and the room plunged into darkness.

FIFTY-THREE

*R*OSE SHRIEKED, and the Viking grabbed her by both arms. "Come here, my lovely."

He stank. Deprived of her vision, she realized many of the people in the great hall stank—all the flowers on her gown couldn't mask the odors of stale sweat and too much perfume. Feeling lost, she held tight to the smelly Viking. Though she blinked and blinked, she couldn't see a thing. Her heart was threatening to pound right out of her chest.

She'd never liked the dark.

"What is this?" she cried.

"It's naught but a bit of fun," he said in a voice anything but soothing. Dropping one of her arms, he scrabbled at her mask. Cool air hit her face, swiftly replaced by wet, rubbery lips.

Gagging, she twisted her head. "Get off me!" She wrenched from his grasp and stalked away—or tried to, but tripped instead.

She fell to her hands and knees, bouncing off a body on the floor. "Ah, the flower girl," a man murmured, his fingers grasping an ankle and working their way up. He gripped her calf and dragged her closer. "Come to me, sweet."

Whimpering with disgust and fear, she scrambled away on

all fours, losing a shoe when it came off in his hand. She kept moving, darting around boots and skirts as she frantically tried to feel her way to freedom. Laughter and exclamations rang through the air along with the sounds of courtiers milling, pausing for a kiss here and a touch there, exploring one another in the dark.

It seemed an enormous, terrifying maze of debauchery.

Someone stepped on her hand, and tears sprang to her eyes. She crawled faster, running headfirst into a pair of legs. Large hands reached down and hauled her up.

"What have we here?" a male voice drawled, sniffing appreciatively. "Oh, the flower girl. Are you not the one guarding the secrets of *I Sonetti*?"

With that, he clamped her ruthlessly, one large hand on the back of her head and the other against her spine, his lips bruising hers as they found their target in the dark.

She pushed against him and kicked his shins, but he kept her clutched tight. Reaching blindly to his right side, her fingers closed on the hilt of his sword. She pulled with all her might, but the peace strings held fast. Tears trailing hot down her cheeks, she bit his lower lip. Hard.

A metallic flavor flooded her mouth.

"Confound you!" he cried, shoving her away with both hands. Spitting blood, she turned and stumbled into someone soft and fragrant—a woman. The vixen squealed and clawed at her face. Rose careened away, bumped into someone else, and screamed.

Hands gripped her shoulders and held her steady. Just held her, not grasping. An anchor in the dark sea of terror.

"Hush," he said. "There's nothing to fear."

Kit. His voice, his hands. Feeling her knees buckle, she leaned against his shoulder, smelling frankincense and myrrh. Kit. Warm and yielding instead of cold and hard, but a knight in shining armor nonetheless.

"Hush," he repeated. "Keep still. It's nothing but a silly

game. The court will tire of it soon enough, and the torches will be relit."

She clung to him, feeling calm begin stealing over her, restoring her world to balance. "Can you help me get out?"

"I'm afraid we'd but stumble over others." His arms came around her; his deep voice soothed. "You're safe here with me, I promise."

Darkness still enveloped her, but she wasn't quite so panicked. "All right," she whispered.

"We'll just wait." Moving closer, he laid his cheek against her hair. She slipped her arms around his waist, wondering vaguely how he'd got in here and managed to find her.

Like at the duel, he'd known just when to show up, just when she needed him.

They were buffeted by other bodies searching, laughing, groping in the blackness. When she mewed in protest, his arms tightened, settling her more securely against him, locking the two of them together. Whatever flowers might remain on her gown were crushed mercilessly between them, but she cared not a whit.

He felt comforting; he felt *right*. The last of her fear evaporated as the moans and groans, the squeals and breathy sighs that echoed all around them melted away. More bodies bumped them, but she barely noticed. She was sheltered within his arms, wrapped in his warmth, enveloped in his soothing, woodsy scent.

At the other end of the chamber, a single torch flared to life. They sprang apart as the glow spread to reveal, in the all-but-darkness, courtiers engaged in various and sundry embraces.

It sickened her, this horde of writhing humanity. The whole court sickened her.

"Take me away from here," she said. One shoe off and one on, she began limping toward the door. Kit swept her up into his arms and wove his way through the crowd, stepping over bodies as he went.

At long last, they made it down the Great Stairs and into

Clock Court. Torches bathed the courtyard in a hazy yellow glow. He strode to the fountain in the center before setting her on her feet.

Her gown was in tatters from the knees down, the few remaining blooms torn and limp. Her face burned in one spot; she touched it and came away with a trace of blood on her fingertip. Her hair tumbled madly over her shoulders, half or more unpinned.

Thank goodness it was only Kit here to see her.

Still shaky, she splashed water on her face before she looked up and blinked. "Good heavens, you were the pirate."

His expression slowly transformed from concern to something darker. "You didn't know? And yet you asked me to kiss you...and pressed against me in the dark..." He looked thoroughly disillusioned. "Perhaps your reputation is well-earned after all!"

"It is not!" Her trembling was swept away by indignation—and maybe a touch of guilt for her actions here at court. "I'm not like that!"

"You could have fooled me," he spat.

"What were you doing in the great hall?" she demanded. "You're not a member of the court!"

"And that's why you won't have me, isn't it?"

"No! To the dickens with the court. I never want to come back here again. Everything here got completely out of hand."

He opened his mouth, then closed it. The fountain trickled in the background while he silently repeated her words.

I never want to come back here again.

Perhaps there was hope for him, after all.

Quite suddenly he felt bone-tired. "I don't want to fight."

She sighed. "I don't want to fight, either."

"Rose, you must be more careful around these men."

"I would never allow—"

"You're a passionate young woman, but for your own good, you must curb—"

"I'm *not* passionate," she interrupted. "Only with you. I

knew it was you, Kit. I've never let anyone else hold me like that. Anyone but you."

He stared, wondering whether to be pleased or angry. Anger won. "How can you lie to me with such a straight face? You expect me to believe that after you admitted you didn't realize I was the pirate?"

"I didn't recognize you during the ball," she returned hotly, "because it never occurred to me you would be there." She shifted her weight back and forth, popping up and down on her single high-heeled shoe. "And you're a deuced hypocrite, do you know that? *You* held *me* when you didn't know who *I* was."

"Pah," Kit shot back, "do you take me for a fool? A sightless nitwit would have recognized you at twenty paces. You smell like a blasted garden. But you could be wearing sackcloth instead of flowers and I'd know you, Rose. Instantaneously. Don't you know that?"

Her dark eyes flashed. "Just as I knew you the moment you caught me in the dark. The moment I touched you, even blind as a bat. I just didn't connect you with the pirate—although I should have, given that I've never wanted to kiss anyone but you, ever!"

Kit stared. She was beautiful in her fury, her cheeks flushed, her agitated breaths puffing in and out between rosebud lips. No one could lie that convincingly.

"I'm sorry," he said. "I mistook your meaning and judged you harshly. You're right."

"Of course I'm right."

He cracked a smile. "You've got a knack for accepting apologies."

Her anger seemed to flee as quickly as it had flared. "It's a good thing, since I still don't want to fight." She answered his smile with one of her own, her gaze raking his costumed form. "You make a very fetching pirate."

"Do I, now?"

Though he'd said it in all good humor, her voice dropped to a whisper. "You appeared like magic, and I was so grateful to have you there. You swept away my fear with a single touch…"

Unable to help himself, he moved closer and touched his lips to hers. A silent apology that was swiftly turning to more—

"Rose?" her mother's voice drifted down the Great Stairs. "Rose!"

Reluctantly Kit drew away. "We're out here, Lady Trentingham."

Her high heels clicked on the cobblestones as she made her way over to them, carrying Rose's missing shoe. "Oh, how I feared for you, my dear. I know how you hate the dark." She kissed her daughter on both cheeks, then drew back and touched the one with the shallow scratch. "What happened here?"

"A lady with claws like a wildcat." Rose's hand went to the injury. "Does it look terribly bad?"

"A little powder and you'll never know it's there," her mother assured her.

Rose sighed. "I cannot imagine what Nell was thinking when she ordered the torches doused."

Lady Trentingham cocked her head. "Did you not know Nell is famous for practical jokes? Why, recently she left King Charles at a brothel—"

"Without any clothes or money," her daughter finished for her. "I heard about that. Remind me never to introduce her to Rowan and Jewel. The three of them together could prove deadly."

"You're all right, though?" Lady Trentingham tried to smooth Rose's hair, but her efforts made little difference. "You're not truly hurt?"

"Kit rescued me," Rose said.

"Did he?" Lady Trentingham shared a furtive glance with him, that one brief look conveying a mixture of emotions: gratitude, congratulations, and a silent admission that she'd been wrong. "I think we should leave," she told Rose quietly.

"Yes," Rose agreed. "There's Judith's wedding, of course… but I believe I'd want to leave anyway."

Lady Trentingham looked back to the great hall. "Then shall we make our good-byes?"

"Please, Mum, just give King Charles my apologies. I'd rather go straight to bed."

Kit was glad Rose didn't want to go back to the ball. "I'll walk you to your rooms," he said, taking her arm.

While her mother ascended the staircase, Rose leaned to put on her shoe. "I look like something one of Lily's cats dragged in, don't I?"

"No." His mouth quirked in a half grin. "Worse."

She winced as she straightened. "Well, thank you for being honest."

"I'll love you no matter what you look like. Always. Would the duke feel that way as well?"

She had no clue what the duke felt, as evidenced by the way she changed the subject. "Did you check all the measurements?"

He took her hand to walk her toward her apartments. "Many. Not all. There are hundreds."

"Have you found anything wrong?"

"Maybe. I'm not sure yet. The set of drawings I keep with me doesn't seem to match the plans I left here, and I'm not certain which is correct or which reflects the actual measurements we took last night."

He couldn't imagine how that had happened. Most builders worked from a single set of plans, but he preferred to err on the side of caution and always made a careful duplicate. Had he been not-so-careful? The discrepancy was more than disturbing, but he'd set aside the problem for the evening when he decided watching over Rose was more important. And he didn't want to think about it again now.

Before she could ask more questions, he stopped beneath the clock tower and turned to face her. "I'll let you know if I find anything conclusive," he said, the pad of his thumb tracing circles on her palm.

Her eyes went soft when he raised her hand to his lips. But

she was still distant, hesitant. She hadn't yet crossed that crucial barrier. She wasn't yet his.

"Come along," he murmured, starting forward again. "It's been quite a night."

Just as they reached Base Court, a shooting star streaked across the sky.

"Look," she breathed, closing her eyes to make a wish.

He wished, too, then turned and took her face in both hands. "What did you wish for?"

"I cannot tell you, or it won't come true."

"Fair enough." It made him smile to think she believed such fancies. "Shall I tell you what I wished for instead?"

"I think I know," she whispered and left it at that.

It wasn't the answer he wanted, but for now it would have to do.

FIFTY-FOUR

*H*AMPTON COURT was quiet in the middle of the night, Kit's building dark now except for the circle of light thrown by his lantern. Scents of fresh-cut wood and hardening mortar assaulted his nose, and his footsteps echoed in the empty rooms as he wandered them for the last time.

Tomorrow the building was coming down.

Two more days spent poring over the numbers had confirmed his suspicions: the building was flawed. He'd double-checked his calculations, remeasured, triple-checked again. The conclusion was always the same. If left standing, the structure would eventually collapse.

Oh, it wouldn't fall today or tomorrow—not even this year. In fact, it could be ten or twenty or fifty years before the inherent weakness resulted in disaster. It would certainly remain standing until long after he was appointed Deputy Surveyor, most likely so long after that he doubted he'd ever be blamed.

But when the collapse occurred, the consequences could very well be deadly.

Was his design at fault? Or had someone tampered with the plans? Since the two copies he had didn't match, he couldn't be sure. The fact that they were different lent credence to the theory that Harold Washburn—or someone else—had sabotaged this project.

But it didn't matter. It was Kit's project, Kit's responsibility.

There was nothing for it. Although it meant he would miss his deadline and any chance at the appointment and knighthood, he'd had no choice but to order the structure torn down and rebuilt from scratch. He couldn't live with himself knowing there were potential deaths looming ahead—not even when he suspected those at risk had yet to be born.

All he had left now was a journey to Windsor and the difficult task of explaining his failing to Wren. Then—while his dreams were torn down along with this building—he would go to Trentingham as promised. Once there, he would finalize the plans for Lord Trentingham's greenhouse…and tell Lady Trentingham why he was no longer worthy of marrying her daughter.

He grabbed an exquisite carved panel—that, at least, could be salvaged—and exited the building without looking back.

He'd long ago learned there was no point in that.

FIFTY-FIVE

"OH, JUDITH," Lily breathed, staring at the gown the maid had just laid out on her friend's bed. Palest blue, Judith's wedding dress had a wide neckline and golden ribbons crisscrossing the stomacher. The underskirt was cloth-of-gold. "It's so beautiful."

A happy sigh escaped Judith's freshly painted lips. "I always dreamed of wearing blue for my wedding."

"Me, too," Violet said.

Lily grinned. "Me three."

Rose's sisters *had* both worn blue, and they were both happily married. Rose brushed her fingers over the gown's shimmering fabric, ordering herself not to be envious. After all, she'd received so many proposals she'd lost count, and she'd probably have more if she hadn't slighted so many gentlemen.

It had been *her* choice to refuse them.

Besides, she would never wear a gown like this. It might be lovely, but it was entirely too pale and insipid. If Rose ever managed to marry, she intended to do so in red.

Judith wandered across her feminine mauve room to her dressing table. "Shall I wear patches?" she wondered.

Rose turned to her pretty, plump friend. "Just one. A heart.

But we must powder your face first." She handed Judith's patch box to Lily so she could find a suitable shape, then dipped a fluffy brush into a packet of Princess's Powder. "Are you nervous?"

"Of course not," Judith said, but her smile was trembly. She held out a wine cup for Violet to refill. "Why should I be nervous? My dear Grenville is a good man."

Rose dusted Judith's cheeks. "Of course he's good. He's titled and has money." And if he wasn't exactly handsome, she added to herself, at least he wasn't pockmarked or ugly. A girl could look at him without wincing.

If she'd gained nothing else from court, she'd learned it wasn't easy to find perfection. Perhaps compromise wasn't such a bad thing.

"No, I mean Edmund is ever so *good*." Judith peered at herself in the mirror. "He adores children, though his first wife couldn't give him any. He makes certain all the orphans on his estate find families and homes. No one, young or old, is ever allowed to go hungry, and—"

"That's just being decent," Rose interrupted.

Violet set down the wine bottle with a little *clunk*. "But decency is important. And rare."

Still riffling through the patch box with a fingertip, Lily nodded. "I'd choose decency over money and a title any day of the week. You have to *live* with the man you wed."

"Husbands and wives don't have to live with each other." Rose fluffed more powder on her friend's face. "At court, it seems hardly any of them do."

Violet stared at her, her brown eyes looking huge through her spectacles. "But those are marriages made for alliance, not love. That's not what you want, is it?"

"Of course not," she said, still fluffing.

"Stop!" Judith laughed, brushing at her dressing gown. White powder flew everywhere. Particles coated the surface of her dark wood dressing table and floated in a sunbeam that came through the window. "Edmund won't be able to find me under all this powder."

"Sorry." Rose dusted more on her own cheeks, though her scratch was all but healed. "Is Lord Grenville nervous?"

"He doesn't seem to be. But then, he's been married before. He's not worrying about tonight."

Violet touched her hand. "Are you worried, Judith?"

"A little." Looking away, Judith grabbed her goblet and took another swallow of wine. A big one.

"I think you're a lot worried," Lily said, prying the goblet from Judith's fingers. She'd downed half a bottle already, and there were still hours left before her wedding. "You don't want to be slurring your vows."

"The marriage bed is nothing to fear," Violet told her.

"Are you sure?" Judith asked.

"Of course she's sure." Rose nervously tweaked the bouquet of flowers she'd made for Judith to carry. "All brides fret about it, but they all survive, don't they?"

"Are *you* fretting?" Violet asked her.

"Why should I fret? I'm not getting married."

"But if you were?" Lily pressed.

"No, I wouldn't fret."

And it was true. She would never fret over the marriage bed —she'd never need to. Because after the humiliating failure of her sojourn at court, she feared more than ever that her wedding day would never come.

"Mama told me it would hurt," Judith whispered.

Having read *Aristotle's Master-piece*, Rose nodded knowingly. "Only for a moment." The *Master-piece* described it as "a little pain," and she believed that was true.

It would be nothing compared to the pain of the empty years yawning ahead of her.

FIFTY-SIX

"*B*ASED ON THE upper floor's loads," Kit said, "I was concerned that with any additional loading the building would eventually collapse. As it stood, it was near the maximum tolerance of the span. I cannot believe I miscalculated something so basic."

"Neither can I," Wren said pointedly, pacing his office in Windsor Castle. Then his eyes narrowed as he stopped and turned to Kit. "Are you saying someone else miscalculated? Purposefully lengthened the span? Altered your plans?"

"I won't say that." Kit met the older man's gaze. "The project is my responsibility. The error is mine, and I'll absorb the costs of rebuilding."

When he first started out, a problem of this magnitude might have landed him in debtor's prison. Thankfully, he could easily afford it now.

Wren nodded as he walked him to the door. "This won't go past this room. I expect the king will be pleased with the final results, even though you'll miss the deadline. You'll doubtless see more commissions, and your reputation won't suffer."

That was some consolation. Thanks to Wren's confidentiality, Kit's career wasn't endangered.

Just his dreams. His knighthood. His chances of winning Rose.

"Thank you," he told Wren as he opened the door. "Though the project won't come in on time, it *will* be done right."

"From you, I expect no less." Wren watched him step outside. "I'm sorry about the appointment."

"I wish Rosslyn well with it," Kit said and closed the door behind him.

So that was that.

He took a deep breath and headed to Windsor's Upper Ward to check the progress on the new dining room. Following a complete inspection, he felt a little better. Everything seemed to be proceeding well and on schedule. He had high hopes that the successful, timely completion of this beautiful chamber would help ensure more commissions from the Crown.

Somewhere in town, a clock struck noon, reminding him he'd best get on his way to Trentingham if he wanted to arrive at a decent hour. But he didn't want to rush to Trentingham—not today. He felt drained. The interview with Wren had sucked the life right out of him.

Tomorrow morning would be better, he decided, heading out of the castle. He was in no hurry to confess his failure to Rose's family, and that greenhouse was hardly an emergency. The groundbreaking wasn't scheduled until tomorrow, anyway.

He looked forward to a long, hot bath, followed by a good night's sleep. Here in Windsor, in his own peaceful, empty house, he'd doubtless rest easier than he had in weeks. Especially since he no longer had to worry about his projects. Or, he thought dejectedly, about whether he'd win the appointment he'd been working toward half his life.

"Good afternoon, Mr. Martyn," the old guard called as he passed through the castle gate.

"Afternoon, Richards," Kit returned.

The next thing he knew he was standing in front of a pawnshop.

His brother-in-law's pawnshop, to be precise. Kit still had a difficult time thinking of Ellen as married. But something inside him knew he had to come to grips with that—the same something that had sent him here without conscious decision.

He hoped she fared well. And there was only one way to find out. He drew a deep breath and opened the door.

At the jingle of the bell, Thomas emerged from the back. "Mr. Martyn," he said, clearly surprised. And apprehensive, Kit thought.

As they were kin now, for better or worse, he'd best set the fellow at ease. "Call me Kit," he said. "Please."

"Kit." The younger man nodded.

"I've come to see my sister."

If anything, Thomas's eyes grew more hooded. "She's upstairs. I'll fetch her."

"No. I'll go up."

"I'm sorry, sir—I mean, Kit. But I'm not sure she wants to talk to you."

That hurt. Kit had hoped Ellen would be over her snit long before now. She'd won their battle, after all. She'd fought to live over a pawnshop, and live here she did.

He wanted to see the place, see how she was living. See whether she and her pawnbroker were happy. They'd be happy after he gave them her dowry, of course, but he hoped they were happy now without it. He hoped his sister hadn't made a mistake marrying for love.

Before he handed over all that money, he needed to see Ellen's happiness with his own eyes. He was not taking no for an answer.

"I'll go up," he repeated. "You can show me the way or I'll find it myself."

"Very well." Thomas handed a key to the youth behind the counter, then Kit followed him through a storage room and up a narrow staircase.

When Thomas opened the door, Kit sniffed appreciatively. "Smells like apples."

"The only thing your sister knows how to cook is apple fritters," Thomas said with a wry quirk of his lips. "I've been eating them till they're coming out of my ears."

Kit looked at him sharply, but the words had been said in good humor. It seemed the man loved Ellen whether she could cook or not.

The living quarters were nicer than he'd expected. The main room was small and the floor was bare wood, but it was polished and everything was clean. There was plenty of fine furniture and, in Kit's opinion, entirely too many knickknacks—all of which he suspected came from the shop. He guessed that some of the best merchandise found its way upstairs. A hidden benefit to this business.

And Ellen doubtless loved all the knickknacks. In fact, he wouldn't be surprised to find she'd dragged most of them up here herself. His heart lifted to think she was probably very happy here, indeed.

"Where is she?" he asked.

"Napping in the bedchamber."

Kit frowned. He'd never known Ellen to nap. "Will you wake her or shall I?"

Her husband drew a steadying breath. "Wait here." Thomas opened a door and slid into the room beyond, closing it firmly behind him.

Kit paced while he waited, peeking into another chamber to find a kitchen with a small fireplace and a scrubbed table for eating.

That seemed to be it—just the main room, kitchen, and bedchamber. He wondered where their children would sleep, though he knew full well that entire families lived in single-room homes—why, this place would seem a palace to the common cottager. He and Ellen had lived like that until the Great Plague had claimed their parents.

But when he built the new shop for his sister in London, he would design it with much larger living quarters attached. A proper house.

The bedchamber door opened and shut again, startling him. "She won't see you," Thomas said.

"Pardon?"

"Ellen doesn't wish to speak with you, Mr. Martyn."

Fuming, Kit didn't bother correcting Thomas's use of his name again. "She doesn't have a choice."

He crossed the room—in all of three strides—and threw open the bedchamber door. "Ellen."

She lay on a huge four-poster bed—much too big for the room—with her back to him.

"Ellen." He sighed. "I don't wish to play games."

She rolled over and stared at him with those eyes that were so like his. Her pretty mouth was thinned into a straight, forbidding line.

She said nothing.

"It's a nice home," he conceded, feeling like an idiot talking to himself. "I hope you're happy here."

Nothing.

A heavy silence hung for a moment before Kit's frustration gave way to anger. "This is about the money, isn't it?"

Not a word. Not even a blink. It was as though she stared right through him, as though he weren't even there.

His heart fisted in his chest as the anger turned to hurt. He swallowed hard. "When you're ready to talk, Ellen, you know where to find me."

Without another word, he turned and left. He wasn't about to give Ellen a fortune when she wouldn't speak to him. Never mind that he hadn't planned to withhold it much longer, if any longer at all—he wouldn't *buy* his sister's love.

Every penny of that dowry had been saved out of *his* love for *her*, but apparently she couldn't see that.

Thomas followed him down the stairs and all the way to the entrance. "She'll come around, sir. I'm sure of it."

Kit opened the door but stopped short of stepping outside. "How is she?" he asked toward the street.

"She's well. We're happy together, sir."

"Kit."

"Kit. I know how lucky I am to have married your sister. I'm going to take care of her."

"See that you do," Kit said, then slowly turned. He measured his brother-in-law a long moment before he decided he trusted him.

Or maybe that he had no choice.

"Tell her I love her," he said quietly, then pushed out into the cool October air, the bell jingling too merrily as the door shut behind him.

FIFTY-SEVEN

STANDING IN THE old village church, Rose shifted on her high-heeled shoes, watching another wedding.

The *third* one this year.

"Edmund Richard Henry, Viscount Grenville, wilt thou have this woman to thy wedded wife, to live together in the holy estate of matrimony? Wilt thou love her, comfort her, honor, and keep her in sickness and in health; and, forsaking all others, keep thee only unto her, so long as ye both shall live?"

"I will." The confident words boomed through the ancient stone sanctuary, binding Lord Grenville to Judith.

But Rose wasn't listening to the ceremony. Instead she was noticing how joyful the bride looked. Judith clutched the flowers Rose had arranged for her, a smile curving her lips, her body ranged close to Lord Grenville's. A *good* man, Judith had described him. Decent.

Rose's mother sighed happily, delighted that this introduction had worked well enough to culminate in marriage. *The Big Book of Weddings Arranged by Chrystabel* was getting thicker. She leaned close, bumping against Rose's left side. "They're perfect together, aren't they?" she whispered.

Rose could only nod numbly. These two were so clearly in

love, Rose knew they belonged together. But she imagined herself standing in Judith's place and the Duke of Bridgewater standing in Grenville's...and she knew she wouldn't be as happy.

Was Gabriel decent? She didn't know. In truth, she didn't know him at all. And she'd tried, hadn't she? He was handsome and kind and generous, but he didn't seem a man who cared to be known.

And he'd kept money that belonged to someone else.

The priest cleared his throat and looked back down at his *Book of Common Prayer*. "Lady Judith Carrington, wilt thou have this man to thy wedded husband..."

Standing on Rose's right, Violet leaned closer to Ford and wrapped an arm about his waist. Ford was decent, too, Rose thought, watching him squeeze her sister around the shoulders. His first love used to be science, but when he found Violet—and responsibilities—he hadn't hesitated to put them first.

Sun streamed through the stained glass windows, glinting off Violet's spectacles. "Oh, isn't this romantic?" she sighed.

"It is," Rose whispered to no one in particular, remembering Ellen's wedding, which hadn't been romantic at all. Yet Ellen had been just as thrilled to marry her love as Judith was today. Ellen's dowry could have bought her a titled man, but she'd wed a pawnbroker instead. Her Thomas was decent. He'd wanted Ellen even though she hadn't come with the money they'd expected.

Lily's husband, Rand, was decent as well. He'd worked hard to become an Oxford professor, but he'd been willing to give that up when other duties were thrust upon him. After falling hard for Lily, he'd even agreed to marry another woman in order to save a man's life.

Thank heaven that hadn't been necessary.

Lily poked Rose from behind. "Your wedding will be next," she whispered.

Rose hoped so. But first she'd have to find a husband who

would make her as happy as her sisters and Ellen and Judith. A decent man. Someone she could admire.

Gabriel wasn't that man. She'd tried her best to fall in love with him, but it hadn't happened. What could she do but keep looking? She'd have to return to court, much as the thought distressed her. But not today. It was too soon. She would ask Mum to take her to the queen's birthday celebration at Whitehall next month.

"...so long as ye both shall live?" the priest concluded expectantly.

"I will," Judith pledged, her voice clear and true. So clear and true that no one in the church had any doubt she meant that pledge with all her heart.

A few more words, a new sapphire ring slid onto Judith's finger, and she was clearly and truly wed now, the new Lady Grenville.

And watching that, Rose knew she wouldn't wed until she found a love as decent and true.

When Lord Grenville lowered his lips to meet Judith's, Rose smiled through a sudden film of tears. She wasn't sure whether they were happy or sad tears...perhaps they were a little of both.

～

*M*ANY HOURS LATER, Chrystabel sighed happily as she closed her bedchamber door. "Another wedding."

Her husband wrapped her in his arms. "Another wedding night." He kissed her thoroughly before setting her away, his hands moving to detach the stomacher that covered her laces. "Will we be celebrating Rose's wedding soon?"

"I wish I knew." She went to work on the knot that secured his cravat. "I'm fairly certain she won't be accepting Bridgewater, but that doesn't mean she'll end up with Kit."

"You sound worried, my love."

"Our daughter is stubborn."

He skimmed one long brown curl off her face. "What will you do next to push Rose and Kit together?"

"Nothing." The fire on the hearth threw his face into shadows. "I've done what I can. The rest is up to them. But with any luck, we'll have another wedding night before too very long."

"Ah, Chrysanthemum." Taking her face in both his hands, he claimed her lips. "You know we've no need of a wedding to have a wedding night."

She sighed into his kiss, thinking this was all she wanted for her daughter. To know that after more than twenty years of marriage, Rose would still feel as loved as she had on her wedding day.

FIFTY-EIGHT

*J*UDITH'S WEDDING celebration had lasted through the wee hours, and Rose had stayed till the end. The sun was high in the sky by the time she awakened the next day, hearing strange noises beneath her window.

Bangs and scrapes and shouts.

Construction.

Kit.

She rang for her maid. "Hurry," she said when Harriet arrived. "The purple gown—no, the red and black damask." The maid pulled it from the wardrobe and helped her wiggle into it. "Hurry."

"I'm going as fast as I can, milady." She laced Rose up the back.

"Tighter." Rose wanted to look her best.

Harriet pushed her onto a chair and began combing through her tangled curls. "Whyever are you in such a rush?"

Rose gulped down some chocolate and nibbled on some bread. "I'd forgotten that today is the groundbreaking."

"I see." The maid twisted up the back of her hair. "I expect you're more interested in the builder than the building, hmm?"

Rose didn't care for the sound of that *hmm*. "Mr. Martyn is just a friend. After the lunacy of court life, I simply crave a sane conversation." Kit had always been easy to talk to.

Harriet met her gaze in the mirror. "Hmm," she said again.

"How is *your* love life?" Rose asked to distract her.

The maid's freckled face lit with a smile as she chose a red ribbon. "Walter has said he will visit. I believe he will ask for my hand."

It was on the tip of Rose's tongue to protest, to tell Harriet she had no business getting married when she needed her. But she was feeling expansive this morning. "Where will you live?" she asked instead.

"We haven't yet decided. And I don't really care. Does it matter, so long as you're together with the one you love?"

Rose's ebullient mood plunged. Even Harriet was in love.

Love, love, love. All around her, people were in love. In that way, it had been easier to be at court. At least there she wasn't constantly reminded just how lacking she was in love. At court, lust ruled the day—no one else at court seemed to be in love, either.

Except maybe Nell Gwyn. And the king's poor, long-suffering queen.

"Are you finished?" she asked.

"One moment." Harriet tied the ribbon and stepped back. "You look lovely, milady."

"Thank you." Rose darkened her lashes with the burnt end of a cork and slicked on some lip gloss from a little pot. She considered a patch or two, but hadn't the patience. In no time at all, she was downstairs, out the door, and hurrying through her father's gardens.

On impulse she paused to pluck a few colorful blooms, gathering them into a makeshift bouquet. Still arranging them, she rounded the corner of the house.

And there was Kit.

Was there anything quite so masculine as a man in charge, giving orders? The greenhouse site looked chaotic, but somehow, at the same time, Kit seemed to have everything under control.

The air smelled of newly turned earth and freshly cut wood. Kit's dark hair glinted in the sunshine, and a metal T-square flashed as he used it to point here and direct workmen there. He'd spread plans on an improvised table balanced across two sawhorses, and he kept looking down at them and back up.

She positioned herself in front of the table, so the next time he looked up, he'd see her.

"Rose," he said briskly, then looked back down.

"Kit?"

"Hmm?"

She shifted uneasily, stepping closer. "Aren't you going to ask me if I want a kiss?" she said, trying to tease one of those glorious smiles from him.

"No." He waved at a man pushing a wheelbarrow full of bricks. "Over there," he directed, pointing with the T-square. Once again, he consulted his plans. "And you've no need to worry," he added toward the neatly inked lines. "I'm not going to try to convince you we belong together, either."

She should be relieved, but she wasn't. Something was wrong. She held out the bouquet. "I brought these for you."

"What for?"

"I'm hoping to celebrate you winning the Deputy Surveyor post."

He finally met her gaze. "I lost it."

"Oh, Kit." The flowers fell to the ground as she moved around the table to lay a hand on his arm. "Tell me."

"There was a problem at Hampton Court." He glanced down at her fingers, then scanned the bustle of construction and sighed, setting down the T-square. "Wait here a moment."

Rose watched him cross the site, looking confident as ever as he consulted with a short, hook-nosed man. Kit gestured with his competent, callused hands, and she wondered when she'd come to prefer them over the smooth, elegant hands of the aristocracy. He ran one of them through his dark hair, and she wondered when she'd come to prefer bold coloring over the pale English ideal.

When he returned, he led her around the house toward the gardens. "It was structural," he admitted flatly. Their shoes crunched on the gravel path. "I ordered the building torn down. It was destined to eventually collapse."

"You could have been killed!" She put her hand to her racing heart, staring at his profile as they walked, imagining her life without him and suddenly realizing it would be tedious and dreary.

When had their friendship come to mean that much to her?

But the gaze he turned on her was sad, not alarmed. "I was never personally in danger." He stopped beneath the huge tree her father called his twenty-guinea oak. "I'll still build it," he said with a half-hearted shrug that didn't fool her. He was more upset than he was willing to admit. "But I'll do it right. And there's no rush anymore, since I've no chance to make King Charles's tight deadline."

"And that's why you lost the appointment?"

He didn't have to answer. His hand slipped into his pocket to grip that little piece of his first building—that tiny symbol of his past success—and in the dappled light beneath the tree, his expression said it all.

Her heart broke for him. "I know how much you wanted that post."

"I wanted the knighthood that went with it. I was hoping…" He sighed. "Never mind." Looking more defeated than she'd ever seen him, he dropped to sit on the grass, his back against the massive trunk. "It was my fault," he said resolutely, and then almost in a whisper, "but it may not have been my mistake."

She sat across from him, carefully settling her skirts. "What do you mean?"

"Do you remember me mentioning the set of plans at Hampton Court didn't match the ones I kept with me? It could have been my error reproducing them, but—"

"Someone could have made changes," she finished for him. "Harold Washburn?"

"Perhaps." He slipped the chunk of brick back into his pocket. "But I should have been there, checking, double-checking—"

"You had too many projects. You couldn't be everywhere at once."

"Which just goes to show that the king was right to test me, because the Deputy Surveyor of the King's Works would have many more projects at a time than I've had these past weeks." He pulled a long green blade from the ground and chewed the end, looking pensive. "But I've been...distracted. It could have been my error. And in any case, it was my project. My responsibility. Which was why I had to tear it down even though the problem would likely have stayed hidden for years—"

"Years?" She blinked. "Are you saying you could have finished the project and accepted the post—"

"I couldn't." At her frown, he tossed the green blade to the lawn. "Can't you see, Rose? When the building collapsed—however far in the future—people might have died. It could have been the mother of the king's children—or his children themselves. And even if it didn't happen until I was long gone—not only from the project, but from our good green earth—I couldn't have lived with myself knowing the possibility existed. Better to lose a post than lose my honor and my very soul."

And suddenly it came clear.

Kit—her dear friend—was the most decent man she knew.

How could she not have seen it? How could she have chased after a title when something better was waiting right here for her? Someone who put others' safety before his own cherished goals? Someone who made her heart quicken with a mere glance and her knees melt with a single kiss?

Someone—perhaps the only one—she could honestly talk to about anything.

"Will you marry me?" she asked.

A thundercloud swept over his face. "That is terribly cruel."

He scrambled to his feet. "Do you know, Rose, I'm usually amused by the way you tend to say whatever comes into your head." Clearly disgusted, he began to walk away. "But that was just plain cruel."

Jumping up to run after him, she grabbed his hand and jerked him to a halt. "I meant it, Kit."

"What?" He swung to her, glaring.

"You're the best person I know. I want to be your wife."

He focused hard on her, searching for the truth, perhaps finding it but unable to believe. It seemed he was also unable to talk. He opened his mouth, but a long moment passed before any words came out.

"I'll never be Deputy Surveyor," he finally said slowly. "I'll never be a knight, let alone a baron, or a viscount, or an earl—"

"You'll be Kit Martyn, the man I love."

His eyes cleared. The tension drained from his face. He took a step closer, and her heart raced.

"No more kissing other men?"

She might have been offended if he wasn't suddenly looking at her in that way that made her stomach dance. "None of them were any good at it, anyway," she said flippantly.

He threw back his head and laughed. "Do you promise to always speak your mind? I do so love that."

"Will you kiss me, already?"

The next thing she knew she was in his arms, their lips clinging together.

And nothing had ever felt so glorious.

FIFTY-NINE

"I'VE ASKED KIT to marry me."

"Oh my," Mum breathed, her eyes growing shiny. "You're supposed to let the man propose."

"Question Convention," Kit quoted with a shrug.

He moved closer, trailing a warm, possessive hand down Rose's back where her mother couldn't see. It took all she had not to shiver with delight. "I was tired of men proposing to me. After the wedding, we're taking a trip to Italy."

Kit's arm stilled. "We are?"

"And France. Everywhere there are beautiful buildings. I have my inheritance—"

"There's no need for that. I've funds enough to travel as long as you'd like. And I shall be free as a bird once my current projects are complete...now that I won't have the Deputy Surveyor post to tie me," he added dryly.

She breezed over that. "We'll leave right after we attend the queen's birthday celebration at Whitehall. I wish to show the courtiers the sort of man it takes to win me."

He laughed, a joyous sound that rippled right through her. "She's planning my life," he told Mum.

"Get used to it," her mother said, delicately wiping her eyes. "Let's tell Joseph the good news."

~

"**S**IX MONTHS. You're my last daughter. This is my last chance to throw a wedding that will be talked of for years."

"Shot in her rear?" Father sat up straighter in alarm. "Holy Hades, who's been—"

"No one's been shot, dear." His wife laid a hand on his arm and raised her voice. "Rose and Mr. Martyn are to be married!"

"Ah!" Though still appearing confused, Father's smile was genuine. "That's wonderful news, darling."

Rose shook her head. "Two weeks, Mum. Violet and Lily only had to wait two weeks for their weddings."

Her mother made a big show of sighing. "Three months."

"I want to be married before the queen's birthday," Rose insisted. "One month."

"Don't I get a say in this?" Kit asked. "I vote for tomorrow."

One month it was, and Rose felt victorious.

Until she heard her mother's next words. "Kit, I wish to commend you on the outstanding job you've done planning my husband's greenhouse. Given your management prowess, I have no doubt the project will finish quickly even in your absence."

Rose's brow furrowed. "His absence?"

Mum blinked at her. "Of course, dear. He cannot very well stay here."

"Whyever not? He's stayed here before."

"Yes, before your betrothal. It wouldn't be proper now."

"But—"

"Besides, Kit must return to his building sites if he's to finish all those projects before you whisk him away to the Continent." Mum turned to him with a honeyed smile. "Isn't that so?"

"Um…" His eyes darted between Rose and her mother. "I suppose—"

"Excellent. I'm sure you two will share a charming correspondence." Mum rose from her chair. "I'm sending for Violet and Lily and their families—we'll have a celebration supper before Kit takes his leave. In the meantime, why don't you two take a turn in the garden before the sun disappears?"

Dropping a kiss upon her husband's cheek, she turned on her heel and left the drawing room.

Rose shrugged and reached for Kit's hand, thinking a walk didn't sound like a bad idea. They'd have some time to themselves before parting.

Mum poked her head back in. "Joseph," she called out, "perhaps you'd be so good as to cut some of those hollyhocks for the supper table?"

Hmmph. So much for privacy.

SIXTY

"*D*ON'T YOU THINK she was acting strange?" Rose asked Kit as they strolled a flower-lined path, staying out of her father's earshot—not that Lord Trentingham had much earshot to speak of.

"Strange?" Kit was only half listening. He held one of her hands, stroking her palm with his thumb and enjoying the way it made her fingers tighten over his. If only her father weren't puttering in and out of sight between the flower beds, Kit would be kissing her right now.

But he supposed there would be plenty of time for kissing soon, after they were married.

He still couldn't believe it.

Rose held a bloom in her free hand, rolling the stem back and forth. "She's trying to keep us apart."

Kit shrugged. "For the sake of propriety, she said."

"There's nothing improper about you staying at Trentingham with my family present."

Kit shrugged again, busy realizing that *she'd* soon be sleeping at *his* house every night. In his room. In his bed. The potency of that thought jarred him, shook him to his very core. Brought home the astonishing truth.

Rose was going to be his...for all time.

Despondency had held him in thrall these past days, but now it simply melted away as his heart took flight. The loss of the Deputy Surveyor post seemed insignificant next to the joy of being with Rose. Perhaps he'd never hold a title, but love, it suddenly seemed, was much more important.

Hang it if his little sister hadn't been right all along.

A shadow fell over them and Kit looked up to see the lovely redbrick summerhouse where he'd spoken with the king's messenger. Had that day—Rand's wedding—truly only been a few weeks ago? It felt like years. Everything had changed, thanks to the breathtaking young woman standing beside him.

His smile faltered when he noticed her frown. "What is it?"

Rose pursed her lips. "I fear Mum might have another reason to keep us apart." Her hand slipped from his to join the other in twisting the delicate bloom. "When we told her about our betrothal, there were tears in her eyes. Might she take exception to the match?"

That was so far from the truth that Kit had to clamp down on a bark of laughter. "They were *happy* tears, Rose."

"You think so?"

"I know so. Besides," he added, catching her hand again with a playful smile, "weren't you raised to make this choice for yourself, regardless of your mother's opinion?"

"I'm *allowed* to choose my own husband, but I don't wish for Mum's disapproval."

"And here I thought you were determined *not* to choose someone she's approved."

"I—" Her eyes suddenly narrowed. "How did you know that? Did I tell you?"

"You must have," he said lightly, though inside he was cursing his carelessness. Lady Trentingham had told him that. Needing to distract Rose—and fast—he pulled her into the summerhouse.

As they stepped through one of the arched entrances to the round structure, her mood shifted. Her arms slid around to draw him in closer, and he felt her warm breath on his lips. He loved that she was tall enough to kiss him without requiring him to stoop.

Her flowery, feminine scent engulfed him, and when their mouths met, she tasted like pure, perfect bliss. The contact jolted through him, leaving his whole body humming with awareness —an awareness of everything she meant to him.

Rose closed her eyes and leaned into Kit, his lips against hers feeling desperately tender. She felt it in her skin, a tight tingling...in her stomach, a melting sweetness...in her heart, an erratic rhythm that sent her senses spinning out of control.

This was right—so right she couldn't imagine what had taken her so long to realize they belonged to each other. She should have known from the first time they'd touched, from that first amazing kiss, from the way he made her feel things no one else ever had.

"I love you," she murmured against his lips, enjoying the feel of the words vibrating between them.

Slowly, a little reluctantly, he pulled back. He gazed into her eyes, that way he had that made her wonder if he could see right into her. She felt the answering flutter in her stomach.

"Are you happy?" he asked, his eyes glittering green and gorgeous in the fading sunlight.

"Happier than I ever dreamed." She licked her lips.

His head tilted slightly in apparent concern, his gaze still searching hers. "Your mother is happy, too. She's thrilled. Trust me."

Rose nodded, feeling reassured. Reminding herself she *could* trust this man.

She laid her head on his chest. "A month without kissing you," she said on a sigh.

"I know." His fingers threaded through her hair, cradling her against him with tender possession. "How shall we survive?"

SIXTY-ONE

*R*OSE QUICKLY realized Kit had been right—Mum *was* thrilled. She often hummed to herself as she flitted about in a frenzy of preparations—penning invitation cards, considering menu options, and perusing fabric samples. One would have thought her in need of a respite after Lily's recent nuptials, but Chrystabel Trentingham was a wedding planning wonder.

After a week without Kit, however, the bride herself was far less than thrilled. Letters simply weren't an acceptable substitute for kisses. Irritable and restless, she saddled her horse and rode over to see her sister at Lakefield.

"It was the same with Ford and me," Violet commiserated, setting aside a fat philosophy tome. "Those two weeks between our betrothal and wedding, we hardly caught a glimpse of each other. It was rather vexing."

"'Vexing' is one way of putting it," Rose grumbled.

"Especially since the whole time we were courting, Mum didn't mention propriety once. She let us go off unchaperoned all the time."

Pacing her sister's pale turquoise drawing room, Rose was listening with half an ear. The rest of her was busy remembering the softness of Kit's lips, the roughness of his hands, the way he liked to touch her dimples...

"Of course," Violet went on, "Mum never suspected he was courting me. Probably because she couldn't imagine Ford wanting me that way."

"Violet!" Rose stopped and turned to face her.

Her sister's eyes looked earnest behind their spectacles. "You know it was so. Mum was certain we were wrong for each other."

"That's right, I'd forgotten she thought Ford was too intellectual for you. Huh." Rose frowned. "It's not like her to be so imperceptive."

"She must have a blind spot where her own daughters are concerned. Even more reason to be glad we avoided her matchmaking schemes."

"I'll say." Rose sighed and resumed her pacing. "Kit and I used to have plenty of privacy, too—Mum even left me at his house once. Perhaps she thought us safe from impropriety because she believed I'd never fall for a commoner."

Violet grinned. "Well, we both surprised her, didn't we?"

~

*A*FTER TEN MORE days, Rose was a ball of restless, squirming tension. Citing concern for the bride-to-be's mental state, Violet dragged her on a day visit to Lily's house in Oxford. It was a journey of two hours, during which Rose's tapping foot never stopped once.

"Mum did the exact same thing to me and Rand!" Lily exclaimed when they were settled in her drawing room. Swiveling on her petit-point stool, she turned away from the beautiful inlaid Flemish harpsichord Rand had surprised her with after their wedding. "Before our betrothal, she insisted on hosting Rand at Trentingham. She even asked me to keep him company, alone, on several occasions. But then after that—"

"Let me guess," Rose said. "You felt like you were the Crown

Jewels and Mum was hired to guard you?" When Lily nodded, Rose slumped in her elegant lemon-yellow chair. "She let you go to Rand at Hawkridge, though."

"With *you* along to chaperone—and spy on us."

Lily's expression dared her to deny the truth. Surprised and sheepish, Rose didn't dare. She wasn't used to being challenged by Lily. My, how her sweet younger sister had changed since she'd won Rand.

"Anyhow," Lily went on, "once Lord Hawkridge had consented to a wedding date, I was only allowed to see Rand *once* before we married. It was torture."

"Sheer torture," Rose agreed.

"I'm not sure the fact that Mum kept us apart once we were betrothed is really most relevant." Violet removed her spectacles and wiped them with a handkerchief. "Frustrating, true, but that can be attributed to propriety, after all. I find it more odd that she left us all together with our men before we became betrothed. As if she had no concerns that anything untoward would happen."

Lily shrugged. "She probably wasn't worried about me and Rand, since everyone thought he was going to marry Rose."

"That's just it." Replacing the spectacles, Violet blinked her eyes into focus. "I mean, no offense to Rose, but even *I* could tell you were the one Rand wanted, and I'm half blind."

Rose pursed her lips. "What are you suggesting?"

Violet turned to her. "I've been thinking about what you said last week. That it's unusual for Mum to misjudge people."

"And?"

"And isn't it curious that, after a perfect record matching dozens of other couples, she was so very wrong about all three of our matches?"

Rose looked to Lily, but Lily was looking elsewhere. "What other explanation is there?" she asked Violet.

"That she only pretended to be wrong."

Rose narrowed her eyes. "To what end?"

"To…" Violet swallowed. "To arrange our matches without our knowledge."

The room went very quiet. Violet stared at her lap, toying with the end of her plait. Lily rubbed an old scar on the back of her hand. Rose's temples began to throb.

Lily's cat rubbed against her skirts, seeming to sense her distress. She scooped it into her lap and rhythmically stroked the cat's striped fur.

"It can't be true," Rose burst out.

"What can't be true?"

The girls turned to see Lily's husband standing in the drawing room entrance, unfastening his academic robe. His sudden appearance spooked the cat, who leapt away to join a sparrow and a squirrel that seemed to be chatting on the windowsill. Lily and Rand had moved to Oxford from his father's estate only last week, just in time for Michaelmas Term to begin, but her animal friends had found her already.

"What can't be true?" Rand repeated, draping his robe over the back of another yellow chair. He wore breeches, a shirt, and a waistcoat underneath.

For once, Lily's big blue eyes didn't soften with love and awe at the sight of her new husband. Instead they looked uneasy.

Rose answered for her. "Violet thinks Mum secretly arranged all our marriages."

Rand's face drained of color while his neck and ears turned bright red. Though his reaction betrayed some shock, it made an even greater impression of guilt.

Rose gasped. "You knew!"

"He only recently found out," Lily mumbled, her eyes trained on her lap.

It was Violet's turn to gasp. "*You* knew?"

Rand crossed to the sideboard and reached for a decanter of brandy.

"Lily," Rose prompted through her teeth.

Lily rose from her petit-point stool. "Truly, we only just learned—"

"When?" Rose demanded.

"The first night Kit came to dinner at Trentingham. Ford told Rand—"

"*Ford* knew?" Violet cried.

"He didn't know everything." Rand pressed a goblet into Violet's hand and watched her take a generous gulp. "Ford only knew that your mother had given him advice on how to win you."

"Mum gave him *advice?*" Violet downed the rest of her drink.

Refusing the brandy Rand offered her, Rose rounded on Lily with daggers in her eyes. "You've known about this for weeks. Were you ever going to tell us?"

"I wanted to tell you, but I..." When Lily finally looked up, she flinched at Rose's expression. "Violet, you have two beautiful new babies, and Rose, you're about to get *married*. I just couldn't bear the thought of spoiling all your happiness. I know I was wrong—"

"You're deuced right you were wrong," Rose huffed.

"Don't blame her, Rose. This isn't Lily's fault." Violet's knuckles were white from clenching the gilded arms of her chair. "It's the fault of the knaves who lied to us."

Rose's jaw dropped. She'd never heard her sister call her husband a name that wasn't nice.

"Who are you calling a knave?" Rand demanded. "*I* never lied. And Ford, he just—"

"Just kept this from me for four years?" Violet regarded her husband's friend with overbright eyes.

Rand fell silent.

Lily rushed to her and wrapped her in her arms. "Oh, Violet, you know Ford hid it out of love for you. Because he feared upsetting you or even losing you."

Violet made no reply.

Rand downed the brandy Rose hadn't taken.

Rose's voice pierced the heavy atmosphere. "And what of Kit?"

Lily didn't release their sister, but turned her gaze on Rose.

"Has Kit kept this from me, too?" Rose's eyes burned with suppressed tears. "Has Mum been advising him?"

The silence blanketing the room was all the answer she needed.

SIXTY-TWO

"WHAT WILL YOU do now?" Rose asked Violet that evening as their carriage neared home.

"Hmm?" Violet said vaguely. She was staring out the window, though Rose wasn't sure why. In the dim twilight, naught was visible but the lumpy outlines of a few squat trees.

Rose tried again. "What will you do now that you...you know. *Know.*"

Her sister turned to look at her and shrugged, her hands twisting in her lap.

Poor Violet. Rose could scarcely imagine how she must feel. Kit's deceit was devastating enough, and Rose had loved him only a few weeks. How much worse would it feel if she'd loved him for years? Shared a home and a life with him? Borne him children?

Good heavens, the children! Poor Nicky and Marc and Rebecca...and poor Rose, too. She'd hoped that focusing on everyone else's woes would distract her from her own, but the tactic was failing utterly.

All through a tense dinner at Lily's house, she'd speared bites of rabbit stew while imagining jabbing her fork into Kit's lying face. She was sizzling with anger. How dare he talk to Mum behind her back? How dare the two of them scheme to influence her decisions? *How dare they?* She wanted to throttle them both.

Right after she told them the wedding was off.

When a little sniffle drew her out of her vengeful reverie, she looked up to see a tear sliding down Violet's cheek.

"Oh, please don't cry." Rose moved across the carriage to sit beside her sister. She patted Violet's shoulder a bit awkwardly, having never been especially good at comforting. "It'll be all right, you'll see." When Violet didn't react, she began feeling desperate. "You can come back to live at Trentingham, you know. And the children, too. There's plenty of room for every—oh, wait!" Rose smacked herself on the forehead. "Mum lives there. That'll never do." She thought for a moment. "I've got it: We'll live off my inheritance. We'll buy a lovely house of our own and live there together, raising the little ones and doing just as we please—"

"Wh-what?" Finally showing signs of life, Violet looked completely baffled. "What on earth are you talking about?"

"You'll have to go somewhere when you leave Ford." Rose took her sister's hand. "It might be hard at first, but I'll take care of you, Violet. We can live quite comfortably on the interest from ten thousand pounds. I'll even help with the children—in fact, I'd love to, seeing as I'll never have any of my own."

"Never have…?" Violet appeared more confused than ever. "You and Kit aren't planning to have children?"

Rose gave a bark of laughter. "Gemini, I'm not marrying Kit! I'm not marrying anybody. I wanted to marry a decent man, but now I see my mistake—there *are* no decent men."

"Oh, Rose, that's not true. Kit's a good man, and he loves you. He made a mistake, that's all. Let's get you back to Trentingham for a good night's rest, and this will all look different in the morning."

Rose pulled a face. "Mum is at Trentingham, and I don't want to see her, given that I'm never speaking to her again. Perhaps I could come with you to Lakefield? Although that might be a bit uncomfortable, seeing as you're leaving Ford—"

"I am not leaving Ford!" Violet shrieked. Shocked into silence, Rose held her tongue while her sister took several calming breaths. "Listen to me, Rose. I know you're angry. I'm angry, too. But I'm not leaving my husband, and you're not jilting Kit."

"So you'll just forgive him?" Rose retorted. "After he kept this secret from you every day of your marriage?"

Her sister winced. "No, I will not *just* forgive him. I cannot. I'm too hurt and too furious. Ford will learn what his mistakes have wrought...and he will regret them." Hearing Violet's tone, Rose almost felt sorry for the target of her sister's displeasure. "Healing broken trust takes time and effort. But at the end of all that, yes, I will forgive him."

"Why should you?"

"Because we're a family."

A jounce of the carriage suddenly sent the sisters careening into each other. "Perhaps you must forgive him, then," Rose said once she'd righted herself. "But I don't think he deserves it. Not after he hurt the woman he's supposed to love."

"Everyone hurts those they love." Violet massaged a spot where Rose's elbow had jabbed her. "We're human, after all. Love is a powerful agent, and we don't always apply it correctly."

"Which philosopher said that?"

"Me, you goose."

Rose rolled her eyes. "Save that one for the book you want to publish."

But she considered her sister's words. *Everyone hurts those they love.* Kit had loved his sister so much, he'd nearly destroyed her happiness. And Ellen had loved Thomas so much, she'd nearly destroyed herself.

And then there was Mum, who'd loved her daughters so much she'd betrayed them all.

"I suppose I cannot stay mad at Mum forever," she muttered, mostly to herself.

"Indeed," Violet said. "Though I expect you'll punish her for a good long while. I certainly plan to."

"As you should," Rose said.

All at once, she felt incredibly drained.

Soon after, as the carriage stopped, she felt a hand on her knee. "And Kit?" Violet asked gently.

"What of him?"

"Will you stay mad at him forever?"

"I don't see why I shouldn't," Rose scoffed. "He isn't family."

Violet sought her gaze in the semi-darkness. "He's family if you love each other."

Looking away, Rose studied Lakefield House's unassuming front gate. Though she'd thought she and Kit were truly in love, had her feelings been manipulated by the clever ploys of a master matchmaker?

Violet sighed. "Think things through before you make any decisions, will you? And talk to Kit. You need to hear his side of the story."

Rose shrugged noncommittally.

"Be well, sister." Violet kissed her on the cheek. "And give Mum hell for me."

SIXTY-THREE

*I*T WAS MID-morning, and Chrystabel paced her perfumery at Trentingham. On occasion she'd pause, select a vial at random, and inhale its potent fragrance. This would quiet her mind for approximately half a second, before it galloped off again in a dozen different directions.

"Mum?"

At the sound of Lily's voice, she turned and seized her youngest daughter in an uncharacteristically fierce hug. "I didn't hear you arrive."

Lily pulled back. "Goodness, Mum, you look—" Stopping abruptly, she sucked in her cheeks. It was the expression she wore when she'd almost said something unkind.

Determined to maintain her composure in front of her child, Chrystabel forced a laugh. "I dare say I've looked better." That was an understatement. She hardly knew what she'd put on this morning, and poor Anne had been in fits trying to keep her still long enough to fix her hair.

"That's not what I meant. You just look tense."

"Well, *you* look stunning, dear. Thank you for coming."

Heaven knew Chrystabel was tense. Rose's future happiness

hung in the balance, and there wasn't a thing she could do to help.

She hated feeling powerless almost as much as she hated causing her daughter pain.

"How is she?" Lily asked, nodding in the general direction of Rose's bedchamber.

"I can only guess." A week had passed since the evening Rose had arrived home from Oxford, full of trembling outrage and bitter recriminations. It was a week Chrystabel had spent in knots, but she knew her daughter well enough to know when she needed solitude. "Most days she stays at Lakefield through supper, or else she has her meals fetched to her room. Though Mrs. Crump tells me the plates come back untouched."

Lily touched her arm. "Rose will come around. I'll talk to her. I'll tell her she needs to forgive you."

"You're sweet for offering, dear." Especially if—as Chrystabel suspected—Lily was still vexed with her mother, too. Her daughter's capacity for kindness never ceased to amaze her. "But I was actually hoping you'd talk to her about Kit."

Lily blanched. "She hasn't called off the wedding, has she? B-because of what I told her?"

"No! At least, I haven't been asked to stop planning it." Though in truth Chrystabel feared the worst, for now she left it at that. She couldn't bear her daughter's guilt-stricken expression. None of this was Lily's fault.

It was nobody's fault but Chrystabel's. She'd been careless and overconfident, and now her girls were paying the price. She should have realized they'd be smart enough to put the pieces together. She should have done a better job covering her tracks. But she hadn't, and now disaster had struck.

She'd hoped her daughters would never discover the truth. Though she'd acted out of love, she'd always known that learning their mother had defied their wishes and schemed behind their backs would bring them pain and confusion. Not to mention send tremors through their blissful marriages, disturbing the happiness Chrystabel had worked so hard to help them secure.

But her clever girls had figured it out—and at the worst possible time. Emotional, headstrong Rose had only just fallen in love. Her bond with Kit was still new and fragile. Fragile enough, perhaps, that a few tremors could break it.

Chrystabel couldn't let that happen, but she couldn't stop it alone.

So she was calling in the reinforcements.

"As far as I'm aware, the wedding is still happening," she assured Lily. "Violet should know more. She should be here any...ah, there she is!" Through the window, Chrystabel was relieved to see a purple-clad figure dismounting a horse. Her eldest daughter wasn't speaking to her, but she'd hoped Violet wouldn't ignore a summons on Rose's behalf.

When Violet joined them, she embraced Lily but kept her distance from Chrystabel. "Good morning, Mum," she said coolly.

Chrystabel nodded, slightly stung though she'd expected no less. "I'm glad you've come."

"You said Rose needed me."

"It's about Rose and Kit, actually," Lily put in.

"Why am I not surprised?" Violet narrowed her eyes at her mother. "If you mean to involve us in some ill-conceived match-making ploy—"

"I don't," Chrystabel said. "I'm out of the daughter-matching business."

"That's difficult to believe," Lily said, her habitual sweetness tempered by a note of steel. It was a recent development that made Chrystabel want to beam with pride. Her youngest daughter was no longer such an appeaser—since finding Rand, she'd also found her spine.

But Chrystabel had meant what she'd said. Having seen the harm she'd caused Violet, Rose, and Lily, she knew interfering further would only lead to more heartache. She couldn't fool her daughters anymore. She could no longer protect them from their mistakes. When she'd said she was out of the daughter-matching business, she'd meant it.

After all, her last child was a son.

"I understand why you feel that way," she told Lily. "And I understand why you three are angry with me. If my mother had tried using trickery to influence my choice of a husband, I would have been just as angry with her."

Of course, *her* mother had been a distant, neglectful sort of parent who would have chosen entirely wrong.

"I owe you girls an apology." Chrystabel selected another oil from her collection as a pretense for sneaking a peek at her daughters' faces. They looked appropriately stunned. She chose her next words with great care. "I'm so very sorry, my loves. I'm sorry for lying to you, for influencing you against your wishes, and for everything you've suffered because of me. I wish things had happened differently."

There. She'd given an honest, heartfelt apology, and she'd meant every word. She *was* genuinely sorry for being dishonest and overbearing, and especially for causing distress.

But she hadn't said she regretted it.

"I don't expect you to forgive me yet. I just want you to know that I've learned my lesson." Her fingers curled around the glass vial. "I will not be interfering in Rose and Kit's relationship again."

Violet's mouth dropped open. "You don't wish them to reconcile?"

Chrystabel's heart skittered at the confirmation of her fears. *Please, dear Rose, don't let love slip away.* "I do wish for that, very much. I still think they belong together."

Lily tilted her head. "Even though Kit deceived her?"

"He didn't want to," Chrystabel admitted, fiddling with the vial. "He was quite resistant to the idea, in fact. I'm afraid I rather ambushed him to force his cooperation." Though her words were matter-of-fact, she had the grace to blush.

Strong-arming Kit was another deed she lamented...but didn't regret.

"Still, as I said, I'm finished meddling in their concerns." Chrystabel put a touch of emphasis on her next words. "If those two are to reunite, they shall have to do so without my help."

Violet and Lily exchanged a look.

Deciding they needed a moment, Chrystabel turned to her work table and busied herself unstoppering the vial in her hand. When the cork came free, she inhaled rose oil. Not the cloying-sweet scent of Maiden's Blush—the dainty white rose after which Joseph had named their second baby girl—but the essence of Damask roses. A strongly floral fragrance, its source had bold red flowers with delicate petals guarded by stout prickles and curved spines.

When her daughters finished their whispered conference, Violet spoke for them both. "We appreciate the apology, Mum. I believe it may be your first," she added dryly.

Chrystabel turned to see both her daughters heading for the door. "If you'll excuse us," Lily said over her shoulder, "we'd like to visit with Rose."

Once they were gone, Chrystabel heaved a sigh of satisfaction. Her stomach unknotted itself for the first time in a week.

They'd got the message.

And though she wished with all her heart she could come to Rose's rescue, she knew compassionate Lily and sensible Violet were more than up to the task. Much as it pained her to admit, her beautiful, extraordinary daughters had grown up. They didn't need their mother holding their hands anymore. They could take care of each other.

But Chrystabel would always be there, just in case.

SIXTY-FOUR

*R*OSE RUBBED HER temples. "I don't really see your point."

"My point is that Kit deserves a chance to tell his side of the story." Perched on the edge of Rose's bed, Lily was round-eyed and earnest. "We all know how persuasive Mum can be."

"The woman could charm the spots off a leopard," Violet put in, rummaging through the chest at the foot of the bed.

Lying on the bed, Rose merely grunted.

Lily's brows drew together. "You've been dithering a whole week, Rose. It isn't like you to hide."

"I'm neither dithering nor hiding. I'm thinking."

Violet snorted. "You've done enough thinking." She transferred an extra chemise and stockings to Rose's traveling case. "It's time to try talking."

"I don't want to talk to him."

"You must!" Violet left off packing to join her sisters on the bed. "For pity's sake, it's only eight days until the wedding."

"And so it is." Though Rose saw her sisters exchange a look, she said no more, toying with the tassels on her bed hangings.

As her wedding day loomed closer, the turmoil inside her was mounting. She couldn't ignore the misgivings that plagued her...but nor could she help loving Kit. What she craved was that sense of rightness, that peaceful certainty she'd felt the day of their betrothal. Now everything felt confusing and wrong.

"Well?" Violet finally prompted.

Rose looked to her with studied innocence. "Well what?"

"*Well,*" Lily burst out, making Rose jump, "*are you still getting married?*"

"Gemini, I don't know!" Fed up with their pestering, she rolled over and jammed a pillow over her head.

"Which is precisely why you must talk to him," came Violet's muffled retort. The thump of her feet hitting the floor underscored her resolve. "Harriet!"

While the maid finished packing Rose's case, Lily ventured forth to procure dinner for their journey and tell Mum they were going to Oxford for a sleeping party. A little fib that proved to Rose just how much her younger sister had changed. Or maybe just how much she was miffed with Mum.

Meanwhile, Violet hauled Rose out of bed and helped her dress. Taking extra care with her appearance, they selected a new gown of lustrous silk taffeta in a red hue so deep it was almost black. Her hair was swept up but for a few sultry tendrils framing her face, and she wore the earrings the duke had given her, knowing that would raise Kit's hackles.

The journey was surprisingly pleasant, whiled away in cozy, sisterly talk over cold chicken, fruit, and fresh bread. Gleeful griping over Mum relieved some of their angst, which eventually gave way to more earnest discourse. Violet confided that she and her husband were still somewhat at odds, though their quarreling had given way to civilized debate—which apparently, in the case of Violet's marriage, was a necessary and promising development. Rose took her word for it.

Newlywed Lily confessed to a lingering unease. "It's not that I'm questioning whether we belong together," she mused aloud, tracing the scars on the back her hand, "but I can't help wondering what would have happened if Mum *hadn't* intervened. Would we have found each other on our own? Would we still have fallen in love?"

Rose stayed guiltily silent, knowing she herself had been an obstacle to her sister's relationship.

Violet wiped strawberry juice from her lips. "I know what you mean. It feels like my connection with Ford was engineered by Mum, rather than having arisen naturally between the two of us. It doesn't make it any less real, but it does change one's perspective on things."

"Exactly." Lily took a strawberry and offered the last one to Rose. "For as long as I can remember, I've been determined to keep Mum out of my love life, and now I find out my grand romance was just another one of her projects. I know it's silly, but it somehow feels less special."

"The feeling will pass," Violet soothed. "The bond itself is what's special, not the story behind it. Besides, I'm certain you and Rand would have got together on your own—faith, the poor fellow had already been in love with you for years! Mum's machinations only sped things up."

Rose's strawberry tasted sour. Would she and Kit have fallen in love on their own? If Mum hadn't dragged her to see his house, where they first got to know each other and became friends? If Mum hadn't—as Rose suspected—arranged all those late-night rendezvous at court, when Kit had seemed to appear like magic whenever Rose needed him? If Mum hadn't brought her to court in the first place?

Swallowing with difficulty, she answered herself: *Not a chance.*

So what did that say about her and Kit?

By the time they were rattling down Windsor's cobblestone streets, Rose's stomach was roiling—and not from champagne bubbles. It was just after nightfall, and when they stopped in front of Kit's mansion, it looked like a shadowy hulk beside the river. Only a few windows were lit. Rose hoped that meant Kit was still at work in the castle, giving her a few more minutes' respite.

On his doorstep, a sister held each of her hands while Violet tapped the knocker. The door swung open almost immediately. Though they were greeted by the butler, Rose saw Kit poke his head out of the drawing room.

When their eyes locked, a surge of emotion slammed into her chest.

SIXTY-FIVE

"*R*OSE?" **LIKE** an apparition, she stood on Kit's doorstep, stark and dramatic in blood-red silk. Bounding forward, he scooped her up in his arms, his heart swelling with relief. It was only after setting her away that he noticed the odd expression on her face.

And Bridgewater's jewels on her ears.

All his tension came coursing back. "Why have you come? Is something amiss?"

When she'd failed to answer his last few letters, he'd tried to tell himself she was simply caught up in the bustle of wedding preparations and planning their Continental tour. But in his gut he'd sensed there was something else, and it had been a struggle keeping his mind on his work this past week. He'd nearly mustered the nerve to defy Lady Trentingham's wishes and call on Rose himself.

She shot a glance at her sisters. "I just missed you is all," she told him, but her smile appeared a bit strained. If she was upset, it seemed she didn't wish to speak of it in front of them. "Lily and Violet stole me away from Trentingham for a surprise visit."

His brows shot up. "Your mother doesn't know you're here?"

"I told her we were taking Rose to my house for a sleeping

party," Lily explained. "We planned to go on to Oxford this evening."

"But then we got a rather late start…" Violet chimed in, blatantly hinting.

Rose gave her a sharp look. "I'm certain we can find an inn nearby."

"I'll not hear of it." Realizing he was being rude, Kit moved aside to let them enter. "You're perfectly welcome to stay here."

"We wouldn't want to intrude," Lily said, ever solicitous.

"No trouble at all. I've plenty of room." Lady Trentingham would undoubtedly disapprove, but what she didn't know wouldn't hurt her.

"This place is stunning," Violet breathed as they stepped inside.

"Goodness, yes, Kit." Lily turned in a circle, taking in the tall entry with its stone walls, white ceiling, and black-and-white floor. "I thought the house you built for Rand was special, but this…" She peeked into the drawing room. "May we have a tour?"

Kit lifted a branch of candles and began walking them through the large house. Though anxious to speak with Rose alone, he found himself charmed by her sisters' lively company. Many chambers hadn't been used in weeks, as he found it wasteful to have the whole house lit each night just for him. Until tonight, he hadn't realized how lonely the place was without Ellen.

Supper was ready by the time their tour ended. His cook had prepared a lovely venison pasty, but Kit hardly noticed what he was eating. Rose was seated on his right, and he was acutely aware of her pushing her food around on her plate. It seemed she hadn't much of an appetite, either.

Supper was followed by port in the drawing room, and though it was still rather early, after one drink Lily and Violet made a show of yawning and proclaiming their fatigue. Kit had had three bedchambers prepared—there were plenty of extras, after all—and he called a footman to show them to their rooms.

While her sisters said their goodnights, Rose didn't budge from her place on the couch. With relief and a twinge of apprehension, Kit refilled their two goblets and settled back into his chair to hear the true reason she'd come.

But it seemed she still wasn't ready for that discussion.

"How is Ellen?" she asked instead, giving him an uncharacteristically shaky smile. "Her room looked so empty without all her things."

"Indeed, it's far less cluttered these days." Kit sipped his port. "Ellen is fine, according to her husband.

"Her husband?"

"She still won't talk to me. I've stopped by six, seven times— but she stares right through me."

"I'm sorry to hear that," Rose said, a little crease between her brows. She looked uncertain and fragile, which did nothing to ease his disquiet.

They sat in silence for a while, sipping port and listening to the fire crackling on the hearth. He waited as patiently as he could, sneaking only the occasional glance at her face. Her eyes inky and unreadable, she looked beautiful in the wavering light.

Beautiful and unhappy.

When she finally spoke, her voice came out stronger than he'd expected. "You lied to me, Kit."

The bottom dropped out of his stomach. There was only one thing he'd ever lied to her about. "How did you—" he started, but then cut himself off.

Because it didn't matter how she'd found out.

What mattered now was fixing this.

His insides wrenched painfully at the thought of losing her, and his hand moved to grip the chunk of brick in his pocket. Did she still want to marry him? He wanted to spring out of his seat and go to her, but sensed it was best keep his distance.

Taking a deep breath, he began again. "Rose, I'm so sorry." Hearing how inadequate the words sounded, he bit back a sigh. "I didn't want to lie to you, but your mother persuaded me it was for your own good."

He winced. *Well done.*

In one single sentence, he'd managed to sound conde-scending *and* too cowardly to accept the blame for his misdeeds.

"That wasn't what I…"

He was mucking this up but good.

Shaking his head to clear it, he tried to start over. "I knew lying to you was wrong, and I felt ashamed. But I did it anyway. There's no justification, but I believed the truth would drive you away, and I was so besotted with you I couldn't—"

"It's all right."

His jaw dropped. "It is?"

Her nod was almost imperceptible. "I'm not angry." Her brows lifted, as though she were surprised by her own words. "At least, not anymore. I probably *would* have run away if I'd learned the truth earlier."

His breath hitched. "But you're not running away now?"

She shrugged. "I-I haven't decided."

Unable to stop himself, he moved to kneel beside her, being careful not to touch her. His throat tight with fear, he struggled to force the words out. "What would make you decide to stay?"

She shrugged again, not meeting his eyes. "I need to know for certain that this is real."

"That what's real, sweetheart?"

"Us. What we are to each other. All along you've said we were meant to be together, and I think I always believed you, even before I knew I had feelings for you. But now I keep think-ing…" Her chin lifted, her fathomless eyes searching his. "Did you truly mean it? Or did Mum tell you to say that?"

He felt as if she'd slapped him. "Of course I meant it!"

"I'm sorry if you feel I'm being unfair." Though the sentence was an apology, her eyes remained determined. "But you *have* lied to me. I can forgive that lie since my mother put you in an impossible position. What I couldn't forgive"—her voice thick-ened as tears flooded her eyes—"is knowing that when you made me feel seen and valued and loved, you were really just telling me what I wanted to hear."

Her words pricked him like needles, her voice raw and vulnerable, her lips quivering with the effort to hold herself together. Kit's insides wound tighter and tighter until he snapped and leapt up to seize her.

The instant he touched her, the air changed in the room. His hand curled around the back of her neck and dragged her mouth to his. The kiss was unlike anything they'd shared before: there was no trace of tenderness, no slow, sweet persuasion. It was a clash of desperate frustration and pure need—the need to be close, to offer comfort, to prove something.

With an effort, he pulled away. "Was that real enough?" he challenged gruffly.

She nodded, and with a grunt of satisfaction he reclaimed her lips.

His mind went blank as it always did when he touched her, his body responding to her of its own accord. She was perfect, thorns and all. She was heaven; she was everything he needed. He was lost in her enveloping warmth and her seductively feminine, flowery scent.

It seemed a long while later when Rose stilled him with firm, warm hands on his shoulders. Leaning against each other, they both sat perfectly still for some time. He listened to her heavy breathing mingling with his own for what seemed like hours but couldn't have been more than a few minutes.

"I'm sorry," she said at last. "Something came over me...I was afraid I'd get carried away. That cannot happen until we're married."

Kit shot upright and turned to look at her. "Does that mean... are we still getting married?"

Her hesitation made his heart stop. But then she nodded, and his heart soared.

And he kissed her all over again.

SIXTY-SIX

*T*HEY HELD HANDS as Rose reluctantly let Kit walk her to her guest chamber. At the door, he gave her such a tender kiss that she felt incredibly foolish for having doubted him.

Would she someday thank Mum for doing whatever it took to bring them together? Now *that* was something to doubt. But she resolved to go a little easier on Mum anyway. After all, if she hadn't been so blind and stubborn where Kit was concerned, all that sneaking around behind her back wouldn't have been necessary.

And it didn't matter now. She and Kit were together again, together for good. She went up on her toes to kiss him again and smiled when he wrapped his arms around her. She felt utterly safe in his embrace. Everything was right.

Well...not *everything*.

Still standing there outside the door, she laid her head on his chest. "Ellen will come to our wedding, won't she?"

"You mean, now that we're having one?" Kit teased, an undercurrent of elation in his voice. But his next words were clipped. "According to Thomas, Ellen has no wish to attend. But let's not talk about my sister, shall we?" He pressed a kiss to the top of her head. "We've much better things to think about."

Her sigh was half bliss, half regret. "I'll go talk to her tomorrow morning before I leave. She's my friend as well as your sister. I want her at our wedding."

"I don't." She felt him tense. "Not if she's going to ignore me."

She found one of his hands and squeezed it, trying to soothe his heartache. "It's only a disagreement. She'll come around."

Privately, she thought he needed to come around, too. If she could forgive Kit's folly, shouldn't he be able to forgive Ellen's? Didn't their bond mean more to him than their quarrel?

She sighed again. "If you'd just give her the dowry you saved—"

"I'm not going to give her eleven thousand pounds when she won't even deign to speak to me."

"Clearly her behavior doesn't warrant it, but for you, Kit, and for me. Because we want her at our wedding." Raising her head, she gazed up at him. "What if she promised to speak to you afterwards—"

"I am not going to bribe her to be my sister. When she's ready to apologize, I'll be here."

Rose bit her tongue, realizing there was no arguing with him. She'd have to convince Ellen to make the first move. But she'd worry about that tomorrow.

Tonight she'd have sweet dreams.

SIXTY-SEVEN

*T*HE NEXT MORNING, after breakfast with her sisters —who were ecstatic and relieved to see them happy together—Kit walked Rose up the hill to the pawnshop.

"I'll wait out here," he said when they arrived.

"I want you two to talk."

"I'll be here if she's willing."

Bent over a tray full of rings, Ellen looked up when the bell jingled. "Rose!" She came hurrying out from behind the counter.

Rose hugged her tight, then set her away. "You look good." Actually, she looked as if she were in her element, fresh-faced and radiant in a simple peach gown.

"Do I? That's funny, because I feel like puking."

"Oh." Rose stepped back in alarm. "Is there anything I can—"

But Ellen was already dashing away, throwing a "Be right back!" over her shoulder.

Though some truly hideous sounds traveled from the back room, Rose allowed her friend the privacy she seemed to want. Her worry mounting, she wondered where Thomas was and if he realized his wife had taken ill.

She was on the point of fetching him when Ellen returned, looking surprisingly cheerful for a girl who'd been retching only seconds before. "My apologies," she said with a blithe gesture. "It comes and goes."

Rose's concern evaporated, replaced by awe. "You're with child."

Ellen's grin was her answer, and Rose immediately pulled her into another bone-crushing hug. "Oh, Ellen, I'm so excited for you!" she cried, bouncing on the balls of her feet. "And Kit will be thrilled—"

Her friend stiffened and pulled away, her giddy laughter trailing off. "I don't want him to know."

"Oh." Rose cleared her throat. "You know we're betrothed?"

"Yes, and I think it's wonderful." Her smile was genuine, if subdued. "I hope you two will be happy."

"You *are* coming to our wedding?"

"No." She fiddled with the tray of rings on the counter. "No, I'm not."

"Ellen, if you don't attend, then someday you'll be very sorry. You cannot refuse to speak to your brother forever."

Ellen slid a garnet ring onto her finger, then pulled it off. "I cannot imagine that he cares."

Rose waited until she looked up. "You know he does."

"Then he should give me my dowry. He has no right to withhold it just because I didn't marry to his liking."

At this point, Rose suspected Kit would hand over everything he owned if his sister would just stop this nonsense. Neither he nor Ellen would budge first. She wanted to knock their two heads together.

But Ellen was just plain wrong. "He has every right. He earned that money."

"I earned it, too," Ellen shot back, her eyes as green as Kit's when he was upset. "I suffered for that money every bit as much he did. More. My parents were dead, and my big brother left me with old Lady St. Vincent. True, I had enough food and a nice place to live, and I was taught to read and write. But I was also forced to wait on her hand and foot. She was nasty and cruel, and she hit me when I displeased her."

"Oh, Ellen." Rose touched her friend's shoulder in concern. Though it was common for parents to beat misbehaving children, her own mother and father had never subscribed to the practice. "Did Kit know?"

Ellen shook her head. "Her ladyship said she'd throw me out if I complained. Whenever he bothered to visit, I used to beg him to take me with him, away from there, anywhere…" Her voice dropped, and she took a deep, shuddering breath. "He promised me that someday I'd live a better life, and I figure it's my due."

Kit considered the baroness his savior, but there were two sides to every story. To his sister, the woman had been a villain. Still, even if Ellen had informed Kit of the abuses she'd suffered, Rose couldn't see where he'd have had much of a choice.

"What do you expect he could have done? How could he have cared for you? Supported you? He was a mere boy, with no money and no livelihood. And he certainly couldn't have brought you along to school—"

"I know," Ellen ground out miserably. Her jaw was tight, her cheeks pink. "He had no choice; I know it. But that didn't make it easy for me."

Rose made a sympathetic noise. "Of course it didn't."

"I earned that money. I mean to have it. He could dictate my life when I was a child, but not anymore."

"How on earth do you expect Kit to understand what you've been through if you don't talk to him? This is childish, Ellen. You're a married woman, an expectant mother. Try to put yourself in his position. And you must come to our wedding. If not for Kit, do it for me."

Tears welled in Ellen's eyes. "I cannot. If he doesn't love me enough to give me my dowry even though I defied him, I cannot."

Rose's gaze strayed out the window to where Kit was pacing

across the street, clearly as miserable as his sister. She wished he would just give Ellen the money and end this painful stalemate, but unlike his sister, she could see his side, too.

Her heart went out to him. "I'm sorry, Ellen, but I cannot keep the news of your pregnancy to myself. I'll not keep secrets from the man I'm betrothed to. I hope you'll understand. And I hope you'll change your mind about the wedding." She gave the girl's shoulder a squeeze and went outside to join Kit.

He whirled when he saw her. "How is she?" he immediately asked.

"Wonderful. She's with child."

Only a slight widening of his eyes betrayed his reaction. "Is she healthy?" he asked in a carefully neutral tone.

"Quite healthy, save for some expected sickness in the mornings. But she still doesn't want to see you."

His jaw tensed as he took her hand to start the walk back down the hill to his house, where Violet and Lily were waiting to take her home.

She squeezed his fingers. "Do you know, it's possible Ellen's pregnancy may be affecting her thinking and her feelings."

"Whatever would make you believe that?" He didn't look convinced—probably because Rose didn't believe the explanation herself. She just hated seeing him so downcast.

She shrugged. "It's common enough for increasing women to be weepy and such. In any case, Ellen is young. Surely when her child is born she will grow up quickly. In the meantime," she added carefully, "if you want her at our wedding, you only have to give her—"

"I cannot," he interrupted. "I won't buy my sister's love."

Rose held her tongue as they walked, listening to the sounds of horses clopping past, children playing chase, and a woman in one of the tall houses scolding her poor sod of a husband.

After a while, Kit sighed and rubbed the back of his neck. "Thank you for trying."

"There's no need for thanks," she said softly.

She hadn't tried hard enough. Someway, somehow, she would come up with a plan to get these two to make up.

Kit had witnessed his sister's wedding, and Ellen would be there for his.

SIXTY-EIGHT

"*R*OWAN, WAKE UP!" Back at Trentingham three days later, Rose shook her brother's bony ten-year-old shoulder. "Wake up!"

He stretched and yawned, opened his eyes, then promptly closed them. "It's still night."

"But it's almost morning. And I need you to do me a favor."

He rolled over, presenting her with his back. "What?"

"I want you to pretend to be ill." She tousled his wavy black hair. "It could be fun."

"Fun?"

"Mum will take care of you." She sat on his blue-draped oak bed. "She'll bring you treats and sit and play cards."

"No, she won't." With a groan, he turned to face her. "She's taking you to London today, remember? To fetch your wedding gown. Being ill alone is no fun at all."

"She'd never leave you ill. You're her precious baby." When he grimaced, she rushed on. "I'll pay you."

He sat up. "How much?"

"A shilling."

He made a rude noise.

"Very well, then, a crown."

"Maybe." At last Rowan looked interested—but skeptical, too. Rose's brother was no half-wit. "I still think Mum will want to go with you to London..." His green eyes narrowed. "You don't want her to go with you, do you? Why don't you want her to go with you?"

"Never mind why. Will you do this for me or not? A crown, Rowan. A nice, shiny—"

"She won't let you go alone."

"I'll take Violet, then. And Lily, too, if Mum insists—she's at Hawkridge at the moment, and it's right on the way. Will you do it?" He still looked hesitant, blast him. "Think of it as a practical joke," she added, grasping at straws.

"A practical joke?" He perked up. He'd loved practical jokes ever since his little friend Jewel, Ford's niece, had played one on him four years ago. In fact, they hadn't been friends at all until the girl had humiliated him with that prank. Rose had never been able to figure that out.

But she wasn't averse to using it to her advantage. "Yes, a practical joke. Jewel will be so jealous when you tell her all about it at my wedding."

"What will I have to do?"

"Hardly anything." She moved aside, revealing the items she'd arranged on his bedside table. "I brought powder to make your face pale—"

"Cosmetics?"

"Just a little. You can run around the room till you're all hot and sweaty. Then jump back into bed, I'll fluff a little powder on, and we'll put a hot cloth on your forehead." She gestured to the bowl of steaming water she'd brought with her.

"I can moan a lot," he suggested with a grin.

"Excellent. I'll hide everything beneath your bed. Then when Mum comes in you'll be all hot and feverish and moaning and groaning...she won't want to leave you, I'm sure."

His eyes brightened with the thrill of conspiracy. "Can I puke?"

She winced. "You can make yourself puke?" She wondered if that was an entirely healthful idea. "Never mind, I'm sure that won't be—"

"For *two* crowns, I'll puke," he said. "Bring me some food."

SIXTY-NINE

*I*N MADAME BEAUMONT'S London shop, Rose twirled in the red satin gown.

"It's gorgeous," Lily breathed. "Whoever would have imagined red for a wedding?"

"Perfect," Madame Beaumont said in her fashionable French accent—never mind the seventeen years she'd lived here since the Restoration. She waved one arm in an expansive fashionable French gesture. *"Absolument parfait."*

The gown had a scooped neckline and full three-quarter sleeves from which a froth of fine white Brussels lace spilled to Rose's wrists. The underskirt and stomacher were both embroidered with thousands of seed pearls in scrolled designs, and the overskirt had love-knots all over it—small satin bows, loosely sewn so they could be torn off by the guests after the ceremony and taken home as favors.

"I can imagine red," Violet said in her practical way, "but what I cannot imagine is Mum allowing you to retrieve this gown without her."

Rose turned so Madame could detach the stomacher. "Rowan was very ill. She'd seen the gown already for three fittings. And it's not as though I had to come alone. I have you two." She glanced over her shoulder and smiled.

Violet snorted. "This is the time third time this month you've dragged me away from Lakefield. Ford is going to be very relieved when you're finally married."

"Rand, too," Lily put in. "He had to travel back to Oxford all by himself."

"Gemini, he's a grown man." Rose carefully stepped out of the gown. "Besides, at least one of our recent adventures involved *you two* doing the dragging."

"You didn't give us any choice," Violet retorted.

Unusually for her, Rose held her tongue. She was truly grateful to her sisters for forcing her to confront Kit. If it weren't for them, she might never have had a chance to wear her exquisite wedding gown.

Minutes later, a footman carried the boxed garment to the Trentingham carriage. "The Strand," Rose told the driver.

"If you wish to visit the shops," Lily said, scooping up her cat as she climbed in, "the Royal Exchange would be better."

Rose pulled a scrap of paper from her purse to check the name and direction. "I wish to visit Abrahamson & Company, the Strand near Charing Cross."

When the door shut behind them, Violet snatched the paper out of her hand. "Goldsmiths? You want to buy some jewelry?"

"No. Mr. Abrahamson has my money."

"I knew that name was familiar." Lily stroked her cat. "He's the man Father sent a letter to when I needed my inheritance."

"Oh, that's right." Violet focused on Rose. "Why do you want money?"

"It's my money. Does it matter?"

Violet and Lily shared a look but dropped the subject until a while later, when Rose came out of the goldsmith's shop with a bag so heavy she could barely support its weight. She climbed back into the carriage and dropped it to the floorboards with a *thud*, dropping herself onto the bench seat with a "Whew."

"How much money *is* that?" Lily asked.

Rose ignored the question, instead looking to the footman. "Windsor," she ordered.

"Windsor?" Violet's jaw dropped open. "You told Mum we would stay at the town house tonight. I heard you with my own ears."

"Well, I wasn't about to tell her we're spending the night at Kit's house." She hadn't planned to from the outset, but when the combination of Rowan's deception and collecting her sisters resulted in a late start that would make an overnight stay necessary, it had occurred to her that she could spend another night at Kit's house and enjoy more of his kisses.

An unexpected bonus, and one to which she was very much looking forward.

"Windsor," she repeated, settling back as the footman closed the door. It would be a lengthy ride, but toward Trentingham, after all, so her sisters had no real reason to protest. They'd arrive at their respective homes earlier tomorrow than if they'd stayed the night in London.

Lily toed the heavy bag with one red-heeled shoe. "How much money?"

There was no point in lying. "A thousand pounds. Do you know, I had no idea how heavy—"

"A *thousand* pounds?" Violet's eyes widened behind her spectacles. "Faith. Whatever will you do with all that money?"

"I'm giving it to Ellen. Kit's sister."

"*What?*" both her sisters burst out. The cat jumped from Lily's lap and cowered under a bench seat.

"I'd planned to give Ellen all ten thousand, but the goldsmith convinced me it would be too much to carry." Rose rolled her shoulders, still feeling the strain. "So I'm giving her just the thousand with a note from Mr. Abrahamson promising the rest is forthcoming."

Violet slumped against the coach wall. "You're giving Ellen Martyn ten thousand pounds."

"Ellen Whittingham. And I'm telling her it's from Kit. At

least I hope she'll believe it's from Kit. He had promised her eleven—"

"Are you out of your mind?" Lily interrupted.

"Yes," Violet snapped at the same time Rose said, "No."

"It's Kit and Ellen who've lost their minds," she continued and proceeded to tell her sisters the long, sad story. "She didn't even want Kit to know about the babe," she concluded. "I told Kit her pregnancy may be affecting her brain, but—"

Violet shook her head. "I never felt better than when I was carrying my children."

"Not everyone is so lucky," Lily put in. "Rand's foster sister Margery is with child, and lately she's been at sixes and sevens. Practically forgets her own name, the poor thing."

"Have you considered," Violet said to Rose, "that Ellen might simply be a spoiled brat?"

"Yes, as a matter of fact, I have. But she has her reasons for feeling the way she does. Reasons I sympathize with."

Violet took off her spectacles and polished them on her skirts. "And you believe Kit is totally blameless in this?"

"Of course he isn't. In his own way he's as stubborn as his sister. But I cannot blame him for the way he feels, either. Nor can I stand to see him so unhappy. It's like a dark cloud hanging over my wedding. The only way to solve this is to give Ellen my inheritance and make her think the money came from Kit. Then she'll talk to him and everyone will be happy."

Lily scooped up the cat again. "But you'll have given up your inheritance!"

"Don't be a goose. Kit will replace it. If Ellen would only speak to him again, he'd be happy enough to hand over her dowry."

"Has he said so?"

"Not in so many words. But I know him," she added, lifting her chin.

"You're certain you know him?" The cat let out a pathetic meow as Lily clutched it tighter. "You haven't lived with him for even a single day. Goodness, I've been married to Rand for nearly two months now, and he surprises me all the time."

Violet slid her spectacles back on. "I've been living with Ford for *four years*, and sometimes I still wonder—"

"I know Kit," Rose repeated, "and there's no chance he meant to keep that money from his sister forever. It doesn't signify whether the ten thousand pounds was mine or his to begin with. It will be ours soon enough either way."

"It signifies," Lily argued. "Unlike a dowry that becomes your husband's upon marriage, according to Grandpapa's will that money is yours to control. Not many women have the advantage of their own funds. By handing it over to Ellen, you're giving that up. You and Kit may have the same amount of money combined, but none of it will be under your control."

"I don't care. This is more important to me." Rose forced herself to calm. Her sisters were only trying to help, no matter that they were wrong this time. "Kit and Ellen aren't speaking, and both of them are miserable. And they're the only family either of them has...can you imagine one of us missing the other's wedding?"

Her sisters seemed to consider that a moment, then Violet tried another tack. "Have you told Mum and Father what you're doing?"

Rose remained quiet.

"Of course she hasn't," Lily said. "They would never in a million years agree."

"I've no need of their permission. I'm nineteen. The money is legally mine."

"But you knew you would have had an argument, didn't you?" Lily's blue eyes lit with sudden understanding. "That's why we're here with you instead of Mum, isn't it? I'd wager Rowan isn't even ill. How can you live with yourself, scheming behind your own mother's back?"

Rose's lips thinned. "She schemed behind all of our backs, as you well know," she pointed out. "I'd rather scheme than have my sister-in-law refuse to attend our wedding. If that happens, Kit may never forgive her."

"Has it occurred to you," Violet asked with concern, "that Kit might never forgive *you* for meddling in his affairs? Isn't this rather similar to Mum's antics that so angered you?"

"No!" Rose exclaimed, though she was taken aback for a moment. "That was different. Mum was manipulating my relationship, while I'm simply..." Rose swallowed. "Well, anyway I've forgiven her, haven't I?" That was mostly true. The two of them had a fragile truce, and Rose was attending family meals again. "*If* Kit is even upset by this, he will forgive me, too."

"You don't know that for sure—"

"I do." This discussion was going nowhere, and Rose was finished with it. "What is it with all this traffic?" she asked, glaring out the window. "At this rate, my wedding day will arrive before we even get out of London."

"Excellent attempt at changing the subject—" Violet started.

"No," Lily interrupted. "Something *is* going on."

The carriage hadn't budged in the last ten minutes. Since they weren't going anywhere anyway, they all climbed out.

"William and Mary," Rose breathed. "The royal wedding! I'd completely forgotten that today is the fourth of November."

William of Orange and King Charles's niece, Mary, rode in an open carriage down the Strand on their way to St. James's Palace. Caught in the crush, Rose and her sisters were swept into the swarm of citizens lining the streets, waving and cheering as William and Mary approached.

"Everyone seems so happy to see them wed," Lily remarked, holding onto her cat for dear life.

"She's a Protestant," Rose said. "Charles is no fool. He has no legitimate heirs, and he knows the people don't want to see his Catholic brother James on the throne. He's wise to marry James's daughter to a Protestant prince like William of Orange."

"When did *you* become so wise?" Violet asked.

Rose lifted her chin. "Just because I don't bury my nose in books about the past doesn't mean I'm ignorant of the present.

This marriage made for much court gossip. Besides"—she shrugged and cracked a droll smile—"I vow and swear, there was little to do at court in the daytime besides read newsheets."

The happy roar swelled as the bride and groom drew closer. But Mary didn't look happy at all. In fact, as she rode by in the royal carriage, wearing a magnificent blue and gold gown and waving to the people, she looked ready to burst into tears.

"How old is she?" Lily asked.

"Fifteen. And William is twenty-seven." Twenty-seven and short with stooped shoulders, bad teeth, and a large, beaked nose. Rose wouldn't want to marry him, either. Her heart went out to the poor princess.

How lucky Rose was to be marrying a man she truly loved. She could hardly wait for her own wedding just five days away. And she knew Kit felt the same.

Of course, that was assuming he wouldn't be angry she'd forced matters with Ellen. Violet's question kept rattling in her brain.

Has it occurred to you that Kit might never forgive you for meddling in his affairs?

But with the wedding so close, she couldn't allow this brother–sister standoff to continue. Not when there was a way to fix it. Standing by meekly was simply not in her nature.

Kit wouldn't be angry; he'd understand why she'd had to act, and he'd be grateful for the result. She knew him well enough to know that.

Didn't she?

SEVENTY

ITH ALL THE excitement and delay caused by the royal wedding, night was falling by the time Rose and her sisters reached Windsor and the carriage jerked to a stop in front of the pawnshop.

Rose roused herself from a doze and climbed down, then turned back when nobody seemed to be following her. Shivering in the cold night air, she stuck her head through the open doorway of the vehicle. "Aren't you two going to come with me?"

Her sisters looked at each other. "I think not," Lily said for them both.

"We don't choose to be part of this insanity," Violet elaborated.

"Oh, do hush up," Rose said. Obviously they didn't appreciate her roping them into her plot, but she couldn't have simply gallivanted about England alone. This was the sort of thing sisters were for, wasn't it?

And she'd done some thinking on the way here to Windsor.

She clutched her cloak tighter around herself. "Do you know," she told Violet, "I seem to remember you meddling in Ford's affairs. For heaven's sake, you patented and sold his invention without his knowledge; you secretly bought that book, thereby giving him your money—giving him your inheritance, Violet, hmm?—without him knowing—"

"It's not comparable," Lily cut in. "She gave the money to Ford, the man she was planning to marry. You're giving yours to Ellen."

Rose turned on her. "And you gave up control of your own money, too, to Rand's father. Quite willingly, if I remember right."

"That's not comparable, either. It was the only way I could marry Rand."

"I see. Speaking of Rand...wasn't Rand the one who came to Violet with the plan to secretly save Ford's estate? It seems to me he's not averse to a little manipulation for a good cause. Are you telling me Rand would leave you if you meddled in his business?"

"Well, no. I am certain we would work it out. But you're not married yet. What if Kit is so angry he calls off the wedding? Then you'll have lost all your money, and—"

"Never mind." There was no reasoning with either of them. Rose reached back into the carriage and hefted the bag of coins with a little grunt. Fuming, she stomped to the pawnshop's door and knocked.

And knocked. And knocked.

She had just about decided the Whittinghams weren't home when Thomas finally cracked open the door, his face illuminated by a single candle.

"We're closed," he said, then raised the candle higher. "Oh. Lady Rose." With his free hand, he clutched the top of his half-open shirt.

She shifted the heavy bag in her arms. "I have something for Ellen. From Kit."

He eyed the bag curiously. "Well, come in, then, will you?"

She followed him through the dark shop and up the stairs, noting his disheveled hair and wondering if she'd roused him from his bed. It was early yet, but he and Ellen *were* newly wedded. Rose's face suddenly felt hot to think that she and Kit would soon be newly wedded, too.

With all the turmoil of the past few weeks, there hadn't been much time to dwell on thoughts of the marriage bed. Now she remembered the other night, when she had nearly got carried away while kissing Kit. A mix of anticipation and nerves made her quiver.

"In here," Thomas said at the top of the stairs, opening a door to a small room crammed full of furniture and decorative pieces.

"Rose!" Ellen jumped up from a chair, dressed in a pale pink wrapper. The firelight behind her left no doubt that she wore nothing underneath.

So Rose had guessed right. She wasn't sure whether to be embarrassed or amused. "I've brought something for you. From Kit." She walked closer and handed Ellen the bag.

Not expecting its weight, Ellen squealed as it slipped through her hands and fell to the floor with a *thud*, flopping onto its side. The top opened a little, and a coin rolled out and across the plain wooden boards, finally landing with a little *clink*. For a moment, it just sat there, glinting gold in the firelight.

Then Ellen rushed to scoop it up. She folded her fingers around it and looked to Rose, a question in her eyes.

"Your dowry," Rose told her. "The first thousand pounds of it. The rest is forthcoming. It's waiting in London whenever you decide to claim it." She handed Ellen the goldsmith's promissory note for nine thousand pounds. "I couldn't carry more."

That last sentence, at least, was the truth. And if the rest of what she'd said was less than honest, it was meant well, for both Kit's and Ellen's good.

Rose sent up a little prayer that Kit would see it that way.

Ellen stared at the paper with the goldsmith's name. Rose hoped she wasn't going to fuss over the missing thousand pounds—ten thousand, after all, was a vast sum of money.

Ellen still hadn't said a word. "Kit loves you," Rose added simply.

"I know." Tears flooded Ellen's eyes. She opened her

clenched fist and stared down at the coin. "I...I don't know what to say."

"Save your words for Kit. Just tell me you'll come to our wedding."

"Of course I will."

Rose opened her arms, and Ellen stepped into her embrace.

"Kit needs you," Rose murmured by her ear. "You're his only family."

Ellen hugged her tighter. "You'll be his family soon."

"It's not the same. You're with Thomas now, but Kit shares your blood." Rose and her sisters bickered all the time, but even irritated as she was with them now, she knew they only wanted the best for her. And they would always be there if she needed them. Always. "You need Kit, too. Sisters and brothers...it's a bond that should never be broken."

"I was going to make her go to your wedding, anyway," Thomas put in.

"He was going to *try* to make me go," Ellen clarified with a strained laugh. She took a deep breath and stepped back. "It was turning into our first fight."

Rose noticed both their gazes stray to the bag of coins and figured they were too polite to dump them all right there and wallow in their new fortune—but also that they were dying to do so.

"I'll leave you, then," she said, concealing a smile. "Use the money in good health."

Thomas followed her back down the stairs. "Thank you," he said at the door.

"Thank Kit."

"We will. But I thank you, too. I'm aware that what Kit gives us comes out of your pocket as well."

He didn't know the half of it. "Kit and I have plenty," she assured him. "It's the love that counts anyway, isn't it?"

He nodded as he locked the door behind her.

It had gone perfectly. She smiled to herself as a footman ushered her into the carriage.

"We're sorry," Violet and Lily said together before she could even sit down.

"Sorry?"

"We talked while you were gone. And you're right," Violet admitted. "We both traded our inheritances for our marriages. And it was a good bargain."

"The best," Lily agreed.

Rose was stunned by their about-face. "It wasn't exactly the same."

"True." Violet started a little as the carriage lurched and began the short drive down the hill to Kit's house. "We both did it to win our men, and you already have Kit."

Rose hoped she still would after she told him of this night's work.

"We've decided," Lily said, "that what you just did was more romantic. And noble."

"Noble?" No one had ever described Rose Ashcroft as noble. "Noble?"

"We traded money for selfish reasons—for what we ourselves wanted. You sacrificed not for yourself, but for your husband's happiness."

"But can't you see? I cannot be happy if Kit isn't. That was the whole point."

Her sisters exchanged a look. "She gets it," Violet said gravely.

"Yes." Lily breathed a languid sigh. "Isn't love wonderful?"

The carriage rolled to a stop. "We're here," Rose announced unnecessarily, her heart suddenly pounding.

Here was her moment of truth.

As she climbed down the steps with her satchel, she ordered herself to relax. Despite her sisters' dire predictions, she'd known from the first this would work. And she was dying to see Kit. Their separation hadn't got any easier since her last visit.

Putting a smile on her face, she marched up the stairs and banged the knocker.

Graves promptly answered. "Lady Rose. What a surprise."

"I hope it's a pleasant one." Surely everything would be all right. "Especially pleasant for Kit."

"I'm afraid Mr. Martyn has gone to Hampton Court," the butler told them. "My apologies, Lady Rose. I don't expect him back until Thursday."

"Thursday?" Rose echoed, her stomach souring with disappointment. Not only could she not see Kit, the roads were too dangerous to travel at night. The countryside was dark as sin, and highwaymen abounded. Standing on the doorstep, Rose looked helplessly at her sisters, then back to Graves. "Do you suppose we could stay the night anyway?"

"Of course, of course." The butler reached for her satchel. "Mr. Martyn would have my head if I turned you away."

In no time at all, he'd called for footmen to take their luggage and maids to ready rooms. He sent word to the cook to prepare a fine meal, then ushered the sisters through the magnificent entry hall and into the drawing room to await supper.

Rose plopped onto the moss green settle. "I cannot believe this."

"All is not lost." Lily shrugged and set down her cat before sitting beside her. "We shall have a nice sisterly evening together."

Rose had wanted to spend the evening with Kit. "I think I just want to go to sleep—" Suddenly an alarming thought occurred to her. "Good heavens, this is terrible. I won't be able to explain to Kit before we leave."

"Explain what?" Violet asked, perusing a book she'd found on a shelf.

"About Ellen and the money. I need to explain. Else he might hate me and call off the wedding—"

"Oh, Rose." Lily covered her hand with her own. "I'm sorry we ever said that. Kit isn't going to hate you."

Violet shut the book and sat on her other side. "As you pointed out, I meddled in Ford's life, too. And he certainly didn't hate me for doing those things. In fact, he thought it was wonderful."

But now that the idea had taken root in her head, Rose couldn't help but worry. "Ford is different," she said. "He thrives on invention, creation—he's not a man driven by ambition, as Kit is. Ford's happiest when other people take care of the details so he can concentrate on his science. But Kit is used to being in charge. He may not take lightly to my arranging his life."

"You said you know him," Lily reminded her. "You said you were certain he wouldn't react badly."

That was true. Her heart stopped pounding quite so hard. "You're right," she said, "I *do* know Kit. He'll probably laugh when he hears what I've done."

But a moment later she was doubting again. She felt as though her emotions were buffeted by the wind.

More than anything, she wanted to talk to Kit and see his reaction once and for all. But she couldn't drag her sisters to Hampton Court, and she couldn't send them home in the carriage and wait here until Thursday, either. Her wedding was Saturday. She had to make flower arrangements, greet the family coming to stay...

"I'll leave him a letter," she decided. "And I'll ask him to send a message as soon as he reads it." She'd be counting the hours until Thursday night when, she hoped, she'd receive words of reassurance. Words that would allow her a good night's sleep.

"The perfect solution," Violet said.

Not perfect, but the best Rose could do.

"He loves you," Lily reminded her.

Rose could only hope he loved her enough.

SEVENTY-ONE

*H*E WAS A coward.

Kit had argued with himself on the entire drive from London. Should he give Ellen her dowry before the wedding, so she'd attend and neither of them would be sorry later? Or wait until she started talking to him again, no matter how long it took?

He wanted to do the latter; he didn't want to give in to her childish behavior, and he didn't want to feel like he was buying her love. But he didn't have the guts. As evidenced by the fact that, following his final inspection of the completed chapel at Whitehall, he'd detoured to visit his goldsmith before driving back here to Windsor.

Not to mention that even though his work had kept him a day later than he'd intended—even though it was nightfall already and his wedding was tomorrow—he was even now heading up the High Street to Ellen's house instead of down the hill to his own.

Still, if he was a coward, at least he was a happy one.

Amazingly, in less than twenty-four hours, Rose would be his. He hadn't needed the knighthood, let alone a more impor-tant title. He'd won her as plain Kit Martyn, and there was satisfaction to be found in that.

No more mishaps had occurred, and, in fact, his work was proceeding extremely well. Lord Trentingham, of course, was enamored of his new greenhouse. Charles was pleased with the chapel at Whitehall, and when he saw the exquisite dining room here in Windsor, which was also now complete, Kit was confident he'd approve. It was unfortunate the new Hampton Court building was so far behind schedule, but as its intended occupant was currently in France, that wasn't exactly disastrous. Kit had double- and triple-checked every detail with his foreman, making certain the project would progress well in his absence. And Kit was certain, too, that, when finished, it would exceed Charles's expectations. Despite losing the Deputy Surveyor post, his future was not at all bleak.

A week from today, he and Rose would attend the queen's birthday celebration at Whitehall, then leave for Italy the day after that. A dream come true for them both. He would learn from the great architects, and Rose would finally get to immerse herself in the Italian language.

But first things first, Kit thought as his carriage drew up before the pawnshop. Before he could be happy with the new woman in his life, he needed to square things with the old one.

He drew a deep breath, hefted the bag of coins, and marched up to the pawnshop's door. It was locked tight at this late hour, but as he was raising his hand to knock, it swung open. Ellen and her husband both stood there, wrapped in cloaks, obviously on their way out.

"What are you doing here?" she asked.

"Where are you going?" he countered—then realized she'd actually spoken to him. Would wonders never cease? Just when he was ready to give in, she'd saved him from proving himself a coward.

"Now that the shop is closed for the evening, I was going to try to see you," she said. "As I've done the past four nights."

"I was away," he said unnecessarily. "Here." He held out the bag. "A down payment on your dowry. I never meant to keep it from you. My goldsmith is holding the rest for you in London."

"I know. I've been trying for four days to thank you." Instead of taking the money, she threw her arms around him, the hard bag of gold between them. "Thank you so very, very much." She kissed both his cheeks. "I love you. I'm sorry I didn't trust you, that I tried to punish you by remaining silent."

Though clearly rehearsed, her words sounded sincere. But Kit was stunned. He pulled away. "How did you know I was about to give it to you?" Until a few minutes ago, he hadn't been sure himself.

Ellen exchanged a confused glance with Thomas, then looked back to Kit. "What do you mean, how did I know?"

"There was no need to bring more gold," Thomas added. "The first bag was sufficient proof of your intentions."

Kit shifted the heavy weight in his arms. "The first bag?"

"The one you sent with Rose." Ellen enunciated slowly, as though he were a half-wit who required the simplest explanation.

Which wasn't too far off from the way he was feeling at the moment. "Rose? What does Rose have to do with this?"

Thomas looked even more confused than Kit felt. "She brought us your money. Or a thousand pounds of it, and a promissory note from your goldsmith for the rest. Abrahamson & Company."

"My money is with Lazarus & Sons." Kit's thoughts seemed to be moving through a fog, until suddenly everything cleared. "Oh, hang it all. It must have been *her* money. Her inheritance."

Thomas blinked. "Is she mad?"

"Clearly," Kit said. "Insane, infuriating—"

"Madly in love," Ellen interrupted with a soft smile.

Reeling, Kit leaned against the doorpost. Not light to begin with, the bag seemed to be growing heavier by the moment. "Do you think I could come in and sit down?"

SEVENTY-TWO

O NOTE HAD come from Kit.

Wearing a sapphire silk dressing gown, Rose paced her crimson bedchamber while her sisters and Judith watched. They were here to help her dress for her wedding.

But she couldn't help wondering if she was going to have one.

She lifted the bouquet she'd made for herself and stroked the soft red and white petals. If she hadn't given all that money to Kit's sister, she wouldn't think twice about the fact that he hadn't arrived yet; in truth, she had no reason to expect him this early. And he wasn't supposed to see her before the wedding, anyway.

But she'd thought she'd hear from him Thursday night. And now it was Saturday...

"You look worried," Judith said.

Rose inhaled deeply of the sweet floral scent before she set the flowers down and forced a smile. "Wedding nerves. You suffered them, too, if you'll remember."

"Did I?" Judith laughed, looking happier than Rose had ever seen her. "But there was no cause for nerves, as I discovered. If it's the wedding night you're dreading...don't. It was ever so wonderful—" She must have suddenly realized what she was saying, because she broke off, her cheeks flushing pink.

Rose struggled to keep a straight face. "Thank you," she told Judith primly. "I feel much better."

"Oh, good." Judith smiled.

Rose's hair was already dressed with pearls and red ribbons, her lashes darkened, and her eyes lightly outlined with kohl. For want of something to do, she sat at her dressing table and fluffed more powder on her face.

"You're going to look like a ghost," Violet said.

"Gemini, you're right." Staring at her pale self in the mirror, she pulled a little sheet of red Spanish paper from a tiny booklet. "Where's Kit?" she asked, rubbing it on her cheeks.

"Now you look like a harlot." Lily grabbed a handkerchief to rub some off. "Let me help you."

Rose sat rigid under her ministrations. "Is it time for me to get dressed?"

"Might as well." Violet swept the red gown off the bed. "Shall I call Harriet?"

"No. You three can help me. I cannot stand any more of her chatter. All she ever talks of is Walter and getting married. I almost wish they'd chosen to live at Hampton Court instead of with me."

"That isn't true," Lily said.

Of course it wasn't. Harriet's chatter hadn't bothered her before she gave the money to Ellen. She just couldn't take so much unadulterated happiness right now. It set her teeth on edge.

She slid out of her wrapper and stood in place while Judith slipped the diaphanous chemise over her head, being careful not to ruin her hair or her carefully applied face. Then her sisters brought the gown over and helped her wiggle into it. Violet smoothed the satin skirts over her hips while Lily stepped close to lace her tightly into the bodice.

"I think I may be with child," she murmured to Rose's chest.

Rose blinked and glanced down to Lily's still-flat stomach. In her dusky pink gown, her sister's body looked as lithe as ever. "Are you sure?"

Lily looked up with a dreamy smile. "I'm two weeks late."

"Oh, Lily!" Violet threw her arms around her.

"Me, too," Judith said shyly.

Lily froze. "You're not jesting?"

"No," Judith said, and they both let out excited little screams.

Beaming, Lily turned from Violet's arms into her friend's. "Remember when you said we should be newly wedded together? Now we're going to become mothers together, too!"

Rose watched them embrace, slowly tying her abandoned laces in a bow while her own flat stomach churned. Lily and Judith and Ellen, all pregnant. And Violet had three children already.

On this day that was supposed to be happy, she felt so left out. She reached for her stomacher and plastered it against her front, beginning to fasten the tabs. When would her turn come? Never, if Kit didn't show up to marry her—

"Edmund is thrilled," Judith gushed. "What did Rand say?"

"I haven't told him yet." Lily hugged herself round the middle as though she were protecting her child. "I wanted to be sure. We've been disappointed before—"

"Oh, heavens," Judith said. "You've been wed just two months. You must tell him. If he's half as happy as Edmund, you'll end up spending a night that makes you wonder if you could possibly conceive a second child when you're already increasing with the first—"

She clapped a hand over her mouth, her cheeks looking like she'd used a whole booklet of Spanish paper.

Lily laughed. "I'll tell him today."

"Tell who what?" came a voice from the doorway.

Kit.

Rose's heart thundered beneath her laces.

"Never mind," Lily blurted.

Kit locked his gaze on Rose, but she couldn't read his face.

"You're not supposed to see me before the wedding," she said inanely. "It's bad luck."

"I'll risk it. I need to talk to you."

He looked so serious. The little breakfast she'd managed to choke down this morning was threatening to come back up.

"Well...we'll leave," Lily said.

"Excellent idea." He waited by the door while the other three women scurried out, then shut it decisively behind them. "Do you need help with that?" he asked, indicating Rose's half-attached stomacher.

"No." Her fingers began moving again, albeit shakily. He was walking closer. "Kit—"

Her sentence was cut off when his mouth crushed down on hers. He kissed her with such heat and urgency that her knees threatened to buckle. By the time he broke contact, she was gasping for air, reeling with the sudden reversal of worry to elation.

He kissed her chin, her throat, her collar bone above her dangling stomacher. "I love you so much," he murmured against her skin. Closing his eyes, he leaned his forehead against hers. "I cannot wait for tonight."

A delicious shiver traveled through her body, even as she felt the itch of tears behind her eyes. "I was so afraid you'd hate me."

"Hate you?" Straightening, he lifted her chin until her gaze was forced to his. His incredible eyes searched hers. "Why?"

"For meddling in your affairs. I only wanted your happiness..."

"Did you think I didn't know that? Did you think I wouldn't fall in love with you all over again when I realized you were willing to give up your inheritance to bring me and my sister together? What sort of fellow do you think I am?"

She'd known what sort of fellow he was—and she suspected she was falling in love all over again, too. "You didn't answer my letter."

"What letter?" His thumb moved from her chin, skimming

tenderly over her cheek. "I never received any letter."

"I left it propped on your washstand."

He shrugged. "No one's ever done anything that touched me the way you have. Hang it all, sweetheart, when I went to give Ellen her dowry and she told me—"

"What?" She forgot about the missing letter as her hand flew up to grasp his wrist. "You gave Ellen her dowry?"

"I tried to," he said with a wry grin. "She told me you already had." His gaze softened. "However was I lucky enough to win a girl as special as you?"

Rose's throat tightened. No one had ever called her special. "I should have known you would do the right thing."

He kissed her again, more gently this time, a tender kiss that brought her tears to the fore. No matter what he said, she knew she was the lucky one—lucky he hadn't given up at the start, when she'd pushed him away for all the wrong reasons.

And she was well aware she had her mother to thank for that gift.

"No crying on your wedding day," he said, wiping a rogue tear off her cheek with a warm thumb. "I'm sure that's worse luck than having me see you before the ceremony."

She managed a watery chuckle.

His hands went to finish attaching her stomacher. "You look beautiful."

"You look better," she said, her pulse thumping madly under his fingers. He wore a deep green velvet suit with silver braid trim on the long waistcoat and the surcoat that went over it. Just enough lace fell from beneath his cuffs, and a tasteful diamond pin winked from the folds of his cravat.

Perfect. If she'd noticed how he was dressed when he first appeared in her doorway, she could have spared herself a few anguished seconds of worry. No one would take him for anything but a groom.

A heart-stoppingly handsome one.

His fingers traced the pearl scrollwork on her stomacher. "I have something for you." He pulled a small wooden box from his pocket. "I wasn't sure what color you'd be wearing, but I think they will match."

She opened the lid to find an exquisite pair of earrings, two teardrop pearls swinging from clustered diamond tops. "They must have cost a fortune," she gasped. She'd never seen such enormous pearls.

He smiled as he took them from the box and moved closer to fasten them on her ears. "I may not be titled, but I'm hardly a pauper."

"I'm not wearing any earrings. I didn't have any I wanted to wear."

"I'm glad to hear it," he said, kissing a bare lobe before he decorated it. "I don't ever want to see you wearing that deuced duke's jewels again. In fact, I think you should pawn them. Permanently. I just happen to know of a pawnshop."

She laughed as he attached the second earring. When he was finished, he drew her close, running his hands over her back and down to her waist. She thrilled at the sensation of his hands on her.

"I love you," he said.

She'd never tire of hearing those three words. "I love you, too."

"I love you in red."

"I'm glad." His scent was making her dizzy. "My sisters both wore blue."

"I'd love to see you in blue, too." He nipped her neck. "I'd love to see you in purple," he said conversationally. "I'd love to see you in green. I'd love to see you in gold."

Each word warm against her skin set off a fizz of champagne bubbles in her stomach. She sighed, tilting her head to give him better access.

His lips found the sensitive hollow of her throat. "But mostly," he whispered wickedly, "I'd love to see you in nothing at all."

If her sisters hadn't knocked on the door just then, she feared he might have.

SEVENTY-THREE

STANDING AT THE front of her family's small, crowded chapel, Rose shifted on her high-heeled shoes and slipped her hand into Kit's.

"Christopher Martyn, wilt thou have this woman to thy wedded wife, to live together after God's ordinance in the holy estate of matrimony? Wilt thou love her, comfort her, honor, and keep her in sickness and in health; and, forsaking all others, keep thee only unto her, so long as ye both shall live?"

"I will." The confident words boomed through the magnificent oak-paneled chamber, binding Kit to Rose.

But Rose wasn't listening to the ceremony. Instead she was thinking that Kit was the most handsome, intelligent, loving, and decent person she'd ever known. She was so glad he'd managed to burst her foolish bubble and make her realize what really counted.

Love, clear and true.

Happy tears brightened her mother's brown eyes. Rose knew Mum believed Kit was perfect for her—and had done everything in her power to get them together. Her sisters, too, had braved Rose's temper for the sake of securing her happiness. She was so grateful to them all.

If she hadn't been blessed with a family who would do anything for her, she wouldn't be standing here with Kit.

Her gaze wandered over the assembled guests, landing on Lily. Her younger sister stood next to Rand, her rich sable hair cascading to her shoulders in glossy ringlets, her lips curved in a way that made Rose think she'd just shared her secret. Beside her, Rand beamed a smile, looking like he wanted to shout to the world that he was going to be a father.

The two were so clearly in love, Rose knew they belonged together—and she was thrilled for her sister. Thank goodness Lily had ended up with Rand, leaving her to find Kit.

The priest cleared his throat and looked back down at his *Book of Common Prayer*. "Lady Rose Ashcroft, wilt thou have this man to thy wedded husband..."

Standing on Lily's right, their older sister Violet shifted one of her twin babies on her hip, gazing up at Ford. Sun streamed through the stained glass windows, glinting off her spectacles as she whispered something in his ear. It seemed they'd returned to their usual state of domestic bliss. No marriage was perfect, but love smoothed out the flaws.

Holding their other infant, Ford squeezed his wife around the shoulders. Seated cross-legged at their feet, their three-year-old son Nicky traced a finger over the patterns in the colorful glazed tile floor, obliviously happy.

Rose couldn't wait to have a family of her own. She flashed a quick smile at Ellen where she stood beside Thomas, one hand in his and the other resting lightly on her middle. The niece or nephew growing there, Rose thought giddily, would someday be cousin to her own children.

"...so long as ye both shall live?" the priest concluded expectantly.

In the hush that followed, Rose's heart swelled. She'd thought her wedding day would never come.

"I will," she pledged, squeezing Kit's hand.

A few more words, a gorgeous ruby ring slipped onto her

finger, and Rose and Kit were husband and wife, Mr. Christopher Martyn and Lady Rose Martyn.

Once upon a time, she'd thought that disparity would bother her. But nothing could be further from the truth. When her new husband lowered his lips to meet hers, Rose threw her arms around him, propriety be hanged.

To think she'd almost settled for being a mere duchess.

Kit made her feel like a queen.

SEVENTY-FOUR

*R*OSE COULDN'T remember ever hating idle chitchat more than she did late that afternoon. Idle chitchat was her nemesis.

Especially when it contrived to keep her from her wedding night.

"Farewell, Aunt Cecily, Aunt Arabel," she said with a forced smile, kissing Mum's sisters on both cheeks. She urged them down the portico's steps to the lawn. "Thank you for coming." As they finally walked away with their children, she leaned close to Kit's ear. "I think that's the last of our guests. We can leave now."

He glanced toward the river. "Soon."

As her curious gaze followed his, Jewel and Rowan stepped onto the portico. "I have something for you," Jewel said.

Rose looked down to find a box, exquisitely fashioned of colored, leaded glass. "It's beautiful!" she exclaimed.

"Jewel made it," Rowan informed them. "Her hands are covered in cuts." His voice rang with admiration, as though blood and gore were badges of honor.

"We'll treasure it," Kit told the girl. Taking the box, he reached to squeeze Rose around her waist. "Won't we?"

"Absolutely." She tingled all up and down her side where he'd pulled her against him. "Thank you so very much," she told Jewel. "I had no idea you worked with glass."

Jewel hid her scarred hands behind her back. "Mama and my little brother both make jewelry. I got tired of doing the same thing. I was looking at the windows in a church, and Papa told me how the lead is soldered like some of Mama's jewelry. I thought I might like to try it."

Mum moved around Rose, plucking the last of the love-knots off her gown. She took the glass box from Kit, lifted the lid, and dropped the little red bows inside. "It's over," she said with a long, drawn-out sigh.

Rose wished it were over. She wanted to be alone with Kit. "It was a beautiful wedding, Mum. Thank you for hosting it. And for...everything else."

The affection in Mum's warm brown eyes told Rose her mother had got her meaning, though she tactfully let the subject drop. "I never really got to plan a big wedding," Mum said instead, heaving a regretful sigh. "I shall have to do so for Rowan. A nice, long betrothal—"

Rose's laugh interrupted her. "Have you considered that Jewel might want to plan her *own* wedding? Or Jewel's mother—"

"Jewel?" Rowan's eyes widened in alarm. "I'm not going to marry Jewel!"

Kit gave the boy an indulgent smile. "Wait till you're older—"

"Never!" Rowan looked at Jewel with such horror, the girl shrank back.

Rose pulled Kit aside. "May we leave *now*?" she asked.

He confused her by glancing toward the river again. "I don't think...ah, yes. Here's our transportation."

Rose turned and stared at the beautiful, gilded barge rounding the bend and approaching Trentingham's dock. "*This* is how we're getting to Windsor? What about your carriage?"

"Ellen and Thomas accompanied me here. I sent them home

in it. You wouldn't have wanted to ride back with them, would you?"

"Not really." She liked Kit's sister well enough, but she was anxious to get her new husband to herself. "This is Ford's barge. Was it his idea?"

"Violet's, actually. Who knew a romantic heart hid inside that intellectual exterior?"

"Violet," Rose said low, "talked of this barge back when she and Ford were courting. There's a bed inside the cabin."

"Is that so?" Kit's gaze intensified. "Well, let's go then," he said loudly, turning back to her family.

"You know," her father said for the third time, "it's traditional for a girl to spend her first married night at her parents' house."

"I'm only questioning convention," Rose shouted.

Her mother smiled. "When are you going to London, dear?"

"The queen's birthday celebration is Friday, so we're thinking probably Wednesday."

"Windy?" Father frowned. "Yes, the wind does seem to be picking up."

"It certainly is, Father." Rose shared an amused glance with Kit. "I think everyone should hurry inside."

A few hugs and kisses and maternal tears later, Rose and Kit crossed the lawn to the river and climbed aboard the barge. He pulled her close, wrapping an arm around her shoulders. They turned to bid farewell to her family, happy to be alone at last.

Well, nearly alone. There was a crew, of course, to guide the vessel to Windsor. And a youth playing a violin, sheltered from the weather by the tall wall of the cabin that sat in the barge's middle.

Anticipation thrummed through Rose's veins. She forced herself to stand at the rail, waving at her family until the barge pulled away. The wind was indeed picking up, whipping her skirts and hair. Her heart was accelerating, too, until it beat in a wild rhythm. Beside her, Kit felt warm and solid, an anchor and a temptation all at once.

"Inside," she demanded the moment Trentingham was out of view. She couldn't get him into the cabin fast enough. No sooner had they slammed the door behind them than she threw herself at Kit.

The kiss, fierce and frenzied, cleared her mind of everything beyond the cabin. Violin music swirled through her head as her focus narrowed to soft lips, strong arms, and the singularly delicious scent of her husband. Somehow, he had become her world.

When the barge rocked, threatening their balance, she took the opportunity to draw him deeper into the cabin, inching them both toward the bed.

His laugh rumbled against her lips. "Aren't you even a tiny bit nervous?" he asked, his fingers moving to detach the tabs of her stomacher.

"A little," she admitted breathlessly. "But that's what makes it fun."

His breath hitched. "My daring Rose," he murmured. Her stomacher dropped to the floor.

She felt the bed against the back of her knees and sank down upon it, pulling him down with her.

But what her bottom rested on was higher than a mattress. And harder. She put a hand back, feeling wood. She twisted in dismay, her eyes flying open. A wedding feast for two was spread on a gorgeous carved mahogany table surrounded by six matching chairs.

There was no bed. "Where in heaven's name is the bed?"

"Hmm?" Deprived of her lips, Kit kissed her throat instead.

"The bed. The bed is gone." Disappointment dulled all the exciting, stormy sensations. "Kit, there's no bed."

He raised his head and blinked. "You're not jesting."

"Can we make do without it?" she asked desperately, though she couldn't imagine how that would work.

Kit laughed again, though with an obvious undertone of frustration. "No, sweetheart. This is our wedding night, for pity's sake. We'll wait for a bed."

His murky, olive-green eyes revealed that he was as vexed as she.

Sconces on the beautifully paneled walls held flickering candles. "I suppose the journey isn't that long," Rose said doubtfully. But now that her heartbeat was calming and her faculties returning, she knew Kit was right. She didn't want to give herself to her husband on the rough wooden deck of an old boat.

"We'll be there before we know it." Pulling her onto his lap, he reached around her to fill two goblets from a waiting bottle of champagne. "I wonder what happened to the bed?"

"I don't know." Rose laid her head on his shoulder. "The barge used to be rather shabby. Violet had mentioned it was being refurbished, but I didn't realize they'd scuttled the bed."

"They have a family now. A table makes more sense."

"Not to us."

"At least we can occupy ourselves with this veritable feast. Did you eat anything at the wedding?"

"I was too busy talking to people." She smiled at the wonderful memories. "But I'm not hungry."

"No? Drink, then." He handed her a goblet, waiting for her to sit up before raising his in a salute. "To a lifetime of love."

"And beds," she said, draining her cup in one long swallow.

He laughed and pulled her near. Suddenly she felt so happy, tears pricked her eyes. "Kit, I'm so glad I married you."

He squeezed her tight. "Then you wouldn't rather be here with the duke?" he teased.

"I expect he'd be puking all over me."

He gulped and swallowed. "What?"

"The duke gets seasick."

"Ah." She heard laughter in his voice. "Good thing you chose me instead."

"Good thing," she sighed in agreement.

Violin music drifted in from the deck, and the boat rocked gently as it made its way downriver. She relaxed against him again, just breathing, existing, enjoying the closeness as he munched cheese and bread and sipped wine.

She must have dozed off, because the next thing she knew, a bump startled her awake. "Gemini, we're here." She jumped off Kit's lap and reached for her stomacher as a knock came at the door.

"Mr. Martyn?"

"One moment," he called, gently covering her fumbling fingers. He moved them aside and went to work reattaching her tabs. "Careful of your dress; you'll want to wear it to the queen's ball." When he'd finished, he swung her up into his arms and began carrying her off the barge.

"Kit!" She laughed, thinking she was much too tall for this. This wasn't just a few feet like in the maze. And there were people watching. "You'll hurt yourself. Put me down."

"I think not." They had docked right beside his house—*their* house—and he walked around to the front. "I've been told I should carry you over the threshold. Else we could have bad luck."

"Only if I trip."

"Well, this way you won't trip, will you?" The wind whipped her skirts, all but blowing them up the portico's steps. "I'm ensuring our future," he informed her as the front door swung open and he carried her inside.

Holding the door grandly, Graves grinned at them both.

"Put me down," Rose said, feeling windblown and silly.

"Not a chance." Kit continued up the stairs. "We've one more threshold before we're safe."

He crossed that one—their bedchamber—before he set her on her feet.

"I feared for your heart," she said and kissed him.

But he didn't even seem winded. "You weigh nothing," he assured her, and she supposed she didn't—at least compared to big beams. She licked her lips, appreciating the way his shoulders filled out his exquisite surcoat. How could she have wanted an idle aristocrat when a working fellow like Kit had muscles that made a girl's hands itch to run all over him?

By the fireplace a small round table sat between two chairs, its polished surface covered with dishes of fruit, a pile of cakes, and bowls of whipped cream and strawberry sauce. Kit dipped an orange slice in both and slipped it between her lips. "Dessert," he said with a smile.

The combination was tart and sweet, but she still wasn't hungry. "I'd rather have a kiss," she told him archly.

He obliged her, thoroughly, so thoroughly her knees felt weak when he finally drew back and turned her around to face a low chest of drawers.

She blinked and focused. "There it is!" she cried, spotting a square of white underneath it. "The letter!"

"The letter?" he said from behind her.

"The note I left for you, explaining about Ellen. It must have fallen off the washstand and somehow wound up under there."

"I don't care about the letter." His hands tightened on her shoulders. "Look up."

And there, on the oak-paneled wall, was an oval gilt-framed painting.

Of her.

The Rose on the canvas was the same one he'd sketched that first day they'd spent together, her lips curved gently, her eyes holding secrets. "I drew a hundred pictures of you," he said softly, "but I always came back to this one."

"It's beautiful," she breathed, staring. She imagined him painting it, his brush stroking lovingly while she worried needlessly that his devotion might have been a lie. Her heart squeezed in her chest. "A thing of beauty."

"It ought to be," he said in her ear, then turned her back around to face him. "Just look at its subject."

When he gathered her close, she melted in her husband's arms.

SEVENTY-FIVE

"*L*OOK AT ALL the people crowding the balconies!" Rose exclaimed.

Everyone who was anyone seemed to be at the queen's birthday celebration. Musicians played at the far end of the chamber while courtiers danced, all dressed in their finest and wearing every jewel they could lay their hands on. From the upper level, more aristocrats and dignitaries looked on.

Kit watched Rose's gaze sweep the classical white and gold room and the stunning ceiling painted by Sir Peter Paul Rubens. "Gemini," she said, "this must be the most beautiful building in all of England."

"More beautiful than mine?" he teased, enjoying her reaction to Whitehall's Banqueting House. In truth, he only hoped to build something as magnificent as Inigo Jones's masterpiece someday. While Rose would be happy here for hours, he couldn't wait to leave and begin their journey to the Continent, where he'd finally get the chance to study the architecture that had inspired Jones.

And yet, this appearance was somewhat of a triumph for him, too. "Shall we dance?" he asked and guided his new wife into the throng. And there he was, plain Mr. Christopher Martyn, dancing at Queen Catharine's birthday ball.

Rose was a masterpiece herself, tall and slender and his. He could still hardly believe he'd won her.

When Nell Gwyn waved at her and winked, she grinned back. "Imagine," she mused. "Nell was born in a bawdy house and ended up the mother of one of the king's sons."

"Very like me." Kit whirled her around. "I was born in a cottage and ended up wed to an earl's daughter."

He'd meant it humorously, but it seemed she was in a reflective mood tonight. "It's odd, don't you think, the way people crave the opposite of what they have? Nell makes Charles happy because her house is his home. A regular home, and a real life when he's with her. She throws parties where he's a guest, not a king. None of his other mistresses do that for him. They take what he has to offer without giving back in return."

Delighted, Kit gave her a quick kiss, right there in front of the king and queen and everyone. "And where did you come by all this information?"

"The ladies here at court. They like me very much, you know. Ever since I started supplying them with lurid sonnets."

He laughed. "The gentlemen like you, too. A bit too much for my comfort."

"No need to worry on that account. I don't even see them anymore." She closed her eyes and leaned into him. "For me, you're the only gentleman in this room."

He laughed again and kissed her again, and fervently thanked God again that he'd won her. He couldn't remember ever feeling this happy.

"Even the queen looks happy tonight," Rose said, as though she were reading his mind. She smiled in Catharine's direction. Dressed in a magnificent cloth-of-gold gown, the queen danced with Charles, gazing up at him with calm satisfaction. On the thirty-ninth anniversary of her birth, she seemed at peace with both the blessings and heartaches of her complicated life.

But William of Orange and his new princess didn't look so

happy. Kit watched them move desultorily around the dance floor. William was shorter than Mary and seemed to have a consumptive cough. Although he was only twenty-seven, deep lines marred his face.

"Poor Mary has been crying again," Rose said with a melancholy sigh.

"Again?"

"I saw her on her wedding day in London. She looked terribly unhappy."

Kit drew her closer. "Their marriage was arranged for diplomatic purposes. Neither of them really had a choice. That's the fate of the important."

Her mood seemed to lighten. "I'm so glad you're not important."

Once that might have hurt, but rank now seemed insignificant next to the joy of wedding Rose.

When they came off the dance floor, Christopher Wren was waiting and handed them both glasses of champagne. "To our queen," he said. "And your successes. The chapel turned out beautifully, just as I'd envisioned it."

Kit toasted him back. "You gave me excellent plans to work from."

"But Windsor's dining room was your own. An extraordinary achievement."

"Thank you."

"I'm sorry about the appointment."

"That's water under the bridge," Kit said, meaning it. He had a new life, new plans.

The Earl of Rosslyn sidled up, a champagne glass in one hand and his ever-present walking stick in the other. "Martyn," he slurred.

Kit wrapped an arm around Rose's shoulders. "Rosslyn. I take it life is treating you well?"

"I find myself overburdened with too much work." He drained the glass and snagged another from a passing maid. "So sad that I won the post in your place."

Kit shrugged and began to turn away. His old classmate had won the post fair and square, but that didn't mean he had to listen to his backhanded boasts.

"A shame you miscalculated the length of that span at Hampton Court," he heard Rosslyn say behind him.

Swiveling back, Kit exchanged a startled glance with Wren. The older man knew Kit had done all his measurements and calculations in private—that besides the two of them, only the perpetrator would know exactly what had been wrong with the building. And Wren had promised to keep that knowledge to himself.

Aghast, Kit turned on Rosslyn. "What sort of man would sabotage a friend's reputation to further his own ends?"

The fellow was drunk and slow, but Kit saw the horror dawn in his eyes as he realized he'd given himself away.

"You set the fire, didn't you?" Kit pressed. "And altered the plans at Hampton Court. I expect you counted yourself lucky that Harold Washburn's greed took care of Windsor for you. By purchasing inferior materials, he lined his pockets and delayed a project without you lifting so much as a finger."

"No, that was me, too," Rosslyn said smugly. "I paid Washburn off."

Kit's jaw tensed. No wonder the old cur of a foreman had been able to throw around so much money.

"Guards!" Wren called.

Leaning heavily on his ribbon-topped walking stick, Rosslyn glared at Kit. A wild sheen in his eyes said he wasn't all there. "Your loss, my gain," he growled. "At last I've proven myself better than you." When a red-coated guard stepped up to restrain him, he twisted from the man's grip. "All those years in school, no matter how well I did, that upstart Kit Martyn always did better—"

He was cut off when a second guard grabbed him and the two began dragging him away. Rosslyn kicked, drawing every gaze in the room with his shouted curses, his useless walking stick banging along the planked wood floor.

Long after everyone else had returned to their revelry, Kit stared after him. "I always thought we were friends," he murmured, stunned.

Rose squeezed his hand. "He never seemed very friendly."

He blinked and looked at her. "Acquaintances, then. Superficial ones, perhaps. But there was never any animosity."

"On your part."

Wren took Kit's empty glass from his hand and shoved a full one into it. "Drink up. I'll be back."

Numbly, Kit followed his advice, taking it a step further by making his way over to a delicate gilt chair and lowering himself gingerly onto it. Realizing petty childhood competition could lead to treachery all these years later was a shock he was finding hard to absorb.

Rose followed and stood beside him, a hand on his shoulder. "He's talking to King Charles."

"Rosslyn?"

"No, Wren. The two of them are making their way outside. Out the same way Rosslyn was taken."

Kit rose to see, but the men had already exited the building. Feeling fatigued, he turned to his wife. "Let's leave. I've had enough. We can get a good night's sleep before we start our journey tomorrow."

"Wren said he'd be back." She peered over Kit's shoulder. "Look, he's coming now. With the king."

Kit drained his glass and set it down as the men approached. Rose took his arm, a silent show of support. The king wasted no time with greetings. "Martyn. I've just learned that in the face of betrayal, you put Barbara's life, and those of our children, before your own interests. I'm very grateful."

Kit's gaze flicked to Wren. "I told him," the older man admitted.

"I gathered that." Kit looked back to King Charles. "The building was flawed. I did only what needed to be done. Any other man would do the same."

"Not any," the king disagreed. "Only the sort of man I was

searching for to appoint Deputy Surveyor. I believe I've found him."

A tiny gasp escaped Rose's lips, and her hand tightened on Kit's arm. It took a moment for the man's words to sink in before Kit swept him a deep bow. "I-I don't know how to thank you, Your Majesty." It had happened so fast, he could scarcely believe his long-held goal was achieved at last. "I shall endeavor to ensure you chose the right man."

"I expect no less."

"There's more," Wren said.

King Charles nodded. "I've stripped Gaylord Craig of his title and properties. I wish to grant them to you. You shall henceforth be known as the Earl of Rosslyn."

Dumbfounded, Kit looked between the king and Wren. "It seems only fitting," Wren said graciously.

Kit's knees locked. He felt all the blood draining from his face.

"Sit down." With a laugh, Rose pushed him back onto the chair.

Clearly enjoying his own magnanimity, King Charles grinned. "I'll accept your gratitude later, Rosslyn." *Rosslyn.* "My queen is awaiting a birthday toast."

"Congratulations, my lord. My lady." Wren bowed and walked off.

As Kit watched them both go, his world slowly stopped spinning and righted itself. Almost.

"Deputy Surveyor and an earldom," he murmured. "Wren is Surveyor General and only a knight."

Rose moved closer. "Wren didn't save King Charles's children's lives."

It still didn't seem real. "You're a countess now," he told his wife. "Lady Rosslyn."

There in front of all the court, she perched herself on his lap and closed her fingers around his cravat, using it to pull him near for a quick kiss. "I don't care," she said gaily, adding "my lord" with an impish grin.

My lord. Two short words that meant so much. He kissed her again for good measure, feeling, at the moment, that she was the only familiar thing he had to cling to. "After all those weeks of putting up with that deuced duke's attentions, you cannot tell me you don't care—"

"I don't," she repeated. "You've been vindicated, and we're off to explore the world together, and that's all that matters."

That sounded wonderful, but too simple. A maid came by with more champagne, and he took a glass, still dazed. "I'm not sure," he said slowly.

"Sure of what?"

"Anything. Where the Rosslyn lands are, for starters."

"Good heavens," she said with mock alarm, "I hope it's not Northumberland."

"And what it will take to care for them."

"I can help you with that." She looked both startled and pleased at that thought.

"And whether I can go *off to explore the world* when I've just been appointed Deputy Surveyor."

Now genuine alarm widened her eyes. "You can go. We're going. Tomorrow. The post will wait. It will be winter soon, anyway, too cold for building, and—"

"Very well, we'll go. Before the king has a chance to say otherwise." It would be the first time in his life he'd acted irresponsibly, but blast if he and Rose didn't deserve their dream of traveling. They could cut their holiday short, but they would go.

It felt strange to be putting the present before his future, but maybe it was about time.

As the courtiers raised their glasses all around him, toasting the queen, he blew out a breath and set Rose on her feet, then stood and raised his own. He was one of them now, and that felt strange, too.

But Rose was right. It didn't really matter. They were together, and that was enough.

She smiled up at him, raising her face for a bubbly champagne kiss. His heart swelling, he leaned her back over his arm and gave her one that had all the jaded courtiers around them whistling by the time he finished.

"A thing of beauty," she whispered, gazing up at him—and she didn't mean the spectacular building.

He knew just how she felt.

AUTHOR'S NOTE

~

DEAR READER,

Perhaps, like me, when you read a historical novel you wonder which characters besides the king and queen might actually have lived. I hope you won't be disappointed to learn that all of Rose's suitors were invented. All of King Charles's mistresses, however, were real people.

Charles II kept many mistresses throughout his life. Although some were disliked by his subjects while others were accepted, never in English history has another royal mistress been as popular as "pretty, witty" Nell Gwyn.

Whether Nell was actually born in a brothel is open to question, but legend has it she came into the world in Covent Garden in February 1650. As a young girl, Nell sold oranges at the Theatre Royal and began as an actress there in 1665. Charles saw her on stage, and by 1668 she became his mistress. Nell bore the king two sons, Charles in 1670, later the Duke of St. Albans, and James in 1671. Charles never tired of Nell, and on his deathbed, his last request to his brother is said to have been "let not poor Nelly starve."

In opposition to Nell's popularity, Louise de Kéroualle was universally disliked. Born in 1649 in France, Louise first came to England in 1670 as a maid of honor to Charles's sister, Henrietta. Charles's interest was apparent, and when Henrietta died later that year, Louise returned to London and was established as the king's mistress, receiving Louis XIV's congratulations on her success. After giving birth in 1672 to another of Charles's sons named Charles, later the Duke of Richmond, she was created the Duchess of Portsmouth.

Though Louise's unpopularity was due mostly to her being French and Catholic, she was also known to be wildly extravagant with the king's money. Her apartments at Whitehall were rebuilt three times, and John Evelyn said they had "ten times the richness and glory beyond the Queen's."

Hortense Mancini, the Duchess Mazarin, was one of five Italian sisters all noted for their great beauty. Two of them became mistress to Louis XIV. Born in Rome in 1646, Hortense moved to France at an early age. Charles proposed to her while there, but her uncle, Cardinal Mazarin, didn't think the exiled king's prospects were good. She later married and then left her husband, arrived at Charles's court in 1675, and became his mistress shortly thereafter. Considered an "adventuress," she was known for her compulsive gambling, her great skill with swords and guns, and her inclination to wear men's clothing.

Christopher Wren was a real person, too. Best known for rebuilding London's churches and St. Paul's Cathedral after the Great Fire, he also designed the Royal Observatory and the Royal Hospital at Chelsea. In 1669, Charles II appointed him Surveyor General of the King's Works, making him responsible for supervising all work on the royal palaces. Wren was knighted in 1673.

Besides churches, palaces, and other famous buildings, Wren also built a family home for himself beside the Thames in Windsor—the house we used as Kit's house in this book. Built in 1676, the home is now known as Sir Christopher Wren's House Hotel. If you're lucky enough to visit, ask to view the original "Oak Room" (Kit's dining room), and see if you find it as impressive as Rose did. Wren's original paneled master bedroom can be booked for an overnight stay. To find the hotel from the castle, just walk down the hill to the river, as Kit and Rose did in the story.

Many other settings in *The Gentleman's Scandalous Bride* are also real places you can visit, and although Kit is a fictional character, all the projects he worked on in the book were actually built for Charles II by different men.

Thomas Wolsey, Cardinal and Lord Chancellor of England, began building Hampton Court Palace in 1514. The best surviving part of Wolsey's palace is Base Court with its forty guest lodgings. By 1528, Wolsey had fallen from favor and was forced to relinquish Hampton Court to Henry VIII, who remodeled the palace to suit himself. Henry's personal lodgings have since been demolished, but you can still see his kitchens, his great hall, and his astronomical clock in Clock Court.

The later Tudors changed very little of the palace, and neither did the early Stuarts or Oliver Cromwell. So the next king to make a major mark on Hampton Court was Charles II. Among other projects, Charles completely redesigned the gardens and also commissioned a set of apartments for his mistress Barbara, the Duchess of Cleveland. This new building, which I have Kit building in *The Gentleman's Scandalous Bride*, is said to have looked completely different from the Tudor gothic architecture of Henry VIII's day.

In 1689, soon after William and Mary took the throne, they followed Charles's architectural lead and asked Christopher Wren to rebuild Hampton Court Palace in a more modern style, to compare with the likes of Versailles and the Louvre. The old Tudor buildings around Cloister Green Court were demolished and replaced by Wren's elegant Fountain Court. The Duchess of Cleveland's lodgings by the privy garden were destroyed at this time as well, and little is known of them now, as no building plans survived.

As for Hampton Court's maze, the one you can visit there now was designed in 1690 for William III, but it possibly replaced an earlier maze, perhaps laid out for Henry VIII. In an inventory of Cromwell's goods at Hampton Court dated 1659, there is mention of a cistern that serves "the fountaine and Maze." Since Charles II was restored to his throne the following year, perhaps the maze still survived at the time of Kit and Rose's story. In any case, we had fun imagining them exploring it!

Hampton Court Palace is open to the public seven days a

week year-round. Just a thirty-minute train ride from Central London, it's a perfect day trip back in time for anyone visiting the capital.

The remodeled east end of the Royal Chapel at Whitehall Palace in London was indeed designed by Christopher Wren—the sketch he made that Kit showed Rose still survives. The actual work was carried out by Thomas Kinward, Robert Streater, and Henry Phillips, for a total cost of a little more than £71. The fire in *The Gentleman's Scandalous Bride* was entirely our invention, but would surely have raised the price of construction.

Sadly, Whitehall Palace was destroyed by fire in 1698. Although a few walls and other original bits of the palace survive as parts of the current government buildings, the only intact part of Whitehall today is Inigo Jones's exquisite Banqueting House. Completed in 1622 and renowned for its architecture and magnificent ceiling painted by Sir Peter Paul Rubens, the building is also famous for being the scene of Charles I's execution.

In Charles II's time, the Banqueting House was used as the ceremonial chamber of the court and the scene of grand receptions. Of the queen's birthday celebration on the 15th of November in 1677, which Rose and Kit attend in the final chapter of their story, John Evelyn noted in his diary: "The Queene's birth-day, a greate Ball at Court, where the Prince of Orange and his new Princesse daunced."

The Banqueting House is open to the public Monday through Saturday except for bank holidays, but it sometimes closes on short notice for government functions. This happened the first time we tried to visit, so do check ahead of time!

Of all the projects we had Kit working on in this book, the only one that can be seen today is the King's Dining Room at Windsor Castle. In real life it was designed by architect Hugh May, who did extensive renovations for King Charles between 1675 and 1678. We chose this particular room for Kit not only because it was actually completed in the year of our story, 1677, but also because it's the most intact example remaining of Charles's rooms, including the original wall carvings by Grinling Gibbons and Henry Phillips and the whimsical ceiling painted by Antonio Verrio.

Windsor Castle is the largest and oldest occupied castle in the world. It has stood for over 900 years, since William the Conqueror chose the site a day's march from the Tower of London. The castle has been inhabited continuously and altered by each sovereign. Some concentrated on strengthening the site against attack, while others, living in more peaceful times, helped create the palatial royal residence you can visit today.

Windsor Castle is open seven days a week year-round, but there are periods, especially in June and December, when the queen is in residence and the State Apartments are closed to visitors.

Trentingham Manor was inspired by the Vyne, a National Trust property in Hampshire. Built in the early sixteenth century for Lord Sandys, Henry VIII's Lord Chamberlain, the house acquired a classical portico in the mid-seventeenth century and contains a grand Palladian staircase, a wealth of old paneling and fine furniture, and a fascinating Tudor chapel with Renaissance glass. The Vyne and its extensive gardens are open for visits April through October.

I hope you enjoyed *The Gentleman's Scandalous Bride*! Next up in The Chase Brides series is Chrystabel and Joseph Ashcroft's story in *The Cavalier's Christmas Bride*, a special holiday prequel novel. Please read on for an excerpt!

Always,

Lauren Royal

Read on for an excerpt from

The Cavalier's Christmas Bride

Book 8 of the
Sweet Chase Brides series
by Lauren & Devon Royal

Christmas has been outlawed by the new Commonwealth government—but that won't stop Lady Chrystabel Trevor from embracing the holiday spirit. When she finds herself snowed in with handsome and intriguing Joseph Ashcroft, the Viscount Tremayne, merrymaking leads to mayhem. In a time of fear and oppression, can the magic of Christmas bring two hearts together?

England
December 23, 1651

THREE DAYS INTO the Trevors' journey to Wales, the weather took a turn for the worse.

Not that the weather had been pleasant to begin with. Chrystabel felt like she hadn't been warm in days, and the churned-up winter roads had made for a bumpy ride. She was convinced their carriage had managed to find every rut from Bath to Bristol.

But today's cold was something else, something malicious, with biting winds and just enough damp to make the chill penetrate down to the bone. Her fingers and toes were achingly numb, though she wore two extra pairs of stockings and kept her gloved hands bundled in her pockets. Even through leather, the lion crest pendant felt like a chip of ice in her palm. Holding it brought her little comfort today.

In short, she was thoroughly miserable. And they weren't even in Wales yet.

When she wasn't too busy wallowing, she was worrying. She worried for her rose plants, which had been carefully wrapped and lovingly secured in the baggage wagon, and for her Christmas decorations, hastily flung atop the load. At the last minute she'd decided Christmas was coming with them, Cromwell's laws be hanged.

In two days' time, she would have her Yuletide celebration. She didn't care where. She would decorate the carriage if it came to that.

But now she worried her treasured roses and hand-trimmed boughs might not make it to Christmas Day. Could any living thing—or recently living, in the case of the boughs—survive such bitter cold and relentless jostling?

Most of all, she worried for their servants, who were bringing up the rear in two ancient carriages with no glass in the windows. Some of the family retainers had chosen to stay behind in Wiltshire, but most feared being out of work in these turbulent times. Though Chrystabel and her sister had loaned them all the spare cloaks and blankets they could find, she feared the poor dears might be icicles by day's end.

If only Matthew had the funds to buy some decent, modern vehicles...

But then, if her brother had had a great heap of money lying around, they wouldn't have lost their home.

"L-look," her sister said through chattering teeth. Hugging herself tighter, Arabel leaned toward the window. "It's s-snowing again."

Chrystabel's sigh made a little puff of fog. "We ought to stop somewhere."

"On account of this bit of fluff?" Matthew's jaw was clenched and his posture unnaturally stiff; he was far too manly to allow himself to shiver. "Regardless, there's nothing nearby—"

"Is that a c-castle?" Peering through the window, Arabel brightened. "Yes, just there off the road, p-peeking up through the woods. And there's smoke rising from its chimneys. Someone m-must be home!"

Matthew leaned to see what she was talking about. "Probably just a skeleton staff who won't want to take us in," he muttered. "And the place isn't 'just off the road,' either—it's got to be nearly a mile away."

"That's certainly closer than Wales," Chrystabel snapped, though in truth, she had no idea where they were in relation to

Wales. She just knew they still had a long journey ahead of them. The ferry crossing at New Passage had been closed due to the weather, the River Severn too frozen for the ferryman to risk. Now they had to go all the way to Gloucester before they could loop around the river and head west to the Trevors' Welsh estate.

"In this weather, whoever's at that c-castle will feel obligated to take us in, even if the owners aren't p-p-present." Arabel was shivering so hard that Chrystabel suspected it was half for show.

Chrystabel nodded. "Think of our staff, Matthew. We must find them shelter. If *you'd* rather freeze to death, you're welcome to wait in the carriage."

"Oh, very well," he grumbled. "But I fear this will prove a waste of time." He knocked on the carriage roof and told the bundled-up coachman to turn off the road, trusting the rest of the train would follow. "If we have to turn back, I'm going to say 'I told you so,'" he warned afterward.

The castle turned out to be *more* than a mile off, and Chrystabel held her tongue the entire way. But her heart sank when they got close enough to see the structure was only half-built.

With its tall, decorative brickwork chimneys and other Tudor architectural touches, she'd assumed the castle belonged to the previous century—but now she feared it might be new and still under construction. What if they found the place deserted and uninhabitable? Picturing her family's carriages turning around to head back to the main road, she felt colder than ever.

But to her very great relief, a footman greeted their arrival. Chrystabel showed remarkable restraint as the man asked their names, scurried off to "consult with milord," and reappeared to graciously welcome them all into the castle. Only then did she turn to her brother and crow, "I told you so!"

Matthew may or may not have looked daggers at her as she led the way inside. She didn't see, because she was too busy noticing the young man who waited in the wood-paneled entry hall.

Or rather, not just noticing. To her astonishment, she found herself *gaping*. Tall and trim, the gentleman had deep green eyes and long, wavy jet-black hair—Cavalier hair, which meant he was Royalist, like her family.

Just occupying the same space with this stranger was having peculiar effects on her body. She didn't feel nervous, as she sometimes had around other good-looking young men. Instead, she felt soft and warm both inside and out. She felt *thawed* in a way that had nothing to do with coming in out of the cold.

She couldn't not look at him. She willed him to glance her way. His gaze met hers—

—and her heart came to a stop.

It just paused, as if suspended in time for as long his eyes held hers.

A sudden truth occurred to her: *This is the man I will marry.*

Which was ridiculous, when she thought about it. Maybe she was overtired.

Yes, she had to be overtired. The frozen, uncomfortable journey had been exhausting.

When he looked away to address her brother, the perplexing moment passed. "Welcome to Tremayne, Lord Grosmont." His voice was deep and as beautiful as the planes of his face, making Chrystabel melt a little more. "I would ask what brings you to my home, except I fear I know the answer. I hope the weather will not delay your travels long."

"My profound thanks, uh…" Matthew trailed off, apparently realizing too late that their host hadn't named himself.

Chrystabel suddenly had to know his name. "Who are you?" she blurted.

Thoughtful eyes fixed on her again, and again her heart paused. "My name is Joseph Ashcroft, my lady. The Viscount Tremayne," he added with a little formal bow she found amusing.

Or maybe it was *be*musing. She was certainly feeling bemused.

Matthew poked her in the ribs. "This is my rude sister, Lady Chrystabel Trevor. My courteous sister is Lady Arabel Trevor. And we are most grateful for your hospitality, Lord Tremayne."

The viscount flashed straight white teeth in a smile that nearly reduced her to a puddle. "The hospitality is my father's. He's regrettably detained, but he hopes you and your lovely sisters will join our family supper tonight."

Lovely! Could he have meant Chrystabel? Or was he just being polite?

"We'd be delighted," Matthew answered for all three of them.

Lord Tremayne nodded. "The dining room is rather hidden, so shall we meet here again at seven? In the meantime, our housekeeper will settle your staff and belongings, and Watkins here will show you to our guest chambers. Please make yourselves at home."

With another droll little bow, the viscount took his leave. Chrystabel stayed rooted in place until he was entirely out of sight. When she blinked herself awake, her siblings were gone.

She caught up to them on a wide flight of stone stairs, which had twisted wrought-iron balusters and a dark oak handrail. The staircase led to a long corridor that appeared to run the length of the building, torches lighting it at intervals.

Though she'd expected a half-built castle would be unfinished inside, too, this portion was a beautiful and sumptuous home. Trailing Watkins, Chrystabel passed a costly gilt mirror and several impressive tapestries, skimming her hand along stone block walls polished to a subtle sheen.

Watkins hurried ahead to open a door on the left. "Would one of the ladies like this chamber?"

Chrystabel peeked into a spacious, splendid room. "I would love it," she said, rushing inside before her sister could claim it.

The first detail that caught her eye was a set of magnificent oriel windows. Why, the glass window panes were *curved.* Marveling, she drifted closer and counted four banks of curved windows projecting out from the back wall, each shaped like a rounded flower petal. She'd never seen anything like them. They afforded a stunning view of the walled Tudor landscape below.

The geometric garden was lightly dusted with snow. "The

grounds were designed by the young viscount," Watkins explained, "in the style of Tradescant the Elder."

Chrystabel loved flowers and knew John Tradescant had brought seeds and bulbs to England from all over the world. She found herself as entranced by Lord Tremayne's gardens as she was by the gentleman himself. "Oh, these grounds must be enchanting in summer!" She longed to see them in full bloom.

Too bad she'd be in godforsaken Wales.

Excusing himself with a bow far more proper than his master's, Watkins ushered Arabel and Matthew back out. "My lady, I hope you'll find the next room over to your liking," Chrystabel heard as he led them down the corridor. "Lord Grosmont, you'll be installed across the way."

When she finally tore herself from the view, Chrystabel closed the room's door and then surveyed the rest of her surroundings with almost equal glee. Her bedchamber at Grosmont Grange had been nice, but not as nice as this one. It boasted a four-poster bed with red curtains and a red canopy, much like her tester bed at home, but newer and finer. A carved stone fireplace blazed merrily on one wall, and a red Oriental carpet cushioned the floor beneath her feet. Besides the bed, she had a carved wardrobe cabinet and a lovely dressing table with another costly mirror. In the cozy rounded space created by the oriel windows sat an inlaid hexagonal table with two well-stuffed chairs.

She was already regaining the feeling in her fingers and toes, and with any luck, she'd get to stay warm and snug in this gorgeous room through Christmas. The impending misery of Wales felt like a distant bad dream. Tremayne seemed no place for such unpleasant thoughts.

Remembering she was overtired, she crawled into the big bed and burrowed beneath the plush counterpane. While waiting to doze off, she pictured Lord Tremayne designing an exquisite new garden. A rose garden. For her.

Goodness, but he looked darling when he was concentrating.

In the summertime, the rose garden he'd planted for her

bloomed. The colors were spectacular, the fragrances breathtaking. And she was here to enjoy it all. She lived here, at splendid Tremayne. And she lived here because—

A knock startled her awake.

Chrystabel scrambled out of bed to open her door. "Is it seven o'clock already?" she asked Arabel, patting her hair back into its austere knot.

"It will be in five minutes. Matthew went on ahead, and he said we're to meet him *on time.*"

Matthew was very punctual and well-mannered and nauseatingly polite out in company. Quite different from the real Matthew that Chrystabel saw at home.

She looked her sister up and down. "Shouldn't we change for supper?"

Arabel shrugged. "What would we change into?"

"Something more elegant," Chrystabel said, though *something more alluring* was what she meant. Her thoughts had returned to the handsome viscount.

Thanks to her nap, she was no longer overtired—and she still wanted to marry him.

Unfortunately, she feared her current attire might hamper her chances. Cromwell had forbidden bright or immodest clothing, so the gowns she wore in public were of plain fabrics in tedious browns and grays. Each one had a vast, stark white collar that tied at the throat and flopped shapelessly about her shoulders, making her appear sallow and bulky. The Puritans couldn't have chosen a style *less* flattering to Chrystabel's ivory complexion and tall stature.

"This will never do," she muttered, looking down at herself in dismay.

"It will have to, at least for tonight." Arabel took her arm. "They haven't brought our trunks up yet."

With a sigh of resignation, Chrystabel let her sister march her down to supper. Oh, how she longed for the fine pre-Cromwell gowns hidden in the bottom of her trunk. "Don't you miss silk, Arabel? I miss silk. And damask. And embroidery and lace. And rosettes and pearls and oh, I could go on all day."

"Please don't," Arabel said good-naturedly. "You'd make us late for supper. Then Matthew would be angry, our hosts would be insulted, and we'd *still* be stuck wearing these hideous sacks."

Chrystabel giggled. "What about velvet? Mmm, wouldn't fur-lined velvet be ever so snug on an evening like this?"

Arabel put a finger to her lips. "You forget we're in a stranger's home. Tremayne folk might frown on such talk."

"They'd better not frown at me," Chrystabel grumbled. "It's Yuletide, and just as soon as my trunk arrives I'll wear red and green whether they like it or not."

"Suit yourself." Arabel shook her head. "But we haven't seen how the lady of the house dresses yet, and I, for one, would rather look dreadful inside a warm castle than ravishing tossed out into the snow."

As usual, Arabel was right. Sometimes Chrystabel thought Arabel should be the older sister. They'd simply been born in the wrong order.

Chrystabel cast about for a safe subject. "How is your chamber?"

"Marvelous. It's done up all in yellow with a very pretty four-poster bed. And best of all, it's *warm*." Arabel was easy to please. "I hope the storm doesn't break tomorrow."

"You'd like to stay longer?"

"I'd like to stay forever."

"Me, too. I think I shall marry the viscount."

That startled a laugh out of Arabel. "Don't be a goose."

"Who's being a goose?" When they passed the fancy mirror she'd noticed earlier, Chrystabel was careful to avoid her reflection. It would only upset her. "I'm perfectly serious."

"No, you're not. You don't know anything about him." Arabel gave her a sidelong glance. "Except that he's handsome and doesn't live in Wales."

Chrystabel lifted her chin along with her skirts as they started down the staircase. For once, her younger sister was wrong. "I'm not wedding him to avoid Wales. I'm wedding him because I love him."

"You cannot be in love with him. You haven't even had a proper conversation with him yet."

"'Who ever loved that loved not at first sight?'" Chrystabel quoted triumphantly. "It seems Shakespeare would beg to differ."

Since Arabel was the academic of the family—she'd read nearly every book in the Grange's library—Chrystabel could rarely best her with scholarship. She relished every opportunity.

"*As You Like It* is fiction, not philosophy," her sister pointed out. "And incidentally, Shakespeare didn't write that line. He was referencing a poem by Christopher Marlowe."

Hmmph. So much for besting Arabel.

"There's no such thing as love at first sight, Chrys. That only happens in plays and poems."

Yesterday, Chrystabel would have agreed with the sentiment. But today she knew differently.

"What a sad, unromantic soul you are, dear sister." She patted Arabel on the shoulder. "Since it's happened to me, I suppose I'll have to prove you wrong."

~

AVAILABLE NOW!
Learn more about *The Cavalier's Christmas Bride* at
www.DevonAndLaurenRoyal.com

ENTER FOR A CHANCE TO WIN
a sterling silver and mother-of-pearl rose pendant!*

Visit the Contest page on Lauren & Devon's website
at www.LaurenandDevonRoyal.com
and answer a question to be
entered in the monthly drawing.

No purchase necessary. See complete rules on the site.

*Please note: Depending on when you enter, the prize may be another piece of jewelry associated with one of Lauren & Devon's books. The authors reserve the right to discontinue this promotion at any time.

ABOUT LAUREN & DEVON ROYAL

~

LAUREN ROYAL decided to become a writer in the third grade, after winning a "Why My Mother is the Greatest" essay contest. Now she's a *New York Times* and *USA Today* bestselling author of humorous historical romance novels. Lauren lives in Southern California with her family and their constantly shedding cat. She still thinks her mother is the greatest.

DEVON ROYAL is the daughter of romance novelist Lauren Royal. After attending film school, she wrote an award-winning TV comedy pilot and worked in digital video production before turning her focus to fiction writing. Devon lives in Southern California with her husband and son. She also thinks her mother is the greatest.

ACKNOWLEDGMENTS

~

OUR HEARTFELT THANKS:

To Ian Franklin and Michelle Griffiths, State Apartment Warders at Hampton Court Palace, for directing us to the right places, and, in Ian's case, giving us incredibly useful information.

To Philip Sidebotham, Adrian Moles, and Tiffany Green at Sir Christopher Wren's House Hotel in Windsor, for graciously allowing and assisting two crazy authors to poke around and take photos of Wren's house.

To Amy and Rick Tanaka, for their expert advice on matters architectural.

To The Landmark Trust, for making it possible for our family to actually live at Hampton Court Palace for a week (how awesome is that?).

To Becca, Blake, Darci Dipo, Dan Mehefko, and Anna Pione, for helping us explore Hampton Court Palace through many different perspectives.

To Andrew Metz, for the video on Hampton Court's history.

To Barry Waller, for converting the videotape on Hampton Court's history so that we could actually watch it.

To Alison Bellach Sonderegger, for sharing a laugh with Lauren over the yipping in the hotel room next door and then challenging her to put it in a book.

To all the honorary Chase cousins in our Chase Family Readers Group, for their enthusiastic support.

And, last but certainly not least, to all our readers, whose wonderful emails, Facebook posts, and tweets inspire us to write more books.

Thanks, everyone!

CONTACT INFORMATION

~

Newsletter

littl.ink / News

Facebook Readers Group

facebook.com / groups / ChaseFamilyReaders

Website

www.DevonAndLaurenRoyal.com

Email

royall.ink / Email